Jr. High
P9-DBN-777

THE MARKED GIRL

THE MARKED GIRL

Lindsey Klingele

HarperTeen is an imprint of HarperCollins Publishers.

The Marked Girl

 For information address HarperCollins Children's Books, a division of HarperCollins Publishers, 195 Broadway, New York, NY 10007.
www.epicreads.com

Library of Congress Control Number: 2015958387
ISBN 978-0-06-238033-3 (trade bdg.)

Typography by Kate J. Engbring
16 17 18 19 20 CG/RRDH 10 9 8 7 6 5 4 3 2 1
❖
First Edition

To my parents, who never once doubted
this dedication page would someday exist.
(At least not out loud.)

THE MARKED GIRL

THE NIGHT THAT STARTED OUT NORMAL

Light glinted off the side of the sword as it arced down in one perfect, sweeping motion. The blade slid into the exposed side of the young man who knelt, frozen, on the ground. Immediately, a small patch of deep red bloomed against his shirt, and he collapsed in a broken heap. The black-haired girl who gripped the sword handle grinned wide and pulled her weapon back, flinging it up over her head so it reached for the night sky—

"Cut!"

Liv Phillips sighed and pushed herself up off of the cement, from where she'd been watching the action unfold. Her knees creaked, and she badly needed to crack her neck. She took two steps toward Shannon Mei, the girl with the sword, who was now twirling the weapon around with lazy flicks of her wrist.

"There isn't enough blood," Liv said.

The boy on the ground—Jeremy—rolled over and sat up. He pulled up the edge of his T-shirt, examining the dark red stain on the side of his abdomen—and, Liv noticed, giving ample view of the abs he flaunted at every given opportunity. *Actors.*

"What are you talking about? It's just as much as last time."

"No, it's not," Liv responded. "The pack must have malfunctioned." She turned around and looked at her crew, which was less an actual crew and more a single camera-operator-in-training nicknamed Tall Tony (for reasons that remained a mystery to Liv, since he was more skinny than he was tall). Currently, Tall Tony was busy blowing dust out of the camera lens. Or maybe he was pretending to be busy so he didn't have to make eye contact with Liv.

"Tony, do we have any more blood packs?"

"Uh, that was the last one," he replied.

"This was my last shirt," Jeremy said from the ground. "And I think she ripped it with that thing." Jeremy nodded up to Shannon, who still twirled the prop sword in her hand. Its plastic edges nearly looked like real metal in the weak light. Kind of. If you squinted.

"Oh, I did not," Shannon said. She used the sword edge to flick strands of her thick, black hair out of her eyes. "See? It's harmless."

"Shannon, you didn't happen to remember to bring any extra T-shirts, did you? Maybe we can do the scene one more time, up until you stab him," Liv said.

But Shannon shook her head. "I'm an actress first, wardrobe lady second. I can't remember all the things."

"You certainly can't remember your lines," Jeremy muttered.

"Excuse me?"

Liv heard the obvious warning in Shannon's voice, but Jeremy had a talent for digging in deeper when anyone with common sense would bail.

"Oh, don't get all offended. It's not like you're a real actress or anything. You're not even *in* the film program. Liv only cast you because you're her friend."

Shannon's eyes narrowed. She swung the fake sword around and pointed its tip at Jeremy's neck. "Jeremy, has anyone ever told you not to piss off a girl with a weapon? It might be plastic, but I could still make it hurt."

Jeremy swallowed, and his Adam's apple bobbed against the sword point.

"Okay!" Liv moved to jump between the two. "I think that's a wrap on tonight." She gently put a hand on Shannon's arm, guiding the sword away from Jeremy's neck.

Tall Tony finally looked up from his camera lens, oblivious. "Did you get what you needed, Liv?"

Liv thought over the last few hours of work they'd put in. She'd shot the climactic fight scene three times, but none of them had felt right.

"No, we'll have to do it again tomorrow night."

"I have soccer practice tomorrow night," Jeremy said.

"And I have a date," Shannon added. When Liv shot her a meaningful look, Shannon gave her one right back.

"This is important, Shan."

"Trust me, so is my date."

Jeremy snorted and turned to Liv. "You know, if you'd just use the available studio space to film this short like everyone else in class, we could work during the day."

Liv put two fingers up to her temples and rubbed a circle. When she'd first taken on this project as part of her summer film program and asked her fellow classmates—and her best friend, Shannon—to help out, she'd known it would be a difficult endeavor. But she hadn't known it would be this hard, that every little step would be like trying to walk with fifty-pound weights attached to each foot. The worst part was that Jeremy was right. Setting up her shots in the basement "studio" at her summer program's office would be much easier, even if the end result wouldn't be as good.

Liv had chosen instead to film her night scene outside, in a place she'd always loved. She glanced around at the familiar landmarks—just beyond where Shannon and Jeremy stood was a concrete ledge that dropped ten feet down into the mostly empty LA riverbed. The ground at her feet was cracked, with small shoots of green leaves working their way up from the dirt underneath. To her right was a packed stone wall, covered with graffiti. The wall led to a small, unimpressive cement bridge that arched over the thin river.

At a glance, the place didn't look like much—aside from slightly resembling the drag race scene setting in *Grease.* But beyond the bridge was a breathtaking view of downtown Los Angeles, the black outlines of its buildings dark against the night sky of early June. In place of stars, the brightly lit windows of downtown LA shone for miles. Streetlights from the top of the bridge cast orangy reflections over the river water.

The spot where Liv stood was nowhere of significance,

really. Tourists didn't come by on buses; joggers stayed away. But to Liv, the place had always felt important. It felt, somehow, like a secret that was hers alone.

And she'd always wanted to capture it on film. She'd gotten special permission from her student advisor to take the equipment out of the studio, so long as she'd fronted an additional deposit. She just hoped it would be worth it.

Liv squared her shoulders and reached down to pick up the boxy floor light at her feet. "Okay, how about we meet here again on Wednesday night? I'll bring more shirts."

Shannon shrugged with one shoulder.

"Fine," Jeremy said. "But we can't go too late. Some of us have actual curfews and homes to get back to, you know."

Liv did her best to ignore the dig, even though it hit below the belt. It was true she didn't have someone sitting at home, watching the clock to make sure she walked through the door on time, or at all. It sucked more often than not, but Liv knew better than to let Jeremy see how much his comment bothered her. For one, she knew he didn't really mean it, and was probably still just pissed that Shannon had gotten the best of him (which, to be fair, happened a lot). And second, getting emotional would make it all the harder to regain some measure of control over the shoot. On set—even if that "set" was just four teenagers playing with fake swords and cameras on a stretch of cracked cement—was typically one of the few places Liv felt like she was able to maintain any control at all. So she resolved to let Jeremy's comment slide.

Shannon, however, had different priorities. "Mommy got

you on a tight leash, Jer-Jer?"

"All right, great night, everyone," Liv said, raising her voice over any possible retort from Jeremy. She clapped her hands a couple of times, which was something her film professor did at the end of class. "Let's pack up and get everything in the van. I might have time to get the equipment back by ten—"

"Liv," Shannon said, her voice suddenly low. "Look."

Liv followed Shannon's gaze over to where the bridge met the stone wall lining the river's edge. Something was moving there. It was like a shadow, but darker somehow. It almost didn't seem like a distant object, but instead like a black spot on Liv's vision, the kind she sometimes saw when she stood up too fast. Liv closed her eyes for a moment, and when she opened them, the dark spot was gone.

"Where did they come from?" Shannon asked, her voice nearly a whisper.

That's when Liv narrowed her eyes and saw the figures standing next to where the spot had just been. Three people, all in a row under the bridge. They wore long, all-white clothing that stood out against the dark gray concrete.

Liv's heart beat quickly. Next to her, Tall Tony swore.

One of the figures broke from the others and started yelling. He beat his left hand against the concrete wall under the bridge and held his right down by his side. Liv could hardly make out what he was screaming, but it almost sounded like he was yelling "um" over and over again. He kept doing it until one of the others moved to restrain him.

"What's that in his hand?" Jeremy asked.

Liv peered closer at the one who did, indeed, appear to hold something in his right hand. It was long and thin, and when it moved it reflected the streetlight on the bridge.

"Holy crap, it's one of our prop swords," Liv said. "They must have taken it from the van." She turned to Tall Tony. "Did you lock it up behind you?"

Tall Tony shrugged.

"Well, they can keep it," Jeremy said. "They look creepy like that, just standing there."

But Liv took a couple of steps forward, toward the figures. The one with the sword had stopped yelling, and they were now eerily quiet, standing in a huddle under the bridge. She could also tell they were young, not much older than her.

"Liv, what are you doing?" Shannon hissed.

"I can't just let them take it," Liv said. "It's rented out in my name."

"So?"

"So it took me three weeks of sweeping up coffee grinds to put down that deposit." She turned back toward the figures.

"Wait," Shannon said, and ran up to Liv. "If you're dead set on going over there, take this." Shannon took the box light from Liv's hand and placed the prop sword there instead.

"I'm not sure that's going to help much," Jeremy said.

"You could always come with me," Liv shot back.

Jeremy raised his hands in a you're-on-your-own gesture. Liv rolled her eyes and walked over toward the bridge. When she was about ten feet away from the figures, she stopped.

"Hello? I think . . . I think you might have something of mine."

From here, Liv could make out the white-clad figures better.

They were definitely teenagers, two boys and a girl. The boy who held the sword was tall, with dark hair and light skin. Standing on his left was another boy, thin, his scowling face partially covered by long strips of dirty-blond hair. The girl stood statue still, her long, dark hair falling in straight lines around her shoulders. The skin above her right eyebrow was stained with something that looked like mud. They all wore what looked like old-fashioned, full-length nightclothes, and they were looking around the riverbed area with wide, transfixed eyes.

Jeremy was right, Liv thought. They did look creepy as hell.

"If you just give me the sword back, no harm, no foul—"

The boy with the sword stepped forward. "Are you the leader here?"

His accent was strange, and one Liv didn't recognize. Close to British, but just different enough to sound . . . off. The boy stared at her, and Liv could see now that his eyes were a clear, light blue.

"Um . . . I'm the director."

The boy's eyebrows furrowed, and he looked first to the girl on his right, then to the boy on his left. They both shook their heads faintly.

"We're shooting a movie over there," Liv said, gesturing vaguely toward where Shannon and the others stood. "It's just a student film thing. It's about these alien samurais . . ."

The teens just stared at her.

"It sounds weirder than it is, honestly."

"Where are we?" the boy with the sword interrupted.

"The LA River," Liv responded. There was no reaction.

"Near Dodger Stadium? Are you . . . lost?"

"Who is in charge of this realm?"

"Um . . ." Liv wanted to look behind her and call to Shannon for help, but she also didn't want to turn her back on this stranger. When he moved his arm, the sword he held shone in the light. The glint was odd, almost too bright. . . .

"I think the girl is simple," the dark-haired girl said in a low voice. The boy with the sword cocked his head slightly, as if considering this possibility.

"Well, I'm definitely not deaf," Liv responded. She was growing less creeped out and more annoyed by these weirdo thieves with every second. "Look, I can help you if you're lost, but you're going to have to give me my stuff back first."

Liv nodded to the sword in the boy's hand. He looked down and, if anything, his confused expression only deepened.

"This does not belong to you."

"Well, technically no," Liv said. "It belongs to the AFI Summer Film Program. But I had to give them a two-hundred-dollar deposit for it, so . . ."

This time it was the scowling boy who responded. "She seems to speak our language, and yet her words are nonsense."

Liv shifted on her feet. "Yeah . . . it's getting pretty late, and I'm not really in the mood to get pranked or robbed or whatever. I mean, two hundred bucks may not be a lot to some people, but to me—"

Liv was cut off abruptly when the earth started moving underneath her feet. It started with a low rumble, but quickly picked up to a shaking sensation. What little water was left in the LA River began to slosh around, and behind her, Liv could hear Shannon's yelp of surprise.

The boy with the sword looked up at Liv, panic spread wide across his features.

"What is happening?"

"It's just an earthquake," Liv responded. She put her arms out to steady herself. "And it seems like a small one—"

At that, the earth seemed to lurch sharply to the right, and Liv was knocked off her feet. Her elbows hit the concrete, hard. The boy with the sword fell also, landing on top of her. He quickly rolled away, and the ground continued to shake.

Liv looked up and could see the bridge above them moving back and forth against the night sky, as though it were being shaken by a giant, unseen hand. Her heart jumped.

"Get out from under the bridge!" Liv yelled. She started to crab-walk down the concrete, back toward Shannon and the crew, who were lying flat against the ground with their hands up over their necks. Liv watched as the cable that connected to the floor light snaked its way past Jeremy's foot and fell over the side of the riverbank, taking the whole light with it.

"No!"

Liv pulled herself over the cracked concrete by her hands, belatedly realizing she must have dropped the prop sword. She turned around to see the strangers following her and staying low to the ground. Thankfully, they seemed to have cleared the bridge.

When the earth finally stopped moving, Liv let out a breath she hadn't even realized she'd been holding. As a Los Angeles native, she'd been through her share of earthquakes. But this had been bigger than most of the little rumbles she was used to. She looked up at the bridge, once again a sturdy, unmoving cement structure.

"Are you guys okay?" Liv asked the strangers, who were starting to get to their feet. "I wouldn't do that yet—" she started, but just as the second boy was dusting off his white pants, the earth started to move once again. Softer this time, but still with enough force to keep Liv low to the ground.

The blond boy—once again scowling—turned to his companions. "I told you! I told you we should not have come to this hell. We are all going to die!"

He took off running in the other direction, his feet slapping against the concrete as he struggled to stay upright through the shaking.

"No!" Liv screamed after him. "Wait till the aftershock stops!"

But he was running too fast and too hard to hear. The blue-eyed boy and the girl exchanged a glance and took off running after him, not even sparing a look back to Liv. The blue-eyed boy scooped up the sword that he must have dropped when he'd fallen to the ground. Liv no longer cared enough to yell out after him. Now that the light had fallen into the river, her deposit was long gone anyway.

After a few moments, the aftershock subsided. Liv pulled herself up to a sitting position and looked back to Shannon and the others.

"Are you okay?" Shannon yelled out across the thirty feet of cement that separated them.

"Yep! You?"

"We're fine," Shannon replied. "But I think Jeremy wet himself!"

"She lies!" Jeremy screamed back, voice breaking.

Liv heard sirens in the distance, which was par for the course after any earthquake. She stood up and reached for her fallen prop sword. But something was off. It didn't feel like the lightweight wood-and-plastic model she'd been holding earlier; the boy must have taken that one as he ran off. But his sword—the one she held now—was different.

It was too heavy, for one. And its hilt felt smooth and hard, like polished stone. Liv held the blade up to the weak light coming from the streetlights on top of the bridge, and she gasped.

The edges of the sword were beveled down to fine points, and they shone in the light. She ran a finger against one of them, lightly, and pulled it back fast when it broke her skin.

This wasn't any prop sword. It was real. It was dangerous.

Liv's head snapped up in the direction that the white-clad strangers had run off. But they were long gone.

THE HOLE IN THE SKY

Earlier That Night and Far, Far Away . . .

They came for him in the middle of the night, the way that cowards do.

Cedric West was deep in a dreamless sleep, the kind he sometimes brought on by drinking one too many glasses of mead with dinner. That night, he'd had yet another argument with his father, which had prompted him to drink not one, but three too many glasses.

So when rough hands wrapped around his arms and shoulders, jerking him out of his bed, Cedric did not wake immediately. He remained in a state of oblivion until hoarse words carried on foul-smelling breath reached his ears and nose, respectively.

"Morning, Your Highness."

Cedric opened his eyes only to find himself in a waking nightmare. The creature holding him had two blunt horns that curled up from its forehead, making it seem impossibly tall as it hovered over the bedside. Its jet-black eyes were set deep into a boulder-shaped head covered with grayish skin.

Only the pain in Cedric's arms was able to convince him that the hideous vision was real. And not only real, but familiar. A wrath.

"Before you think of screaming, look left," the wrath growled in a voice that sounded like rocks falling over steel.

Cedric struggled against the creature and looked to his left, where another bulky wrath blocked the entire frame of the doorway. The creature held tightly to a slight figure. She stood still, her white nightgown the only bright thing in the dim room.

"Emme," Cedric whispered.

"Take one wrong breath, and your sister will pay," the wrath holding on to Cedric said.

Though Emmeline was only two years younger than Cedric, she looked small and childlike in the wrath's grip. The sight of the creature's dirty claws on her thin arm brought up such a sudden rage in Cedric that the edges of his eyesight blurred red and black. He forced himself to focus. How was it possible these monsters had invaded the castle? His whole life, Cedric had been trained to fight off the threat of the wraths and keep the creatures outside the borders of the realm's towns and villages. Never once had a wrath stepped so much as a foot within the main city's walls. That they had somehow invaded not just the city, but the castle itself, was unthinkable.

"What do you want?" Cedric asked, trying his best to make his tone sound commanding and imperial, like his father's.

Emme whimpered, and Cedric looked over to see the second wrath gripping her neck with its taloned hand.

Cedric jerked toward her, but the first wrath put a knife to his throat.

"Want to speak again?"

Cedric shook his head once, his shoulders clenched tight with anger. The wrath dragged Cedric through his room, keeping his arms pinned behind his back. It pushed him into the hallway, directly behind the wrath that half held, half carried his sister. The stone halls were quiet and dark, their smooth walls impassive to the plight of the young prince and princess being dragged past them in their nightclothes. The wrath holding Emme continued to jerk her arm roughly, as if reminding Cedric not to struggle against his own captor.

As they reached the main corridor of the castle, Cedric cast a glance toward the giant wooden doors on the far side of the room, in front of which two long, bulky shapes lay in heaps on the ground. The guards.

"You do not know what you have done," Cedric said. "When my father catches you, the punishment—"

Cedric stopped talking when he heard his captor laugh. Actually laugh.

"Your father already waits for you in the dungeons," the wrath said. Its craggy face stretched into what was either a hideous grimace or an attempt at a cruel smile. "Do not worry that he is being mistreated, Highness. He was given the largest cell, after all."

From the opposite side of the corridor, Cedric watched a series of figures emerge from the shadows. Another wrath appeared, its twisted horns catching the flickering light from the torches on the wall. The wrath was dragging behind it Katerina Esson and Merek Harcourt, both in town with their parents for the annual peacekeeping summit.

Katerina's teeth clenched as the wrath pulled her by the arms. She wasn't making its job any easier, but was digging in her heels and trying to wrench her arms free as she was dragged over the stone floor. Her proud, sometimes haughty family stood as wards of the large northern holdings, and she had been betrothed to Cedric since her birth. Watching her struggle now, Cedric couldn't help but think of when he first saw Katerina—his Kat—enter the palace three days earlier, surrounded by ambassadors. She'd grown significantly since he'd seen her last, and her customary twin plaits that he used to pull on to tease her had been combed out to fall around her shoulders in a gentle wave. Now Kat's dark hair was a loose, messy tangle that flew about as she tried to yank her arm from the wrath's grip.

If only she had a weapon in her hands, Cedric knew the wrath that held her would not be smiling.

Behind Kat, Merek was being ushered along much more smoothly by another wrath. The youngest son of the king's cousin, a duke, Merek had always been better at cutting with words than with swords.

Cedric was thankful to see both of the nobles unharmed, and prayed that their parents were still alive as well. His eyes met Kat's as the two groups converged in the hall. She scanned the space just as Cedric had. They were evenly matched—four of them versus four wraths. Not great odds, but not terrible, either. Kat cocked one eyebrow up and smiled.

"This is the last of them," one of the wraths said to the creature who was still gripping Cedric's arm. "Take them to the dungeons."

"Wait," Cedric said to the wrath that held him. "What if I have something to offer you instead? Something incredibly powerful."

The wrath made a grunting noise that might be construed as a laugh. "What might that be?"

In response, Cedric aimed his knee upward and connected solidly with the wrath's middle. Before the wrath could rebound, Cedric spun slightly, extended his leg and kicked it, hard. The creature doubled over, and its grip on Cedric loosened. Cedric drove his elbow into its neck, forcing it to the floor. He took the creature's knife and tossed it to Kat, who caught it with her free hand. She sunk the knife into her captor's side and twisted out of its grasp, so quick that her nightgown looked like a white blur against the backdrop of shadows and stone. She was sparring with the wrath that held Merek before her captor even hit the floor.

Cedric spun quickly to the wrath that held his younger sister. It tightened its hold around her throat as Cedric approached and Emme's blue eyes bulged slightly. Her mouth opened, but only a small, gasping sound emerged.

"Stop, or I choke the life from her body," the wrath growled.

Cedric put his open hands up. The wrath's black, bulging eyes flicked between Cedric and Kat. It didn't even notice as Emme lifted up her own hand, raking her fingernails violently down the creature's arm. The wrath howled, and in that instant,

Kat came up behind it and slashed across its shoulder. A spurt of blackish blood flowed from the wound. Howling in pain, the creature released Emme, who crumpled to the ground, gasping for air.

While the wrath clutched at its shoulder, Kat lunged forward again, plunging the knife into its neck. The creature clutched uselessly at its throat as it slumped to the ground, joining the other three fallen wraths.

"Something incredibly powerful?" Merek turned to Cedric and raised one eyebrow, which transformed his thin face into its usual expression of mild disdain.

Cedric looked to the wrath lying at his feet, then gave his own leg a light pat.

"I was referring to my high kick." He grinned. "Was that not clear?"

Merek rolled his eyes and bent down to take the knife from his fallen captor's hand. His nose wrinkled as he got closer to the creature.

"This one actually tried to *bite* me," he said.

"They will not stay down long," Kat said, brushing strands of dark hair out of her eyes. She left behind a dark streak of blood on her forehead.

Cedric glanced down at the wraths as their blood leaked onto the stone floor. The creatures could only be killed with silver, which was why all Guardian blades were made with the substance. But these knives belonged to the wraths and were made only of common metal. Sharp, but common. The wraths' wounds would heal in a matter of moments, and they would rise again. The one near Emme's feet was already starting to stir. She made a slight noise in her throat and moved away from it. Cedric took the creature's knife from its hand and stabbed it again for good measure.

"We should get out of here," Merek said, pointing toward the corridor's main doors. "Before more of them come."

"No," Cedric said. "First we find my father." He started running down the hallway toward the dungeons and didn't look back to see if the others would follow.

He knew they would.

When they neared the entrance to the dungeons, Cedric stopped. He motioned for the others to be quiet and then poked his head around the corner of the entryway.

Another wrath stood there in the hallway, holding a large sword. Its posture was relaxed, as though it didn't expect any trouble.

With one hand, Cedric gripped the handle of his borrowed knife. With the other, he reached under the collar of his nightshirt and pulled a golden chain from around his neck. On it sat a betrothal ring, one he'd worn since he was a child. He shot a look of apology to Kat, who wore its twin, before tossing the ring to the ground on the other side of the entryway. Cedric held his breath as the ring clattered against the stones.

"Who's there?" The wrath's footsteps echoed as it made its way nearer. As the creature approached the entryway, head turned toward the ring, Cedric ran up from the other direction and thrust the knife up under its ribs. He saw its head whip around and its coal-black eyes widen in surprise before it fell to the ground in a bulky heap.

Cedric threw the bloodied knife to the ground and picked up the fallen wrath's sword, as well as his betrothal ring. He signaled the others, and the group moved into the dark hallway. From the main corridor, Cedric could hear shouts and yells. The original wrath guards were waking up.

The stone walkway tilted downward, and the air grew colder as they moved closer to the dungeons. Finally, the dark bars of the cells came into view.

The first person Cedric saw was his father. The man was well over six feet tall, with arms thick as the massive rafters that ran across the dungeon ceiling. He was the kind of king that men wrote songs about—and Cedric would know, as he'd been forced to listen to most of them. But now, King James swayed unsteadily on his feet, his left leg twisted at an awkward angle. Dried blood covered the left side of his pale face and matted his beard.

"What are you doing here?" the king rasped.

"We got away from the wraths—"

"And you did not get your sister to safety immediately?"

Cedric tried to swallow the flicker of disappointment that ignited at his father's harsh words. "I'm freeing you," he said.

The other royal children moved to their own parents' cells, and Cedric heard a chorus of relief and fear as hands clutched hands through the bars. Emme reached out for their mother, who was held in the same cell as the king. Emme's long hair—the same deep brown color as Cedric's—swung forward as she leaned her forehead against the bars of the cell.

"Where are the keys?" Cedric asked.

King James met his eye. "Malquin has them."

Cedric shook his head, confused.

Malquin wasn't a wrath, but a man. He'd been known to haunt the city's bars and sometimes disrupt royal events spouting drunken nonsense. He was a nuisance, but considered mostly harmless, and a few years before he'd packed up and left the city altogether to make his own way in the wilderness. Cedric could barely even remember what he looked like.

"He led the wraths here," the king continued. "He calls himself their leader."

Cedric struggled to wrap his mind around his father's words. Malquin? Leader of the wraths? It was so . . . nonsensical. But then again, so was a wrath invasion of the castle.

"Where is Malquin now?" Cedric asked. He looked down at the thick metal padlock that hung from the cell door. The steel sword he clutched was no match for it.

"You have to run," the king said. "Leave us, and go."

Cedric shook his head. "No."

The queen pulled away from Emme and turned to Cedric. Tears tracked down her bone-white cheeks. "You must. Take your sister and the others. Get free of here. Get help."

Cedric looked back toward the entrance of the dungeons.

"You cannot go that way. Hundreds of wraths surround the palace," the king said.

Emme let out a small cry. "Hundreds?"

"But . . . how did we not notice them approach the city? How did they get in?" Cedric asked.

The king shook his head. "By the time we saw them coming, it was too late. They have infiltrated the whole city. We did not even have time to take up defensive posts before they overtook the castle. I have never seen so many in one place before, so organized, so armed . . ."

"We can fight them," Cedric said. He gripped the hilt of the unfamiliar sword in his hand and forced himself to meet his father's gaze.

"You cannot," the king responded. His tone was certain and harsh, and Cedric tried not to feel the sting of it. "There is another way out," the king continued. "The portal."

Cedric shook his head, uncomprehending. The rest of the jailed royals all stared at the king.

"But that is madness," said Lord Esson, Kat's father. "No one knows for sure where the portal leads. And the rumors . . ."

Cedric knew as well as anyone what rumors surrounded the portal. It had been found just outside the palace grounds some twenty years earlier, at the beginning of his father's rule. Many believed it led to the hellish ancient world of their people's origin, though there was no way to prove that claim. No one who entered the portal had ever returned.

The king's face was set. "It is the only chance they have—"

A clamor of noise from the top of the hallway interrupted him.

The king pulled himself up against the bars, close to Cedric. "Go to the portal, Cedric. The wraths will not need all of us as prisoners, and they will likely kill those they do not need."

"Father—"

"I am not only your father, but your king, and for once you will do as I say. And, Cedric . . . remember the scrolls!"

Cedric didn't have time to puzzle out his father's words before a group of wraths were upon them, led by Malquin himself.

"You know, a wise prince would have run away from his captors," Malquin said, looking at Cedric with a thin-lipped smile. He took a small handkerchief from his pocket and used it to wipe a smudge of dirt from his crippled left hand. Aside from the hand, and the shriveled, twisted arm to which it was attached, Malquin looked much like any other man in the realm. It was hard to tell his age—though his face was smooth and unlined, his shoulder-length hair was a shocking white.

"But then again," Malquin continued, "wise isn't exactly your reputation."

Cedric clutched the sword in his hand. Malquin's quick eyes caught the movement. "Now, now," he said. "This need not get messy."

Malquin gave a slight nod, and three wraths broke off and made for Cedric. Each was armed.

"Go," the king urged Cedric in a low, ragged whisper.

Cedric startled at the king's tone—his father wasn't commanding him this time. He was pleading. Cedric made up his mind in an instant and reached to grab Emme's hand.

"Run!" he yelled.

Instead of trying to charge through the wraths and up out of the tunnel, Cedric turned to head deeper into the dungeons, pulling Emme along. He looked behind once to ensure Kat and

Merek were following him. Few knew the location of the portal. Many even doubted its existence, as the king had kept it a close secret since it was discovered. He'd erected an entire hidden courtyard around it, accessible only through a series of tunnels that led through the dungeons. Even Cedric had not known how to access the tunnels before his seventeenth birthday a few months earlier. On that day, he'd finally convinced his father to show him the portal's location. After all, Cedric had reasoned, if he was going to rule Caelum someday, he should know of its secrets.

The dungeon tunnels twisted and turned, gradually leading the group upward once again. Cedric took intersections and offshoots quickly, struggling not to stumble over the loose rocks strewn across the floor as he ran. He heard the pounding footsteps of wraths chasing after them and only hoped they would get lost in the labyrinthine tunnels.

He arrived at one last intersection and turned left, coming up abruptly against a thick, wooden door. Cedric reached out to the wall on the left-hand side. He pushed on one stone after another, feeling nothing but cold rock under his fingers. Finally, one of the stones pushed inward, and the heavy door swung open.

Cedric stepped through it and into the hidden courtyard, lined with thick, high stone walls. It had no roof or ceiling, and when Cedric looked up, he could see stars glittering in the distance. At the end of the courtyard sat a large wooden box.

"Is that it?" Emme's voice broke through the still night. The others came through the door after her, panting.

"We cannot honestly be considering this," Merek said.

Cedric darted across the courtyard, lifted the box off of the ground, and tossed it aside. Hovering there an inch above the grass was a thick, swirling black mass roughly the size and shape of a man.

"It . . . it is real," Kat breathed.

A clatter of footsteps echoed from the tunnel.

"If we are going through, we must do it now," Cedric said in a hushed voice.

But he didn't move. No one did. All four of the royal children stared wide-eyed at the portal. Its whirling mass was mesmerizing. It seemed as though it was actually sucking in the darkness of the night, leaving all traces of moonlight behind.

"I am absolutely not going in there," Merek said.

"Stay behind and get skewered by wraths if you like," Kat replied.

"No," Cedric said. "We are all going." He held Merek's gaze for a moment before the other boy finally looked away.

"I do not think I can," Emme whispered to Cedric.

"It will be all right," Cedric replied.

"Promise?"

Cedric opened his mouth to respond, but was interrupted by the noise of the wraths pushing into the courtyard. They were followed by Malquin.

Malquin's eyes gleamed in the moonlight. He turned to Cedric. "I would not recommend going that way, young prince."

Cedric held up his sword. "That seems enough reason to go."

With an air of complete calm, Malquin reached into the pocket of his trousers with his good hand. He brought out a small, metal object that glinted in the moonlight as it moved. Cedric had never seen anything like it before. Part of the object was shaped like a small tube, cut open at one end and attached at an angle to a handle that vaguely resembled a sword hilt.

"Step away from the portal." Malquin aimed the device at Emme while the wraths formed a circle around their group, closing them in.

Cedric gripped the edge of his stolen sword's hilt, but didn't move.

Malquin shrugged. "Or have it your way." His finger moved slightly against the device in his right hand. Moving on instinct, Cedric dove and knocked Emme to the ground just before the night air was filled with a loud bang that reverberated off the stone walls.

A wrath standing just behind Emme crumpled to the grass, a black stain growing on his chest.

"What . . . ?" Cedric stared at the creature on the ground, then to Malquin's device. "What is this magic?" He got to his feet, directly between Malquin and Emme. The circle of wraths tightened around them, though some looked down at their fallen comrade, expressions of confusion flashing briefly across their gnarled faces.

Malquin merely smiled and raised the device again. Cedric shot a panicked look to Kat, who nodded once. Kat grabbed Merek by the arm and jumped into the swirling dark hole, pulling him behind her. One moment, they were standing on the solid, moonlit grass. The next, they were gone.

Emme gave a little scream as the pair disappeared into the

portal. Malquin's eyes fixed on the empty, dark mass, his mouth a small O of surprise. Even the wraths looked stunned. For a moment, no one moved.

Cedric heard another gasp and whipped around to see that a wrath had captured Emme from behind. It grasped her wriggling form and moved toward the dungeon doorway.

"Emme!" Cedric shouted.

Emme wrenched her head in his direction. "Go! Cedric, go!"

Cedric sprinted instead toward Emme. Two wraths jumped in front of him to block his way, but Cedric swung out wildly with his sword. His blow hit one wrath in the shoulder, cutting through mottled leather and hitting skin. Before Cedric could brace himself, the other wrath swung out with a stonelike fist and hit him in the chest.

Cedric stumbled backward. He looked up just in time to see Malquin aim the small, dark device directly at his face. He took one more step backward and prepared himself for another loud bang that would shatter the night, and likely his skull. But he never heard it. Instead, his momentum kept him reeling backward until he no longer felt grass beneath his feet. He was only falling, falling, falling . . .

At first, Cedric felt nothing, saw nothing, heard nothing. Once he realized he wasn't dead, he turned to look for the others, but he saw only black. He tried calling out to them, but no noise would escape his throat.

Then the space around him exploded into brightness. He landed, hard, on his hands and knees. Underneath him was a type of strange gray stone. He hurried to stand on unsteady feet.

Cedric spun around to the portal, which was no longer hanging in the air, but was now a dark circle against a stone wall. It grew smaller and smaller as Cedric stared.

"Emme!"

The portal shrank down to the size of a pebble and then blinked out, leaving only the stone behind. Cedric ran to the wall, to the place where the black hole had been, and threw his fists against it.

"Emme! Emme!" His scream seemed to tear from his throat of its own accord. He beat the wall with his fists until a pair of hands pulled firmly on his shoulders. Cedric turned to see Kat, whose eyes were fixed on the space where the portal had been.

"It's gone," she said, her voice flat.

"No. No. She is . . . We have to go back!"

Kat just shook her head, her expression grim. Behind her, Merek looked like he might be sick.

It was still night outside, but the air felt different, smelled different. When Cedric looked up, he couldn't see stars, only a frightening orange glow in the sky, and beyond that, a darker, empty blue. He could hear water running nearby, and when he looked for it he saw a small stream flowing over odd-looking stone. He was standing at the edge of a riverbed, only there were no trees, no shrubs, no dirt. Just flat gray and white all around—under his feet, over his head, on the wall behind him. It was cracked in some places, smooth in others, and altogether foreign.

They had actually made it—the other side of the portal.

The unfamiliar landscape grew fuzzy as Cedric tried to fight down a rising wave of panic. He gripped the hilt of the sword he'd stolen from the wrath guard, trying to think of a single thing to say, to find someplace solid for his mind to land—

"Hello?"

Cedric turned toward the sound of the tentative voice and saw a girl standing nearby. She wore a bright blue shirt covered in strange markings and trousers that fit tightly around her hips. She carried a sword but held it strangely, dangling by her side as if it weighed nothing. Her light brown hair was loose, and strands of it flew across her face in the breeze.

The girl spoke again, but Cedric could not make out her words. Behind him, he heard Merek shift. One of them would have to step forward, and Cedric knew who it should be.

"Are you the leader here?"

The girl's eyebrows rose, and she was close enough that Cedric could make out her greenish-brown eyes. "Um . . . I'm the director."

The girl began to babble then, using a mix of words Cedric recognized with ones he definitely did not. She gestured to a group of people who stood a distance behind her, and Cedric assumed she must be acting on their behalf. He looked again at her shirt, trying to make out what appeared to be a drawing on its front. It was a star inside of a blue circle, with larger red circles outside of that. He was still trying to interpret its meaning when he realized the girl had stopped talking and was looking at him, expectantly. Had she asked him a question?

"Where are we?" he asked, trying to sound more in charge than he felt.

"The Ellay River," she responded, then added a few more of her nonsense words. *Could this be hell?* Cedric wondered. Would hell have rivers? Maybe his father had been right, and the rumors of the portal land were false. Cedric tried to ask more questions of the girl, and received only frustrating answers in response.

Then the very ground he was standing on began to . . . shift. His first thought was that the portal was opening again, but no. The sky didn't open in a black, swirling mass. The sky stayed exactly where it was. It was everything else that moved.

How could the ground move?

"What is happening?" Cedric called out to the girl, who also looked startled. He struggled to maintain his balance. It felt as though someone were roughly pulling the ground back and forth, right underneath him.

Then he fell. It happened quickly. One moment he was using every muscle in his body to stay upright, and the next he was flying forward, as if he had been pushed. He landed hard onto something soft and realized he'd fallen onto the girl. He had just enough time to register that she felt like a normal human—skin and hair and bones—before he pushed himself away from her, hard.

Cedric looked around to see Merek and Kat on the ground as well, and that's when he realized his sword was no longer in his hand. He searched the area beneath him as it continued to shudder. The girl screamed something then, and he looked up. Her eyes were focused on the large piece of stone that ran over their heads—a bridge? It was moving as well. Could it fall on them? Could this whole realm be falling apart?

What sort of world was this?

Cedric reached for Kat's arm and pulled her out from under the stone structure. Merek followed as well. The whole world seemed to be shattering around them. And then, without warning, it stopped.

Cedric was breathless, and his heart was racing. It felt as though he'd just run for miles. He looked around him and saw the ground was intact, and the girl was staring at him with concern. Cedric looked to Kat and Merek, and they seemed unhurt.

Then the earth jerked again.

Before Cedric could speak, Merek whirled to face him. His hands were shaking and his eyes were wild with fear and panic.

Merek directed that panic right at Cedric, who tried not to flinch under his words. "I told you! I told you we should not have come to this hell. We are all going to die!"

Cedric wanted to say something back to calm Merek down, to contradict him. But wasn't he right? The king had told Cedric to go through the portal, but in the end, it had been his own decision that pushed them through. And now they had wound up in a place far worse, a place that seemed to want to shake them apart from their own skins.

They *were* in hell. Merek was right.

And then, Merek was gone. His body jerked, and then he was moving, running across the shaking ground.

Everything in Cedric wanted to stay right where he was and

wait for the world to still itself again, but he knew he couldn't. Merek was his responsibility. He looked at Kat, who seemed to understand. Together, they stood up and ran. Cedric spotted his sword lying nearby and stopped to pick it up by the hilt.

Cedric and Kat chased Merek across the gray stone, leaving the odd girl behind. Eventually, the earth stopped shaking again, but Merek didn't slow. He ran wildly, blindly. When the gray stone in front of him reached an end, he pulled himself up a low wall and onto a patch of brown earth. Cedric followed, then Kat.

Merek only stopped when he reached a point where he could run no farther. A long, low fence spanned the length of the ground in front of him. It looked like no fence that Cedric had ever seen, however. It wasn't made of wood, but of pieces of iron that shot from the ground and wound around each other, creating diamondlike patterns. Merek clutched at the thin pieces of interwoven iron with both hands, his chest heaving.

"Merek . . . ," Cedric started. But Merek wouldn't look at him. He threw one fist against the fence, which made an echoing, clinking noise in response.

"You think you know everything," Merek said, his breath ragged. "But you were wrong. Now look at us."

"We will get home again," Cedric said. "We will find a way to open the portal, go back and take Malquin by surprise—"

"How?"

Cedric said nothing. He thought of his father's words back in the dungeon, something about scrolls. He hadn't had much time to think about them while escaping through the tunnels, but now he tried to remember.

The only scrolls he could think of were part of a legend. They could supposedly open new portals from the Old World to Caelum. Cedric had always thought they were myth, but maybe . . .

"Cedric will find a way," Kat responded. She sounded confident, sure.

"My father told me how to get home," Cedric said, trying to sound just as confident. "We *will* go back."

Merek narrowed his eyes, but he was either out of responses or was too angry to form words.

A noise like screaming cut through the air and grew louder. Lights shone in the distance, coming from the same direction as the screaming. The lights weren't from torches, however; at least, they were like no torches Cedric had ever seen. To begin with, they were red and blue. Also, they rotated. As they grew nearer, Cedric could see the lights seemed to be attached to something—something large that hurtled toward them, just on the other side of the fence. It was boxy, big, and moving fast. A beast?

"What is that?" Merek screamed. "What is that?"

Cedric said nothing as the beast approached. He could see now that it was black and white underneath the swirling lights. Cedric held out his sword, but it felt off, different. How had he not noticed sooner? The sword wasn't the wrath's weapon he'd brought from Caelum. It was lighter, and under the hilt it was wrapped in a dense fabric instead of leather. The blade itself was no blade at all. It was not any kind of metal that Cedric knew—not steel or silver or bronze. Cedric ran his finger easily over the blunted edge.

It was worthless.

Cedric's grip on the nonsword loosened, and it fell to the ground. Again, he wondered what kind of world this was, where everything seemed false and unreal.

The beast with red-and-blue lights moved toward them, and now Cedric could see actual letters along its hide—LOS ANGELES—and smaller writing underneath.

He looked at his hands, which were empty, open. Exposed. His sword was gone. His last link to Caelum was gone. A fear stronger than any he had ever known gripped Cedric, and he couldn't move. He stood between Merek and Kat, frozen, watching as the beast grew closer, knowing they had no way to fight it off. They had no backup, no weapons, no knowledge of anything around them.

They were entirely alone.

THE ARTIFACT

Two months later

Liv pulled the curtains wide to let in the harsh morning light.

As she crossed her small bedroom, she avoided looking into the cracked mirror above her cheap flea-market bureau. She didn't need confirmation of the dark circles under her eyes or the knots in her hair. She knew from experience that looking into a mirror in direct California sunlight after getting only three hours of sleep could not end well for anyone.

Stretched across Liv's tiny twin bed, Shannon slept on, face smushed against the pillow, last night's clothes twisted around her body. Liv smiled, grabbed her phone from her nightstand, and clicked open the camera app. She turned on the flash, inched closer to the bed, and lowered the phone until Shannon's half-open mouth was centered in the screen.

Shannon groaned as the bright light flashed across her face.

"What're you doooinnng?" Shannon mumbled, half turning over and crossing her arms over her face. "Too early."

"Actually, we're late." Liv smiled and snapped another

picture. "Gotta get up."

"Ugh, no."

"Come o-on," Liv said in a singsong voice. Then, less quietly, "You promised, remember? You said if I went out with you last night, you'd drive me to my appointment in the morning." Liv pulled the comforter off of her best friend, causing her to curl up like a worm exposed to sunlight. "And it is now officially morning."

Shannon groaned, her eyes still closed. "You're so not my favorite person right now."

"What if I buy you a coffee . . . ?"

"Hmmgh."

"From Coffee Bean?"

Shannon exhaled, then opened her eyes. "Fine."

Liv laughed as Shannon finally sat up and ran her hand tentatively through her newly shortened hair. It was matted to her head, and its tips—which had also recently been dyed red—stuck up in funny angles around her ears. Her mascara ran from the corner of her eye down to her ear on one side, and her long, dangling earring had left an imprint in her cheek from when she'd slept on it in the night.

Shannon looked in the cracked mirror and shook her head. "Ugh. This is gonna take some time."

"We don't have time. I'm supposed to meet with the museum acquisitions lady at ten."

"Ten a.m. During the last week of summer. Just feels so wrong." Shannon picked up a limp strand of hair and let it fall back against her forehead. Then she pulled out the tube of red lipstick she'd worn the night before and reapplied it to her lips, smacking them together when she was done. While Liv only really dressed up when Shannon dragged her out to all-ages clubs, Shannon treated every single day like it was a Saturday night.

Liv slipped a jacket over her shoulders to cover up what Shannon mockingly called the only evidence of her "inner wild child," an ill-gotten tattoo that she preferred to ignore. She slipped on a pair of Chucks and went systematically through her room, erasing any signs of mess. First, she made up her bed, pulling the sheet into tight hospital corners and arranging the pillows by the headboard. She collected a few stray hair ties from the floor and piled them neatly on her dresser, next to the one decoration in the room that was truly hers—a framed photo of herself and Shannon they'd taken during an excursion to Amoeba Records. Every other decoration in the room had been placed there by her foster mother, Rita.

The small guest bedroom still had the mothball-smelling floral bedspread and generic framed pictures of kittens on the walls that were there when Liv had moved in a year before. Most of her important belongings were hidden away in the closet—her meager camera equipment, sketchbooks, and photographs. One of the first things she had learned as a foster kid was to keep anything she valued hidden away or locked up. It also helped to know that she could always pack up her whole life with five minutes' notice.

Liv's eyes tracked over the nearly spotless room. The only item truly out of place was the heavy sword, which rested against the wooden bureau. She picked it up for the first time in weeks and was again instantly surprised by its weight. At first glance, the sword could almost pass as fake, the kind of cheap item sold at Comic-Con or a ren faire, until she actually felt its heft in her hands.

Liv was relieved to finally be getting rid of it. She'd had a hard time shaking that weird night of the film shoot from her mind. Not only had she had to completely change her shooting plans—thanks to Jeremy being too freaked out by the earthquake to return to the river—but now she had this unwanted prop as a reminder of that night. Every time she saw it, she thought of the strangers in nightgowns who'd shown up out of nowhere before disappearing just as quickly, the shaking ground, the lost equipment. Hopefully once the sword was out of sight, that night and its unanswered questions would be out of her mind as well.

Right after bringing the sword home, Liv had immediately called her caseworker, Joe, to tell him about what had happened. She'd first thought to call the police, but then realized that a teenage foster kid in possession of a deadly weapon probably wasn't the most credible witness. So Joe had called the police for her, and they'd said the sword hadn't been reported as stolen. They'd agreed to keep an eye out for the weird teens or reports of missing weapons, but after two months, Joe hadn't heard from them. He was the one who suggested that Liv donate the sword to a museum if she wanted to get rid of it so badly. It looked old enough to probably belong there anyway.

"Let's go," Liv said to Shannon as she carefully walked across the room, holding the sword and its crazy sharp edges as far from her skin as possible. She led Shannon through the tiny hallway with its nicotine-stained walls and into the kitchen, where she frowned at the dirty dishes in the sink. As soon as they reached the living room, Liv came to a halt. Rita was passed out cold on the sofa. Just like Shannon, she was still wearing last night's clothes. Her heels and purse rested under the coffee table near two empty bottles of wine.

"Looks like we weren't the only ones out late, celebrating the end-time," Shannon said.

Liv pulled Shannon slightly away from the doorway and lowered her voice to a whisper. "Shh, don't wake her. And enough with the dramatic apocalypse stuff."

"Well, what would *you* call four earthquakes in three months?" Shannon asked, her voice as close to a whisper as it could get. Which was not very.

"I call it summer in LA. Now come on."

Liv set the sword carefully against the wall and walked slowly toward Rita, navigating around some tubes of lipstick that had somehow found their way out of Rita's purse and onto the floor.

Up close, Rita looked peaceful. Her usually teased and sprayed hair was flattened into submission against a couch pillow, and her eyes fluttered as if she was dreaming. The heavy curtains in the living room were slightly parted, letting in a crack of daylight to fall across Rita's face. Through them, Liv could see Rita's useless, broken-down car sitting in the driveway. Next to it was Liv's still crappy, but at least functioning, Toyota. It wasn't pretty, but it had taken Liv two after-school jobs to save up for the down payment, and she was proud of it. Ordinarily, she'd be driving her own car to the museum. But this week, she'd lent it to Rita until Rita made enough tip money to get her own car fixed. Liv figured it was the least she could do.

Rita wasn't the best foster parent Liv had ever had. That honor went to Chuck and Marty, the elderly couple who'd taken her in when she was eight. They were the ones who'd bought her her first camera, who'd shown her *E.T.* for the first time. They had encouraged her obsession with movies, even letting her stay up late to watch old classics like *The Godfather* and *Casablanca* with them on their sixteen-inch TV. Liv could have stayed with them forever, but unfortunately Marty had to move back to Australia to take care of his sick mom, and Chuck had gone with him. They left Liv behind.

Since then, though, the foster family situation had seriously declined. Liv had moved from house to house, getting bounced out of some, running away from others. Rita wasn't perfect, but she treated Liv with respect and left her alone most of the time. They got along.

Liv drew an old afghan down from the back of the couch and spread it across Rita. She picked up the empty wine bottles and carried them into the kitchen, careful not to clank them against each other as she lined them up neatly on the countertop. Now that her summer program was over, she'd have some time to spend cleaning up the house before school started up.

Sparing one last glance at her foster mom, Liv once again picked up the sword and motioned to Shannon. Together, they slipped out through the screen door and into the hot late-August morning.

⁂

Shannon pulled her mom's minivan over to the side of the road, right across the street from the Natural History Museum. She yawned, then reached out to take a gulp from the iced coffee that sat in her cup holder.

"How long will this take, you think?"

Liv shrugged. "Maybe like an hour or so? I haven't exactly done this before. Sure you don't want to come with?" Liv asked.

"Tempting, but since I already have this baby out of the house," Shannon said, patting the minivan's steering wheel, "might as well take advantage. Think I'm going to swing down through the fashion district, see if there's any sales."

"Your mom's gonna kill you."

Shannon shrugged. Her parents had grounded her when they discovered Shannon had spent her summer not volunteering at the library like she'd claimed, but acting in Liv's movie. Both conservative Minnesota transplants, Shannon's parents weren't too pleased about their daughter's obsession with becoming the next Jennifer Lawrence. Not that their disapproval stopped Shannon. Nothing ever stopped Shannon.

"What are they going to do, lock me in my room? There's, like, laws against that," Shannon said with a grin. "Text me when you need me to pick you up?"

"Sounds good." Liv opened the door handle, maintaining a careful grip on the sword. Before she got out, Shannon reached over and grabbed at her sleeve.

"Are you sure you just want to give that thing up? I mean, it could be worth something."

Liv lifted an eyebrow. "Yeah, and getting mixed up in the

arms market is exactly what I need on my college resume."

"For all you know, that thing could pay for college. Or your next movie."

This gave Liv pause for just a moment, but then shook her head. "Not worth the trouble."

"Please. You love trouble."

"Uh, I think you're confusing me with you," Liv said as she hopped out of the van.

"If you say so. See you in a bit."

As Shannon pulled away from the curb, Liv turned to face the museum. Though she'd lived in Los Angeles her whole life, she'd never actually been here before. She walked up the path toward the front door, passing vendors selling fruits and bags of chips. She was quickly surrounded by families and groups of kids trailing stressed-looking nannies.

Liv's eyes flicked over the crowd. Her mind went through its regular mental checks, running through the same questions it did whenever she saw the unfamiliar faces of kids around her age—how many of them were fair-haired, bespectacled boys a couple of years older than her, and how many were freckled young girls who tripped over their own feet when they walked? It had been nearly ten years since Liv had seen her biological brother and sister, and it was unlikely she'd run into them by chance, and unlikelier still that she'd recognize them when she did.

But she couldn't help checking, every time.

No boys or girls she saw matched the outdated images of Peter and Maisy that she clung to in her mind, and Liv breathed a sigh of both disappointment and relief. Once the flickering hope had passed, it was easier to get on with her day. She gripped the sword closer and made her way quickly inside.

The first thing Liv noticed was a giant skeleton of a T. rex, one she recognized from dozens of television shows and movies that had been shot at the museum. As she walked around it, Liv got that strange feeling she always got when she encountered something in person in LA that she had first seen on a television screen—a sense of inclusion, like she was being let in on a secret that no one else knew. Like she was seeing behind the scenes of something amazing.

Liv pulled out her phone and rechecked the email she'd been sent by the assistant to the museum's acquisitions director. She was supposed to meet with the director, who would appraise the sword and hopefully take it off her hands as a donation made to the museum in her name. The hilt of the sword felt hot in Liv's hands as she made her way up to the museum's member desk. An older woman with glasses looked Liv up and down, raising one eyebrow when she saw the sword point dangling down by Liv's knee. Liv cleared her throat and explained she had an appointment. The woman said nothing, but turned to a monitor on the desk. She typed into it for a few minutes, then gestured for Liv to follow her.

The desk woman led Liv through a series of hallways and deposited her on a wooden chair outside of a door labeled "Acquisitions."

"Should I just wait?" Liv asked.

"Dr. Clark knows you're here," the woman said, before

turning around and leaving Liv alone in the hall.

She didn't see another person for forty-five minutes.

Though the entrance to the museum had been bustling, this back hallway was nothing but stillness and silence. Liv's ears perked up whenever she heard the sound of footsteps in the distance, but they always trailed off before coming her way. The Acquisitions door remained firmly shut. She played with her phone until finally the door creaked open, and a mousy-looking man peered out into the hall.

"Olivia Phillips?"

"That's me," Liv said, standing.

The man motioned for her to sit back down. "I'm so sorry, but Dr. Clark is running behind this morning. We just got a big shipment from Egypt."

"Oh," Liv said. "Do you know what time—"

"Hard to say," the man interrupted. "Maybe you could visit the exhibits, and I'll call you when Dr. Clark is ready?" he suggested. A phone rang in the background, and the man's eyes twitched in the direction of the sound.

"Uh, sure," Liv said. She held up the sword. "But what should I do with this?"

The man paused for a moment, thinking. The phone kept ringing, and he held out his hand. "We'll keep it here. Don't worry. Dr. Clark is eager to meet with you; she's having an extremely busy morning."

Liv put the sword hilt in the man's outstretched fist.

"Sure, I understand. My number is—"

"I have it," the man said, then shut the door again in Liv's face.

"O-kay," she said to the closed door.

Liv found her way back to the visitors' portion of the museum and texted Shannon with an update. She ate at the museum grill before passing through several rooms, gazing over shiny rocks in the gems and minerals room and passing a hundred-year-old trolley in the Los Angeles exhibit. She checked her phone every two minutes as the day slid by.

At 4:47, Liv officially passed from irritated into fully pissed off. She had been hoping to spend the afternoon storyboarding ideas for her next short film project, but now those hours were lost. Liv pushed against the flow of exiting museum traffic, trying to make her way back to the Acquisitions Department one last time. She was going to tell the mousy man that Dr. Clark could just keep the freaking sword, and leave her out of it.

Liv turned in the general direction she thought would lead her back to the office. Every hallway she stepped into was less crowded than the one she'd just left. The voices of the crowd behind her began to filter out and then fade altogether.

After twenty minutes, Liv looked up to discover she was completely alone, in front of a doorway with a banner strung up over it. The banner featured an odd symbol, a small, dark circle with two lines drawing down from it like daggers. Liv stared at the mark for a moment, unable to look away. It seemed so familiar, and yet she couldn't place where she'd seen it before. The words below the mark read "**LOST LANGUAGES EXHIBIT, JULY–OCT.**"

Liv pushed the door open and stepped inside. The room was empty—lost languages not having quite the same draw as velociraptor bones. Lining the walls of the room were long, glass cases filled with yellowing books and pieces of parchment. The door at the far end of the room was propped open slightly by a small rock. Gold letters stretched across its metal surface, reading "**MUSEUM ARCHIVES ROOM—PERMISSION REQUIRED**."

Liv checked her watch—past five thirty now—and cursed under her breath.

Just as she turned to go, Liv saw a flash of blue from beyond the nearly closed door at the end of the room. She walked toward it, and through the crack between the door and the wall, she saw a dimly lit corridor. Walking quickly in the opposite direction down the hall was a tallish boy wearing a blue shirt—the uniform of the museum security guards.

Liv briefly thought to call out and ask for directions to the Acquisitions Department, but then the security guard turned to a door on his left. And Liv's mouth dropped open.

She knew that profile. It wasn't just familiar—it screamed out from her memory. Dark hair, square jaw, and blue, blue eyes. It was him. The boy from under the bridge. The sword boy himself, here in the flesh.

Momentarily stunned, Liv could do nothing but stare as the boy quickly slipped into a side door from the hallway. She hadn't expected to ever see him again, let alone here, in the back hallway of a public museum, dressed as a security guard. It was surreal enough to stop her in her tracks, but there was no mistake—it was the same boy.

"Wait!" Liv called out, finally finding her voice. But she was a moment too late, and the door slammed behind him.

Her mind raced. What was Sword Boy doing here? Had he been following her? Maybe to get the sword back? But if so, why had he waited two months? And what was with the uniform? Nothing made sense.

Without even thinking, Liv stepped into the hallway. She let go of the metal door, and it fell backward. It knocked aside the rock that had been propping it open and hit against the doorjamb with a small click. Liv reached out to try the handle, but it held firm. Locked.

"Of course," she whispered.

There was nowhere to go except forward down the hallway, in the same direction as the sword boy / security guard / walking unsolved-mystery person. She had definitely entered an off-limits area, one that wasn't meant to be seen by paying guests. Unlike the cool marble corridors of the museum proper, this hallway was covered with old, scuffed linoleum. Fluorescent lights hung from metal cages in the ceiling. Instead of glass cases or displays, the walls of the hallway were lined with closed doors.

Liv reached the area of the hallway where the boy had turned. On her left-hand side was a scuffed-up wooden door with a glass pane located at eye level.

At first, all Liv could see through the grimy glass pane were books. Rows and rows of books, arranged on overcrowded metal bookshelves that were set up haphazardly around the room. Some of the books looked old, with cracked leather bindings and yellowed covers. Others seemed to be held together just by rubber bands.

Liv couldn't see the boy. But in the far corner of the room, something was moving. A tall metal bookshelf seemed to be gliding across the room. Liv leaned closer to the windowpane to get a better look, almost smacking her forehead on the glass.

At the bottom of the metal unit, she could see a hand, pulling the bookshelf. The hand was attached to an arm, which disappeared . . . into a hole in the wall. No, not a hole, Liv realized. A tunnel. The mouth of the tunnel was rough and jagged, and only about three feet high. It obviously wasn't an official passageway—it didn't look like it belonged in the museum at all. The boy had crawled inside it, and was now dragging a bookshelf back to cover the hole. One book fell from the shelf and landed on the ground with a smacking noise, which made Liv jump.

The bookshelf was once again resting immobile against the wall and covering the tunnel as Liv pushed her way into the room and over to it. For a moment, she looked at the bookshelf, as if willing herself to see beyond it.

She was debating whether or not to call out again when she heard the muted sounds of voices coming from behind the bookshelf. Liv strained to listen, but couldn't make out what the voices were saying. She gripped the edges of the metal bookshelf and pulled with all her might. After finally budging it a few inches away from the wall, she stopped to listen again.

". . . hear that?" The voice sounded young, like a teenage girl. Someone responded in a gruff voice that Liv couldn't make out.

The girl's voice continued. ". . . cannot keep going on like this . . ."

Liv leaned closer, but the voices were moving in the opposite direction, getting harder to hear. She could turn around right now, somehow find a way around the locked door and back to the main part of the museum and then home, leaving the sword and this whole incident behind her forever. But seeing the boy again felt like too big, too strange a coincidence to ignore. What if she left now and spent the rest of her life with unanswered questions about that night under the bridge and the white-clad sword switcher who'd somehow morphed into a museum security guard?

"Oh, hell," she said under her breath, as she peered into the wall tunnel. "If Indiana Jones can do it . . ."

Positioning herself to the side of the bookshelf, Liv put her shoulder against it and pushed with all of her might. The shelf inched backward from the wall with a screeching groan. Liv stopped when there was just enough space between the bookshelf and the wall for her to slip through. She took a deep breath, crouched down, and stepped into the dark tunnel.

THE LABYRINTH

At first Liv saw only blackness and shadows, but as she inched farther into the tunnel, her eyes began to adjust to the darkness. The walls around her were rough, and sharp edges of brick, cement, and metal pressed out on either side.

Liv took out her phone and pressed the 9 and 1 buttons, then left her thumb hovering over the glowing numbers. If following a potentially unbalanced—if admittedly hot—stranger boy down into the unlit bowels of a quiet museum turned out to be a huge mistake, she at least wanted to be prepared.

Liv slowly moved forward, almost convincing herself she was fully in control of the situation. After a few more steps, the tunnel opened up into what appeared to be an old hallway, one with smooth cement floors and actual, constructed walls, albeit ones that looked like they might crumble apart at any second. The hallway didn't seem to have working lights or doors. It stretched on into the darkness as far as Liv could see, and she took one turn after the next, following the distant sound of voices as they moved away. After a few minutes, they became clear again.

". . . know I heard something . . ."

". . . please, just trust me . . ."

". . . too dangerous . . . someone could get killed. . . ."

Liv stopped in her tracks. Although she couldn't see them, she could feel the hairs rising on her arms. Killed?

It hit her all at once, how dumb it was for her to come down here. Though she was in the exact same position she had been in moments earlier, everything suddenly looked different. Her flimsy sense of control slipped away completely like the unreliable companion it was, leaving her alone in an underground tunnel with a smartphone for a weapon.

What had she been thinking? Pretending to be all Indiana Jones–confident, when this could just as easily be a *Silence of the Lambs* situation?

Liv raised her phone's screen to shed light on the darkness in front of her and took a step backward. Her foot landed on something hard and pointy, and she winced when it cut through the bottom of one of her Chucks. A rock. The sound of the rock scraping against the cement floor issued a faint echo through the tunnel.

"There, I know I heard something that time," the girl's voice said in a harsh whisper.

The male voice replied, but Liv couldn't make it out. She stopped in her tracks, straining to hear. At first there was nothing. Just the sound of her own breathing. But then, heavy footsteps echoed out in the hallway. They were heading in her direction, and they were running.

Liv started moving backward quickly, away from the rapidly approaching footsteps. She brought her thumb down on the 1 on her phone, pressed send, and waited for the emergency call to go through . . .

The call didn't connect. She had zero bars.

Obviously.

Liv sucked in her breath and picked up her pace. She kept her eyes on the darkness in front of her as the running footsteps got louder and louder. The light from her phone bounced wildly along the tunnel walls, and Liv couldn't make out where she was going. Her foot hit a bump in the floor, and she pitched forward.

A hand reached out and grabbed Liv's arm from behind, jerking her backward. Just as she started to scream, another hand clapped against her mouth, trapping her cry against her throat, unheard.

Liv tried not to panic.

That was one of the first things she'd picked up in her self-defense class, which she'd taken at a community center when she was fourteen and had been placed in a particularly unsatisfactory home along with two handsy sixteen-year-old boys. To panic is to waste valuable time. It's far better to stop, wait to catch your breath, and then strike your assailant in the place they're most vulnerable.

Liv counted to three, then bit down hard on the fingers that were clamped over her mouth.

"Ow! You bit me!"

Liv whirled around, arms up in defense mode, and found

herself facing a tallish figure. She swung her phone's screen around to light him up and saw it was him, of course. The boy from under the bridge. He winced in the bluish light, and put his finger up to his mouth, sucking on the space where Liv had bit into his skin.

"You grabbed me!"

"Only to stop you from screaming," he said in his strange, unplaceable accent. "Who are you? What are you doing down here?"

"Um . . ." Liv's hand shook as she tried to think of a single good answer, and the light from her phone bounced around the walls of the tunnel. The boy tracked the light to her face, and his eyes widened in surprise.

"You," he said. "You are the girl from the night we . . . but how did you come to be here? Did you follow me?"

"No. I mean, technically, yes," Liv replied, feeling flustered. "But I only followed you to see why you were following me."

The boy blinked. "What?"

Liv shook her head. "What are *you* doing here?"

"I believe I asked you first."

"What are you, twelve?" Liv took a deep breath. "Let's start over. A couple months ago, I was shooting my movie when I saw you and some other kids in pajamas down by the river. You acted sketch as hell, somehow switched swords with me, and ran away, so again I ask, what are you doing *here*?"

The boy's eyes widened. They looked almost black in the tunnel, and remained fixed and intensely focused on her. He grabbed Liv's arm.

"You have my sword?"

"Are you sure it's yours? You didn't steal it from anywhere?" She looked around the tunnel, wondering what other rooms in the museum it might connect to. "Like, say, from a museum? Are you some kind of security guard grifter who peddles stolen swords on the side?"

"A . . . what?"

Liv grimaced. "I don't think I could say it again."

The boy shook his head, as if trying to clear it. "I did not steal the sword. You did."

Liv pulled her arm free.

"I didn't steal it. You left it behind. And I was just delivering it to the museum, where it probably belongs."

"It is here?" The boy asked, his eyes lighting up in the darkness. "Where?"

Liv realized she wasn't likely to get any satisfactory answers out of this strange boy. Talking to him was like trying to have a conversation with the staticky, disembodied voice that took orders at the Fatburger drive-through. Frustrating and near impossible. Now what she wanted most was to get out of this cold, dirty tunnel that she regretted walking into in the first place. And she certainly no longer cared what became of that stupid sword. It was officially time to bail.

"Tell you what," Liv said, summoning courage. "I'll tell you where the sword is if you tell me the fastest way out of here."

The boy seemed to consider her for a moment, then nodded. He looked behind him once, into the blackness of the tunnel, and Liv wondered if the girl he had been talking to was still back there, listening. Was it the same girl from under the bridge? Then the boy turned again toward Liv.

"We have a deal."

And then he bowed. Actually, truly, bent at the waist and bowed.

"Uh . . ."

The boy didn't wait for a better response. He started off in the direction Liv had come from without turning around to see if she was following him. They walked in silence for a few moments, Liv following the careful bobbing of his dark head as it ducked beneath low-hanging sections of the ceiling.

The boy came to an abrupt stop, turned right, and put his hands up against the wall. Through the dimness, Liv could just make out the outlines of a wooden panel—one she hadn't seen on the way in. The boy grabbed the edges of the panel with both hands and pulled, yanking it free. Behind the panel there was another hallway, also dark and abandoned. He stepped through the opening and then put his hand back for Liv.

"This isn't the way we came in," Liv said.

"It is the fastest way out."

Liv hesitated a moment, then reached out for the boy's hand and clasped it. His palm was warm and she felt strength in his rough, callused fingers. Liv looked up from his hand and saw that he was watching her, his eyes slightly narrowed. He gave a light shake of his head—like he was trying to clear it of something—and pulled her into the second tunnel after him. When she was through, the boy let go of her hand, and Liv let it fall back to her side. She felt strangely conscious of it then, of its weight and feel, of the sweatiness of her palm. She balled it into a fist and continued walking.

After a few minutes, Liv saw an opening far up ahead and what looked like the late afternoon light filtering in. Finally, they reached a grate in the worn concrete wall, about two feet high and two feet wide and located just a few inches off the ground. The boy reached down to loosen the edges of the grate and ply it away from the wall.

"Out you go," he said.

"Wait," Liv protested. "Are you serious? Where does this even lead?"

"To a side alley, east of the museum. Turn left and walk true, and you will eventually find the main thoroughfare. It is the fastest way out."

Liv was about to duck to go through the grate when the boy reached out and touched her lightly on the shoulder.

"The sword?"

"Last I saw it, it was in the Acquisitions Department. It's probably still there."

Relief washed over his face. "Thank you," he said.

"Sure, uh, anytime," Liv responded. "You're kind of a weirdo, and possibly a criminal, but I guess I'm sorry I bit you."

For the first time, Liv saw the boy smile. It was a nice smile, a slightly uneven one that turned up on the right side of his face more than the left. It made him look younger. "I will heal."

Liv dropped down lower to the ground but turned back toward the boy once more.

"I'm Liv, by the way."

The boy paused before responding. "Cedric."

"Well . . . 'bye, Cedric. Enjoy your sword."

"Good-bye, Liv."

With that, he turned and started walking back through the tunnel. Liv hesitated, stopped by the strange urge to call something out after him that would make him turn around. Instead, she watched Cedric disappear around a slight curve in the tunnel before ducking her head through the grate and crawling into the alley beyond.

It was still light out, but the sun had fallen behind the museum wall, casting shadows over the narrow space. On the opposite side of the alley was a brick wall separating Liv from a small park. Down at the far end to her left, she could just barely make out a few cars driving by on Exposition Boulevard. Liv started walking. After a few moments, she thought she heard footsteps treading behind her. She turned around, expecting to see Cedric, but saw only the brick walls of the alley and an overturned recycling bin. She turned back and hastened her steps.

There it was again. Definite footsteps.

"Cedric?" Liv called out.

No response. It sounded as though the footsteps were getting closer. Liv whipped her head around, trying to see who was following her, and ran smack into something solid and large. She bounced back and nearly fell to the ground. The solid figure—a man—reached an arm out and steadied her.

"Sorry," Liv gasped. "I thought there was . . . something."

The man stared at Liv. He was more than six feet tall,

dressed in simple jeans and a T-shirt. Dark, thinning hair curled around his ears and dropped to the edges of his shoulders. For a moment, his face betrayed no expression. Then he smiled.

Or no, *smiled* wasn't exactly the word for it. His lips curled up, exposing his teeth, and the skin crinkled around his eyes. But there was no warmth there. It was the approximation of a smile, like something you'd see on a Halloween mask. The man was still holding on to Liv's arm.

"Um, I think I should go—"

Liv tried to wriggle her arm free, but the man just gripped tighter.

"Where you headed, little girl?" he asked. Liv shivered at the hollowness in his voice. A familiar warning sign went off in the back of her head. Danger.

Many people felt it at some time or another, when they passed homeless men muttering to themselves on the street, or a group of teenage boys walking by with their pants hanging low. But Liv knew the most dangerous people were often the ones you didn't expect. Signs of hunger, mental instability, or bad fashion choices weren't the things to watch out for. It was a certain tone of voice, a calculated attempt at humanity. An emptiness.

Liv twisted her arm free with a violent yank, sprinted around the man, and took off running down the alley toward the main street. Her heart burned against her chest. The man was close behind her; she could feel it. She could hear him gaining on her.

And then, without warning, something landed squarely against Liv's back, knocking her to the ground.

Liv struggled to breathe, but she couldn't find air. She squirmed and rolled around until she was facing up, and saw the face of the man leering down at her. He had her pinned to the ground by the arms and was smiling that awful smile. She knew how to get through this—she just had to find the most vulnerable point and strike it. The man's throat was defenseless, and the hand pinning her left arm to the ground was loosening. If she could just free her hand, she could jam her fingers into the skin there. . . .

Liv prepared to swing up her left arm, but then froze when she saw the man's face. His smile stretched wider and his eyes . . . his eyes changed colors, turning from dark brown to black. It was as if the pupils completely dilated and spread, overtaking first the irises, and then the whites of his eyes. Pooling slowly outward, like ink spilled in a glass of milk.

After a moment, the man's eyes were completely black. His smile stretched, opening wider than any mouth should. And his teeth—there was something wrong with his teeth. There were . . . more of them than there should be.

Liv blinked rapidly, trying to clear up this image that was so obviously wrong. It didn't work. She wondered if she had a concussion. The man leaned in, his teeth getting closer and closer to her face.

"I've been waiting for you all day," he said. "So tell me quick, girl, where are the rest of your little friends?"

Liv tried to control her ragged breathing, tried to curb the panic running through her limbs. "I don't know what you're talking about," she choked out. "Please . . ."

"No need to beg," the man continued. "Answer my questions, and I will let you go. Fight me, and I will leave your mangled body behind as a warning for the others."

Liv struggled to suck in air as the man leaned down even closer and whispered into her ear. "Personally, I hope you choose to fight."

He gripped her jaw with his hand, and Liv screamed.

THE MONSTER

Teeth. Hot breath and so, so many teeth.

Liv was still screaming, but she doubted anyone would come running. The opening to the alley was too far away.

The man's lips curled back. He put his mouth against her cheek, and she felt those teeth touch her skin. Liv braced herself for the pain . . .

But it didn't come. Instead, the man jerked backward. He flew through the air and landed on the ground a few feet from Liv. Standing behind him, brandishing a shining knife the size of a forearm, was Cedric.

Cedric's eyes blazed, and he spared just one glance to Liv before advancing on the man.

Liv scrambled to her feet at the same time her attacker did. A voice in the back of her brain screamed at her to *run, run*! But she couldn't move; she was frozen solid, a statue in jeans and Chucks. And even if she could run, she didn't know which direction to go. The hulking man blocked her exit to the road.

Liv couldn't look away from the man's face. His eyes were still entirely black, reflecting zero light. He hissed at Cedric, a completely inhuman sound.

Cedric lunged at him, and for a moment, he seemed inhuman, too. His movements were so fast, so sure. His face was entirely altered from the one she'd seen in the museum tunnel. He wore the rigid expression of a seasoned boxer, calculating his opponent's next move. One second he was standing flat on the pavement, knife in hand, and the next he was at the man's throat.

The man tried to dodge Cedric. He, too, was moving fast. Much too fast. But he wasn't as fast as Cedric.

Liv tried to keep up with the tangle of limbs, heads, and legs, but she had a hard time telling Cedric apart from her attacker in the fading light. Every few moments she saw the gleaming blade whip through the air before plunging down again. She couldn't tell if it was connecting with anything.

Then she saw an arm in blue sleeves—Cedric's—reach out in a slicing motion. She heard more hissing from the black-eyed man as he leaped away. He was holding his neck, and blood was trickling through his fingers. He was no longer smiling.

"You cannot defeat me with that toy," he growled.

Cedric actually smiled in response, the right side of his lips pulling upward. "No, but I can have a great deal of fun trying."

The man lunged for Cedric again, but at the last second he altered his attack, sliding toward the ground and kicking out straight to knock Cedric off his feet. Cedric hit the pavement with a hollow thud, and his smile fell from his face. The man got up and crouched over Cedric's back, pinning his neck to the ground with one hand.

"Help!" Liv screamed. She turned toward the museum, but saw no doors or windows nearby. "Please help us!"

But even as she screamed her voice raw, she knew there was no time. The black-eyed man was reaching for Cedric's right hand, the one with the blade. He pinched Cedric's wrist hard and weakened his grasp. Liv could see that it would only be a matter of seconds before the knife was ripped free.

"Cedric!" she yelled. But this time, she moved as well.

Concentrate on the weak points. The weak points. The weak points.

The black-eyed man was focused on Cedric. He didn't see Liv approach, didn't see her kick out with all her might toward the side of his knee.

Liv's right foot connected hard, sending vibrations up her leg. The black-eyed man's leg bent inward. He let out a long, horrid cry and clutched at his knee. Liv reached into her pocket and closed her fist around her keys. She fumbled a bit with the biggest key, the one that unlocked Rita's front door, and situated it between her ring and middle fingers, pointing outward. Before the black-eyed man could get to his feet, Liv punched out with her fist, key first, toward his left eye.

He pulled away just in time, jerking backward so that the tip of the key caught the skin under his eye instead of its intended target. His lips curled and he made a noise that sounded like a cat growling. And not a small cat, either.

Liv's mind raced to think of her next move. The man swung

out with alarming speed and grabbed for Liv's arm, getting a grip on her jacket sleeve. She pulled backward, maneuvering herself out of her jacket and pulling her arm free. The momentum sent her spinning, and she crashed to the ground, landing hard on her forearms. The chilly night air blew across her neck and back, exposed in just a tank top.

Liv twisted her head around to face the black-eyed man. But he stood still, his mouth hanging partially open. He was staring at Liv with wide, rounded eyes that now seemed more human than feral. He almost looked surprised. Liv's torn jacket dangled limply in his hands before falling to the ground.

Before either the black-eyed man or Liv could make another move, Cedric leaped out of the darkness. He brought his blade down hard into the man's back and pulled it out again. The man let out a ferocious scream that bounced off the walls of the alley. He cast one last glance to Liv before turning on his heels and sprinting away.

"How do you like that for a toy?" Cedric yelled to the man's retreating form. He turned to Liv as she slowly stood up. Her eyes were fixed on his bloody blade, which he quickly slipped into his pocket.

"It is gone now," Cedric said.

It took a moment for his words to register. "It?"

Liv realized she was struggling to breathe, and saw dots begin to circle in front of her eyes. The shapes in front of her—the building, the recycling bin, Cedric—all started to get a little hazy around the edges.

Cedric stopped a few feet away from Liv. "Sorry, I misspoke.

I meant *he*. He was trying to hurt you and—"

"No," Liv said, her voice coming out firmer than expected. "There was something really wrong with him. His mouth, his eyes . . ."

Cedric's eyes widened. "You could see that? You saw his true face?"

"Of course I saw his face. It was totally jacked, like he was on some crazy kind of drugs or something. But why did he attack me? And, and . . . how did you get to me so fast? And that knife? You moved so quick—"

Cedric reached a tentative hand out to Liv. "You are injured."

"I just hit my head, I think."

Cedric shook his own head a little, and gently lifted up her hand. Liv looked down, and at first all she noticed was a patch of red. The skin of her left hand, reaching from the fleshy area beneath her thumb down to her wrist, had been partially peeled away. She hadn't even felt it until just now.

"Whoa," she whispered.

"And yes, your head," Cedric added. He reached up and moved a lock of her hair to get a better view of the side of her face. He moved slowly, gently, brushing Liv's temple with his thumb. When she lifted her hand to her head a moment later, to the place where his fingers had just been, she felt something warm and sticky. Blood.

"Oh," she said, and her voice sounded shaky to her own ears. "I don't do so well with . . ."

Liv pitched forward a little, and Cedric caught her, one hand on her arm and another circling around her back. He held her steady and slightly away from his body, but Liv was still close enough to feel the heat coming off him, his breath as it ruffled her hair. She righted herself quickly.

"It's okay, I'm okay. It's only my own blood that brings on the embarrassing dizziness."

"There is not too much of it," Cedric said. "I can retrieve some clean cloths and bandages. If you wait here, I'll be right back—"

"Are you kidding? There's no way I'm staying alone in this alley."

Cedric considered this, then nodded.

"All right, come with me, but stay quiet. It would be best if the others did not see you."

"The others. That's what the man, the—whoever, that's what he said. That he was going to leave me for 'the others' to find."

A look of concern passed over Cedric's face, but he said nothing. He picked up her discarded jacket and handed it to Liv. She threw it over her shoulders and followed him back down the alley.

"You don't seem really surprised by that," Liv said. "Do you know who he was? Why he . . . what he wanted?"

Cedric hesitated before answering. "Not exactly."

"Not exactly?" Liv fought to keep her voice calm, but could hear hysteria edging in. She breathed in deep. "What *exactly* is it? Drugs? Gang stuff?"

"It is . . . difficult to explain. And trust me, you really do not want me to."

"Trust you. You want me to trust you. You know how crazy

that sounds? We were just attacked. We have to report it."

"Report it to whom?" Cedric said, looking genuinely confused.

"Uh, the police?"

They'd reached the grate in the wall of the museum. Cedric turned to face her, and his expression was difficult to read in the darkness.

"You mean the men in blue. With the lights that flash." He made a circular motion in the air with his hand, as if he was trying to demonstrate police lights. Liv's eyebrows shot up, sending a spark of pain across her hairline. She winced.

"Yes. Here in . . . well, pretty much all English-speaking countries, we call those men *the police*." Liv put a finger to her temple and rubbed, trying to ease the pain there. At this point, she wasn't sure how much of it was caused by her head cracking against the concrete and how much was caused by trying to carry on a conversation with Cedric.

"You may call the men in blue if you wish, but if you do, we will be long gone before they arrive," Cedric said. "We have already had interactions with those men—the police—and they only tried to separate us. They threatened to send us away. Though to where, I know not."

Liv flinched reflexively. *They only tried to separate us.* She thought of Peter and Maisy, then pushed them quickly again from her mind.

"They cannot help us," Cedric continued. "We are alone."

Cedric's voice wavered when he said this, and Liv felt her frustration ebb a bit. She knew what it was like to feel that there was no one who could help. She also knew exactly how the LAPD could be when dealing with street kids. Still, she couldn't shake the physical memory of how the black-eyed man had pinned her to the ground, how he'd fought . . . something was wrong with him. Really wrong.

"Okay, I won't call the police. But only if you explain what the hell just happened. That's all I ask. Give me one straight answer."

Cedric breathed out. "Okay, I will try," he finally said with a short sigh. "But not out here. Let us go inside. We will clean your injuries, and I will tell you what you want to know. Though I promise you will not believe me."

"Don't be so sure," Liv said. "I mean, maybe it's the gaping head wound, but I'm feeling pretty open-minded."

She smiled up at Cedric, but he shook his head, confused.

Liv dropped down to the grate. "No one ever gets my puns."

Careful not to touch her injured hand against the concrete, Liv crawled through the grate hole and out the other side. After a moment, Cedric came through behind her.

"What is this place, anyway?" Liv asked.

Cedric's voice was hushed when he answered. "It is an old part of the museum, I believe, that has been closed off. I found the opening in the alley wall, and it led to this." He gestured to the tunnels.

"And the other opening, to that room with the books? Did you just find that too?"

"That was originally a small hole in the wall that I . . . helped along. I needed access to—" He cut himself off.

"To what?"

"Shh, we are getting closer."

They walked back through the wooden panel that led to the main blocked-off hallway. Wordlessly, Liv followed Cedric through the tunnel entrance, past the bookshelf, through the small room, and into the hallway beyond.

The door to the archives room was still locked, so Cedric took Liv through another series of halls before leading her to the public portion of the museum. Once there, he quickened his steps and craned his head to look around every few seconds. He only slowed down when they got to a large black door labeled with an **M**. He pushed the door open and made to go inside.

"Wait, what are you doing?" Liv hissed.

Cedric turned around, confused.

"We will need water to wash your cuts."

"This is the men's room."

For a moment, Cedric just blinked, uncomprehending. Then his mouth burst open with a laugh that completely transformed his face. His serious features melted away, leaving him looking almost like a different person. A different person who was still frustratingly attractive. And just plain frustrating.

Cedric clapped his own hand over his mouth, silencing the laugh. His eyes still gleamed as he walked into the room and motioned for Liv to follow.

"I apologize," he said, still smiling as he shut and locked the door behind them. "But the girls here have the strangest sense of propriety. They walk around half-dressed in the middle of broad daylight, but refuse to share a common toilet."

Liv looked down at her own clothes, frowning. Her outfit

was perfectly respectable—tank top, jeans, and jacket, now a little worse for wear, of course.

"I'm not half-dressed."

Cedric shrugged. He walked over to the sink and ran the water, putting a paper towel under the stream. Liv moved cautiously toward him and tried not to get too grossed out as she passed the urinals.

Cedric reached out with the wet towel and gently pressed it against the left side of Liv's forehead. It brushed against her torn skin, causing her to wince.

"Hold still just a moment, I have to clean some of the dirt away," Cedric said, his voice gentle. He was no longer laughing, but his face wasn't as closed off as it had been in the tunnels, either. As he moved the paper towel down the side of her head, Liv tried to sneak glances at his face. His blue eyes covered by dark—almost black—lashes, his long nose, his lips slightly parted in concentration. A spot of skin near one cheekbone seemed to be inflamed, bright purple in the middle and spreading into red as it reached his ear.

"You're hurt, too," Liv said.

"I've had worse."

"That's . . . not comforting."

Cedric didn't respond, but continued to gently wipe bits of dried blood from the side of Liv's head. He moved closer to get a better angle, and Liv was hyperconscious of how his whole body was just a few inches away from hers. For a moment she felt lightheaded and short of breath. Weren't people supposed to sit down while bleeding from the head?

Cedric's fingers pressed gently against her temple, at the worst of the cut. He leaned in even closer, so close that his features blurred before Liv's eyes. Was it just her imagination, or was his breathing getting quicker, too?

Liv wanted to say something to break the thick silence that had fallen between them, but couldn't think of a single thing. Her gaze rested on a gold chain around Cedric's neck. It extended down beneath his shirt, and she could see the outline of what looked like a ring hanging from the edge of it.

"Nice necklace."

The moment the words left her lips, Cedric stepped back from Liv sharply, taking his hands from her forehead. His left hand went immediately to where the outline of the ring pressed against his heart.

Liv knew she had said something wrong, but didn't get it.

"What is it . . . a ring?" she pressed on.

"Yes, it is." Cedric averted his eyes and turned to throw the wadded-up paper towel away. "It is a betrothal ring."

Liv laughed, sure he was being sarcastic. "You mean, like, an engagement ring?"

"Yes."

"Wait, what? Aren't you a little young for that?"

"I am nearly at the proper age."

"Yeah, in Kentucky, maybe. But that's not exactly a Southern accent you've got. So where are you from? Eastern Europe or something?"

"Or something. I think you can probably clean your hand yourself."

"Oh. Right."

Liv rolled up her sleeve and set to washing dirt and small pieces of gravel from the scrape on her hand. Under the fluorescent lights, it looked even nastier than before. She wrapped it in a paper towel, trying not to look at the blood flecks soaking through.

"Okay, I'm ready."

Cedric peeled himself away from where he'd been resting against the tile wall, watching her.

"Good. The museum will be cleared out and mostly locked up now, so we will have to go out through a side door," he said. "Quietly."

Liv nodded. Cedric had almost reached the door of the men's room when a thought occurred to her. "I heard you talking to a girl in the tunnels. Is that the one you're . . . betrothed . . . to?"

"Yes, that was her. Katerina."

Liv felt a small pang as she pictured the girl under the bridge. She'd been beautiful, all dark hair and fierceness. That girl seemed a perfect match for Cedric, with his rigid posture, untended wounds, and an actual betrothal ring. Liv imagined them in elaborate wedding gear, like two engravings from a fairy tale book sprung to life.

As the male half of the living fairy tale pushed open the scuffed door of the men's room, the image faded away.

"She said something about being killed?" Liv asked. "And now with the not-so-friendly alley attacker . . . what kind of trouble are you guys in?"

Cedric turned to her, his eyes concerned.

"You were eavesdropping."

Liv shrugged.

"You should be careful when you do that, you know. You could overhear something you might not want to." With that, he started walking quickly down the empty hallway, toward a door marked **EXIT**.

"Okay, I can see you're really, seriously committed to this whole man-of-mystery bit." Liv said, her voice low. "But the vagueness stopped being charming around the time my face hit pavement. Don't forget you owe me some answers."

"I have not forgotten, and I will keep my end of the bargain. If you are absolutely sure you want to know everything, follow me."

Liv hesitated, but only for a second.

THE PRINCE'S TALE

The diner just down the road from the museum was mostly empty, so Liv and Cedric took one of the orange vinyl booths by the window. It was mostly dark now, and when Liv looked through the plate glass, all she could see was her own reflection.

Cold, recirculated air pumped down onto their booth from a grate in the ceiling, and Liv shivered. When the waitress came by to drop off some laminated menus, Liv ordered a coffee. She raised her eyebrows at Cedric. He just shook his head.

"Aren't you hungry at all?" Liv asked.

"I am fine."

But she saw Cedric's expression as he glanced over the pictures of pancakes and French toast on the menu. Liv had seen that look before—hunger was hard to hide.

"Look, I can't decide between the Hash Brown Surprise and the Chocolate Waffles Supreme . . . split them with me? My treat."

Cedric tore his eyes away from the menu, but said nothing.

"Come on, you'll really be helping me out," Liv continued. "I don't feel like eating alone, and it's not like my foster mom is going to have a hot dinner waiting for me. Rita has many gifts, but cooking? Not among them."

Cedric's eyes narrowed in confusion. "Foster mom?"

"You know, a foster parent. Legal guardian."

"Guardian?" Cedric's voice was pitched unnaturally high. Liv wondered if he was messing with her. Had he really not heard of the foster system?

"Yeah, like, appointed by the state. She takes care of me because my parents can't."

"Oh," Cedric answered, his eyes clearing. "Why can't they?"

"They're dead."

Liv kept her eyes on the table, feeling a little bad about her blunt reply. She knew just springing the dead-parent thing like that could freak people out, reduce them to stammering, pity-filled gazes, or worse—follow-up questions. Liv had become adept at steering entire conversations away from that inevitable next question—*what happened to them?*

She finally lifted her eyes to Cedric's. He was looking directly at her, his mouth turned slightly down. He sat very still.

"I am sorry."

Liv shrugged and pointed to the menu again. "So are you going to help me with my pile of carbs or what?"

"Maybe I will have a little," he finally said.

When the waitress came back with coffee, Liv put in the order. She warmed up her hands on the side of the white ceramic mug for a moment before opening up a packet of creamer and pouring it in. Cedric watched her with an intense concentration, as though he'd never seen anyone put cream in coffee before.

"Okay, so level with me. Were you, like, raised in one of those really strict religions that doesn't let you watch television or go outside on Sundays?"

Cedric shook his head, slowly.

"So what *are* you, aside from a museum employee? If you're even that? I mean, I saw how you moved in that alley . . . that must have taken some serious training."

Cedric looked out the window. Liv didn't know what she expected him to say. Was he a martial arts expert? A speed freak? When he spoke, his voice sounded tired.

"I am a Guardian . . . and a prince."

Liv tried not to react, but knew her eyebrows had shot up nearly into her forehead. She tried to hide it by taking a sip of coffee.

"Never seen a prince work for minimum wage before."

Cedric shook his head. "I told you that you would not believe me. No one has, not since we arrived."

"By 'we,' you mean you and Katerina, right? And there was another boy under the bridge. Is it just the three of you?"

"Only us," Cedric said, then looked abruptly away, toward the window.

"Cedric, are you . . . are you living down there? In the tunnels?"

Cedric's eyes flashed over to Liv. "You cannot tell anyone where we are. If they found out . . ."

"Who? The people at the museum?"

"Yes. And others."

Liv's voice dropped low. "So what kind of trouble are you in?"

Cedric looked away, and Liv sighed. He wasn't going to make this easy on her.

"We only want to get home."

"Okay. Where's home?"

Cedric knitted his eyebrows together, as if he was trying to solve a complex problem.

"Caelum."

Liv brought the cup of coffee to her lips, running the name over in her mind. "Is that in Canada?"

Cedric shook his head. "It is difficult to explain. . . ."

"Well, the night is young, and Rita doesn't exactly give me a curfew, so . . . take your time."

"Caelum is another place . . . that is not this place. Another world. I came to this world through a portal."

"Oh, a *portal.* Well, that makes sense."

Cedric's jaw tightened. "You are mocking me."

Liv felt a tug of guilt. "No, sorry, it's just . . . a portal, you say?"

It didn't seem like Cedric was intentionally messing with her, and anyway, why would he do that? Why make up such an elaborate lie for a complete stranger?

Maybe he didn't think it was a lie at all. Liv had seen kids with mental illnesses before. Schizophrenia, delusions, even just drug-induced craziness. She remembered a boy named Ryan who'd lived with her in the same group home for a while. Ryan's story was tragic—his mother had died right after he was born, and his father had been abusive—and Ryan had a tendency to retreat into a fantasy world in his mind to survive. The social worker who ran the home had explained to Liv that whenever Ryan talked about being afraid of "the dragon," he was really referring to his father. Ryan had never frightened Liv, and he really was a generally sweet kid to be around, so long as you didn't touch his Fruit Roll-Ups.

Whatever his situation, Cedric, too, seemed more sad than dangerous to Liv as he stared down at a plastic carton of sugar packets. She definitely wasn't afraid of him.

"That thing that attacked you tonight . . . it is called a wrath," Cedric continued. "And I was born to fight them."

Cedric reached for Liv's torn-up packet of creamer across the table. He spoke quickly, and he kept his eyes focused on his hands, which ripped the creamer packet into tinier and tinier pieces.

"In my world, the wraths are more easily recognizable. Big, ugly things with horns and teeth and claws . . . they've plagued our lands for centuries, for as long as anyone can remember. We have never been able to defeat them completely, but we are—or were—able to keep them away from our cities and rule the realm in relative peace. I do not know if they followed us here or were in this world all along, but . . . they are different here. They walk around looking like men, and most people cannot even tell that they are different at all. . . ." Cedric looked up. "But you could. You saw its eyes? Its face?"

Liv recalled the all-black eyes of the man in the alley. Something had felt wrong about his face, deep-down, in-the-gut wrong.

"He looked . . . like there was something the matter with him," she finally conceded. "But you're saying he was some sort of . . . monster? Like an actual monster, of the horror-movie variety?" It was hard to keep the skepticism from her voice.

"The wraths started hunting us shortly after we came through the portal. We did not know who they were at first, because they look so different here. But they are the same evil creatures from our realm. At least, they smell the same. What I do not understand is what they are doing here, or why they are tracking us."

Cedric stopped talking when the waitress came back and set down two plates, each heaped with food. Liv pushed the waffles toward Cedric and pulled the plate of hash browns to herself. She moved the potatoes around on the plate with her fork, but she wasn't as hungry as she had been a few minutes ago. Cedric, on the other hand, had no such problem. He took one bite of the waffles and closed his eyes, as if savoring the taste. When he opened them again, he dove back into the food with a fury, cutting through it so hard that his knife made a screeching noise against the plate.

"Why do you think he attacked me?"

Cedric tilted his head, swallowing before speaking again. "It must have thought you were one of us. I do not know why, but I am sorry for it."

"Yeah, me too," Liv said, touching the strip of paper towel still wrapped around her hand. Whether or not Cedric truly believed in his weird delusion, the man in the alley had certainly meant business. He'd wanted to hurt Liv for real. She remembered the gleaming blade that Cedric had wielded with such skill. She swallowed, trying to sound casual. "And your . . . knife thing?"

"I . . . acquired it," Cedric said. "After losing the only sword we had. Getting it back will be helpful for fighting the wraths off, though it will not kill them. Only silver can do that. I used to have a whole arsenal of my own back in Caelum; you should see it, beautiful things—"

Cedric stopped when he saw Liv's expression. "But here, we could not find anything like that. We have only managed to find a few knives in the museum, and paltry ones at that, old and made of steel." Cedric stuck a giant forkful of food in his mouth and chewed, then swallowed it down in a giant lump. "What did you say this was called again?"

"Waffles?"

"Waffles," he repeated, savoring the word. "Amazing."

"Yeah," Liv responded, thrown. She felt a dizziness overtake her again, and realized she was having a hard time keeping track of Cedric's tale. She nodded to his plate.

"You should put syrup on them."

Liv grabbed the syrup carafe and poured some onto his waffles in a long string. Cedric watched her carefully before shoving a syrupy forkful in his mouth. When his lips closed around the bite, he actually closed his eyes and let out a light *mmmm* noise.

When he opened his eyes, he looked directly at Liv and gave a small smile. "You do not believe me, do you?"

Liv averted her eyes. "Well . . ."

"I expected as much," Cedric said, his voice kind of smug. "This is such a strange place, filled with so many things I can neither understand nor explain, and yet we learned very quickly that people here are unable to believe us. It is odd, though . . . they can speak to each other through devices smaller than this—" Cedric picked up the saltshaker on the table. "And yet the notion of a portal is unthinkable!"

"Well, cell phones are possible through science. Portals are . . . fantasy."

"They both seem like magic to me. But I suppose I understand your reluctance. Sometimes I try to imagine going home and telling my sister, Emme, about some of the things I have seen here, and I know she would never believe me."

Cedric shoveled the last bit of waffles into his mouth. Liv pushed the plate of hash browns over to him and smiled. He licked a bit of syrup off of his fork and dug into the new food.

"So why the museum? What would make you stay there, of all places?"

Cedric contemplated while chewing. Then he told Liv a story, about a man named Mal-something who had led a group of the creatures—wraths—into his home in the middle of the night. "A small group of us managed to escape our guards, but there was no way out of the castle. So we left through the only means we could think of—the portal."

Now Cedric looked up, eyes blazing. But it wasn't Liv he was looking at. It seemed as though he was focused on something behind her, though there was nothing there but the vinyl booth. "We had to run in the moment, but I will not run forever. I will find my way back home. Create a portal back to Caelum, and once there, I will raise my father's army. Malquin will not see us coming, and we will defeat him and the wraths."

The silence that followed Cedric's tirade was heavy, and Liv felt that she should say something. "Well that sounds like . . . quite the challenge. So why haven't you gone back yet?"

Cedric looked away, the anger draining from his eyes. "We are looking for a set of scrolls, very old ones, that will open the way for us to get home."

"You can't just go back the way you came?"

Cedric shook his head. "We tried. It does not work like that. The portal is closed from this side, and we need to reopen it. And the only way we can is with the scrolls." He paused to swallow another bite of waffle.

"The scrolls. Right." Liv once again put a hand up to her temple. One glance at Cedric's face revealed his complete earnestness. He truly believed all of the crazy things he was saying.

"So you thought these . . . scrolls . . . would be at the museum?"

Cedric sighed. "I do not know, truthfully. When we first arrived, our only goal was to stay alive. But the people we met were . . . not always helpful. None of them knew anything about the scrolls, or our world, or even wraths. I knew the scrolls were very old, and that I should look for them in a place where very old things might be stored. The museum is so large and has so many artifacts, I thought I would be bound to find them eventually. But I have so far only found old parchment, rocks, and monster bones."

Liv tried to stifle a smile.

"But how did you get a job there, at the museum?"

Cedric looked sheepish. "I did not, exactly. I took this uniform. So long as I keep my head down and move quickly, only coming up from the tunnels at night or when we really need to acquire food, no one has stopped me."

"Acquire food? Is that, like, a fancy way to say stealing?"

Cedric leaned back against the booth with a heavy sigh. "We were so hungry . . . I have never known hunger like that, not in my life. But food was everywhere. Everywhere we looked—in stalls, in buildings, safe behind glass. We did not have the ability to pay for it, so . . . we took it."

Cedric swallowed, looking down at the two now-empty plates before him.

"I get it," Liv said. And she really did. Though secretly, she wondered whether Cedric's stealing habit had led him into more trouble than he was admitting. Was that why the black-eyed man was really after him and his friends? Had Cedric stolen from the wrong people?

"We are good at it," Cedric continued, "because of our speed. You asked me earlier how I could move so fast . . ."

"Crazy fast."

"It is because of who I am," Cedric continued. "All Guardians are naturally strong, but we are also well trained to move quickly—it is how we can fight the wraths."

"Well . . . sure," Liv said, unable to keep the sarcasm from her voice. "That makes sense. . . ."

Cedric smiled. "You sound like Merek."

"Who?"

"My . . . friend, I suppose. Although he would die before admitting it. He does not think it a good plan to stay in the museum. Neither does Kat."

"They may be right. Regardless of whether or not there are portals and wraths and other worlds and whatever, it sounds like you're a little over your head here."

The second the words were out of Liv's mouth, she regretted it. Cedric leaned back in the booth, and it was like a wall had gone up suddenly between them. Liv felt a small pang of knowing that it was partially her fault, for not playing along anymore.

"I know I cannot convince you I am telling the truth. But thank you, for the waffles," Cedric said, his voice stiff. He started to rise.

"Wait," Liv said, her voice just barely above a whisper. "All I meant was that the museum basement's probably not the safest place for you to stay. It seemed really dank down there, and it didn't look like there were any lights. Probably hard for you to sneak food in and out on a daily basis. And plus, if you get caught by the museum, they'll call social services . . ."

Liv trailed off, wondering if maybe that wasn't the worst thing that could happen. . . . But no—ratting out another street kid was out of the question, even if he was just a touch delusional. She had no idea what he was really running from, but it had to be pretty awful for his brain to make up such a far-fetched scenario. And calling social services might get him sent right back into whatever situation he was working so hard to flee.

Liv opened up her satchel purse and took out her notebook, tearing out a piece of paper. On it, she wrote down her phone number, then slid the paper over to Cedric.

"I may know of a few places where you could stay. They're out of the way, but they have beds and sunlight, at least. Will you call me if you need help?"

Cedric looked down at the paper, his eyebrows knitting.

"I do not have one of those . . . things. You know, a . . ." He put his hand up to his ear.

"A phone?"

"Yes, that."

"Right," Liv said, deadpan. She pulled the paper back. "Do you know how to get around the city?"

Cedric nodded. "I have acquired a map, although I do not travel around much during the day."

"If I give you my address, will you promise not to come rob me?"

Cedric started at her words, genuinely taken aback.

"Well, you did just admit to being a thief," Liv said, trying to keep her voice light. "Though it's not like we even have much to steal. I own next to nothing, and Rita likes to spend all her tips the second she gets them, so unless you're looking to score a bottle of Jack, there won't be much to take."

Cedric looked down again, as if trying to hide an emotion on his face. This time, she was sure it was shame. "I would not steal from your foster mother's home, or from this Jack fellow. I would never take anything from you, Liv."

The sound of her name on Cedric's lips rang in Liv's ears for an extra beat, and she made an effort to push it aside. "Okay. I didn't mean . . . anyway, come find me if you want to check out one of those places. . . ." Liv trailed off, awkwardly. As she slipped her notebook back into her purse, she caught a glimpse of her phone lying against the bottom of the bag. She picked it up and turned it over. Four missed calls and nine texts. All from Shannon.

"Crap," she said. "I really have to go. My friend Shannon's probably having a heart attack."

Cedric looked up in alarm, until Liv quickly clarified. "Not literally, it's just an expression . . . never mind." She smiled and stood up. "Take care, Cedric."

He nodded, and Liv went to go pay the check at the counter. Before she left, she turned around one more time to find Cedric still in the booth, pouring syrup directly onto a spoon and then sticking it into his mouth. She shook her head and then pushed through the door, escorted out into the night by the sound of the diner's ringing bell.

Liv's eyelids grew heavy as the bus moved ever nearer to the small house she shared with Rita in Los Feliz. She leaned her head up against the glass window of the bus, letting her eyes unfocus as the cars and lights sped up and slowed down outside.

She'd just hung up the phone with Shannon, who'd spent half the call yelling at Liv for not returning her calls sooner. Liv had lied and said her phone was accidentally turned off, not wanting to explain that she'd actually forgotten all about Shannon during her time with Cedric. When Shannon asked why she'd been at the museum so long, she lied again and said she'd lost track of time.

"You've never lost track of time in the history of, like, ever. It's one of your most annoying traits."

Liv had sighed. "I don't know what to tell you."

"Tell me the truth. You decided to keep that sword, didn't you? Don't pull the good-girl act on me, Liv Phillips. You may have all our teachers and parental figures fooled, but I know you. I know where you keep your fake ID. I know about that back tat you keep covered up—"

"Okay, okay. You caught me. I've decided to become a really authentic *Lord of the Rings* cosplayer."

Shannon had scoffed and offered to pick Liv up, but she said she'd take the bus instead. Really, she didn't want to answer any more questions—she just wanted to sit and think about her ridiculous night in silence. She didn't entirely know why she wanted to keep Cedric's story to herself. It wasn't that she thought Shannon would rat him out to the cops. Shannon might not have grown up in the foster system, but she still had a pretty healthy distrust of authority figures in general, and she would never turn Cedric over if Liv asked her not to.

Still, she didn't want to imagine what Shannon would say if she knew the whole story. That Liv was attacked by a stranger in an alley and saved by a mysterious boy who dresses as a security guard and thinks demon creatures are chasing him. . . . She wouldn't even know how to begin that conversation.

Liv could feel a headache building up in her left temple. A part of her wanted to turn back and take a different bus to her favorite spot along the LA riverbed, just so she could be alone and think in peace for a few hours, but she knew she should go home first and put actual disinfectant and bandages on her cuts.

The bus was mostly empty. An elderly woman sat with her eyes closed a few benches up. In the back, a large man sat with his back straight against the seat. Liv glanced over and gave a small start when she realized he was looking directly at her.

The man's face was craggy and lined, his shaggy hair a light gray that bordered on white. His hands were folded neatly in his lap. But it was his eyes that rattled Liv—they were dark, too dark, and still, and they didn't break contact with hers. The faint lines around the edge of the man's mouth deepened a bit, revealing the tiniest of smiles.

Liv looked away and tried to calm her heartbeat. Just a creep on the bus. Happens all the time. After a few moments, she risked a look back at the man. He was still staring at her.

Paranoid or not, she wasn't taking any chances. The events of the night had left her too on edge. The bus came to another stop, and Liv jumped up at the last minute and ran toward the front door as it opened. She looked behind and saw that the man had also risen from his seat and was standing at the opened door in the back of the bus. She took a deep breath and started down the stairs to the street.

As soon as her feet touched the ground, Liv looked to her right and saw the man had exited the bus also. Just as the bus door started to close behind her, Liv reached up and stuck a hand out, stopping them. She slipped her body back in through the door just before it swung shut.

"Hey," the driver called out to her. "You can get hurt doing that."

"Sorry," Liv murmured. "Wrong stop."

The driver shook her head and pulled away from the curb and back into traffic. Liv looked out of the window at the man, now standing motionless on the sidewalk. He was still staring at her.

Liv sat at the very front of the bus until it arrived at her actual stop. As soon as the doors opened, she jumped out and started running toward home. It wasn't until she pushed through the chain-link gate outside of her house and jogged up to the front door that Liv really let out her breath.

Inside, the living room was stuffy, and the curtains were still closed from this morning. No sign of Rita.

Liv locked the door behind her, then leaned back against it and reached for the light switch on the wall. Warm yellow light fell over the room, resting on the familiar couch and coffee table. She suddenly felt silly for running home.

With a sigh, Liv pushed off from the door and headed to the bathroom. Once inside, she put Neosporin and a large bandage over her hand. She then washed her face and ran her finger along the cut on her head, cautiously. It wasn't as bad as she'd originally thought. In the end, she was able to affix a small, beige Band-Aid just over her left temple. She moved a chunk of hair over her forehead to hide it.

Liv walked into the kitchen and was still scratching the

corner of her hand bandage when a movement caught her eye. The green-and-white-striped window curtain was blowing in a breeze. Liv swiveled to the patio door and saw it was open to the night. Or no—not open—but gaping, hanging off its tracks. As if it had been torn from its place.

And lying just beyond it was a small, dark shape, barely visible in the moonlight. Liv took a few quiet steps forward. It was a single, black tennis shoe. The kind Rita wore to work every day. And just a few feet beyond the shoe was Rita herself, sprawled out on the concrete patio.

Liv gasped and ran to Rita's side. An empty liquor bottle was lying near the side of the house, just inches from Rita's outstretched arm. A plastic patio chair was tipped over on its side, with one leg broken. Rita was sprawled out underneath it, her head resting half on the concrete stretch of patio and half on the browned grass beyond.

Liv took hold of Rita's shoulder and turned her over. The overwhelming stench of hard liquor and vomit hit her at once. Rita's body moved limply, her eyes half open but unmoving.

"Rita, please," she cried, fighting against the rising lump in her throat. "Help! Somebody!"

The windows in the neighboring condo remained dark.

Liv ran back inside to call 9-1-1, while Rita's half-open eyes continued to stare vacantly at a world they couldn't see.

THE ORPHAN'S REFUGE

When Cedric woke up, he had no idea whether it was morning or still night. Though his eyes had mostly adjusted to the natural darkness of the living space under the museum, it was still difficult to see more than a few feet in front of him. With a groan, he pulled himself up from his nest of blankets and rubbed at a crick in his neck.

He heard a click, and then a small, bright flame flared up in the darkness. It illuminated the face of Merek, who leaned against the wall near Cedric's makeshift bed.

"He rises," Merek drawled.

Cedric rubbed his eyes. He was definitely not awake enough yet to deal with Merek. "Watching me sleep?"

Merek scoffed. "Hardly. Katerina asked me to come fetch you from your royal slumber."

"Fetch me?"

Merek clicked the little metal device in his hand again, this time closing the cap that extinguished the fire. Then he clicked again, relighting it. He'd found the device in the alley outside of the museum and couldn't be parted from it. Partially, Cedric suspected, because he knew how much the constant clicking noise irritated Cedric.

"I am merely the messenger." Merek kicked off from the wall and slipped through the doorway, blessedly taking his clicking fire device with him.

Cedric sighed. Whenever he went outside, into the wild, chaotic mess of a world that existed out there, he was terrified of running into a new threat or doing something that would expose them. He was constantly confused by new words, places, and situations that made little sense, and every day threw him something new to try to comprehend. But when he was down here, surrounded by Merek's endless barbs and the stress in Kat's eyes, he longed to climb up to the surface of the museum, escape through his tunnel hatch, and run down the streets, free.

Cedric lay back down against the tangle of old blankets, trying to prepare himself for another fight. If it were the kind involving swords and fists—like the one he'd had last night against that wrath—he'd be up and ready to go. But this kind of fight, the kind that involved labored discussions and endless complaints, was one he would rather do without.

Again and again, the king had tried to prepare Cedric for leadership, telling him that he must be firm with his subjects as well as fierce with his enemies. The second part had always been the most appealing. He had wanted to be a great warrior, like his father. He'd just assumed all the leadership stuff would easily follow.

It wasn't really working out that way.

Cedric pulled himself up and put on a shirt—he was now in possession of two of them, in addition to the nightclothes he'd worn through the portal and his stolen museum uniform. The shirt he wore now was faded and old, emblazoned on the front with bold letters that read, inexplicably, "The Rolling Stones." He had seen many people in this world wearing clothes with words and pictures on them, but as far as he could tell, they only sometimes designated their wearers with particular meaning. The museum guards wore shirts that read "Security." That, Cedric could understand. But the day before, he'd seen an old woman with a walker wearing headgear that read "Oakland Raiders," and Cedric doubted highly that she was in the process of raiding anything at all. Some shirts even had nonsensical directions, which were even more confusing.

Honestly, what did "Come at Me, Bro" even mean?

Cedric ducked to avoid the low ceiling and walked carefully out into the common living area, where stolen lanterns provided some light. Kat was making a meal out of something called "trail mix," which Cedric had stolen from the museum gift shop. Next to her was the sword Cedric had taken back from the museum's Acquisitions Department—by breaking through its door the previous night.

On the handle of the sword was a series of fresh markings Kat must have just etched into the wood. They were a vestige from the Guardians' own ancient, mostly lost language. More ceremonial than anything else, the language was now used to decorate weapons and draw up formal announcements. It was a fairly useless tradition to mark weapons meant for battle, but seeing the familiar language on the sword hilt made Cedric feel closer to home, if even just for a moment.

Seeing the marks in this realm also boosted his confidence—when he'd come across pieces of the Guardians' old language in one of the museum's rooms, he'd felt closer than ever to finding the scrolls. Convincing Kat and Merek of that was another task altogether.

As Kat worked, Merek lay back against some wooden boxes by the wall, examining his fingernails. He flicked his long hair away from his half-lidded eyes and blinked at Cedric.

"Good morning," Cedric said.

"If you say so," Merek replied.

Kat shot him a withering glance. "Enough, Merek. You promised to remain civil."

"Of course," Merek shot back. "We are stuck in a dingy cavern on some foreign hellhole of a dimension, but let's do remain civil."

"Anything constructive you want to add today, Merek? Or just the regular complaints?" Cedric asked.

No one said anything for a beat. Cedric took in the faces of his friends, the only reminders he had left of home. They looked dirty and tired and older than they had a mere two months ago. He knew he should say something uplifting, something to inspire confidence in their search. But Merek's smirk pushed all hopeful thoughts out of his mind.

Merek shrugged. "You call it complaining. I call it maintaining a voice of reason in this chaos. Someone ought to."

"Merek," Kat said, her voice filled with warning. "Cedric is doing the best he can."

"The saddest part is I believe that," Merek said.

Cedric gritted his teeth, knowing that defending himself would only encourage Merek to continue. Not that he necessarily needed encouragement.

"Our Cedric may be the best possible example of why blood and birth order don't necessarily translate into intelligence. Let's not forget it was his ludicrous plan to jump into the portal in the first place—"

"And you would have had us, what? Do nothing? Get put in the dungeon along with our parents?" The last of Cedric's fragile patience had fallen away.

"At least we would be home."

Cedric turned away. He hated the part of himself that knew Merek was right. Everything that had happened since he'd knocked down that first wrath guard in Caelum and escaped through the palace tunnels had been his doing. And now here they were, hungry, cold, tired. Every day it was getting harder to rally his friends. Every hour that passed took more of their hope from them.

Cedric took a deep breath. "We will get back home."

"Do you know every time you say that, you sound less and less convincing?" Merek said. "You know as well as we do that those scrolls do not exist. We need to figure out another way to get home that does not involve sleeping in this stone cellar that stinks of mildew and underarms."

Cedric gritted his teeth and resisted the urge to sniff himself.

"Merek." Kat's voice was at its most dangerously calm. "We agreed to limit this discussion to whether or not we should stay at the museum. Leave the scrolls out of it."

"Why should I? They are all *he* ever talks about," Merek shot back. He pushed his dirty hair out of his face with one hand.

"They exist," Cedric said, clenching his fist.

"If you want to lie to yourself, fine. But stop forcing us to suffer." Merek stood up from his box and moved toward Cedric. "Just because you had the good fortune to be born within the castle walls does not mean your plan is inherently the best one."

"Do you have a better idea?" Cedric shot back, then instantly regretted it. It was the opening Merek had been waiting for.

"The wraths that followed us must have come from a portal as well. If we can leave the damned scrolls alone and find where they came through . . ."

"How do you propose we do that?" Cedric asked, his voice rising. "We do not know how many of them are here or where they are coming from. We don't even know that they came through a portal! Wraths might have existed here all this time."

"Maybe we should ask them," Merek said.

Cedric clenched his jaw. Didn't Merek know how hard he was trying? He didn't want to be here any more than the rest of them. But no matter what Merek thought about Cedric's ability to lead, the responsibility of getting everyone home fell to him.

"No," Cedric finally said, slowly. "The wraths are not to be trusted."

"You cannot just dictate—"

"He can," Kat cut in. "Whether you like it or not, he is still our prince, in Caelum and in any other realm. If he says we need to keep looking for the scrolls, then that is what we will do." She looked over at Cedric, and he felt instantly buoyed by her support.

"But," Kat continued, "staying here, at the museum, might not be the best idea anymore."

Cedric shook his head. "We have been safe here. Safer than anywhere else . . ." His voice trailed off. The weeks after they had come through the portal had been chaotic, confusing, and dangerous. They'd slept wherever they could those first few nights—under bridges, in small clusters of trees. On the fifth night, the wraths had found them, and they'd had to flee again.

The museum at least offered them a brief respite from being out on the streets. They were still overly hot and hungry most days, but at least they weren't constantly on the run.

"We *were* safe here," Kat said. "But the wraths have gotten closer and closer. They tracked us somehow, Cedric. We have no idea how large their numbers are and we have no weapons to damage them permanently. It is only a matter of time before they break into the tunnels and find us. Like they almost did last night."

Cedric tried not to betray any emotion at the mention of the previous night. He had told Kat about the wrath in the alley, but at the last minute, had decided to leave Liv out of the story entirely. It wasn't just because Kat was untrusting of everyone in this realm and would be angry with Cedric for risking their cover to protect one stranger. There was something more than that. Cedric's conversation with Liv had been the only enjoyable (though still extremely confusing) one he'd shared with a non-Guardian in months, and it felt precious to him somehow. He didn't want to offer it up to Kat and Merek for dissection.

"The wrath yesterday didn't see me climb from the grate, I promise," Cedric finally said, sighing. "They still do not know the way in."

"How convincing," Merek muttered.

Kat looked at Merek, her eyes flashing. "Cedric would not lie."

"Thank you," Cedric said to Kat.

She turned to him and sighed. "Do not mistake my defending you for agreeing with you. You are our leader, and I will support you; you know that. But, Cedric . . . we cannot go on like this. At the very least, we should find a place that Merek and I can get into and out of without being detected, so we can look for the scrolls as well. We cannot stay in this . . . hole."

Cedric closed his eyes, trying to gather his thoughts. It was all so much—keeping everyone alive and looking for the scrolls at the same time. And he really had no idea why the wraths of this dimension were following them, or what they might do if it turned out that Merek was right, that the scrolls didn't exist . . . and it was so hard to think when he was so, so hungry.

Although he tried to focus, Cedric's thoughts drifted back to the wonderful food he'd eaten the night before with Liv. He could practically taste the sticky, drippy syrup still. He recalled the way she'd smiled when she watched him eat, and how she'd let him have both meals, and how she'd offered to help. . . .

Cedric opened his eyes and sighed. So much for his secret.

"All right. Just give me the afternoon. I might have an idea on where we can go. But you will have to trust me."

Kat gave a slow nod, but Merek just continued to flick his fire device, staring at the flame as it appeared and disappeared. In Caelum, Merek had always been quick to contradict Cedric, and yet he had always followed the prince's lead in the end. Cedric could only hope that here in this new world, his friend would follow that tradition of talking a lot and acting little.

It wasn't trust, exactly, but it was the best Cedric was going to get.

Liv's chin rolled down and smacked into her chest for what must have been the twentieth time in an hour. She jerked her head back up and willed her eyes to stay open. She shifted against the hard, plastic hospital chair and clutched her Styrofoam cup of now-cold coffee. It had been a long, anxiety-filled night, and she'd been trying to stay awake until the doctors brought news of Rita.

An older woman in light blue scrubs finally entered the waiting area and made her way toward Liv.

"Is she okay?" Liv asked, as soon as the doctor reached her.

The doctor nodded. "She'll be fine. We had to pump her stomach and put her on fluids, but after a long rest, she'll be okay."

Liv exhaled one long, ragged breath. "Thank you."

"She's awake for the moment. Would you like to see her?"

Liv nodded and followed her out of the waiting room, down a narrow hall lined with faded, pink-framed posters of seasides and meadows. After a few moments, they went past a hallway with a placard reading "**BURN UNIT**." Looking at those words, everything else in the world seemed to fade away at the edges. Liv struggled to breathe in, but her throat felt tight and hard, like there was something stuck in it. The walls of the hospital grew fuzzy, and the only thing she could concentrate on was that black-and-white placard with those two words—*Burn Unit*.

Liv nearly walked right into the back of the doctor, but caught herself just in time. As soon as they moved past the burn unit, the knot in her throat loosened. After a few minutes, it was like it was never there at all.

The doctor finally stopped in front of a room and ushered Liv inside. Rita lay in the center of a hospital bed, her body a small, straight line under a tight sheet. Various tubes connected into her arms, which looked so drained of color they almost matched the white fabric of the bed. Her face looked equally drained, its only distinguishing color coming from the greenish-yellow tinge beneath her eyes.

Liv walked closer and carefully took Rita's hand.

"Oh, kid," Rita said, her voice raspy, "I'm so sorry."

"It's okay. The only thing that matters is you're okay."

"No, I really messed up," Rita said, then coughed. "I never meant . . . you have to know I didn't mean for this . . ."

"I know," Liv said. She thought back to those panicked moments when she'd seen Rita lying on the concrete outside of the kitchen patio door. Her first thought had been, crazily, that it was her fault. That the wrath had followed her home and hurt Rita. And she hadn't thought *the man in the alley*, or *the black-*

eyed man; her brain had immediately gone to Cedric's word. The *wrath*.

It wasn't until she saw the empty liquor bottle that she knew what had really happened. And in that instant, she'd felt a bit of relief that she hadn't been responsible, but she'd also felt a sense of the inevitable, like some part of her knew the second she'd been placed under Rita's care that this moment would occur. Rita was kind, but she wasn't happy. And she wasn't good at taking care of herself.

"It's okay," Liv whispered again. She leaned closer to Rita and grasped her hand tighter. "It's going to be okay."

Rita closed her eyes tightly and shook her head. "No, Liv, you don't understand . . ."

Liv shook her head in confusion. It wasn't until she heard a familiar voice calling her name that she understood what Rita was trying to say.

Liv turned around and saw Joe, her caseworker, standing in the doorway. Joe wore his typical flannel shirt, jeans, and work boots. He carried a tattered leather satchel under one arm. His beard had grown slightly longer since the last time Liv had seen him.

"Joe," Liv started. "What are you doing here?" But she already knew. Just the fact that Joe had shown up at the hospital could only mean one thing.

"I've come to see how you are," Joe said, his voice gentle, but wary.

"I think we're going to be okay," Liv said, speaking fast. "Honestly, the doctor says she just needs a couple days of rest, and Rita didn't mean for it to happen. It was an accident, and I think if we just go home—"

"Liv." Joe shook his head.

"Please." Liv looked directly into his eyes. "I don't want to go to another home. There's got to be some way, please . . ."

"You know you can't, Liv. The hospital had to call us straightaway, so it's already on file. You're only sixteen, and the rules—"

"Please, Joe. Please." Liv could hear the desperation rising in her voice, and she struggled to get it under control. "Who's going to take care of Rita while she gets better?"

"It should have been me taking care of you," Rita whispered. Liv knew she should turn around and look at her, should try to relieve Rita's guilt in some way. But she couldn't face her. She kept her eyes trained on Joe.

"Rita's agreed to enter a thirty-day rehabilitation program. She'll be just fine. Can you wait in the hallway for a few minutes, Liv? I have some matters to discuss with Rita, and then you and I can talk about what happens next."

Liv nodded, numb. She braved one last look at Rita, who shook her head, mouthed the word *sorry*, and looked away. Liv dropped Rita's hand and walked out of the room. Joe shut the door behind her.

Liv took a few steps down the hallway and waited just a beat before breaking into a sprint toward the stairwell. She felt a pang of guilt for ditching Joe. He was one of those rare caseworkers who always went a step beyond his duty, and he'd been looking out for Liv from her first day in the system. She'd always tried to forget the very first foster home she'd stayed in after her parents died, but it was impossible to erase the memories of how terrified she'd been. How her foster parents were strictly religious and unforgiving, how they'd considered her "unclean." How they'd left her marked forever.

It was Joe who'd saved her from them, and she'd always remember the way he'd looked at the couple when he saw how they'd treated Liv. The fire in his eyes when he took her away.

He'd been trying to look out for her, in one way or another, ever since. He'd placed her with Chuck and Marty and checked up on her more regularly than most caseworkers would have. He never forced Liv to go to group therapy when she really, really didn't want to go. He told Liv he knew what it was like to lose family, and she didn't have to talk about it if she didn't want to.

Liv knew that she owed a lot to Joe, and things could have gone much worse for her without him. But still . . . getting placed in another temporary group home just wasn't something she could handle, not right now. Any choice of her own was better than that.

Liv's feet beat against the linoleum as she raced down the hospital staircase. Shoving open the heavy, metal door, she was instantly bathed in the bright morning sunlight. She took off like a shot across the parking lot.

She'd apologize to Joe later.

THE EXILED

Liv sat on the edge of her bed at Rita's house and stared at the worn, packed duffel lying at her feet. She knew she should get moving—this was the first place Joe would look for her—but she couldn't help looking around her room one last time. She thought about that idea, of it being her room. When she'd woken up that morning, the room was definitely hers. But by tomorrow, it would be just a guest bedroom once again.

Liv pushed her palms up against her eye sockets to stop angry tears from falling. She was mad at herself for caring, for letting herself get comfortable in this home for even a moment, for believing in the notion of a home at all. She knew better than that—she had more than ten years of practice in knowing better than that.

All of Liv's clothes and books fit in her duffel. Her camera equipment was already safely packed away in the trunk of her car, which she was reclaiming. Rita wouldn't need it in rehab, anyway. Liv lifted the photo of her and Shannon off the dresser and tucked it in her bag, officially leaving the room exactly as she'd found it. She left quickly. It never helped to look back.

She was halfway through the kitchen when she heard a low creaking noise coming from the living room. Footsteps? Liv stopped in her tracks and turned her head in the direction of the noise. But all she could make out now was the sound of a car horn in the distance.

Carefully, Liv set her duffel bag down on the kitchen floor. She looked around for something solid and heavy to grab, eventually choosing the tea kettle on the stove. The noise sounded again—the same creaking, only for longer this time. She pictured the face of the man who'd followed her down the alley, and her heart pounded hard.

Liv gripped the kettle and slowly made her way toward the living room. She got to the doorway, then inched her head into the room and peered around. Couch, television, drapes. Nothing out of the ordinary.

Sighing, Liv felt the tension leave her shoulders. Just as she was beginning to feel silly for getting so worked up over a noise, she saw a blurring motion moving toward her from her left-hand side.

Without thinking, Liv swung the kettle with all of her might. She felt it connect, but didn't realize who or what she'd hit until she heard a loud groan and a male voice crying out in pain.

"Cedric?"

"Ow. Again." Cedric stepped forward and rubbed his shoulder. "Should I always be prepared for violence when we meet?"

Liv let out a breath of relief and loosened her grip on the tea kettle. "Meet? You broke into my house!"

"The door was open."

"So you just came right in?"

Cedric shrugged, and then instantly winced in pain, reaching up for his shoulder again.

"Well, here's a pro tip for living in LA: knock before entering."

Liv set down the kettle and picked up her duffel. Cedric was still rubbing his shoulder.

"What are you doing here?" she asked him.

"You told me to come if I needed to find a new place to stay."

Liv raised an eyebrow. "Well, as it happens, I'm looking for a new place to stay, too."

Cedric looked around at the living room and Rita's modest belongings. "What is wrong with this place? It seems . . . very comfortable."

"It was." Liv kept her eyes trained on the floor. "It's not anymore."

He didn't push the issue.

"We should probably get out of here," Liv said. "I'll drive, obviously."

Cedric followed her to the door and reached out an arm for her bag. "Here, let me."

"No, it's okay," Liv said, swinging the duffel in front of her body. Instead of grabbing the bag's straps, Cedric's outstretched fingers instead brushed against Liv's hip, briefly touching the skin between her T-shirt and jeans. He pulled his fingers back quickly, and Liv felt her face redden. She was glad for the dim lighting of Rita's living room.

"I apologize. I did not mean . . . ," Cedric started.

"It's okay. I just don't like people touching my stuff," Liv said, then felt her blush deepen. "I mean, my bag. That's what I meant. By stuff."

Cedric nodded, but Liv could see confusion written on his face. She shook her head. "Let's just go."

Liv led Cedric out of the house and down the short driveway to her rust-red Corolla. She opened the back door and threw her duffel over the seat, then got into the driver's side. Cedric slowly opened his door and sat down, his back rigid against the passenger seat. He placed his palms down flat on his knees and stared through the windshield.

"You okay?" Liv asked.

Cedric swallowed and nodded, but kept his gaze forward. "I am still unaccustomed to these."

"To . . . cars?"

"Yes. They move . . . much faster than I prefer."

Liv shook her head and put her keys in the ignition. "Not this one, trust me. I saw you moving in that alley, and you could probably outpace my Corolla any day."

Cedric smiled, that lopsided smile Liv remembered from the night before.

"So how did you get here?" Liv asked as she reversed the car down the driveway. She noticed Cedric's eyes following the movements of her hands as she turned the wheel.

"It took several hours, I admit. I ran part of the way—"

"Ran? That's, like, miles."

"And then I caught up to one of those large cars. The orange ones."

"You mean a bus?"

Cedric nodded, his eyes darting around the road as Liv pulled into traffic. A car moved in front of Liv's, and Cedric flinched.

"Somehow I have a hard time picturing you in a bus," Liv said.

"I was not really in it, so much as I was riding on the back end, where no one could see me."

"Sure. Like you do."

Cedric didn't notice her sarcasm. "It went fairly slowly, so it was easy to hang on. I probably could have run here faster, truthfully."

Liv just shook her head and decided to let it go. She would help Cedric find a place to stay, as promised, but she wouldn't help to actively encourage his delusions.

"So I want to try this house in Echo Park first. I stayed there for a couple of weeks when I had this foster situation that . . . well, let's just say it sucked."

"We must go to the museum first and get the others." Cedric's voice was tense as the car picked up speed.

"Of course we must," Liv muttered. She waited until she was stopped at a red light before looking over at him. "You know, it might help you relax if you buckle up."

"Buckle what?"

Liv sighed.

All of Cedric's muscles ached from sitting so stiffly in the car. Just a few feet away, Liv seemed perfectly at ease. Her hands worked the controls in confident, easy motions that were completely foreign to him, no matter how much sense he tried to make of them. Whenever Cedric looked to his left or right and saw objects flying past the window in a series of blurred motions, he felt his stomach roll over on itself.

"You really need to chill out," Liv said, glancing over at him. Cedric had no idea what she was talking about, but he didn't want her to know that. Even though he had spent time at the museum eavesdropping on patrons to better understand the language of this world, it still took him some time to puzzle out certain expressions. He had to go by facial expression and body language to figure out what Liv was saying half the time. Now, her voice was calm, but her eyes looked worried. She was concerned for him.

Cedric breathed out when he saw the familiar shape of the museum.

"Looks like the museum's closing, so I'm going to park on the street," Liv said. She maneuvered around a turn so fast that Cedric went flying across the center portion of the car and practically landed on her seat. He reached out a hand to steady himself, but it somehow landed on her thigh. He could feel the warmth of her skin radiating through the fabric of her pants, and he felt his stomach swoop the way it had when he'd accidentally brushed against her in her house earlier. It was a strange feeling, like taking a step and finding a bottomless hole where the ground used to be. Like jumping through the portal all over again.

Cedric pulled his hand away quickly and pushed himself over to the far side of his seat. Liv kept her face turned forward, though Cedric thought her cheeks were a bit pinker than before.

"See? That's why we buckle up."

The car came to a stop near the alley that led to his secret living space. The area was mostly deserted. In the distance, Cedric could see cars pulling away from the main museum entrance in one long trail, their red lights blinking on and off in a strangely beautiful pattern.

Just as Cedric got out of the car and put his feet on the ground, he heard the sound of yelling.

"Cedric!"

Cedric turned around and saw a lone figure running toward the museum. Merek.

And he wasn't alone. Four, five—no, six men were chasing him, their footsteps echoing along the street.

"Cedric!" Merek yelled again, waving his arms. That's when Cedric realized that the men following him weren't actually men at all.

Merek barreled forward, nearly running smack into Cedric and Liv, who had also exited the car. Cedric grabbed his shoulders.

"You led them here?"

Merek's face twisted. "No! I just—"

And then the wraths were upon them. Cedric vaguely heard the sound of Liv crying out as he squared off to push back the first wrath he saw. There were too many of them to fight easily—they outnumbered him and Merek three to one.

Instead of panicking, a sense of familiar calm washed over Cedric. Finally, finally, here was something he knew he could handle. He didn't have to devise an elaborate plan, search for a secret artifact, defend his leadership, or try to make conversation with an alluring girl from a strange hell dimension. He only had to calculate strength and response. Defend and attack.

This was a language he knew. And one he was good at.

The first wrath to approach Cedric gripped a long, metal pipe. As he swung it out, Cedric easily ducked away. He used the spare second to retrieve his knife from the hidden pocket Kat had sewn into his pants. He cut the knife down toward the wrath's midsection, but the wrath skidded backward.

Cedric turned quickly to Liv, who seemed frozen in place as a tall wrath, muscled and wearing a thick red beard, reached out for her. Just as she put up an arm to defend herself, Cedric spun around and kicked out with his right leg, connecting with the red-haired wrath's face. The creature was only momentarily stunned, and Cedric was just positioning himself to land another blow when he felt something heavy slam into his back. He nearly dropped to his knees before forcing himself back up to face the first wrath, who still held the metal pipe in its clawed grip.

Though his back was on fire, Cedric straightened to face both the red-haired wrath and the wrath with the pipe as they advanced on him. Through their figures he could just barely make out Merek dodging a series of blows. The wraths were pushing them back, toward the alley that led to the tunnel entrance.

Blocking the metal pipe with his left arm as he swung his

knife out with his right, Cedric yelled out to Liv. "We need help—get Kat!"

He wasn't even able to turn around and see if she had followed his direction before the two wraths smashed into him with astonishing force. He pulled both wraths to the ground, and the next noise he heard was the harsh crack of breaking bones echoing off the alley's brick walls.

THE WARRIORS

The red-haired man who had tried to grab Liv now lay on the ground, writhing in pain. A jagged, yellowish piece of bone stuck out through the span of skin just below his elbow. But it was his eyes Liv couldn't stop staring at. They were all-black, shiny and empty, just like those of the man who'd attacked her in this very alley the night before.

The *wrath.* The word bounced to Liv's mind easily, but she pushed it away just as quickly.

Cedric rolled away from where he had landed on top of the man and got to his feet again. "Run, Liv! Go!"

Liv whirled around and sprinted toward the grate. She was halfway there before she stopped to look behind her. Her heart flipped as she realized how outnumbered they were.

With shaking fingers, she reached down into her purse and pulled out her cell phone, then punched in three buttons.

"Nine-one-one, what is your emergency?"

"I need help. My friend is being attacked by a group of, um . . . bad men. They're really strong—I think they may be on drugs or something . . ."

"I need you to tell me exactly where you are."

"The natural history museum, downtown. They're in the alley on the right-hand side of the building."

Liv could hear clicking noises as the woman typed into a keyboard on the other end of the line. She reached the grate in the alley wall and bent down to swing herself through it. A tinny voice echoed out through her phone.

"Sorry, what was that?" Liv asked, sliding ungracefully into the tunnel. It was completely dark in there, with only a bit of afternoon light filtering in from the alley. Liv made her way through the tunnel slowly—it was much more difficult without Cedric to guide the way.

The woman's voice came through insistent and firm. "Can you tell me if any of the attackers have weapons?"

"I . . . I don't know. But there's a lot of them. Please hurry."

"Dispatch is on the way. Tell me what's—"

The woman's voice cut out, leaving only a buzzy silence in Liv's ear. She looked down at the phone as she continued walking. No reception.

Liv clicked on the flashlight app, and a bright beam of light flickered over the walls of the concrete tunnel. Securing her phone in her right hand, she started to run.

Eventually, she saw a warm glow of light coming from around the corner, and she sprinted toward it. She rounded the corner and found herself at the entrance of a wide, dimly lit room filled with wooden crates and blankets.

A teenage girl jumped up from where she'd been sitting at

the edge of the room, assuming a fighting stance as she did so. It was the girl from under the bridge. Kat.

Liv's flashlight app lit up the strange girl's features. Even though Kat's face was contorted with confusion and she wore what looked like a loose nightgown over a grimy pair of jeans, she was still one of the most beautiful girls Liv had ever seen, outside of a movie screen. Her dark eyes scanned Liv's face as she approached.

"Who are you?" Kat asked, her voice high and forceful.

"Cedric sent me," Liv choked out.

"Cedric?" Kat moved forward, closer to Liv. Her eyes narrowed. "Wait, I remember you . . ."

"Cedric's in trouble," Liv breathed out. "He's right outside fighting this group of men. Of . . . um, wraths. There's so many of them . . ."

Understanding dawned on Kat's face. In a movement almost too quick for Liv's eyes to follow, she dropped to the floor and picked up something shiny. It was the sword that had sat in Liv's room for two months—Cedric must have reclaimed it from the Acquisitions Department. Kat gripped the hilt and pushed her way past Liv without a second glance.

"I'll just, uh . . . follow you, then," Liv called after her, weakly.

Kat's footsteps were already fading away through the tunnel.

When Liv finally made her way back to the grate and crawled back into the alley, the first thing she noticed was that the fight had gotten closer. The men had pressed in toward the recesses of the alley, blocking off the view of the street.

Someone yelled out in pain.

"Cedric," Liv whispered, then took off toward the fight. The logical part of Liv's brain screamed out at her to stop, but she ignored it, running faster and faster down the concrete alleyway. It was only when she finally reached the tight circle of fighting that she halted abruptly, her shoes screeching against the pavement. Instead of jumping in to help, she could only stare in amazement at what unfolded around her, bright and strange as a movie sequence.

The alley was only about ten feet across from wall to wall, and nearly the entire width of the space was filled with the sights and sounds of fighting. Liv saw Kat toss Cedric the sword through the air. He caught it in one hand midwhirl, and somehow seemed more balanced with the large blade than without it.

Kat squared off against a burly, blond man in a torn Metallica T-shirt. Just like the others, he had jet-black eyes and a pointy grimace. He slashed out with one of his hands, aiming for the smooth skin of Kat's right cheek with fingernails that were sharpened to pointed bits, almost like claws.

Kat held up her hand to ward off the blow, then ducked under the man's grasp. Clenching his arm in her own small hands, she wrenched it downward, snapping it over her knee. Physically, it shouldn't have been possible. For someone as slight as Kat to get that kind of leverage over her attacker and to exert enough force to break his arm . . . it went against the laws of nature. Liv wouldn't have believed it had she not heard the crack of bone from where she stood.

Against one wall, Cedric and Merek were fighting more of the wraths. One of the black-eyed men charged at Merek, and before the two collided, Merek swerved to his left, grabbed the man from behind, and used his momentum to throw him against the side of the museum. When the man's head hit the wall, the bricks behind him cracked and crumbled, falling in pieces to the ground. Again, it shouldn't have been possible. It shouldn't have happened. But it had.

And Cedric, he was all speed. He moved so fast between two of the hulking men that Liv could barely see him, aside from a kick here or a whirled blade there. The two attackers grunted in frustration as their fists missed their target, again and again. Cedric moved with precision and accuracy, but also with a kind of grace. And his face . . . though his expression was set in determination, Liv could swear he was almost smiling. He leaped off the ground—higher than Liv thought a person should be able to leap—and kicked a man in the jaw. Then he landed on his own feet with hardly a grunt and kept fighting.

Liv sucked in a breath as her eyes bounced from Cedric to the others, watching them break the laws of physics as they fought. They looked like, well, like superheroes, fighting off the bad guys in the third act of the movie.

Except this wasn't a movie. This was real.

Everything in the world seemed to shift slightly. Liv couldn't argue with what she was seeing happen with her own eyes. But none of it made sense, either. It didn't fit into the real world that she knew, the world that she'd always known. Was she going crazy? Or was it that . . . was it that Cedric wasn't lying? That everything he'd told her was true?

And if that was the case, then . . .

Liv struggled to think straight. Cedric said he'd come through a portal from another world. That he'd been raised to fight monsters with all-black eyes and superstrength. Liv looked at the disfigured men around her, letting the truth sink in. They weren't on drugs; they weren't part of a strange cult or a group of Anne Rice fan boys. They weren't human at all.

"Holy. Shit."

The whispered words were barely out of Liv's mouth before something knocked into her from behind. Liv fell face-first to the ground and hit it, hard. She tried and failed to cry out, unable to pull in a breath. Craning her neck, Liv saw one of the wraths perched over her, knee pressed into her back. It was the black-haired wrath who had attacked her the night before.

"I've got her!" The wrath called out in a rough voice.

"Hold her there," another low voice responded.

Liv looked to the others, but they were all still busy fighting. No one had noticed her go down.

The second wrath approached. A large one, with a shock of white-gray hair. The man who'd stared at her on the bus. He looked down at Liv with hungry eyes, then to the black-haired wrath. "Well?"

Liv pushed up off the ground with all her might, but the black-haired wrath still had his knee located firmly in her back, and one hand clutching tightly at the back of her jacket. He pushed her back down to the pavement, and Liv heard her jacket tearing. She looked back again and saw the wrath staring down at her exposed skin. His black eyes narrowed, his features contorting into something that might be construed as a smile.

"Well done, Varl," the wrath from the bus said. "You were ri—"

The wrath's head whipped around at a sound in the distance—sirens. In the instant he was distracted, Cedric appeared and slammed his entire body into the black-haired wrath, Varl, knocking him off Liv in one ungraceful yet effective movement.

Liv scrambled to her feet, just in time to jump away from the grasp of the white-haired wrath. His grin revealed a row of overcrowded, pointy teeth. Liv screamed.

"Kat!" Cedric called out, still fighting with Varl on the ground. "Help!"

The white-haired wrath grabbed for Liv again, his smile contorting into a snarl. The sirens grew louder. Liv curled her hands into fists, hoping she could keep the advancing wrath at bay until the police arrived.

Kat got there first.

She jumped into the white-haired man's path and aimed a roundhouse kick that he quickly dodged. Kat pursued, throwing punch after punch until one landed on the wrath's jaw.

Kat stopped punching when red and blue lights fell over the brick and concrete. Liv looked up to see two squad cars pulling up to the mouth of the alley.

"Finally," she muttered.

The wraths noticed the police, too. Many of them stopped fighting, instead looking from the cop cars to one another, as if deciding what to do. Cedric disentangled himself from Varl and jumped up.

"We must leave," he said. "Now."

The white-haired wrath whipped his head back in Cedric's direction. He'd made his decision. Turning his back on the cops, he squared off to face Cedric and his friends. The other wraths quickly followed suit.

"You're not going anywhere," he said.

"Chath, what about—" Varl said, gesturing toward the cops.

The white-haired wrath, Chath, snorted. "They cannot hurt us. And neither can the royals. If they had silver, they would have used it by now." Chath grinned. "But we can hurt them."

Chath nodded his head in Liv's direction, and Varl leaped out toward her.

This time, Liv didn't wait for Cedric or Kat to jump in the way of the charging wrath. She ran. She dodged around Varl and nearly collided with the alley wall. Instead, she pushed herself off it and kept racing ahead, straight toward the cops.

"Help!"

"Liv, no!" Cedric was running right behind her.

Liv turned around in surprise as Cedric caught up to her easily, grabbing her wrist.

"Everybody stay where you are!" a gruff voice called out. Two officers jogged toward them from the mouth of the alley. One talked into his walkie-talkie as he ran.

"Liv," Cedric said, his voice low and urgent. His eyes darted between the cops and Kat, who was once again fighting with the wraths nearest to her. "Those men cannot help us. We must run."

"But . . . ," Liv sputtered. She looked up and saw Kat getting knocked to the ground by a hulking wrath.

"Trust me. Please," Cedric said. His eyes raked over hers, intense. He didn't seem to notice that he was still gripping her arm.

Liv looked back at the police as they took formation along the alley.

"He's got a weapon."

Liv's chest seized as the officers nearest to her pulled out their guns. They were looking at Cedric, who still held the long sword in one hand. His eyes were on her, begging. She nodded.

Cedric lifted Liv off the ground and sprinted backward before she could say another word. They moved so fast that the shapes passing by Liv condensed into one unfocused blur. In just a few seconds, they were standing back with the others, who continued to grapple with the wraths.

"Move out, now!" Cedric screamed. His voice blended into the commands being shouted by the police officers. Chath was also screaming orders, but Liv couldn't pick one voice from another in the chaos. She saw Kat free Merek from the grip of a wrath. Varl stood frozen, eyes bouncing between Cedric and the officer who was quickly approaching him. He charged the officer, knocking his gun down and throwing him back against the brick wall in a fraction of a second. The officer smashed into the wall and crumpled to the ground, motionless.

Liv let out an involuntary gasp, her breath catching in her throat.

And then they were running, racing toward the back of the alley, away from the cops and the wraths both. Liv knew they were running in the opposite direction of her car, but she couldn't get her mind to work right to say something. It was stuck on the image of the police officer's head hitting the brick wall. She heard one gunshot, then another, but refused to look back.

Cedric still carried Liv, tight against his side, as they finally reached the back of the alley. He turned left just before the fence, running down a second alley that butted up against the rear of the park. Another turn, this one toward the massive USC Coliseum, and soon the sounds of the fight faded behind them. Liv could only hear the labored sound of Cedric's breathing, the racing of his heart, the paces of his friends as they ran and ran and ran.

They finally made it to a large parking lot, and Liv found herself breathing normally. Her thoughts were less muddled by fear. "Cedric," she said, turning her head to face his. "Cedric, stop," she said.

His body slowed from a sprint into a human-capable jog, and then a walk.

"You can put me down, please," Liv said.

Slowly, Cedric's arms released from around her waist, and he set her down on the pavement behind a giant parked SUV. She felt better the instant she was once again standing on her own two feet. The others came up behind them, slowing to a stop as well.

"Is anyone injured?" Cedric asked. Merek shook his head, but Kat motioned to her shoulder.

"Dislocated," she said, matter-of-fact. Liv could only detect a hint of pain in her face when Cedric gently reached out and touched her shoulder.

"I can put it right when we get somewhere safe," Kat said. "Where did the men in blue come from?"

Cedric shook his head and ran a hand through his hair.

"Oh, uh . . . I called them . . . ," Liv said.

Kat muttered something under her breath. Liv looked around at each of them, shaking her head. "You were being attacked. By a group of seriously pissed-off looking guys—"

Cedric looked at her in disbelief. "Wraths. I told you they were wraths!"

"Well, I know that now!" Liv yelled back. "But at the time, I didn't believe they were . . ."

. . . *Monsters.* Liv had called the LAPD to fight a gang of monsters. She saw the police officer again, the way he'd hit the brick wall, the way he'd slid to the ground. That was her fault.

Cedric let out an exasperated sigh and turned away from Liv, toward Merek. "What I don't understand," he said, in a strained voice, "is what those wraths were doing chasing you?"

Merek's face drained of color.

"You went after them, didn't you? You went against me and sought out the wraths to speak to them, as though they were creatures to be reasoned with!"

"Not exactly," Merek said.

"Merek," Kat put in, "you told me you were looking for food."

"I was not going to talk to them, only to see if they were still near the museum and maybe try to track them. But then they found me—"

"You expect me to believe that?" Cedric looked incredulous.

"I honestly do not care what you believe," Merek retorted.

"Do you care about anything? We could all have been killed tonight."

Merek's jaw tightened, and he averted his eyes to look at the ground.

"We do not have time for this now," Kat said. "We cannot stay here."

Cedric and Merek continued to glare at each other, but neither said another word.

Liv looked back in the direction of the museum. "The police are right by my car. We'll never get past them. I think we should get to a busy street and try to blend in with the crowd."

"And why should we do what you say?" Kat's voice turned from sensible to biting as she turned to Liv with narrowed eyes. "Who *are* you, anyway?"

"I'm the only one here who knows my way around this city," Liv shot back.

For a moment, Cedric looked between the two girls. His gaze finally settled on Liv. "Do you know somewhere safe we can go?"

Kat's jaw clenched, and she looked away. Liv ignored her and pulled out her phone.

"Not only that, but I know who can get us there, too."

THE UNAVOIDABLE TRUTHS

The gray minivan pulled up twenty minutes later, then skidded to a halt just outside of the Laundromat doorway where Liv waited with Cedric and the others. The passenger-side window rolled down, revealing Shannon's black-and-red locks and her incensed face.

"Liv! What the hell?"

Liv stepped forward and rested her hands on the van's window. "Hey, Shannon."

"Hey, Shannon? *Hey, Shannon?* I don't hear from you since yesterday, Joe's been calling me to see if I know where you are, and then I steal my mom's van—which was much more difficult the second time around, by the way—to come pick you up halfway across town and all you can say is 'Hey, Shannon?'"

Liv waited for Shannon to take a breath. "Thanks for coming. And for covering with Joe. And for stealing the minivan. But . . . we kind of need a ride. Then I can explain."

"We?"

Liv gestured to where Cedric and the others stood behind her.

Shannon looked past Liv, and her mouth fell open. "Oh my God, is that . . . are they who I think they are?"

"It's kind of a long story," Liv said.

Shannon continued to stare. "I'm sure."

"But we really need to get out of here, like, five minutes ago. So . . ."

Shannon shook her head in slow disbelief, then leaned back in the driver's seat. "Okay, get in. But I'm going to need more details."

Liv waved her hand to Cedric, who stepped forward, the others close behind. One by one, they all climbed into the van.

Shannon turned to Liv in the passenger seat and whispered, "Are you in trouble?"

Liv swallowed. "Kinda. Can you take me to Echo Park? Near Alvarado."

"Curiouser and curiouser," Shannon mumbled, rolling her eyes, but she put the car into drive and slipped back into the traffic on the street. Liv took the opportunity to pull out her phone and saw six missed calls from Joe. Damn. She put the phone away.

While she drove, Shannon sneaked peeks at the others through the rearview mirror. Her eyes landed on Cedric, and then on the sword he still gripped in his hands. Her eyebrows shot up.

Liv wondered how much of the truth she'd be able to tell Shannon. Certainly nothing about wraths or portals or teenage royals from another world. She'd seen that insane fight go down with her own two eyes and she still had to remind herself every few minutes that it was all actually real, and not just a weirdly vivid hallucination.

"So what's in Echo Park?" Shannon asked. "Since we're already on the way and all."

"Remember freshman year, when I was staying with the Hopmans?"

Shannon's hands tightened on the wheel. "Yes," she whispered.

The Hopmans were a particularly mediocre set of foster parents Liv had lived with for about six months. They were drunks, but not like Rita. Not like her at all.

"That was when I tried to set you up in my garage and my mom caught us."

Liv nodded. "And I had nowhere else to go, so I ran."

Shannon's eyebrows wrinkled. "I thought Joe put you in a group home?"

"He did, eventually," Liv said, careful with her words. "But I was on my own for a while. I fell in with some kids who helped me out. . . ."

"Like, runaways?" Shannon pursed her lips.

"That's what I was too, remember? Anyway, these kids let me in on some places I could stay—abandoned houses, foreclosed places. It's kind of like . . . a network. I just hope this place we're going is still empty."

"Why did you never tell me any of this?"

Liv couldn't meet Shannon's eye, and was glad that they were having this conversation while Shannon was driving. "I don't know. It was just . . . easier that way. To keep that part of my life separate from everything else."

"You know I'm here for you, right? You can tell me anything." Shannon's words were comforting, but her voice sounded slightly accusatory. And hurt.

"I know that, Shan. I really do."

They drove on in silence. Liv gazed out the window at the small, artsy boutiques and coffee shops lined up next to 99-cent stores and fast-food restaurants on Sunset Boulevard. Nearly every corner was populated by a homeless person, a hipster in skinny jeans, or both.

"Here." Liv nodded to a street on the right. Shannon turned and the van moved slowly uphill, past single-level houses painted orange, purple, and green. Some of the houses had small front lawns covered with furniture, while others were hidden behind fences bearing Beware of Dog signs. Nearly every third house was still decorated with Christmas lights, even though it was August.

The abandoned house sat, dark and empty, at the very top of the hill, all peeling paint and a sagging front porch. A foreclosure sign leaned against the front door. The house had an unusually large lawn in the front and on the sides, almost as if the houses on either side were trying to get their distance from it. It backed up to a grove of trees so thick that Liv couldn't see through them.

"We're here."

The doors opened and Cedric and his friends climbed out of the van. Before he was fully outside, Merek turned to Shannon. "Did you know that your hair looks like it's bleeding?"

Shannon made a face. "A simple 'thanks for the ride' would have been fine."

Merek shrugged and jumped out of the van.

Shannon whipped her head back to face Liv, who put up a hand, speaking first. "I told you I would explain everything, and I will. But right now, I have to get them set up."

Shannon bit her lip, then nodded. "I trust you. What should I tell Joe, if he calls back?"

"Don't tell him anything. Just till I can figure things out."

"Okay . . . Oh, here's that shirt you asked for. What happened to yours, anyway?"

Shannon handed a folded-up, long-sleeved T-shirt to Liv. Her eyebrows creased as she looked at the tatters of Liv's shirt.

"Caught it on a nail. You know me, never met an outfit I couldn't destroy in less than a day." Liv let out a shaky laugh and opened the passenger-side door.

Shannon eyed Liv's bandaged hand, too. "Right," she said. "Hey, Liv? You would tell me, wouldn't you, if something was really, really wrong?"

"I'd tell you. Everything's fine. Weird, but fine," Liv said, getting out of the van and closing the door quickly before Shannon could figure out she was lying.

The house had four bedrooms in total, but the three located upstairs were deemed unusable because the staircase leading to the second floor was almost entirely rotted through. All of the downstairs rooms were empty except for two tattered couches in the living room. The electricity wasn't connected, and the water was shut off. Liv searched the kitchen cabinets, just in case whoever had last passed through left some cans of food behind. No luck.

Liv found a bathroom on the first floor and shut herself in. It was getting dark out, but the curtainless window let in a good amount of twilight, enough for Liv to check herself out in the mirror above the sink. Her face looked drained of color, all whiteness and shadows. A tiny bandage was still affixed above her eyebrow, from when she'd first been attacked by a wrath the night before. It already felt like weeks ago.

Liv wished she could splash some cold water on her face to freshen up, but she settled for running her fingers through her hair. Her brush was locked in the backseat of her car, along with the rest of her things. She'd have to figure out a way to get it all back the next morning. And then . . . well, she wasn't exactly sure what she'd do then. School started in a week, and she was once again homeless. That was enough of a problem *without* thinking about the fact she'd just been attacked by monsters from another world.

Liv slowly shrugged out of her jacket and turned around so that her back was to the mirror. She craned her neck, trying to see the area where the wrath had clawed at her. Her T-shirt hung from her shoulders in shreds, but the skin underneath was undamaged. She reached up a hand and pulled the pieces of T-shirt away. She brushed her fingers against the dark, twirling lines of her tattoo.

"You're fine," she said to her reflection. "One thing at a time."

Liv put on Shannon's shirt, took another deep breath, and opened the bathroom door. In the living room, Cedric was holding Kat's arm out in a straight line, while Merek gripped her other side.

"Ready?" Cedric asked.

Kat nodded, her face set and pale.

Cedric quickly pushed Kat's arm, and Liv jumped at the resulting cracking noise. Then Kat let out a long, ragged sigh and sank onto one of the sagging couches.

After a moment, Liv cleared her throat and looked to Cedric, who sat down as well, as close to Kat as he could be without upsetting her shoulder.

"Okay. Now that I know—or at least am pretty sure—that you're not a crazy person, I'm going to need some more answers."

Cedric nodded. "I tried to tell you before."

Liv sighed. "I know. But after seeing you fight . . . and those things, they weren't just men. I wanted to believe they were, but . . ."

"They most definitely are not," Cedric finished for her.

"You said you came . . . from another world?" Liv asked.

"Caelum," Kat said. Her voice was clipped, and she gently rubbed at her shoulder.

"Right. Well I guess that's the part I'm having a little trouble with. The 'other world' part. So does that make you . . . aliens?"

"What's an alien?" Merek asked. He'd moved to perch at an empty window seat across the room. His fingers worked over a tarnished metal lighter in his palm.

"An alien is like . . . you know, from another planet." Liv

gestured out the window, up toward the moon. "Like E.T."

Blank looks all around.

"Have you never seen *E.T.*? It's one of my favorite movies of all time." Liv put one finger in the air. "Phoooone hooome."

"Movie?" Cedric's lips formed the word awkwardly, as if they'd never spoken it before.

"Wait. Are you telling me you've never . . . seen a movie? Ever?" Liv asked, incredulous. "*The Avengers, Star Wars . . . Mean Girls?* Any combination of moving pictures that tell a story, any one at all?"

Nothing.

Liv shook her head. "That's just . . . so sad. How can you have an entire planet with no movies? I mean, is Caelum really that different from here? You do seem to speak English pretty well . . . for the most part."

"We speak the same language because we originated from this realm," Cedric replied. "Many, many years ago our people lived here as Guardians. They were here for centuries, fighting off the wraths and keeping peace. But it was a hard, bitter place, and our numbers were small. The wraths had the advantage. And that is when the first portal was opened."

Liv raised her hand. "Um, sorry to interrupt, and I'm not saying that history is my area of expertise or anything, but if wraths came from this world, I think I would know."

Cedric shrugged. "This is what we have always been told. Our people crossed through a portal to seek a new world, leaving this one behind. But the wraths followed us. And they did the one thing they're good at doing, aside from causing destruction. They populated."

Liv pictured the all-black eyes from the wraths in the alley . . . not to mention the teeth . . . and fought off a shiver.

"I come from a long line of Guardian kings, who have ruled over Caelum for centuries. We keep the wraths from entering our territories and send out hunting parties to destroy those who come too close. That is the way it has always been, until . . ." Cedric's voice faltered, and he looked out the window.

"Until recently," Kat finished for him.

"Until Malquin," Cedric added, his voice hard. Kat reached out and laid her hand on top of his. Liv couldn't help thinking of how it had felt to hold that same hand of Cedric's briefly in the tunnels. She pulled her eyes away.

"The only chance we have of getting back and reclaiming the palace is to find those scrolls," Cedric went on.

"Right, you mentioned them at the diner," Liv said.

"We do not know much about this world, Earth, or what life was like here before our people left it," Cedric continued. "But it is rumored the first portal was opened by a series of scrolls—"

"*Rumored* being the operative word," Merek cut in. "There is always a chance the scrolls are imaginary, and we do not actually have a way home—"

"But we choose to believe they are real," Kat said, glaring at Merek. She turned to Liv. "According to legend, there were three scrolls originally used to open the portal to Caelum. And those scrolls were left behind on Earth when our people crossed through. We need them to open a portal again."

Liv's mind raced, trying to keep up. She struggled to fit the details into a larger picture, the way she would when trying to piece together a movie. "Okay, so . . . the scrolls are the MacGuffin."

Cedric's face was blank. "Mac . . . what?"

Liv sat up straighter. "Oh, it's a filmmaking device. A thing that everyone wants to get, like the briefcase in *Pulp Fiction* or the Ark of the Covenant in *Indiana Jones.* "

"You are speaking nonsense again." Cedric shook his head, but inched forward on the couch, his attention only on Liv. She leaned forward, too.

"*I'm* speaking nonsense? Portals and monsters and scrolls—that's nonsense. Movies have internal logic at least. They have rules so you know what's going on. Like, imagine your life is a story—"

"Now that *would* be good," he said, and grinned.

"I can see it now. The waffle-eating prince who loved his sword too much."

"Said the girl who spoke gibberish and drove much too fast—"

Kat cleared her throat loudly, and Cedric and Liv both shut up and sat up straight, as though they'd been caught at something.

"Anyway," Liv continued, "if your life were a movie, the MacGuffin would be the thing you really, really want."

"Fascinating. But I believe we have things of actual import to discuss," Kat said, her voice cold.

From the other side of the room, Merek scoffed. "Like jealous fiancées."

There was an awkward silence, and Liv took a deep breath, choosing to pretend she hadn't heard Merek. "So I get you're looking for scrolls, but . . . why didn't your people just come back here years ago, once they realized the, um, wraths followed them to Caelum?"

Merek snorted and gestured outside. "Why do you think?"

Cedric shifted uncomfortably. "We were taught that our people left this place when it had grown uninhabitable. Though the wraths followed us, returning here was never even an option."

"You do not escape hell only to return," Merek said, his voice low.

"Well, I think that's a little harsh. I mean, yeah, we may have a lot of wars and a disturbing amount of reality TV shows based on botched plastic surgeries, but . . . hell?" Liv laughed. "I mean, Earth is where you all came from. It's your home."

"It is *not* our home," Kat said.

"Okay, but . . . it's not *hell*." Liv turned to Cedric. "Is that really what you think?"

Cedric sighed. "What I think is we have to get back, at any cost. It is not only our own lives in the balance. All of Caelum is at risk."

For a moment, no one spoke. Another thought occurred to Liv. "Wait, you said these wraths followed your people into Caelum. But if that's true, how did they end up in that alley? And why are they after you now?"

Cedric's eyebrows furrowed. "I do not know the answer to that."

"Or to anything else, really," Merek muttered, looking out of the window.

"Yes, Merek, I think you have made your opinion on the matter quite clear. You continue to be extremely helpful by repeating it."

"Well," Liv said, with a forced laugh, "at least when your people went through that portal the first time, they remembered to take sarcasm with them."

To Liv's—and everyone's—surprise, Kat was the one who laughed at that. She quickly squelched it, forcing her expression back to a more grim one.

"It has been a long night," Kat said. "And we are all a little tense. Maybe we should get some rest."

Liv still had so many questions to ask, but more than that, she wanted a few quiet moments to think, and to wrap her head around everything that had happened. "That's a good idea," she said. "This place is relatively safe . . . I mean, from cops, anyway. As for the wraths . . ."

"They cannot have followed us," Cedric said. "We moved too quickly on the way here."

"Yeah, well, Shannon believes that speed limits are more of a suggestion than a rule." Liv laughed, but it was hollow. She tried to ignore the way her stomach flipped around uncomfortably at just the thought of those creatures with the pitch-black eyes, and the way that black-haired one had stared at her hungrily as it pinned her down to the ground . . . she shook her head to rid herself of the image.

They ended up spreading out around the couches or on

the torn carpet in the living room. Liv lay down against the cushions in the darkness, her eyes barely making out the sloping shapes lying around her. As the minutes stretched on, she could tell that the others were falling asleep, one by one. She wanted to stay awake and sort through all of the images of the day, get them into some kind of recognizable order, but instead, she slipped into half-dreams full of black-eyed monsters and dark holes that tore open the sky before waking up each time with a gasp.

After a few hours, Liv gave up trying to think or even trying to get a good night's rest. None of the sleeping forms so much as twitched as she got up and crept out of the room and through the kitchen.

Through a window in the kitchen door, Liv could clearly see the backyard area, dim and tranquil in the moonlight. She opened the door and walked out onto the back patio. A few plastic lawn chairs surrounded a glass-topped table with an old, dirty ashtray sitting on top of it.

Liv took a seat and shut her eyes. She suddenly longed to go down to her spot by the river, which she knew would be isolated and calm at this time of night. It was her go-to place whenever life was feeling a bit . . . much. But even if she had her car with her, it wouldn't have felt right to leave Cedric and the others behind on their own.

A small scraping sound made Liv jump. She whirled around and saw Cedric coming through the back door, which he closed behind him.

"Cannot sleep?" he asked.

"Nope. Lots going on up here," Liv replied, pointing to her head. She tried to let out a small laugh, but it got caught at a lump in her throat and came out sounding strangled.

"Do you mind?" Cedric pointed to the chair next to hers.

Liv shook her head.

"I find it can be hard to sleep through the night in this world. We usually rotate in shifts." Cedric leaned back in his chair, tipping his head toward the sky. Liv followed his gaze. She'd always loved how the night sky in Los Angeles could look different depending on where you were. By the beach, it was a deep blue. In the center of Hollywood, with its roaming searchlights and congestion, the sky turned purple-gray, almost the color of slate. Here, in Echo Park, it reflected the orangy glow of the streetlights.

"Do you believe what Merek said in there?" Liv asked, her eyes still on the sky. "About thinking this place is hell?"

Cedric waited a moment before responding. "I did at first, but not anymore. There are some things here that seem far too lovely to exist in any type of hell . . ."

"Like syrup?"

"Among other things." Cedric flushed and looked away. "I suppose this realm is not like any kind of hell I have ever heard of. Then again, how would one really know? Maybe hell is just a myth we ascribe to worlds we cannot imagine."

"Whoa. Deep."

"I am more than just a pretty face."

Liv snorted, and Cedric gave her that half-smile she was coming to recognize. His eyes looked dark blue in the moonlight, half covered in shadow. She remembered how fast he had run in the alley, and nodded toward his outstretched leg.

"I guess that's true. Does everyone have superpowers where you're from?"

"Superpowers?" Cedric chuckled in the darkness. "I like that. All Guardians are fast and strong, to better fight the wraths. Several generations ago, the fastest and strongest of us joined forces to rule over the others and ensure peace in the kingdom."

Liv was about to interject with a snarky comment about fascism, but decided against it.

"For years, the royals would intermarry to ensure that the next generation would be just as capable of leading," Cedric continued.

"Thus . . . arranged marriage."

"It is of the utmost importance. The wraths grow in number every year, and we have to maintain the power to fight them."

"So, you were all trained to fight? The way you all moved in that alley . . . I've never seen anything like it."

"We were all trained, yes. Kat and I had royal training for years. Merek trained as well, although he never showed the same aptitude as his older brother. I think it bothered him more than a little."

Liv choked down a laugh. "Well, that explains the majorly chipped shoulder, I guess."

"The what?"

Liv waved her hand. "He just seems to go out of his way to be kind of a dick. You know, rude for no reason? So remind me to keep him away from Shannon. That's exactly her type."

Liv had meant it as a joke—sort of—but Cedric didn't smile. "I suppose he has his reasons to act as he does. As a second son, Merek will not take over his father's place as duke. Without superior fighting skills, he will never lead a guard, either. Still, he is royalty. And my responsibility"—he paused—"'dick' or not."

Liv pursed her lips to swallow her laughter at Cedric's labored pronunciation of the word. They sat in silence for another moment. Liv batted a fly away from her leg as she tucked both her legs up underneath her in the flimsy chair.

"What's it like, where you're from?"

"Caelum . . . ," Cedric started, his voice turning softer, "is not as bright as here. We have a sun, but it is not so big, nor so intense. It is also colder there, though not in a bad way. Everything is . . . clearer. And cleaner. Bigger and yet . . . sharper, somehow."

"No smog, huh?"

Cedric shook his head, though Liv wasn't quite sure he even knew what smog was. "It is both simpler there . . . and more complicated, in some ways. We ride in carriages to get from the palace to the town, and we hunt in giant forests with trees that reach as tall as that." Liv followed Cedric's finger to where it pointed at a series of hills. "Taller, actually."

"What do you do for fun?"

"Besides hunting? We go to feasts and dances on high holidays, but we also just . . . spend time together."

"Like hang out."

Cedric shrugged. He was still staring at the sky, but it didn't look like he was really seeing it. His eyes were much farther away.

"And what about Kat?" Liv asked, trying to keep her voice light.

"What about her?"

"Well, the whole lifelong betrothal thing . . . it's just, it's kind of difficult to understand. We don't really do that here. Not in LA, anyway."

"Kat and I . . . that is simply the way it has always been for us."

They were silent again, and Liv could hear crickets chirping from the trees. The air around her felt thick.

"What about love?" she asked, her voice low. "Doesn't that exist in Caelum?"

"Of course it does. But Kat and I, we are different. We have responsibilities to our families, to our nation. Our union will make our entire kind stronger against the rising wrath forces."

"Oh," Liv managed. She wasn't sure what else to say. It seemed like a lot for a teenager to take on.

Cedric's eyebrows stitched together as if he was trying to work something out. "Kat and I are lucky. We have always cared for each other, which is more than a lot of people in our position can say. I trust her. More than anyone."

Liv tried to think about the people in her life she really trusted. Just Shannon, really. Joe, too, although she didn't really want to think about him right now, or the half dozen voice mails he'd left on her phone.

"I get it," she said. "But do you think you two will still . . . I mean, if you don't get back—"

"We are getting back." Cedric's voice was firm.

"Right, sorry. I didn't mean . . ."

"Of course." Cedric shook his head, but his tone had changed. He stared off into the distance again, his expression hard. Liv felt something strange, then, just an all-consuming need to make him feel better somehow, to erase the past few moments.

"I can help you, if you want."

Almost startled, Cedric looked over at her. "You have already helped."

"I mean, I can help you track down the MacGuff—the scrolls. I assume you've Googled them already . . ."

Cedric just raised an eyebrow, and Liv took that as a no.

"Right. Well, we can start with that. Tomorrow morning, we'll go pick up my car—it has my laptop in it—and we'll do some research. Can't promise anything, but there's all sorts of crazy stuff on the internet. Who knows, some of it might even be true."

Cedric still looked confused. "The internet?"

Liv didn't think she was up to the task of explaining how computers worked to someone who'd never even used a cell phone before. "I keep forgetting how much I have to teach you." She tilted her head and put on a mock-condescending voice. "So innocent."

Cedric smiled. "Not *so* innocent. I am sure I could teach you a thing or two, as well."

"Um."

Cedric's eyes widened, as though he'd just realized what he'd said. "I only meant . . ."

Liv looked away quickly, hoping her face wasn't turning strange shades of red. "No, I know. You could probably teach me how to use a bow and arrow, or something."

"Exactly, yes. That is what I meant." Cedric's voice was still a bit high-pitched, but the worst of the embarrassment seemed behind them. For now. "Do you really not know how to hunt at all?"

"Not unless you count going through the Fatburger drive-through," Liv replied weakly.

"My sister, Emmeline, could hold a bow properly by the time she was seven years old." Cedric chuckled to himself. "She loved that bow so much—it was a birthday gift from my father. She used to actually sleep with it in her bed. One day I accidentally stepped on it and broke it. When I told her, I was holding it in pieces, and I thought she was going to burst into tears. Instead, she punched me—right here." Cedric pointed a finger to his nose. "My father just laughed. Said no one would ever mess with his daughter . . ." Cedric's smile faltered.

Liv swallowed. "Sounds like a nice family."

"They are my home," Cedric said, his voice almost a whisper. He cleared his throat, as though eager to change the subject. "Though I am sure everyone feels that way about their family." Cedric looked up quickly, his eyes apologetic. "I am sorry, I forgot . . . your family . . ."

For a while, Liv didn't respond. She felt a familiar lump rise in her throat, and then got angry with herself, angry that her body could still react in this way, even after all these years. Cedric lifted his hand up and moved it a few inches closer to where her hand rested against the plastic arm of the chair, but then pulled it back. He didn't ask, but Liv knew the story was coming up anyway.

"There was a fire, when I was six," Liv said, tentative. "Both of my parents died. I had a brother and a sister, too, but we were split up. No foster family wanted to take all of us. I've been on my own since then."

This time Cedric did reach out and take her hand. His skin felt warm in the cool night air. He wrapped his fingers around hers and held them there.

"I truly am sorry," he said.

"It was a long time ago," Liv said, breathing in deep. The lump in her throat was almost gone now. "Besides, I just lost my family. You lost your whole world."

Cedric looked down at their hands, pressed together in the darkness. "Seems like the same thing to me."

They didn't talk for a while after that, but sat in stillness, watching the few stars that were visible in the sky and listening to each other breathe. Liv didn't remember closing her eyes, but the next thing she knew, she was waking up and looking around at the backyard, which was full of light.

She looked down at her hand, but Cedric was no longer holding it. His own hand had fallen down and was dangling against the edge of his lawn chair. It was close enough to reach out and grab, and yet felt very far away. After staring at it for a moment, she curled up in her chair in the sunshine, feeling a small ache in her chest she couldn't begin to explain.

THE MAKINGS OF A PLAN

Later that morning, Liv's biggest hurdle was trying to convince Cedric not to bring a sword on the LA city bus. He'd insisted on going with her to pick up her car, just in case there were any wraths still in the area. He also insisted on being "prepared."

"We can't just get on a bus holding a deadly blade the size of a baseball bat," Liv argued.

"It is a sword."

"I know that, I just—" Liv took a deep breath to start again. "I'm trying to explain how insane you'll look."

"It isn't insane to be ready for our enemies."

"Okay, sure. But how do I tell that to the kindly bus driver who thinks you might chop his head off?"

"I doubt this blade is sharp enough to chop anyone's head off."

"Now you're just *intentionally* missing my point."

Cedric grinned. Eventually, he'd agreed to wrap a large trash bag around the weapon to hide it. He still looked like a crazy person, but one who would at least cause less panic.

Cedric had hoped to retrieve his few belongings and remaining food from the museum while Liv got her car. When they got to the alley, however, they saw the way was blocked off by a police cruiser and a line of bright yellow crime scene tape.

"They won't be there forever," Liv told Cedric as he narrowed his eyes in the direction of the alleyway. He sighed heavily and got into her car.

From the museum, Liv made a trip to the ATM, bought some water and blankets for the house, and dodged more of Joe's calls. Running errands helped clear her head a bit, and made her feel useful again. Whenever she wondered whether it was a good idea to help out Cedric and his friends—and maybe put herself in danger in the process—she just remembered the alternative plan. Call Joe, get placed in a new home, start from scratch following another stranger's rules and eating another stranger's food. Staying at the Echo Park house seemed like a pretty good idea by comparison. At least there she'd be making her own decisions, even if those decisions involved arguing with a cute otherworldy prince about the safest way to hold a sword in a moving car.

Plus, she didn't like the thought of abandoning them now.

On the way back to the house, Liv drove through the In-N-Out drive-through. By midafternoon, she and the others sat sprawled out across the living room, surrounded by red-and-white discarded burger wrappers and soda cups. Liv had changed into fresh jeans, a tank top, and a light jacket, and had lent a T-shirt to Kat as well. The boys still had to wear their clothes from the day before.

"We should go back to the museum tonight to retrieve our belongings," Kat said. She was studying the plastic top to her soda cup, pulling the straw in and out. "It will be easier under cover of darkness."

Cedric nodded, but his mouth was too full of burger to respond.

Liv had her laptop open, and in between bites of fries was working to connect to a neighbor's unprotected Wi-Fi system. Finally one hit.

"Bingo."

She pulled up a search box and typed in *Caelum* and *scrolls*. She could feel Merek over her shoulder, looking intently at the screen.

"It's magic, then?" he asked as the screen popped up with search results.

"No," Liv said, her eyes on the screen. "It's Wi-Fi."

"What is the difference?"

"Um," Liv tilted her head. "Electrons? Shh, I'm concentrating."

The first few links to come up on the page were obvious misfires; one was for a popular fantasy video game, and one was a fan page for an actor named Tyler Callum, whose name was misspelled on at least three occasions throughout the site. Cedric came to sit on her other side, and their shoulders touched. The heat from his arm radiated out to hers.

It was a bit distracting.

Liv tried to keep her arm that was next to Cedric's still as she scrolled down the list of links. She was afraid that by moving it or calling attention to it in any way, Cedric might move a few inches away and take the warmth with him.

Eventually, she came to one from the University of California, San Diego. It was a link to a professor's biography page, but the word *Caelum* was featured in its two-sentence description.

On the page, the professor's name, Leonard Billings, PhD, was in bold type next to a picture of an older man with dark skin, a big smile, and a scraggly white beard.

Professor Billings taught a class in ancient cultures and myths, from the Greeks to the Celtic Druids. Liv continued to scroll down through a list of the required reading materials for students. At the very bottom of the page was a blurb with the professor's own qualifications, including the title of a dissertation he had written: "Origins of the Knights of Valere and the Search for Caelum's Scrolls."

"What are the Knights of Valere?" Liv asked.

"It does not sound familiar." Cedric shrugged, and the movement of his arm against Liv's raised goosebumps on her skin. She hoped he didn't notice.

She hoped Kat didn't notice, either.

"Do you have knights in Caelum?"

"Yes," Cedric replied, matter-of-fact. "But Valere? Never heard of them."

Liv went back to Google's main page, and typed the professor's name into the search box, along with the word *Caelum*. Only one more site came up, and it contained an abstract from the professor's dissertation. Liv read:

The ultimate representation of this ancient belief system exists in the legend of "Caelum," a fantastical realm that is connected to our own, but that cannot be accessed without a key, represented in this instance by a series of secret or hidden scrolls. Much like the Nordic myths of the mystical land of Asgard, Caelum is a concept brought into being by ancient pagans and perpetuated into the Early Middle Ages. . . .

There the text cut off. The site went on to explain that the actual dissertation was available for purchase in hard copy from the UC San Diego bookstore.

"It doesn't say much," Liv murmured. She clicked back to the main search screen but couldn't find anything else helpful. She tried typing in *Knights of Valere*, but kept getting linked to websites authored by conspiracy nuts, with pages that featured white text on a black screen and that focused on alien abductions and robots in the White House.

"This professor seems to be the best lead," she said.

"We should find him," Cedric said.

"Well . . . San Diego isn't that far away. Just a couple of hours. Maybe I could drive you in the morning?"

Cedric's hand gripped the sword that lay by his side. "We have several more hours of sunlight left. Let us go now."

Liv sighed. "I guess now works, too. But we're leaving all swords behind. This isn't a wrath we're facing, it's a college professor. And I don't want to get arrested for walking into some old guy's office with a two-foot blade in a Hefty bag."

"Liv—" Cedric started.

"No." Liv crossed her arms. "I'm serious. I'm the one with the car, and if you want to get to San Diego by tonight, we go without an armory."

Cedric drew in a long breath. "Fine."

Kat gave him a hard, calculating look, but then nodded as well. "Let us go, then."

Cedric turned to Kat. "I think it might be best if you and Merek stay here."

Kat's expression was one of disbelief. "What?"

"You were right earlier, that we need to retrieve our belongings from the museum. But it is more than that. . . . I have been thinking about what Merek suggested, back in the tunnels of the museum," Cedric said quickly, talking over Kat's shocked sputters. Merek turned one cool glance in his direction. "Last night was not simply a few wraths tracking our whereabouts. It was a whole group, and they were on the attack. I do not think we can sit back and wait for them to find us again. Now *we* need to track *them*, picking up their trail from the museum. And it cannot wait another night, else the trail might fade."

Cedric fixed his eyes on Kat. "You are one of the best trackers I know, Kat. If anyone can find a wrath and determine where they are coming from and what they want, it's you."

Kat appeared torn. She was nearly glowing from Cedric's praise, but her eyes darted back and forth between Liv and Cedric, sitting side by side on the couch.

"And the two of you will journey alone?"

Merek smiled. "Ah. And the true purpose of the mission becomes clear."

"Merek, enough," Cedric said. But he got up, moving away from Liv. The cold rushed into the space where he'd been, and Liv tried not to let her disappointment show.

Cedric walked to Kat and touched her lightly on the arm. "We will be back tonight, hopefully with more information about the scrolls. The sooner we can find them, the sooner we can get home."

"And leave this place, forever?" Kat said. Her words had a challenge in them, but Liv had a hard time understanding the conversation that Kat seemed to be having with Cedric just under the surface. Their eyes were speaking a hidden language the way that only two people who had known each other a very long time could do.

"Yes." Cedric finally said. "Forever."

Something twisted in Liv's stomach—just for a moment—and she turned her head away. At the same time, the tension went out of Kat's shoulders. She exhaled and murmured, "Going after the wraths is a good plan."

"It's a brilliant plan," Merek said, kicking his legs up over the edge of the couch. "Which is what I said when *I* thought of it yesterday."

Cedric and Kat rolled their eyes at exactly the same time.

"Will you go with Kat and provide backup?" Cedric asked.

Merek shrugged one shoulder, but didn't say no.

Cedric turned to Liv. "Are you ready?" His eyes looked bright and almost fevered, the way they had just before he'd fought the wraths. He had a mission again.

"Sure," Liv said, trying to convey an excitement she didn't feel. "Let's get this show on the road."

"Show?" Cedric asked.

Liv sighed, heavy. "Never mind."

THE QUESTING

Cedric was getting used to riding in cars.

When Liv first pulled onto the main thoroughfare she referred to as "the five," one look at the number of cars rushing toward them and past them at such an incredible speed made Cedric regret the second "animal-style" hamburger he'd eaten at the house. But after traveling for an hour, he was getting used to the feel of sitting still while the entire world flew by almost too fast to see.

Right out his window were trees and fences and houses and ocean, all blurring together and connected by an odd series of black wires that cut through the sky. He had to admit, the sight was almost beautiful. So often in this realm, Cedric had to grapple with confounding mysteries (Who put those black wires there, and for what possible purpose?), but when he stopped trying to puzzle it out, he found this world could be surprisingly interesting to look at. In calm moments, it was breathtaking.

Cedric turned to Liv and began to study the slight movements she made to control the vehicle. It didn't take much—just one hand on the wheel, one foot working controls. Much easier than controlling horse-drawn carts, actually. Just as soon as you got used to the speed.

"What does this do?" he asked, pointing to a lever between the seats that could move between different slots, labeled *P*, *D*, and *R*. Liv smiled and explained, going on to answer more of his questions about various buttons, pulleys, and keys, as well as the GPS on the dash that directed them where to go.

"Does not seem all that difficult, really," Cedric said.

"Nice try. But no way are you driving my car."

Cedric shrugged. "What's this?" He reached over and turned a dial, and suddenly the car was filled with a noise that rolled and pounded through his skull.

"That's music!" Liv yelled as she leaned over to twist the dial. The noise level fell instantly.

"Music? You call that music?"

Liv shook her head. "Not just music. The Beatles. I'm guessing you've never heard of them?"

"Cannot say that I have," Cedric countered. "But then again, you have never heard of the Rackling Quartet."

"The what?"

"The most famous and talented group of musicians in our kingdom. My mother had them to play for Emme's fourteenth birthday feast." Cedric looked back out the window, smiling at the memory. "It was a surprise. I'll never forget the look on her face when she came down the grand stairway and the Quartet started up with 'Love Song in Green,' and dedicated it to Princess Emmeline. She turned white as a sheet, nearly tripped over her own gown coming down the steps. I teased her about that for a week."

Liv smiled, a far-off look in her eyes, as if she, too, could see his memory. Cedric replayed it in his mind, the way his father had taken his sister's hand and led her through the first dance. He'd later snuck swigs of his father's wine when no one was looking, and then danced all night with the pretty twin daughters of the aging Duchess Carroll.

"What did they sound like?" Liv asked.

Cedric struggled to think how to describe it, the twinkling sounds of the instruments that floated across the airy ballroom, the almost ethereal voice of the singer, a young woman with braids that twisted down almost to her knees. He could just barely make out the melody of the song in his own mind, but he didn't know enough about musical terms to explain it to Liv.

"It sounded like summer," he finally said.

Liv just nodded, as if she knew exactly what he meant.

Cedric looked out the window again, but this time, instead of seeing lines of black wire or the endless blue sky, he could only see Emme's face. The sneaky grin she used to wear when she stole Cedric's toasted bread right from his plate at the breakfast table. The terror in her eyes just moments before Cedric stepped through the portal. He wondered what she was doing now. Was his family chained up at this moment, dreading whatever future awaited them? Was Emme getting enough to eat for breakfast? Was she missing him?

"Do you ever think about your brother and sister?" Cedric asked.

Liv stared straight ahead, her eyes focused on the road. If the sound of his own voice hadn't still been ringing in his ears, Cedric would have wondered if she'd heard him at all.

"I try not to," she finally said, her voice barely above a whisper.

Something in the set of Liv's jaw warned him to let it alone, but then he thought of Emme's face again, and how he would do anything to get back to where she was.

"But are they not still alive?"

Liv swallowed. "We were split up after the fire," she said, her hands gripping the steering wheel. "I suppose I could go through the records at social services, track them down if I wanted. I think my caseworker, Joe, would help me, but . . ."

Liv paused and bit her lip.

"Why would you not look for them? If I knew I had family near, and that I could find them . . ." Cedric's voice warbled off. "You could *find* them."

Liv stared straight ahead. "They probably wouldn't want me to."

"I do not understand. Is this . . . another Earth custom?"

"No. It's . . ." Liv swallowed, and for a while she didn't speak. Then she sighed, and her story flowed out of her as if a dam had broken. "I used to be afraid of the dark when I was a kid. It was pretty bad, actually. My older brother, Peter, he used to watch these horror movies late at night in his room, ones with killer dolls and evil leprechauns. Definitely not kid-appropriate. And I used to sneak into his room at night and watch them with him, even though I knew I wasn't supposed to. I started having these nightmares, and every morning I would tell myself that I would stop watching, but every night I was, like, compelled to go back for more. I had to watch what Peter was watching, you know?"

Liv shook her head a little and smiled. Still she kept her eyes locked straight ahead, and in the intense sunshine coming in through the car's front window they looked more golden than green-brown.

"Anyway, I developed this terrible fear of the dark. I started keeping a flashlight in my nightstand, just in case I had to get up and go to the bathroom in the middle of the night."

Cedric tried to picture a younger version of Liv, vulnerable and afraid. It was difficult to do.

"One night, I got up and grabbed for the flashlight, but it wouldn't turn on. The batteries were dead. So I went into my closet and opened up this secret shoe box of stuff I had, just, you know, old arrowheads and junk like that."

Cedric didn't know, but he didn't say anything.

"I had this old lighter of Peter's, one he had from his Boy Scout days. I used it to light a candle that I could take with me to the bathroom. I know it sounds dumb, but it helped. The flame was like this weapon I had against the dark. So I went to the bathroom with my candle and put it on the counter next to the sink. When I was done, I raced back to my bedroom and jumped into bed. I didn't remember that the candle was still in the bathroom. I just . . . fell asleep."

Liv stopped and took a shaky breath, eyes never veering from the road.

"When I woke up, it was dark and my room was filled with smoke. I could barely breathe, and I was so terrified I kept inhaling these huge lungfuls of ash. I cried out for my parents, but it was Peter who came into my room. He had Maisy, and he pushed open the window and dropped us out of it. That's when the fire reached my bedroom door. I could feel the heat from the flames from where I was sitting on the grass outside.

"Peter didn't have any choice but to jump through the window. He took Maisy and me each by the hand and led us to the street. The fire trucks appeared moments after, and I remember how happy I was to see them. How sure I was that they would put out the fire in my room, and then my parents would come out the front door and join us.

"They did put out the fire. But my parents never came outside. It wasn't until I was in an ambulance on the way to the hospital that I remembered the candle."

Cedric had stayed completely silent throughout Liv's story. Toward the end, her voice sounded scratchy and harsh, as though she was trying not to cry. As though she were still choking on ash. He struggled to think of something to say, but nothing felt appropriate. "Liv, I am so sorry—"

She cut him off with a wave of the hand. "It was a long time ago. But every time I think of Peter and Maisy, all I can think of is how I ruined their lives, ruined everything."

"You were just a child."

"A child who killed our parents, even if it was an accident. How could they ever forgive me for that? I don't think I'd be able to forgive someone for that. In fact, I know I couldn't."

Cedric waited again. He wanted to reach out and take Liv's hand, but both of hers were clutched tight against the steering wheel. Her eyes didn't waver from the road. "I don't know what I'd say if I saw them again. I don't know if I'd want to hear what they have to say to me."

After a moment, Liv finally turned her head and looked at Cedric. Her eyes caught the glare of the sun, which was lowering itself past Cedric's window, and lit up bright. He could see moisture border the edges of her eyes, but not a single tear fell.

"I've never told anyone that story before," she said. "Not even Shannon."

Cedric's mind raced as he tried to think of what to say. He finally just settled on the first thing that occurred to him. "Why tell me?"

Liv paused before turning her attention back to the road. "I don't know. I really don't," she whispered.

THE RULES OF THE UNIVERSE

The campus of UC San Diego was much bigger than Liv had anticipated. It took them at least a half hour before they were able to track down the history building, a squat, brick structure with patches of old vines clinging to its front wall.

Inside, Liv was surprised by how quiet it was, its halls nearly empty. She looked at a wall clock and saw it was nearly seven p.m.

"The website said that his office hours end at seven. We have to hurry." Liv's voice sounded smaller than usual to her own ears. She felt hollowed out and raw, having spilled her guts to Cedric. Why had she shared that story with him? The lull of the car on the highway, the heat of the sun, the gentle way he'd asked her questions—everything had just flowed out of her. After she'd finished talking, it had felt like waking up from a dream. Was it too late to take those words back? What could he possibly think of her now that he knew what she'd done?

To have her deepest secret spoken aloud in the world instead of held tight and safe inside of her was unthinkable, as wrong as wearing her very nerves outside of her skin.

But still, Liv pushed forward, through the university building's hallway to Professor Billings's office. Maybe she could will the conversation away by never thinking of it or acknowledging it again.

At the professor's office door, Liv gave one last look to Cedric. He nodded and reached up to knock.

"Come in," a voice called out.

The room was small and warm and cluttered with books. Four bookshelves of various sizes and designs lined the walls, and each was overflowing with large, leather-bound tomes, reference books, paperbacks with cracked spines. They spilled out of their shelves and onto the floor. They covered the cushions of a small love seat and curled around the legs of a worn desk.

Professor Billings sat at the desk, looking slightly older than the picture on the UC San Diego website. His hair was whiter and his skin more lined, but his dark eyes were bright and vibrant. He carefully placed a bookmark between the pages of his book and set it aside as Liv and Cedric approached his desk.

"I was beginning to think no one would take advantage of my office hours today," he said with a smile. He looked them over more carefully and gestured for them to take the two seats in front of his desk. "Sorry, I can't seem to place you. Are you in my eleven a.m. class?"

"No," Cedric said as he sat. "We are not pupils."

Liv shot him a quick look. "Well, we are pupils—I mean, students," she continued for him. "Just not in your class."

Professor Billings raised one eyebrow, but said nothing.

"We're actually here hoping you could shed some light on a subject we're interested in learning more about," Liv added, then cleared her throat, unsure how to begin. "Well, we read that you know a lot about a . . . mythical land called Caelum."

"And a set of scrolls that lead there," Cedric added. He sounded a little too eager, so Liv kicked him gently under the desk.

"Well," Professor Billings said with a chuckle. "This is a surprise. I haven't taught that particular lore in years. It's fairly obscure, you know."

"But you wrote your dissertation on it?"

Professor Billings's eyebrows shot up in surprise. "You certainly have done your research."

Liv smiled and gave a half-shrug.

"Can I ask what brought about your interest? Most students who come see me are here to bargain up their grades, not to hear more about my dissertation subject. And you look . . . very young. Are you freshmen?"

Cedric shifted in his seat, and Liv shot him a quick side glance.

"When I said students, I meant . . . high school students, from LA. We're . . . writing a research paper on ancient myths, and we happened across Caelum online and were really interested in it. But there's so little information out there, so we thought we'd come straight to the source. . . ." Liv's voice trailed off, and she wondered if she'd just blown their chances. Why would a college professor care about a stupid high school project?

Professor Billings studied Liv's face for a moment, and she squirmed under his gaze. But then his expression cleared and he smiled an easy smile once again.

"Well, it's nice to see high school students so interested in the lesser-known historical myths," he said warmly. "What in particular would you like to know about?"

"The scrolls," Cedric cut in.

Professor Billings nodded. "Well, to understand about the scrolls, you really need a background of the legend. Written accounts of Caelum can be traced back to the early thirteenth century, although its oral history began before that time. It was at its most pervasive around the same era as the Knights of the Round Table and all of that business, sort of medieval Britain's latent response to . . . sorry, is this boring you?"

"No," Cedric said quickly.

"Well, let me know if I get too dry. I tend to go on sometimes," he said, smiling and leaning back in his chair. "Anyhow, the legend begins with the once widely held belief that devils roamed the Earth, spreading terror and destruction. Mostly ruining crops and taking firstborn babies, that kind of thing. Some cultures referred to them as evil spirits, or sprites, or wraths."

Cedric sat up straighter, and Liv wished she could tell him to chill out. The professor didn't seem to notice, however.

"According to this particular lore, these creatures have been on this planet in some form or another since its creation. In response to their growing numbers, a group of men banded together and mixed their bloodlines with those of the wraths, in order to incorporate some of their otherworldly strength for the purpose of fighting them—"

"That's not true!" Cedric burst out, jumping out of his seat. He bumped against the desk and disrupted some nearby papers as well as a small bronze figurine. The trinket swayed on its stand, coming perilously close to toppling before the professor reached over and steadied it. He looked at Cedric, a bit discomfited.

"Well, obviously none of it is really *true*, son."

"Sorry," Liv interrupted. "He gets really excited about . . . ancient myths." She made a motion for Cedric to sit down, and he reluctantly did.

"I can understand that, I suppose. After all, these ancient stories are nothing but metaphors for how we live our lives. In this instance, it's a metaphor for how good men must necessarily become corrupted in some way in order to be strong enough to protect their people. To fight devils, man must become part devil himself. . . . Quite fascinating, really . . ."

Liv did her best to look fascinated while the professor continued.

"So with their tainted blood, these mythical men had the strength necessary to fight off the scores of wraths. At first, they acted in secret, but over the centuries, other groups of men joined in the fight against the wraths. Scholars and religious sects, mostly. They wanted to find a way to not only fight the wraths off, but to expel them from this world for good. And then, according to legend, they did. They found a way to send the wraths somewhere . . . else."

"Caelum," Cedric whispered. His tone was hushed, almost reverential.

Professor Billings nodded. "That's right. You know the story?"

"We'd still like to hear it from you, if that's okay," Liv said after Cedric didn't respond. "For our assignment."

The professor nodded again and continued. "One particular sect was known as the Knights of Valere, and they were believed to have true mystics in their midst. Sorcerers, you know."

"Sorcerers?" Liv asked. "You mean, as in wizards and magic and all that?"

"You could say that. Myths of sorcerers certainly abounded during that time. Just look at Merlin!"

"But Merlin's fictional," Liv said without thinking. "I mean, I guess all this stuff is fictional . . ." she added, trailing off. But really, she wondered how many other "fictional" things actually fell in the nonfiction category. After everything she'd seen the last two days, anything was possible. For all she knew, the North Pole was real and Santa Claus was up there right now, making presents for all the nice children of Los Angeles. Or holding on to a set of mythical scrolls.

The professor leaned forward, his words picking up the pace as he continued. "We know that now, but at one time, people really believed these legends were true. The documented accounts of wraths and the superpowered men—who were referred to as Guardians—tapered off around the same time that stories of magic drifted into the stuff of legend. Most historians agree that advancing technology allowed human beings to become more rational, more able to explain the phenomena around us and less likely to write it off as magic."

Liv nodded, trying to follow along.

"There is another theory, however," the professor continued.

"Put forth by, I'll admit, mostly discredited historians, who believe that magic does exist—that it has existed in some form on Earth since the beginning of time. These historians believe that, centuries ago, around the time the Guardians left Earth, the planet became overwhelmed by magic and developed a negative reaction to it. So it went into a sort of survival mode, you see, by hiding magic or expelling magic when necessary. A type of evolutionary response. It's called the Quelling Theory. Similar to the way different species evolve and adapt in order to survive, the Earth evolved to get rid of its magic when it became too powerful and too dangerous. The Quelling Theory might explain why the Knights of Valere were able to banish the wraths and Guardians from Earth when they did—the wraths posed a threat to the planet's existence and had to be expelled. So, when the Knights went looking for the means to banish the wraths, the planet supplied it. They were able to craft a series of scrolls that opened up a portal to another world. And they used that portal to push all the wraths through."

"Just pushed through? Like some sort of mystical trash chute?"

"A trash chute!" Professor Billings chortled. He leaned back in his chair and looked at Liv, almost wonderingly. "Yes, that's perfect. Mind if I write it down?"

Liv shrugged and ignored the angry glare Cedric was aiming in her direction. The professor's story was shaking out a little differently than the one Cedric had shared with her about his people finding the portal and leaving the hell dimension of Earth behind.

"Anyway," the professor continued, "the portal also had an

unintended effect. Instead of just drawing out all wraths, it drew out all living things with wrath energy, or wrath blood. The earth's protective, magic-quelling instincts went into overdrive, so to speak. And thus the Guardians disappeared forever too. Along with much of Earth's magic, of course."

For a moment, the room was silent. Professor Billings seemed lost in thought, staring down at his folded hands.

It was Cedric who eventually spoke up, his voice strained. "What about the scrolls? What happened to them?"

Professor Billings threw up his hands and shrugged. "The same as what happened to the Holy Grail, I'd expect. They're lost to time, if they ever existed at all." The professor put one finger into the air. "But!" He turned around in his seat and started to rummage through a filing cabinet behind his desk. He opened and flipped through drawer after drawer, finally letting out an exclamation and pulling up a manila folder.

"You might find this of interest for your report," he said, putting the folder down on the desk. Liv almost asked him what report he meant before she remembered their bogus cover story.

"What is it?"

"I bought it at an auction some years back, but have never been able to authenticate it. It's a document connected to the Knights of Valere, rumored to be a partial copy of the scrolls in question."

Liv's eyebrows furrowed. "I thought you said they were just legend."

"Mystical scrolls that can open a portal to another world? Those are legend. But the Knights of Valere were a real sect, and they left real artifacts behind. Whether or not we can read them is another matter . . ."

Cedric leaned forward eagerly, just barely stopping himself from bumping against the desk edge again. "Can I see it?" he asked, gazing down at the manila folder with an eager expression.

"Of course."

Liv braced herself. She didn't even notice that she was holding her own breath as Professor Billings flipped over the front of the manila folder with a flourish. Although she didn't know what she had been expecting, the plain sheaf of slightly yellowed copy paper was a bit of a letdown.

At first, she could only make out faint, scribbled lines in an unknown language. But then they came together to form a sort of pattern. An eerily recognizable pattern. At the bottom of the page, one line of text caught her eyes. She had no idea what it meant, and yet it was as familiar to her as her own skin.

Her skin.

Liv rocked back in her chair as black dots swam in front of her eyes. The professor droned on about an authentication process, but it seemed as if his words were coming from another room, from another place entirely.

The marks at the bottom of the paper—she'd seen them before.

Unconsciously, Liv reached a trembling hand up over her shoulder and under her thin hoodie, barely touching it against the hollow between her shoulder blades. She rubbed her fingers there lightly, over the place where she knew her tattoo to be. The tattoo that bore the exact same foreign marks, in the exact same order, as the ones printed on the yellow papers below.

THE LONELY INN

Liv heard blood rushing in her ears.

She understood with a dim sort of awareness that Cedric and Professor Billings were still talking, but their words didn't penetrate the cloud that had fallen over her.

It didn't make any sense. It couldn't be true.

And yet it was. The figures on the paper in front of her were an exact replica of the tattoo she'd had for years—the one she never talked about. Because no matter what Shannon might think, the tattoo wasn't a symbol of her hidden "wild child" nature. Instead, it represented what she hated most about being a foster kid and having such little control over her own life—even her own body.

"Are you all right?" Cedric's voice cut through the fog. She looked over at him and saw concern flicker across his blue eyes.

"Yeah, it's just . . ." Liv looked over at the professor, who also seemed concerned. His hands spread across the replica of the scrolls on the desk. Was it possible that she had found the one man who could finally explain what the symbols of her tattoo meant? And if it was somehow connected to Caelum . . . she had to take this chance. "I have to show you something."

Before she could lose her nerve, Liv twisted around in her seat and drew her jacket off. She pushed the straps of her tank top down, giving Cedric and the professor the best view of her shoulder blades.

She heard Cedric make a sound behind her, sort of a quick exhalation of breath, but didn't turn around to face him.

"Oh . . . my . . . ," the professor murmured.

She heard the rustling of paper and knew that one of them was lifting up the copy of the scrolls, comparing it to her back . . . but she didn't need to look at it again. She'd long ago memorized the strange slashes and swooping lines that crawled just over her shoulder blades in a straight line.

"Young lady, where did you get that?" the professor asked.

"I don't remember physically getting it, I just remember what happened afterward. I was so young, and it was right after my parents . . . died. My memories from then are hazy. All I know is my first foster parents were these religious nuts. They're the ones who gave me the tattoo. As soon as my caseworker found out about it, he pulled me out of there . . ."

Liv trailed off, thinking of the few memories she had from that time. She had been so young, and so deep in grief over her parents. But she remembered Mrs. Hannigan, in her tight bun and floor-length skirts. Mr. Hannigan with the thick Bible he read from every night. She remembered scouring the floors in her bedroom because cleanliness was next to godliness. She remembered the way they used to look at her, like she was something . . . dirty. And she remembered the day Joe came and got in a huge fight with the Hannigans, screaming at them about the tattoo before picking her up and swooping her out of there forever. In the years since, she'd asked Joe about it, but all he'd told her was that the Hannigans wouldn't ever hurt her again. She'd been saving up money to get the tattoo removed as soon as she turned eighteen.

Cedric was silent. Liv suddenly felt self-conscious and pulled her tank top strap back up. She sneaked a look at Cedric, but his expression was hard to read.

"It's quite . . . unusual," Professor Billings whispered.

That, Liv knew. She'd heard it said so many times in her life, mostly from foster parents who thought it was strange that so young a child had a tattoo. Many of them were creeped out by it, and Liv had always secretly thought that it was one of the reasons she'd never been asked to stay in any one family for very long.

Shannon teased her about it, of course. Some other classmates had asked her about it as well, passing acquaintances and boys she'd gone out with for small stretches at a time. They saw it and they always asked her the same question—what did it mean? And she'd smile in what she hoped was a mysterious way, and shrug. *It's a secret.*

And it was a secret, from everyone and from her, too. Only the nutbag Hannigans knew what the tattoo meant, and she certainly never planned to track them down and ask them. She'd always assumed it was some weird religious thing.

"Is this why you came to see me?" the professor asked.

"No," Liv whispered, head spinning. "I know it sounds crazy, but I've never seen anything like my tattoo until just now. I've never even known what it means."

The professor's eyebrows raised. "Quite a coincidence," he murmured.

"Yes. It is," Cedric said. His eyes weren't on Liv, but were focused on the floor, as though he was thinking hard.

"How did you say you heard about the legend of Caelum again?" the professor asked.

Liv felt stuck. She couldn't tell the professor the real reason they'd come to visit him without making Cedric look crazy, and she couldn't convince Cedric that she'd had no idea her tattoo was in any way connected to his home realm with the professor sitting right there. She had to think quickly.

"I saw it online," Liv said. She avoided looking over at Cedric, but hoped he would go along with the story. "It just . . . sounded really interesting."

The professor still looked skeptical.

"Maybe reading about it kind of reminded me of my first foster parents in some way," Liv lied. "Because the legend's so crazy, and they were so crazy . . ."

Then something occurred to her. She sat up straighter. "They were really into random Bible passages and weird stuff. . . . Do you think maybe they believed in that group? The Knights of . . . whatever . . . the ones who wrote that?" She gestured to the marked piece of paper on the professor's desk. "Maybe that's why they put this thing on me?"

The professor looked at her with sympathy. "Hmm. It's

possible, though the legend of Caelum isn't associated with any modern religion. And I certainly don't know how it would compel them to mark a child in that way."

Liv could feel the answers slipping away, and realized with a sharp pang how much she wanted them.

"And you don't know what exactly it means? The tattoo?"

He drew in a breath. "That's part of the reason this copy hasn't been able to be authenticated, see, because it matches no complete written language that scholars can find. Snatches of these symbols have been found here and there, but nothing to really cling to. It's a language out of time."

The professor sighed and moved the papers closer, shaking his head a little as he looked down at them.

"I have an associate," the professor said, looking off and scratching his chin. "He also has a minor archive of documents related to the scrolls and the legend . . . I could give him a call, maybe see if he could provide any additional information?"

Liv's heart jumped with hope again. "That would be great."

The professor stood, and, numbly, Liv followed. Cedric rose too, scraping his chair back against the floor.

"I'll call him tonight. Maybe you could drop by tomorrow morning? My first class is at ten a.m., so anytime before then."

Liv and Cedric exchanged a quick glance, but there was no need for discussion. They both nodded.

"We'll come back," Cedric said.

The professor shook Cedric's hand, and then Liv's. He pressed his hand against hers for an extra beat, looking right into her eyes. "It really was nice to meet you." When he smiled, his eyes crinkled in the corners.

"You too," Liv said, trying to manage a smile as well.

She and Cedric stepped out of the office, and the professor shut the door behind them. They stood alone in the hallway, which seemed emptier and darker than before. A fluorescent light flickered overhead. Without saying a word, Cedric moved toward the exit, and Liv followed.

⊱⊹⊰

Liv figured it would be much easier for them to find a cheap motel in San Diego than to try and drive all the way home only to turn around and drive the two and a half hours back the next morning. She didn't want to admit it to Cedric, but she was pretty sure the professor was only being nice and really wouldn't have any more information to share with them the next day. If anything, he was probably just as weirded out as she was. But heading home now without making absolutely sure was *not* an option.

They drove around for about twenty minutes until they were able to find a motel off the highway that was small and seedy enough to not ask for a driver's license or credit card information. Not only was Liv under eighteen, but she knew there was a possibility Joe had put a watch on her debit card to try and track her down.

Liv used the rest of her cash to pay for the room and scrounge up a dinner from the motel's vending machines. She and Cedric sat on one edge of one of the room's twin beds, facing the only window, and silently divvied up the food between them.

They hadn't spoken much since leaving the professor's office, which had been fine as long as they were in a car that could be filled with radio music. But once they were alone in the small room with its dingy walls, the quiet fell heavily around them.

"Do you think the others will worry when we don't come back tonight?" Liv asked as she opened up a bag of pretzels.

Cedric's brows knitted together for an instant, but then relaxed. "They might, but Kat will know to stay put until I return. I only wish I knew how she was faring on her mission."

Liv nodded. "We should probably get everyone disposable cell phones. Cheap, but they work."

"I am not sure we would know what to do with them."

"I could show you."

Cedric nodded absently and chewed slowly on an Oreo. After a moment, he put the cookie down and turned to Liv. His normally bright eyes looked dark in the dim light of the room.

"Tell me just one more time. About your . . . back."

Liv sighed. "I told you everything I know. And trust me, it's not much."

"You never thought it strange, that this family would brand you in that way?"

Liv pushed the bag of pretzels away from her, suddenly not hungry anymore. "Of course it's strange. But it's just one strange thing in the long list of strange things that is my life."

"I am sorry . . . I did not mean to offend."

Liv's eyes dropped to the remaining junk food wrappers that rested between them. "I know you didn't."

"But I really must ask you . . . for so long, all we have been trying to do here is to find the scrolls so we can get home. And we have hit nothing but dead ends. Then I discover the first person we saw upon entering this realm just happens to have text from the scrolls printed on her back, and . . ."

Liv crossed her arm protectively across her chest, suddenly wanting to look away. "Spit it out. Ask what you want to ask."

He took a big breath before continuing. "Are you sure you have never heard of us before, or of the scrolls or Caelum? I only ask because . . . how is it possible?"

That same question had been running through Liv's head since they'd stepped out of the professor's office. How was it that her tattoo was a copy of the very scrolls Cedric was looking for? How much of a coincidence was it that they'd met? Because if it wasn't a coincidence, but something larger at work . . . the thought was too terrifying. Liv couldn't stand the idea that she had even less control over her life than she'd thought.

"I don't know how it's possible," Liv said, her voice shaky. "But I've never even heard the word *Caelum* until a few days ago."

Cedric nodded, though he didn't seem especially reassured. "But you were drawn to the very museum where we were staying."

"No, I had an *appointment* at the museum. Because I wanted to get rid of the sword *you* left behind. I wouldn't have even seen you that day, except . . ."

Liv thought about the day at the museum, the moment before she'd followed Cedric down into the tunnels. She'd been wandering and was drawn into the languages exhibit. . . .

She turned to Cedric. "In the museum, I was lost, and I found this symbol—" Liv broke off and grabbed the complimentary pad of paper lying on the motel's nightstand. She tore off the cap of the cheap pen next to it and started drawing the symbol on the pad. She remembered it clearly—the circle, the two dagger-like extensions that reached from its bottom half. "I didn't know what it meant. I still have no idea. But it looked . . . familiar somehow. I was curious and couldn't shake it . . ."

Cedric reached over for the pad of paper, his hand brushing slightly against Liv's. His eyes widened in recognition.

"Yes, this is one of our ancient symbols, in Caelum. I saw it at the museum as well. It is why I thought we were on the right track to finding the scrolls. Although, aside from this one symbol and a single piece of paper containing a few others, I couldn't find anything else related to Caelum or my people at the museum."

"What does it mean?"

"Knowledge," Cedric said. He traced the edge of the symbol with his finger.

"That's not one of the symbols on my tattoo. I'm pretty sure I've never even seen it before. So why did it feel so familiar?"

Cedric shook his head. "I do not know, but maybe you saw it somewhere else? Possibly with those . . . people who marked you?"

"Maybe?"

Cedric looked as though he was on the verge of figuring out a mystery. His eyes bore into Liv's, and his knee edged closer to hers on the bed. She was suddenly aware that he was just inches away, and she felt a flush creeping up the back of her neck.

"Once you had seen the symbol in the museum, what

happened next? Try to remember everything."

"Um . . . I followed you."

"Why? Do not leave anything out."

Liv raised an eyebrow. "You think I would?"

"You did fail to mention the markings on your back."

"I didn't exactly know they were relevant."

"Yes, and maybe there were other things that happened that day that are relevant as well. Try to remember everything. What made you follow me?"

Cedric's eyes met hers, and their blue was so bright, she had to turn away, toward the motel window. His reflection there was muted, easier to handle.

"I don't really know," Liv said, "I guess I wanted to finally figure out who you were, and what you were doing under the bridge that night. Why you were crawling into a hole in a museum wall. That was pretty weird. And then there was . . ."

"What?" Cedric leaned forward, eager.

Liv gestured to their reflected images. There she was, with her flyaway hair and well-worn jeans. And there was Cedric, with his broad shoulders and annoyingly clear skin.

"That. There was also that."

Cedric's reflection looked confused, while Liv's turned red.

Liv barreled on. "I mean, look at you. You look like you just stepped out of an Abercrombie ad."

Cedric tilted his head. "I do not know what that means."

"You were hot, all right?"

His eyes remained blank.

"Cute. Handsome. Stupid good-looking. Do any of those

words mean anything in Caelum?"

Cedric didn't move a muscle. Then, one corner of his mouth twitched upward. "Some of them, yes."

"Good." Liv's voice was sharp. "I doubt any of that matters, but is it honest enough for you?"

"Yes," Cedric said, still smiling. "And at least part of it *does* matter."

"Yeah, and what's that?"

"You finally admit I'm good-looking."

Liv's jaw dropped, and when she looked over to Cedric—the real Cedric, not his reflection—she saw he was barely suppressing a grin. She could feel one starting to spread across her face as well. She picked up the pillow from the bed and threw it at him. He dodged it easily.

"You're hilarious," Liv said, deadpan.

"Yes, and good-looking, don't forget."

"And humble."

"Oh, extremely humble. The most humble in all the land." Cedric's voice broke into laughter on the last word.

Liv buried her face in her hands, trying to smother the laughter bubbling up. But it was a losing battle.

"Ah, yes," Liv said, trying to suck in a deep breath between laughs, "this is definitely a normal reaction for a person to have to all of this. Hysterics. Is this a sign that I'm finally going crazy?"

Cedric shrugged. "How should I know? You all seem crazy to me here. You know, I looked into a building once, with a huge window that faced a roadway. And I saw hordes of people running in place on these large machines. Just running and running and not going anywhere. That is crazy."

"I actually agree with you on that one," Liv said.

"And I've seen women walking along, pushing dogs in carts. Dogs."

Liv burst into a fit of laughter again. Cedric joined her, and this time it took longer for the two of them to recover.

"I think I needed that," she said, finally catching her breath.

"Me too."

Listening to her breath normalizing, Liv felt lighter, like she always did after a laughing fit. But then she looked around the room, with its grim curtains and years-old bedspread. The confusion of their situation, and all of their unanswered questions, began to rise up again.

Without thinking, Liv reached for her shoulder blade. Cedric was watching her. The remains of his smile slipped from his eyes. They took on that dark, hooded look again, following her hands to where they rested near her back.

"Can I see it again?" he asked.

Liv thought for a moment, then removed her jacket for the second time that evening. She half turned on the bed so that her back was facing Cedric, then slipped down the straps of her tank top.

She heard him behind her, inching closer to where she sat on the bed.

"If I had seen your tattoo before, I might have noticed . . ."

"I don't really make a habit of showing it to people," Liv said, trying to keep her voice light.

"If the professor has no more information to provide, maybe we can locate these foster parents you spoke of," Cedric said. "Perhaps they know the whereabouts of the true scrolls."

"Maybe," Liv responded. She didn't really want to think about the Hannigans right now. She couldn't think of anything with Cedric's body so near to her own. The small hairs rose on the back of her neck, and she tried not to shiver. Which became harder when he reached out a finger and placed it gently on the skin just over her shoulder blade, where the tattoo began.

"Is this okay?" he asked in a hushed voice.

Liv struggled to remember how to talk.

"Yes."

"I do not know what these symbols mean. We no longer have the whole language, just pieces of it. My tutor tried to teach me the ancient symbols, but I never paid as much attention to our studies as Emme. I only remember a few."

"Like the one for knowledge," Liv said, glancing down at the pad of paper that sat at the edge of the bed.

"Yes. And the markings we carve onto our weapons. Some others."

"Like what?"

"There is an ancient word carved above the main entrance of our castle. It means *protector*, and it begins with a letter that looks sort of like this one . . ."

Cedric's finger moved lightly from the tip of her shoulder blade, tracing down across her skin, following the swoops and arcs of the tattoo. Liv shut her eyes tight, blocking out everything in the room that wasn't the motion of his hand.

Then his finger stopped moving, having reached the end of the tattoo. Liv shifted slowly, turning on the bed so that she was facing him. His face was only inches from hers, and she could make out with perfect clarity the lines of his cheekbones, the shape of his eyes, his mouth . . .

"Liv," Cedric whispered, his voice hoarse. He reached up with one hand and touched her cheek. She leaned in closer. She couldn't help it. It wasn't even a thought, really. Thoughts were gone. There was just his face, and his touch, and his breath.

"Who are you?" he whispered again, this time so low she could barely make it out. But if there was an answer to that question, she didn't know it. She didn't say anything back. Instead, she leaned forward, her lips getting closer to his, then brushing against them . . .

All of a sudden a huge, shattering noise cut through the night, breaking through their perfect, near-silent bubble. Liv and Cedric flew back from each other, both turning to look at the wide, gaping space where the hotel window had been just moments before.

Pieces of glass fell across the rough carpeting of the room. It was dark out, but Liv could make out the shapes of men standing outside the window frame. They were wearing dark robes with hoods that covered their faces.

Cedric jumped up first, blocking the bed and Liv from the group outside. He reached into his waistband and pulled out a small knife. Liv couldn't even be annoyed that he'd gone against her wishes and brought a weapon with him on the trip. Cedric had been right all along.

They were never safe.

Liv looked around for an exit, but the only thing on the far side of the room was a windowless bathroom. A connecting door led between the motel room and the one right next to it, but Liv knew it would be bolted shut from the other side. The main door was right next to the window, and therefore right next to the advancing figures.

Liv counted five of them, and as they moved forward, she could see that their robes were actually a dark red. None of their faces were visible under their hoods.

"Halt!" Cedric yelled out. "Come no closer." He waved his knife in the air with his right hand. With his left, he reached to pick up a lamp from the nightstand by the bed. He held it clenched in one fist, aiming the bright bulb toward the figures.

The hooded man closest to them—he could reach an arm through the window and touch the bright end of Cedric's lamp if he wanted—gave a low laugh.

"And you will fight us all off with a toothpick and a lamp, then?" The man stepped right across the threshold of the window, and in one quick movement his right arm shot out and twisted Cedric's knife hand. Cedric swung out with the lamp, but the man ducked. Another figure came forward and grabbed the knife from Cedric's trapped hand.

Before Cedric could react, the first man reached up and removed his hood. The lamp lit his face from below, making his features look hideously distorted. Dark, triangular shadows rose from the sides of his nose and the lids of his eyes. It took Liv a couple of seconds before she recognized him, with his face as warped-looking as it was. But once she realized who it was standing before her in a blood-red robe, she was finally able to release the scream lodged in her throat.

Professor Billings did nothing but laugh.

THE KNIGHTS OF VALOR

"Run!" Cedric cried. He wrenched his arm free and stood to face the professor.

Liv scrambled off the other edge of the bed, looking desperately for some place to run to. She saw Cedric swing his arm down and smash the lamp against the hotel room floor. The shade popped off the end, and the lightbulb smashed, sending the room into darkness.

Through the dim light that trickled into the room from the street, Liv saw Cedric swing out with the remains of the lamp, which now had broken shards of lightbulb sticking from its end. Professor Billings jumped back from the sharp edge of the lamp, and it whirred past him harmlessly.

The robed figures swarmed into the room behind the professor. Two of them moved to block the front door. Liv turned and ran across the room, to the connecting door.

"Help! Help us!" Liv pounded her fist against the door, but the men were right behind her. One thick arm reached out and clamped down on her shoulder, while another wrapped itself around her waist, squeezing the breath from her lungs.

"Cedric!" she choked out. She tried kicking her legs out at the two men who held her, but every time she flung a limb, one of them was there to grab it and hold it still. Soon she was completely immobile.

Liv twisted her head to see Cedric standing on the bed, brandishing his lamp down at the professor and two more robed figures who flanked him.

"There's no point in fighting," Professor Billings said, his voice calm.

Cedric responded by thrusting the end of his lamp up to the edge of the professor's jaw, just centimeters from the skin of his neck. The professor merely smiled in response. In the dim light pouring in through the broken window, the whites of Cedric's eyes grew in fear.

"Who are you, really?"

"Did the robes not give us away? We are the Knights of Valere. An ancient sect, tasked to keep this world safe from its most dangerous threat." The professor smiled, his eyes once again twinkling like they had in his office. "We're the good guys."

Cedric clenched the lamp tighter. "I have a little trouble believing that at this precise moment."

"I understand that you're frightened. But put that thing away before anyone gets hurt," the professor said, his voice calm.

One of the robed men holding Liv squeezed her arm, and she yelped. Cedric's gaze flashed quickly to Liv, and after a second's pause, he pulled the broken lamp a few inches from the professor's neck.

“We are not your enemy,” Cedric said, voice tight. “We only wanted answers.”

Professor Billings shook his head slowly. “You know, I do believe you. At first, I even believed that ridiculous story about doing research for a paper. . . . But then, when I saw her back . . .” The professor looked to Liv, his eyes narrowing. “I had to call reinforcements and follow you here. I cannot stand by and risk her being used to open a portal and let the greatest evil ever known filter back into this world.”

“Use her to open the . . .” Cedric trailed off as he shook his head faintly. Then his body went completely still. He looked over at Liv, meeting her eyes. Seeing the understanding and fear written all over his face, Liv couldn’t deny the truth of the professor’s words. The truth etched upon her back.

She was the one who could open the portal to Cedric’s world. She *was* the scroll.

“No,” she whispered.

“Yes,” Professor Billings said, and he sounded almost gentle. Except he obviously wasn’t. It was the worst kind of pretending. “I imagine it comes as quite a shock to you. After all, I don’t believe you would have shown me your markings if you knew what they really were, or who I really was. Poor child, you really did believe it was a tattoo, didn’t you?”

“But . . . ,” Liv sputtered. Of course the markings were a tattoo. They were permanent, after all. She didn’t remember getting them, but that’s because she’d been so young. At the mercy of crazy foster parents. It had to be a tattoo. What else could it have been?

"Everything I told you at the office is true," the professor said. "Though the mythical scrolls of Caelum are real, very much so. And they're not printed on any ancient paper lost to the centuries. No piece of paper could hold that kind of power. Only human energy could contain the power of the scrolls. Don't you understand?" The professor looked at Liv, his eyes imploring. "Don't you see how dangerous you are?"

"No," Liv managed. "I'm not. Honestly, there's been a mistake . . ."

The professor shook his head, and the arm around Liv's throat tightened.

"Our ancestors used willing sacrifices to create the first portal and expel the wrath threat from our world. What they didn't know—what none of them could have foreseen—was that their acts would outlast them. Twenty years after the portal was opened and wraths were banished from the earth, a group of children was discovered in an outlying village. They were covered in marks, the same marks that had been imprinted on the first human scrolls. The magic didn't die, you see, but tied itself to the human race. Earth magic can be . . . tricky like that. Even when you think it's completely gone, it can pop up in the most unexpected of places. Like that carnival game, Whac-a-Mole."

The professor grinned at his own joke. Liv felt sick.

"Every twenty years or so, a group of new children with the markings would be discovered. Which meant they had the power to open a portal."

Liv wanted to fight the words he was saying, to convince

herself they were lies, but so much of it was starting to click. She remembered the wrath in the alley, the one who had let her go moments after tearing the back of her shirt. . . . And then returned the next night with backup. They'd come back looking for her. They knew. They knew what she was.

Cedric's hand tightened on the lamp end. "What happened to them? The children?"

Professor Billings's eyes flashed for just a moment, and his face was grave once again. "The order did what had to be done. To prevent horror from falling upon us. The scrolls did not belong in this world." He gave a tiny shake of his head. "We had to whack the moles."

A shiver shot down Liv's back. Her voice cut through the room. "You killed them."

The professor lowered his eyes to the floor. "Yes. To protect the world, yes."

"But every twenty years since the Middle Ages, that's . . . so many . . ."

"It is a terrible but sacred birthright to find the scrolls in every generation and eliminate them. It was the job of my father before me, and his father before him."

Everything in the room seemed suddenly hazy. It was only when her eyes caught Cedric's that Liv was able to regain some focus. Even in the darkened room, his bright eyes shone out. But instead of fear, they were shining with anger.

They held eye contact for just a moment before Cedric flicked his eyes over to the door behind her that connected their room to the next room over. Cedric gave a tiny raise of his eyebrow, and Liv gave the briefest of nods in return.

Professor Billings looked in mock sadness at his own hands, clasped before him. "And now, my dear, you must know what happens next."

Liv stayed perfectly still, waiting for any movement from Cedric.

"It's not that we want to, of course," the professor continued. "You seem like a perfectly lovely girl. But even if you yourself mean no harm, it would be too easy for you to fall into the wrong hands. That's why we cannot let you leave this room alive."

The professor reached down into his robe and took out a silver object that reflected the light of the street lamps outside the window. He flipped it open, revealing a long blade, sharpened to a point.

It was then that Cedric started to laugh. At first it was low, almost disbelieving. Then it grew louder and louder. The robed men standing behind Liv shifted uneasily. She used the small amount of room this afforded her to situate her elbow between herself and the ribs of the man closest to her. She kept it there, ready.

As Cedric laughed, the professor's features pulled taut in annoyance. "What do you find so funny?"

"You," Cedric said, shaking his head and grinning. "You really love to hear yourself talk. And after all your self-righteous speeches, this is what you've come to threaten us with? A single blade?"

"You think this is amusing?" the professor asked, his voice

dropping into a low growl.

"I think I know something you do not," Cedric said, keeping his voice light. "You may know what she is, but you clearly have no idea what *I* am." Cedric's mouth curled up into a smile. "Allow me to educate you, Professor."

Cedric's arm was moving before he even finished the sentence. He swung it around so fast that Liv could barely tell what he was doing. Only when the professor stumbled and fell to one knee did she realize that Cedric had hit him in the face with the blunt end of the lamp.

One of the robed men near the bed bent down to aid the professor, while the other advanced on Cedric. He spun around and kicked out straight. Liv heard the crack as Cedric's foot connected with the face of the robed man. Cedric leaped off the bed toward Liv.

She was ready for him. Before Cedric's foot even hit the floor, Liv jammed her elbow up into the abdominal area of the closest man holding her. He doubled over, groaning and releasing his grip on her ever so slightly. The other man holding her tried to tighten his grasp, but by the time his thoughts translated into actions, Cedric was already there.

He was so fast, so impossibly fast, that Liv could barely make out his expression as he kicked out at the man who still held her, while the man she'd elbowed reached into his robe and brought out a short, gleaming knife.

"Kill her!" the professor gurgled from beside the bed. He had one hand over his face, and Liv could see blood streaming through his fingers.

The robed man with the knife lunged at Liv, but Cedric pulled her away just in time. The knife sliced nothing but air.

Before Liv could blink, Cedric kicked at the connecting door's lock with one powerful blow. The cheap wood cracked inward, separating from the deadbolts on both sides. Liv put her hands over her face to protect it from shards of wood as Cedric shouldered his way through the remains of the door.

Liv barely had time to feel hot, angry breath on her neck before her head went snapping backward—one of the robed men had grabbed her by the hair and yanked. She kicked out at his kneecaps, but his grip only loosened a tiny bit.

Already through the door, Cedric grabbed Liv's arm and pulled her through into the next room. She yelped as some of the hair tore from her head. The robed man who held on to her hair tumbled over the broken remains of the door and fell into the room. Liv saw two others preparing to crawl over him, including the one with the knife.

Liv barely had time to take in the room's occupant—an elderly woman wearing a patterned bathrobe was lying on the bed, her mouth open in shock. Liv saw her reach up with one hand to adjust a hearing aid.

Cedric raced through the room's outer door to the parking lot, lifting Liv clean off the ground to sprint the few paces to the car. Liv had never moved so quickly in her life. She didn't even risk a quick look back at the motel as she fished her keys out of her pocket and jammed her shaking fingers onto the Unlock button. Cedric was already seated in the passenger seat by the time she got behind the wheel.

Liv locked the car doors just as the robed men gathered around it. One tried to open the driver's side door as Liv turned the ignition key. When it didn't budge, he pounded his fist against the glass.

Another robed man jumped up onto the hood of the car, and Liv screamed. She could see the rounded outline of his face, the lines of his long nose, the dark of his eyes. He wasn't like the wraths who'd tried to kill her—he was disturbingly human. She threw the car into reverse and pumped on the gas. As she spun the wheel, the man went flying off the hood and onto the pavement.

For just a moment, through Cedric's window, Liv saw the professor standing in the doorway of the motel room, one hand gripping the frame. Blood still poured from his nose. Liv barreled out of the parking lot onto the highway's on-ramp, merging with the free-moving traffic.

"Are they following us?"

Cedric turned in his seat and looked out the back window.

"There are so many lights . . ."

Liv cursed under her breath and checked the rearview mirror. Cedric was right—she saw a line of headlights stretching out behind them, but couldn't tell if any of these cars belonged to the robed men. She pumped the accelerator, trying to put more distance between her car and the approaching lights. Wondering how much distance it would take before she would start to feel safe.

If she'd ever feel safe again.

"You realize what this means, right? I'm the MacGuffin. The MacGuffin is *me*."

Cedric didn't seem to hear her, or maybe he wasn't paying attention. Which made sense, since he'd been busy staring out the back window to make sure no one was following them for the past two hours while Liv prattled on in panic mode.

"I mean, a scroll? I'm a scroll? What is that? What even . . . what am I?"

Cedric finally turned around in his seat and faced forward. "You are still you. Still Liv," he responded. His words were reassuring, but his voice sounded like he was on autopilot.

Liv wasn't sure if she believed him. A few hours before, they'd been alone on a motel bed, Cedric and Liv, just a boy and a girl, about to . . . and now, now, she wasn't just a girl anymore. She was something else, something more. Or maybe something less? If she really was some kind of ancient scroll, then, well . . . what did that even mean? That she could open portals? The professor said that every generation, children had exhibited markings like hers. But she hadn't been born with the markings—of that, she was sure. But if the Hannigans hadn't tattooed her, then how and when did the markings get there at all?

Liv gripped the steering wheel tighter. She had so many questions that only the professor could answer, but there was no way she was going back to ask him. And she couldn't bring herself to ask the questions out loud, although she knew Cedric must be thinking at least some of the same things. His only goal since coming over to this world was to find a scroll, and now he had. But if he was thinking about somehow using her to get back to his home world, he wasn't saying so. Instead, he kept his mouth closed and his eyes trained on the rearview mirror.

And one more thing Liv couldn't say out loud—that the thought of him leaving, the thought of physically helping him to go, made her feel strangely empty, scooped out inside.

That was something she obviously had to keep to herself.

Liv tried to keep her attention on the Los Angeles skyline as it rose in the distance, its tall glass buildings twinkling in the night. It was better than seeing her own pale face in the rearview mirror, with the brand-new bruise she had just under her chin. She was collecting injuries at an alarming rate.

"I thought for a second I was going to die back there," Liv finally said, her voice nearly a whisper.

Cedric's expression was stony. "I would not have let anything happen to you."

"Because I'm the scroll?"

He tensed beside her, but she didn't know if it was because he was angry, or because she was right.

"That is not what I meant."

Liv spotted their exit sign and watched as it grew nearer and nearer.

"Almost home," she whispered, more to herself than to Cedric.

He looked away from her, out the side window.

"Almost."

THE REVELATIONS

Although it was nearly midnight when they finally got back to the house in Echo Park, Cedric and Liv weren't able to rest. Merek and Kat—who were still wired from their own mission—wanted to hear every last detail of what happened in San Diego, the professor, and their escape that almost wasn't.

When Cedric explained about Liv's "tattoo" and what it could mean—a one-way trip back to Caelum—Kat let out a whooping noise.

"You were right! The scrolls exist! I knew you were right," Kat said, clapping a hand on Cedric's shoulder.

"And she never shut up about it, either," Merek said, but his heart clearly wasn't in his customary sarcasm. He couldn't keep the smile—an actual smile—off his face. He didn't even flick his ever-present lighter as he eagerly took in Cedric's story.

"We still do not know what the next step should be . . . ," Cedric began, sitting up straighter. Surrounded by his friends, he seemed more sure of himself than he had during the anxious car ride home.

"We will figure it out," Kat replied. "We have a scroll now. And there are other things we know now, too."

Cedric's eyebrows furrowed. "You found something at the museum?"

Kat smiled. "A wrath was waiting there, just as we thought."

"Wait until you hear what she did," Merek put in. "Even I can admit it was brilliant."

Kat grinned. "Merek and I split up. He went to get the rest of our belongings, and I looked around the perimeter. The wrath was alone, and unprepared for me. I do not believe they really thought we would return. It was one of those who attacked us last night. I dragged him through the grate and into the tunnels, and I threatened him, but only a bit—"

"A bit?" Merek gave a sly grin. "When I caught up to you, the wrath looked more than 'a bit' scared."

"I would not want to be that wrath," Cedric said.

"Anyhow," Kat continued, clearly pleased, "the wrath said they were under orders to find 'the marked one,' which I did not understand at the time—"

"He meant me," Liv interjected. She was sitting a little outside their circle, and they all turned to look at her.

"That makes sense," Kat finally said. "He also said he was not from here. He came from Caelum, like we did. He came through the portal shortly after us, on the orders of Malquin."

"Malquin?" Cedric immediately became alert.

Kat nodded. "But he claimed he did not know where Malquin is now. He said only that his orders were to find us and discover what we knew about the 'marked one.'"

"So Malquin is looking for the scrolls as well. Not only that, but he knew the scrolls were in human form . . . ," Cedric said. "Where is this wrath now?"

Kat averted her eyes. "Gone. When it had no more information to give, I thought it would be a good plan to let it go and then follow. I wanted to know if it was telling the truth, or if it might lead me to Malquin."

Cedric nodded. "Smart."

"It might have been," Kat continued. "But the wrath got away from me in the alleyways several blocks from the museum."

Cedric was quiet for a moment before shooting Kat a reassuring smile. "You did well. We know so much more now."

Kat smiled. "And we might have finally found a way home."

Liv could practically feel the mix of tension and excitement coursing off everyone in waves. She was just tired.

"Excuse me," she said, standing up in the middle of a conversation about what their next steps should be, now that a scroll was "in their possession." She knew that her input was important, and that, as the scroll in question, she should voice her opinion about what to do next. But whenever she closed her eyes to think, she instead pictured the professor's unnerving smile, the righteous look in his eyes when he had promised to end her life.

"Are you all right?" Cedric asked. He looked at her directly for what felt like the first time in hours.

"I just need some air," Liv said and left to make her way toward the back porch.

Cedric stood. "Maybe I should go with you . . ."

Liv blinked. "Why?"

Cedric looked taken aback. After a moment, he straightened. When he spoke again, he sounded less filled with concern and more like he was giving orders to an unruly soldier.

"Those knights are after you. And from what Kat said, the wraths are definitely after you, too. If Malquin wants to get hold of a scroll—I mean, of you—it cannot be for a good reason."

"I know all this."

"Liv, it is not safe," Cedric said.

"It's the porch. Like, ten feet away. Besides, I've been taking care of myself for ten years, and I can take care of myself now. I don't need you to hold my hand."

Hurt flashed across Cedric's face for a moment. But it was gone as quickly as it appeared. He opened his mouth as if he wanted to say something, but Kat put a gentle hand on his elbow.

"Give her a moment. It has been a long night."

Surprised, Liv shot Kat a grateful smile before leaving the room. She pushed the back door open, relishing the feel of a light breeze on her face. She didn't turn around to see whether or not Cedric was still looking at her as she firmly shut the door.

Staring at the night sky, Liv was overtaken by a disorienting, but familiar, feeling. It was the same one she always got the instant the lights came up in a theater at the end of a movie. During those moments, it would take a few seconds to disengage her mind from the make-believe and readjust to the reality around her—the too-bright room with sticky floors that smelled of stale popcorn. For those few seconds, her brain was confused. Stuck in a place between real and fake.

That's what it felt like now. She tried to focus on something real. Almost immediately, she knew what to do.

Shannon picked up after just one ring.

"Where are you?"

"Exactly where you dropped me last night. Sorry to call so late."

Shannon scoffed, and Liv smiled in the darkness. Though it had been barely twenty-four hours since they'd last spoken, it felt like much longer.

"You promise me answers, and then I don't hear from you for a whole day?"

"I know, I'm sorry. I've sort of got . . . stuff going on."

"Obviously. Although if you could clarify what the 'stuff' is, I'd feel much better."

Liv could hear the lightest amount of hurt in Shannon's voice. But how could she tell her best friend the truth without Shannon thinking she was crazy? Or worse, what if telling Shannon put her in danger?

"I know everything with Rita was hard," Shannon said after a few moments. The compassion in her best friend's voice made Liv's chest feel like it was being squeezed by a large fist. A tear formed near the corner of her eye, causing the backyard to blur. Liv put the palm of her hand up against her eye and pressed down hard before the tear could fall.

"It was," she whispered. "But there's more than that."

"Tell me, Liv. Tell me what's going on."

Liv hesitated, thinking about how good it would feel to say a single real thing out loud to Shannon. But she couldn't tell her one piece of the puzzle without telling her everything—the tattoo, the portal, the wraths, the motel . . . Cedric. Most of all she wanted to talk to Shannon about Cedric.

But she couldn't. If she started talking about Cedric or any of it, who knew what else would come pouring out? Not just the details of the last few days, but everything? Her past? Her parents?

Once the truth was out, she wouldn't be able to stuff it back inside, just like she hadn't been able to put it back after revealing the truth about the fire to Cedric in the car. Could she really stand Shannon looking at her any differently?

Even if her best friend deserved the truth . . . what if she got a glimpse of what was really inside of Liv and ran?

"I wish I could, Shan . . . I really do."

Shannon sighed. For a while, both girls were silent.

"What if we meet up tomorrow morning, face-to-face?" Shannon asked.

Liv glanced back over her shoulder at the back door. Beyond it, she knew that Cedric and the others were still endlessly discussing what to do next. She wondered how long it would take them to decide exactly how and when they would use her to get home.

Would they leave her here when they were done with her, used up and alone for the wraths or the Knights or whoever got there first? Who would she have on her side then?

"Liv?"

"I'm here. Yeah, tomorrow sounds good."

"The usual spot?"

Liv frowned as she thought of the familiar piece of concrete down by the LA river. Her usual spot. How many times had she and Shannon met there to hang out, do homework, or complain about life? A part of her longed to go back there, but now even her favorite place was too wrapped up in this madness—after all, it was where she'd first seen Cedric and his friends. A portal had opened in the exact spot where she and Shannon used to paint their nails and talk about movies. She wanted to go somewhere else, somewhere untainted by the past few days.

"No, not there," Liv said. "How about that spot we went to on our ninth-grade field trip? Where we tried cigarettes for the first time?"

"And then threw up?"

"Yeah. That was a good day."

"Um . . . because of or despite the vomiting?"

Liv laughed. "Both, I guess. We were just two regular teenagers, doing something dumb. I miss that."

"We're still regular teenagers."

Liv didn't respond, and Shannon got quiet.

"You're kind of freaking me out."

"I'm sorry. Will you still come? Noon?"

"Of course I will. Tomorrow, Liv."

"Night, Shannon."

Liv hung up the phone and looked around the backyard. It had been a relief to hear Shannon's reassuring voice in her ear, to hear something normal. But it only took a few minutes for that feeling to pass. The emptiness of the yard seemed to stretch and grow into the night, past Liv's field of vision. Still, she wasn't ready to face the others yet. She decided to wait until they'd fallen asleep before going back inside to rest herself.

Liv sunk down low in a lawn chair, feeling even more alone than before.

⊱⊰

The next morning, Liv found that getting out of the house wouldn't be so easy.

"There are not one, but two groups of enemies trying to capture and probably kill you," Cedric said. He made emphatic movements with his hands, which reminded Liv of Joe at his most serious. It also made her angry.

"You think I don't know that? I was there in the motel room last night, just like you. I was scared, too—"

"Motel room?" Kat cut in.

"I was not scared," Cedric shot back.

Liv just raised an eyebrow.

"Why were you in a motel room?" Kat asked.

No one answered her. Instead, a quiet tension fell over the living room of the Echo Park house. Merek watched Liv face off with Cedric and Kat, an almost bemused expression on his face.

"A motel is like an inn, right?" Kat asked, her eyes bouncing between Cedric and Liv.

Cedric waved his hands. "We were attacked there. What is important now is that we work together to try to figure out our next step. We cannot let Liv fall into the wrong hands."

Kat pursed her lips, but said nothing.

"I don't intend on falling into anyone's hands," Liv said, crossing her arms over her chest. "But I'm not going to sit around in this house and wait until you come up with some grand plan on how best to use me, either."

A part of Liv knew that Cedric was right, that she was in way over her head here. She doubted that the Knights would be able to track her down to this house after she and Cedric lost them in San Diego, but the wraths had been distressingly good at keeping up with Cedric and his group. A group that now included her.

Still, the thought of getting away by herself for just two hours, to sit in the sunshine with Shannon, being normal for just a little bit . . . it was too tempting to pass up. Especially since it was starting to really sink in that her previously "normal" life was about to change, probably forever. After all, being a scroll made her a fugitive from the Knights. Could fugitives do senior year? Or go to college? Or make movies?

The future she had so carefully planned and waited for was slipping away, and she wanted—needed—to see Shannon and hold on to what she could. But how could she explain that to Cedric?

"I must agree with Cedric on this," Kat said, though her face was still stormy, probably because she was thinking about the motel. "I am sorry, Liv, but you cannot think only about yourself right now. You are no longer just a girl. You are our only means to get back to Caelum."

"Right. Just some scroll. Some ticket home," Liv shot back. She could feel the force of her argument against the two of them wavering as they stood side by side. They looked impressive, almost regal.

And in the end, she knew they could keep her here in this room as long as they wanted. She might be a supernatural scroll thingy with one or two self-defense moves up her sleeve, but she still had all the muscle of a sixteen-year-old girl who'd taken her gym class pass/fail.

She'd have to try another tactic.

"I'll help you get home, but I won't be your prisoner," Liv said. At the word *prisoner*, Cedric winced slightly. "All I want is to see my best friend in a safe, public place for a couple of hours. You can even come with me if you want. Then, if any wraths somehow manage to find us, I'll have just as much protection there as I would here." Liv met Cedric's eyes as she continued. "Unless you don't think you can take them."

Cedric's jaw tightened. "That is *not* the problem. I can handle the wraths—"

"Good. Then there should be no issue with us going."

"Cedric—" Kat turned to Cedric.

But Liv spoke over Kat, looking directly into Cedric's eyes. "You need me," she said. "But I need this, Cedric. Please."

Cedric looked at her for a few moments more before he gave a slight nod. "Liv is right. We cannot cower in fear of them—the wraths or the Knights. We need to determine what Malquin is up to, but we need Liv's cooperation as well if we want to get home."

Liv let out a long breath.

"Well, isn't this an interesting turn," Merek said. He smirked as he looked between Kat and Cedric. "And do you agree with him now, Katerina? Haven't you always said we should follow him in all things, because he is our leader?"

Kat looked stretched tight, like a rubber band about to snap.

She turned to Cedric. "You are sure about this?"

A flicker of doubt rose up in Cedric's face, and Liv felt guilty. She remembered him telling her how hard it was to be the leader. To have every decision fall to him.

"I am," Cedric said, then looked to Liv. "I will keep you in my sight at all times. And we will only be gone for a couple of hours?"

"Yes," Liv said as she exhaled sharply, afraid to say anything else that might work against her.

"I guess it is all decided then," Kat said, her voice brittle. "Though I am going with you should there be any trouble."

Merek swung his legs off the side of the armchair and onto the floor. He tilted his head up at Liv. "I think I will go as well."

Cedric narrowed his eyes. "Why?"

"To see more of this world, mostly," Merek responded with a lazy grin. "Now that I know we are close to going home, I find myself interested in exploring more of this place than its dungeons and dusty rooms. Besides, I prefer to be present should things come to fisticuffs between Kat and our suddenly interesting new friend here."

"Then you will be disappointed," Kat said. Merek shrugged.

"We should go soon," Cedric said, raising his voice a little louder than necessary to cut through the tension.

Liv explained they'd just have to make a quick stop at the Walgreens on the corner, where she'd withdraw more cash and buy some cheap disposable phones for everyone, just in case. As they started to get ready, Liv slipped out onto the front porch.

She wanted to enjoy a little precious time alone in the

sunshine, without feeling weighed down by the expectations of everyone in the house. Without feeling watched.

She got about fifteen seconds.

The front door of the house opened, and Liv heard someone walk out onto the porch. Without even turning around, she said, "Cedric, I'm okay—"

"It's not Cedric."

Liv turned to see Kat shut the front door and move toward her.

"Oh. Hi."

Kat wore a faded T-shirt and jeans that were torn at the knee. She looked comfortable in them, and confident, though they must certainly have been different from her regular clothes of, what—armor? Tiaras? Liv couldn't picture it. She suddenly wondered what type of girl Kat would be if she'd been born on Earth. If she wasn't a medieval warrior princess. Would she have been stuck-up? Artsy? A cheerleader?

Would they have been friends?

Kat stopped next to Liv by the porch railing. She looked out over the street and the houses across the way. "I saw what you did in there. With Cedric."

"What?"

"Stop," Kat said, then turned to look at Liv. "Do not pretend. I have seen the way he looks at you. I know you have seen it, too."

Kat's dark eyes bored into Liv's, and Liv looked away. She could feel herself flushing.

"I'm not sure . . . ," she started. "I mean, I don't think he and

I . . . he talks about you. A lot."

Kat gave a small smile. "I am not jealous. Despite what Merek might believe."

Liv just nodded. "Okay."

"Whatever . . . flirtations Cedric has now, they do not matter. None of that matters." Liv could hear the unspoken pronoun in Kat's words. *You don't matter.*

"Cedric and I are going to be together. We have known it since we were children, and nothing can change that. It is what is best for Caelum, which means it is best for us." Kat paused, then looked back toward the front window of the house. Nothing was visible through the window, but she and Liv both knew Cedric was in there.

Kat turned back to Liv. "He will make a great leader someday. I know it. A king has to be able to make the hard decisions, to do what is right even if he does not want to. Cedric is capable of that, but here . . ."

Kat gestured to the space around them, to the street, the houses. To the very air. "Here, it is harder for him. It is confusing."

Liv didn't know what to say.

"I know he cares for you," Kat continued, "but you cannot use that to turn him away from his responsibility."

"I didn't use anything," Liv said, defensive. But she remembered the way Cedric's eyes had softened when she pleaded, right before he gave in. "And I don't plan on getting in the way of anyone's responsibility."

"I am glad," Kat said, her voice cool and even as her dark

eyes stared down into Liv's. "Because that is a good way for people to get hurt." With that, Kat turned around and walked back into the house.

And Liv suddenly knew what type of girl Kat would be if she had been born on Earth.

One to watch out for.

As soon as the Griffith Park Observatory came into view through Liv's windshield, she felt immediately lighter. Cedric, Kat, and Merek had barely spoken as she made the long, winding drive up the steep hill overlooking the whole of Los Angeles, and by the time she reached the top and parked the car, they were all looking around with wide eyes. The observatory stood directly in front of them, a massive half-globe structure filled with tourists and surrounded by hiking trails.

They walked toward the railing on one side of the observatory and looked out, taking in the view of the hills, of the Hollywood sign, of the downtown skyscrapers off in the distance.

"It's like the view from the Westing Mountains in Caelum, only . . . more," Merek said, eyes wide.

"When have you ever climbed the Westing Mountains?" Cedric asked.

Merek's face transformed from awestruck into his trademark sneer. "You do not know everything about me."

Cedric shrugged and turned back to the view.

"I'm a bit early to meet Shannon," Liv said, then pointed to the top of the observatory. "Up there."

Cedric scanned the roof, putting his hand to his eyes to

shield them from the bright sunlight as he did so. "I will keep my eyes on you from here."

Merek snorted. "I am sure you will."

Cedric opened his mouth to reply, then seemed to think better of it. He turned to Kat. "Come, let us check the perimeter." He pointedly turned his back on Merek as he walked off with Kat.

As soon as they were gone, Liv turned to Merek. "Why do you have to do that? Go and make everything all awkward?"

Merek shrugged with one shoulder. "Everything is already awkward. I am merely giving it voice."

"No, it's more than that. You always give Cedric such a hard time—"

"Believe me," Merek said, turning back to face the Hollywood sign. "In all of Cedric's life, he has never known a hard time."

"That's a bit unfair."

"Unfair? You have known him just a few days, and already you rush to his defense, though he does not need it. I have seen Cedric turn mathematics problems into gibberish and still earn top marks from his tutors. I have seen him cut into his dinner with a sword just to show off, and receive only applause as response. I have seen him flirt with every girl in Caelum while treating his own future bride like a hunting mate, and yet she stays by his side. No matter what he does, his future is assured. He will one day rule an entire kingdom, and all he had to do to earn it was be born. And you speak of *fairness*?"

Liv quietly studied the darkened expression on Merek's

face. She remembered what Cedric had said about Merek a few days earlier, that he was a second son, and what that meant for his future.

"You're right," she said. Merek turned to her, shocked. "It is unfair. I forget, sometimes, what a different world you guys came from. I mean, things aren't all equality, sunshine, and rainbows here, but at least most people can make their own futures."

Merek shook his head. "How do you mean?"

"Here, it's not supposed to matter where a person comes from or who they are. They can be a leader anyway. Or a business tycoon or a YouTube star. Anything. Not that it's always easy. I mean, less than ten percent of all film directors are women, but I fully intend to break through the system, and no one can stop me. Like Lara Croft, but without all the killing people . . ."

Merek looked confused.

"Sorry. Got a little rant-y there. But my point is that here, ideally, anyone can be anything. Especially in LA. That's kind of why this city is awesome."

Merek didn't respond with a snarky comeback. He looked out over the city, his expression thoughtful. "Anything . . . ?"

"Anything. So long as you work at it. And aren't such a dick all the time."

Merek either didn't notice the insult or didn't know what it meant. He continued to stare out over the Hollywood Hills, still lost in thought.

Liv checked the time on her cell phone. "I gotta go meet Shannon . . ."

Merek nodded, and Liv turned and walked toward the observatory. She passed the statue of James Dean's head and the group of tourists who were posing around it. She made her way through families and amateur photographers, slipping inside and taking the elevator that led to the rooftop observation area.

Although it was easily the coolest part of the whole building, the rooftop was often empty of visitors and tourists. Liv walked to the waist-high cement wall that lined the area and sat down before peering over. From up high, she could see Cedric and Kat rejoining Merek, tiny shapes in the parking lot.

It was five minutes before she and Shannon were supposed to meet, so Liv expected her best friend to show up anytime within the next half hour. She was surprised to hear footsteps approaching from behind just a few minutes later.

"The world must really be ending if you showed up on time—" Liv turned, her words cut short when she saw who was approaching.

"Hello, Olivia." Joe stopped a few feet away. He clasped his scuffed leather briefcase in front of him. His expression was so full of disappointment that Liv averted her eyes.

"Shannon told you I'd be here?" she asked. "She set me up?"

"Don't blame her. She's worried about you. Plus, I was pretty persuasive."

Joe took a seat on the half-wall next to Liv. She didn't move over to make more room for him, and he perched there awkwardly.

"There was once a time when I didn't have to stoop to subterfuge to see you," he said, and set his briefcase down on the roof. He opened it and pulled out a manila folder.

"I have to show you something," Joe continued, his voice somber. He flipped open the folder and put it on Liv's lap. She assumed the folder would contain information on her next placement, but the second she looked down at it, her stomach dropped. Cedric's face was staring back at her. The image of him was grainy, taken from a security camera that must have been outside the museum. He was facing off against a man in a torn T-shirt. Although his back was to the camera, Liv knew the man was actually a wrath. In the photo, Cedric was very clearly aiming his sword in the wrath's direction. Liv flipped through the rest of the pictures quickly, and in one she saw herself in the corner of the frame. Her back was to the camera, her hair flying behind her. But it was definitely her.

"They haven't identified you yet," Joe said, rubbing his hands over his eyes. "I hope it's not a mistake that I haven't turned you in—"

"Joe, I can explain."

"Your little friend with the sword is wanted for assault and battery, and for connection to the assault of a police officer."

"That wasn't him! It was the—"

"The what?"

Liv breathed in deep. How could she explain this in a way that wouldn't cause Joe to label her as "potentially deranged" in her file?

"Do you have any idea what you've gotten yourself into?" Joe's voice started to rise. But not in anger, Liv realized. In fear.

"I know what it looks like, Joe, but you have to trust me.

This boy—Cedric—he wasn't the one who hurt that cop. . . ."

Liv trailed off, and she looked away from Joe. He took the folder back and flipped to the last picture, a blown-up image of Cedric and his sword. Its hilt had markings carved onto it; they were visible, though grainy.

"And where did he get this?"

Liv tried to think up a quick answer, but Joe didn't wait for her to respond. "Look at the markings on this sword. Do they look . . . familiar to you?"

That was odd. Joe should have been asking why Liv was hanging around guys with swords, but instead he noticed the markings?

Liv's throat suddenly felt dry, and her mind was spinning. She knew that Joe had seen her tattoo before. He was the one who had taken her away from the Hannigans after they'd given it to her. In fact, he was the one who told her the tattoo had come from the Hannigans in the first place. And she'd always believed him. Why wouldn't she? He was Joe, solid, reliable Joe . . .

"There are things I have to tell you, Liv." Joe set the file down and turned to face her. "Things I wanted to protect you from. But I think that maybe not telling you has put you in even greater danger."

Joe's voice grew fuzzy in Liv's ears. "What are you saying?"

Joe reached out and took one of her hands into his. He looked directly at her, with those same clear, comforting eyes that she had been able to count on for almost her entire life.

"What are you saying, Joe?"

"I'm saying that you're special. You were born with a type

of . . . ability. A strange and rare ability. But one that could attract dangerous people . . ."

Joe's eyes searched Liv's face as she tried to process what he was saying. She yanked her hand from Joe's and looked down over the edge of the wall, at the ground and the people milling below. She couldn't focus on any one person . . . they all seemed to be spinning, going in and out of focus, as she stared. For just a moment it seemed as though the bottom of the world had just dropped out beneath her, and she was just seconds from tumbling down, down, down . . .

"You know?" she managed to whisper, tearing her eyes away from the ground and back to Joe. "You know what I am? What the tattoo does? Everything?"

"Liv . . ."

"No." She pushed herself backward from him. "I almost died last night. We went looking for information and some Knight tried to kill me, and all this time you knew everything?"

Joe looked like he might be sick.

"They found you? The Knights of Valere?" He ran his free hand through what was left of his hair. "Thank God you're still alive."

"I wouldn't have been in danger at all if I'd known. We would never have gone to the professor, never put ourselves in that position. Why didn't you tell me? And how . . . how did you know?"

"I only ever wanted to keep you safe," Joe said, his whole body sagging like a puppet whose strings had been cut. "I promise, Liv."

"Don't promise. Explain."

"I don't even know where to start."

"Let's start with the tattoo. Or the scroll, or whatever it is," Liv said. "Did the Hannigans even have anything to do with it, or was that a lie?"

Joe looked at the ground for just a moment. "They didn't give it to you. It's not really a tattoo at all. You were born with it, although it was probably faint and small enough to pass for an odd birthmark at first. That's the way it works with all children of the scrolls. They're born with the markings, but they don't start to darken until the fifth or sixth year."

Liv blinked furiously, trying to reconcile her own memories with this new truth. "So there's no way to get rid of it? The . . . marking?"

Joe shook his head, his eyes sad. "Your marking didn't really show itself until you were already with the Hannigans. When they found it, the way they treated you . . . they said you were 'marked by the devil,' they called you 'unclean.' I took you out of there as soon as I could, Liv."

"But you let me believe it was just a tattoo, that they'd given it to me . . ."

"It was safer for you to blame the Hannigans than to know the truth."

"I'm gonna have to disagree," Liv said, unable to keep the acid from her voice. "But since you mentioned the truth, let's have it. Start from the beginning."

Joe shifted slightly on the wall. "It's not a coincidence that I'm your social worker. I got into this job with the express purpose of tracking down more scroll children, so that I might protect them before it was too late."

"More children? So you've met people like me before?"

"Liv . . ." Joe said, his voice taking on a weary, resigned tone. "It's easiest if I just show you." With that he turned on the half-wall so that his back was facing Liv. He reached up to the collar of his T-shirt and pulled it down just below his neck, so it showed a line of skin just above his collarbone. The skin was marked with thin, dark writing.

"I knew what you were because it's what I am, too," Joe said, his face still turned away. "A child of the scrolls."

THE LEGEND OF THE SCROLLS

Joe turned back around to face a still-speechless Liv.

"You're . . . You . . ." Liv struggled to form a complete sentence. The sun beat down on the roof, and she could feel a bead of sweat drip down from the edge of her hairline.

"My parents discovered the markings shortly after I was born. My brothers, John and Eric, were born with them as well. At first they were faint, just white lines like you might see from a fading scar. The doctors didn't know what they were. No one knew. But the markings grew deeper and darker, and by the time each of us was six years old, they resembled full-on tattoos."

Liv tried to picture Joe as a child, but it was impossible to see him as anything other than the fully grown, bearded, responsible Joe he'd always been.

"My parents weren't marked," Joe continued. "The children of the scrolls are born randomly to one family in each generation . . . there are always three of them."

Liv's breath caught in her throat. She saw the image of a skinny boy pushing her through a window, a toddler sitting on the grass as her house burned down in front of her eyes.

"Peter . . . Maisy . . ." She couldn't finish the sentence. Their names stuck to the side of her throat.

"Yes. Your brother and sister are marked as well. After your parents died, you were immediately taken into protective care, your information entered into a social services database. I had flagged the system to report any instances of children with unusual markings or tattoos. Peter already had full-fledged markings. I immediately signed on to take your case. Since the day I first met you, Liv, I've done nothing but try to keep you safe."

Liv swallowed, looking away from Joe's concerned face. Her eyes scanned the empty roof. She thought she saw a slight blur of movement next to the nearest telescope structure that jutted out from the building, but the next instant, it was gone.

"I only wish I'd found your family sooner, before it was too late."

Liv turned her eyes back to Joe. "What do you mean, too late?"

Joe reached out and laid one hand gently on Liv's arm.

"I know there's no excuse, Liv. I was looking for scroll children, but the Knights were looking, too. They've been doing this for years, centuries, and have more resources than I do. They find scrolls early, and they . . ."

"I know what they do," Liv whispered.

"Unfortunately, they've gotten good at it. If any scrolls before me have ever slipped the Knights' notice and survived, I have not been able to find them. The Knights probably check schools or doctors' offices . . . from his medical records, I know Peter was taken in for consultations because of his markings. Your parents must have been concerned, scared even, to not know what the markings meant or why they were getting darker."

Doctor's visits? She searched her memories, but came up with nothing. "I don't remember that," Liv said.

"You were so young," Joe responded. "Your parents might not have told you. But they did see doctors, and one of them may have contacted the Knights, given them your address . . ."

Joe looked Liv in the eyes, and suddenly she knew what he was about to say. She shook her head in disbelief, even as the words fell from his mouth.

"Liv . . . they set fire to your house. Trying to kill you all—you, Peter, and Maisy. The Knights wanted you dead."

Liv's shoulders fell, her muscles suddenly slack. She felt as though her throat was closing up, squeezing out all the air . . .

"I'm so sorry. So, so sorry," Joe reached out to steady Liv, and she realized she was slumping downward.

"But it was me," she choked out. "It was . . . I . . ."

With effort, Liv sucked in a breath around the apple-sized lump in her throat, and continued. "The candle. I lit a candle that night. That was why . . ."

Joe's eyes widened. "No! Oh, Liv, no . . . it wasn't you." He looked at her with more pity in his eyes than she could handle.

"I lit a candle that night. I remember doing it. I remember."

"Even if you lit a candle, the police found your house doused in kerosene and ruled it arson. It was the Knights. . . . I'm so sorry, Liv, I just—I didn't want you knowing your parents were murdered. You were so young, and I figured it would be best if you thought it was an accident . . . but you didn't. All this time, you thought . . . oh God, how could I not have known?"

It wasn't a question Liv was meant to answer, but she could feel her head making a tiny, jerking motion anyway. "I didn't tell you. I didn't tell anyone. I couldn't."

Liv thought of all the nights she had closed her eyes before going to sleep, trying to conjure up the images of her parents' faces in her mind so that she wouldn't forget them. She thought of all the other nights that she tried to scrub their images from the backs of her eyelids, so that she might.

"It wasn't your fault, Liv. Not at all."

Something broke open inside of her. And she realized that it was too late and too hard to close it back up in time. The cry tore from her throat and muffled itself against Joe's shoulder when he reached to hug her. And once she started, she couldn't stop. Sobs built in her throat and exploded outward, seeming to rip up her insides as they did so.

It hurt.

She cried and cried, her eyes burning, mouth open against Joe's flannel shirt. Eventually, her breathing began to even out; the tears dried up on her cheeks. She had no idea how long she had been leaning against Joe, although it had felt like a long time, endless.

She pushed herself upright and wiped at her eyes, taking in one long, shuddering breath.

"Are you okay?" Joe asked.

Liv sniffed deeply and nodded. A new thought occurred to her then, one that caused a flash of fear to pulse through her body. She jumped up from the half-wall, looking down at Joe.

"The Knight who threatened me—he said he would kill me for being a child of the scrolls. Do you think he would go after Peter and Maisy? Are they safe?"

"After the fire, I split you up immediately and gave you new last names. I'd hoped it was enough to keep the Knights at bay. They would have known you survived the fire, but I made it difficult to track you down. Peter had recognizable markings by that point, so I sent him north. As a younger child, Maisy was adopted pretty quickly. You were trickier . . . but bouncing around from foster home to foster home has helped, I think. I kept your markings out of the system, and there's no sign they had any idea where you were."

"Until now," Liv whispered. Without thinking, she started to pace in front of where Joe was sitting. "I should never have gone to the professor. If I hadn't, none of this . . ."

"Why *did* you go there?"

Liv paused, conflicted. She glanced out over the green yard in front of the observatory, looking for Cedric. But he wasn't standing where he had been before. It wouldn't betray him, really, to tell his secret, would it? They needed all the help they could get. And Joe was a scroll, too. He would believe her.

Liv took a deep breath and launched into her story, starting with the day she first saw Cedric down by the riverbed. When she mentioned the LA River, Joe's eyes flashed briefly, as though he wanted to interrupt, but he let her continue until the end. When she finished, she sighed heavily and sat back down on the half-wall.

"I couldn't tell anyone," she said. "I thought you'd think I was crazy. I kind of still think I might be."

"You're not," Joe said. "But you may be in even more trouble than I realized."

Liv snorted. "That should be the subtitle of my autobiography."

"I've never seen a wrath before. Or a . . . what did you call them? Guardians?" Joe continued, looking down again at the sword. "The lore I've learned about Caelum and its origins was always murky. The only dangers I knew of firsthand were the ones that existed in this world—the portals, and the Knights, of course."

"The portals? How are they dangerous?"

Joe once again ran a hand through his hair. "I told you that I was one of three brothers, each of us children of the scrolls. When our markings darkened, our parents were confused and scared. They took us to specialists. And that drew the attention of the Knights.

"The Knights picked up Eric and John as they walked home from school. I was out sick that day." Joe paused, his eyes dark and far away. "They just drove by in a dark van and swooped my brothers up, so quickly that no one on the block even noticed. John, my older brother, managed to escape when the van stopped at a red light. He couldn't get Eric out, and he just ran. We never saw Eric again."

"Oh my God," Liv whispered. "I'm so sorry, Joe."

Joe nodded, but seemed eager to move on with his story. "John was convinced the Knights would come back for him. He'd heard them talking and knew they would never leave him alone. My parents and the police thought the people who kidnapped my brother belonged to a fanatical cult, and I guess in some ways that was true. But my brother shared with me the truth that my parents couldn't accept. Because the Knights had told him what he was, and what he could do.

"We ended up moving to Los Angeles to start over. My parents wanted to grieve for their lost son and get on with their lives. So did I. But John could never get past what had happened. When the hunt for Eric stopped, he grew angrier and more obsessed with the Knights. He devoted his life to learning about the organization. What little information I have about them, I got from John.

"Once he was out on his own, John finally found a way to use the scrolls on our backs to open a portal. As far as he could tell, no portal had been opened on Earth in hundreds of years, and he was determined to give it a try. He said it's what we were born to do."

Joe paused and took a breath, shielding his eyes as he looked out over the edge of the observatory wall at the hills rising up beyond. While he looked out, Liv's gaze drifted back over to the opposite wall of the roof. Behind the small building that housed the telescope, she once again saw a blur of movement. Only this time, it didn't move quickly enough. She saw exactly what—or rather, who—was listening to her conversation with Joe. Cedric hadn't been content to watch from a distance, after all.

Joe sighed. "John was always . . . persuasive. Especially when he was passionate about something. And it was exciting to think we might have some kind of power, that we had been chosen for something bigger. We were both so young, barely in our twenties, then."

"Did you manage to do it?"

"Yes. Though I wish every day that we hadn't." Joe sighed. "John had to go to a lot of shady people to find the right documents to translate the markings . . . and when he did, he used them to open a portal on the banks of the LA River."

"The river . . ." Liv murmured, remembering the night Cedric and his friends had come through the portal. Could it be the same place? The very same portal?

"Yes, when you mentioned it earlier, I thought it was quite the coincidence too," Joe said, with a sigh. "We wanted to find somewhere out of the way. I really only half believed opening the portal would work, but John never had any doubts. For him, it wasn't a matter of if he could travel to another dimension, but when."

Joe exhaled in one long, shaky breath. Liv realized it was possible that he'd never told this story to another person before; she wondered how different things might have been if she and Joe had been honest with each other from the beginning. How much less alone they might have been.

"The portal itself was terrifying, a giant black hole that opened up right in the middle of the concrete wall under a bridge. It scared me, and I changed my mind, right then. Not John, though. I'll never forget the way his eyes looked when he stared into the portal. He was hypnotized. I asked him to stop, to think about what he was doing. But John didn't even turn around. I watched him walk into the portal as easily as if he were walking into another room. And then I saw it swallow him. And then I heard him scream."

Joe closed his eyes, as if he was trying to shut out the image once again.

"I ran to the portal to try to pull him back, but I was too late. I couldn't see him, but I could hear him crying out. I could hear the sound of bones breaking. . . . I yelled after him, but I'll never know if he heard me. Because that's when the bridge came down."

"What?"

Joe opened his eyes, but they were far, far away. "The ground began to shake, and the foundation of the bridge began to split. It was so old, it smashed to pieces when it hit the ground. Emergency workers searched through the rubble, but they never found John. He was just . . . gone."

"Oh." Liv wanted to apologize or say something comforting, but before she could think of the right thing, Joe grabbed her shoulder.

"You have to listen to me, Liv. You and I were born to open portals, but the portals aren't meant *for* us. They're meant to use us, to chew us up and spit us out. Wraths and apparently even the Guardians might be able to cross through them unharmed, but not us. Do you understand? That earthquake . . . I don't think it was a coincidence. What John did was against the laws of nature, and the earthquake was a reaction to that."

The laws of nature . . . something in Joe's words reminded Liv of the professor, and how he spoke of the Quelling Theory. He had said magic didn't belong in this world anymore. But where did that leave Cedric? She remembered the way his face looked whenever he talked about his home.

"Cedric and his friends don't belong here," she finally said, her voice quiet. "They need to go back."

Slowly, Joe shook his head. "I'm sorry that your new friends are stuck here, but I won't risk losing you. Not that way."

"You won't, Joe. But they've saved my life—more than once. What if I just open the portal for them—if you show me how to open it—but not go through it myself?"

"It's still dangerous. The consequences—"

"We could go somewhere far from the city. If there's another earthquake, it won't hurt anyone. . . ."

Joe breathed in through his nostrils, eyes focused hard on the ground.

"I'd rather do it with your help than without it. But no matter what, I'll figure out a way," Liv said. "I have to help them. Like you've always helped me."

"All right," he finally said. "You and I will figure out a safe way to send your friends home. Just as long as you promise not to make any moves without me."

Liv nodded, solemn. "There's something else, too," she started, careful to keep her voice neutral. "I get that you kept all this a secret from me to protect me. But . . . it didn't work. Who—what—I am, it caught up with me. I don't want it to be that way for Peter or Maisy. The less they know, the less safe they are."

Joe still looked doubtful, so Liv kept pushing.

"Especially now. The Knights know for sure that I'm alive

and in LA. What if they start looking for Peter and Maisy again, too? They have a right to know what might be coming for them."

Joe sat still for a moment, then nodded. "They might not believe us."

"We can make them."

Liv stood up, and together they started to make their way back to the roof's main doorway. Liv let Joe walk a few paces ahead as they rounded the telescope building. Without breaking stride, she turned her head and saw Cedric standing there, leaning against the building. When she saw his face, her heart thudded painfully. How much of the conversation had he heard? She sucked in her breath and held his gaze. She wasn't paying attention to where her feet were taking her, and she smacked hard into Joe's back.

"Sorry," she said, turning her head back around and giving Joe an apologetic smile. He smiled back and reached for the door handle. Liv whipped her head back around to find Cedric again, but the space was empty.

As they walked down the stairs and into the observatory's main lobby, Joe explained to Liv that Shannon was waiting for them in the parking lot. She'd told Joe where he could find Liv, but only on the condition that she could come along.

"I want to tell her about all this," Liv said. "I don't want to keep any more secrets."

Joe considered this as they wove their way toward the exit. "It's up to you."

Shannon had obviously not been content to wait in the car.

She dashed up the steps toward Liv and Joe, with Merek and Kat close behind her.

"I'm so sorry, Liv," Shannon started. "I was worried about you, and Joe kept calling and I'm so—"

Liv held up her hand. "It's okay. You don't need to apologize."

"Great, so now will you please tell me what's going on?" Shannon's face was such a mixture of confusion and impatience that Liv nearly burst out laughing.

"You're sure you want to know?"

Shannon raised her eyebrows. "Are you joking? You're joking. You can't be asking me that question in any kind of seriousness. When have I not wanted to know what's going on?"

"Can she be trusted?" Kat asked.

"Excuse me? Can *I* be trusted? Who even *are* you?"

"Yes," Liv said quickly, cutting off Shannon's outrage. "She can."

A shadow fell over her. She looked back up the steps and saw Cedric coming down.

"You must be Cedric," Joe said, reaching out to shake Cedric's hand. "I'm Joe." Cedric nodded in response.

"How much did you hear?" Liv asked Cedric.

His eyes flicked over to Liv briefly. She tried to imagine what he was thinking, and failed.

"I heard that Joe can help us open the portal," Cedric replied.

"Portal?" Shannon's voice rose in pitch.

A couple passing behind Cedric on the steps looked over at them.

"Let's move clear of the crowds, maybe," Liv said, directing their small group to a small side lawn.

"I can open a portal," Joe said once they were away from the tourists and schoolkids, "But my first priority is to protect Liv and her brother and sister," Joe said. "Then we'll figure out how to open the portal as safely as possible. Without anyone getting hurt."

"And again, I say—*portal*?!" Shannon's eyes were wide.

"Okay, calm down," Liv said, putting a hand on her arm. "I'll tell you everything. But you have to wait a few more minutes. Please?"

Liv turned back to Cedric and Joe. "We need to make sure Peter and Maisy are safe, that they know about everything so they can protect themselves." Her eyes went to Cedric. "That's the way it has to be."

He nodded slowly. She wondered if he was thinking about Emme—did he understand why she was putting her siblings' safety before his desire to go home, or did he resent that she was keeping him from his own sister with every passing second?

"Peter's up near Fresno," Joe said. "His life was a lot like yours, Liv. He moved from foster home to foster home. He graduated from high school this year, but I know how to find him."

Liv's insides swelled at the thought of her brother, grown up now. Quiet Peter with the serious, worrying eyes.

"You're going up there?"

"Somehow I don't think this is information to deliver over the phone," Joe replied.

"And Maisy?"

"Your sister's . . . much closer," Joe said, hesitation in his voice. "I don't think we need to worry much about her safety.

She should be highly protected already. Peter's more vulnerable. More alone."

"What do you mean, Maisy's highly protected already? Where is she?"

"Beverly Hills. Her adopted family lives there."

"Wow. That's . . . good for her." Liv tried to keep the tinge of jealousy out of her voice. "Doesn't really answer my question, though."

Joe ran a hand through his hair. "Maisy's family is a bit . . . high profile. She has lots of security. And another thing you should know . . . her new family changed her first name as well."

"*What*?" Liv shook her head. "Why? How? You can't just change a four-year-old's name—she's not a dog."

"This family could. They only changed a letter, though."

Liv couldn't understand why Joe was being so cagey. Before she could think it over, Shannon burst out with a sudden yelp.

"Oh my God. Is your sister Maisy actually . . . Oh my God."

"What?" Liv whirled on Shannon. "Out with it!"

"*Daisy* Ratner? As in the third adopted daughter of Michael Ratner and Shana Cole?"

Joe nodded.

"Oh my God," Liv said.

"Who are they?" Cedric asked, brow furrowed. Next to him, Kat shrugged. Merek looked bored.

"Movie stars," Liv answered, finally understanding Joe's warning. "Very, very famous ones."

"They adopted, like, all these kids, and then they named them after flowers," Shannon continued, in a rush. She turned to Liv. "Didn't you know that? Everyone knows that."

Liv shrugged. "I mean, I know how their last two films did at the box office, but gossip stuff? I never really paid attention . . ."

"I *told* you to get that *Us Weekly* app. But *no*, you said it would clutter up your precious screen—"

"Shannon."

"Sorry." Shannon looked just a bit chastised. She pulled out her phone. "But if you did have the app, you would know Daisy's not even in the country. Michael Ratner is in Nicaragua right now shooting a movie. And he always brings his family with him on location."

Shannon turned the screen to Liv. She saw a small picture of the movie star Michael Ratner, all sunglasses and big teeth, moving through an airport. A group of people trailed him, but Liv couldn't pick out Maisy, or Daisy, among them.

Liv took a deep breath, then forced herself to look away from the screen and toward Joe. "Okay, so Maisy's safe for now. And you're going to tell Peter what's going on."

"What about you?" Joe asked.

Liv looked past him to Cedric, who looked like he was still desperately trying to figure out what *Us Weekly* was. But even in his state of obvious confusion, his posture was all readiness. His shoulders were back, his fingers just inches from where his knife rested against the inseam of his jeans. Always prepared for battle.

"I'll be protected, too."

THE LAST MEAL

Joe offered to give Shannon a ride home from the observatory, but she insisted on staying with Liv and hearing the whole insane story.

"Shan, aren't you still grounded?" Liv whispered to her as they walked to her car.

"Probably," Shannon replied. "But Joe doesn't know that."

Before they parted ways, Joe pressed a few fifties into Liv's hand and told her to stay near her phone. Liv used one of the fifties to buy some pizzas and take them back to the Echo Park house. She, Cedric, Kat, Merek, and now Shannon hungrily attacked the food while sitting around the table on the back patio.

Shannon had listened silently—well, mostly silently—as Liv caught her up on the main details of how she'd met Cedric and what her "tattoo" really was. She seemed skeptical, but at least she hadn't run away screaming yet. Liv was glad to have her around, especially since Cedric and his friends were casting pointed looks in her direction every few moments or so while they discussed strategy over bites of sausage pizza.

Liv tried to pay attention, but her mind kept drifting to Peter and Maisy—or *Daisy*, now, as if she'd ever get used to *that*. She kept picturing them as she last saw them, tired and worn-looking in a temporary children's home. For so long, thinking about her brother and sister had only brought up feelings of shame and fear—shame for what she thought she'd done to her parents, and fear of what her siblings thought of her.

It was difficult to replace those long-standing emotions with what she now knew. Besides, the fear was still there, only attached to new worries. What if Peter and Maisy-now-Daisy didn't believe they were in danger? What if Joe couldn't figure out a way to keep them safe? The questions were eating her up.

"This meal is not as good as yesterday's," Merek said, putting down a piece of pizza crust and dragging Liv's attention from her thoughts.

"Yeah, LA is really more of a burger town," she replied, trying to force herself to pay attention to the conversation.

"Or kale, if you're into that kind of thing," Shannon said.

"What is kale?" Merek asked.

"It's best you don't know," Liv said.

Shannon smiled, but briefly. She seemed to be handling this pretty well, Liv thought, although if this were any other day, Shannon would be taking this opportunity to list all the celebrities she knew of who were on all-kale diets.

Across the table, Kat put her slice of pizza down as well. "Enough nonsense. We need to determine what to do next. We should open a portal as soon as possible—"

"We said we'd wait for Joe," Liv interrupted.

"Yes, but we should have a plan ready to put in action immediately upon his return." Kat spoke slowly, as if to a small child. Liv pursed her lips to keep from saying something snarky.

"The next step should be to make sure Liv is safe from the wraths and the Knights of Valere before we leave for Caelum," Cedric said.

"That could take days, or longer. We have nothing to do with these Knights. Meanwhile, our kingdom, our home, is under siege." Kat looked back and forth between Cedric and Merek, her dark eyes alight with energy. "You know I am right. We have the scroll. We could be going home tomorrow."

"We cannot ask Liv to help us get home and then leave her in danger. We wait—just until we know she is safe," Cedric said, definitively. "That is final." Kat flared her nostrils, but didn't respond.

"Not so fun when he does that to *you*, is it?" Merek asked Kat with a smug smile.

"And there is more to consider," Cedric continued, ignoring Merek. "We want to go home as soon as possible, of course. But think about it . . . what are we going back for, if not to fight Malquin? Yet we still know so little about him."

Kat leaned back and crossed her arms, but didn't argue.

"Always know your enemy," Cedric continued. "My father always said—*says*—that. Know not just your opponent's strengths and weaknesses, but their desires. And right now, all we know is that Malquin invaded the palace and he wants Liv. But we do not know why."

"And that matters?" Merek piped up.

To Liv's surprise, it was Kat who responded, though she still sounded pissed off. "We cannot defeat him if we do not know what he wants."

"Why he aligned with wraths to invade our castle in the first place, and what he wants with Liv—they might be connected," Cedric added.

"So what do we do?" Kat asked.

Cedric let out a relieved sigh, like he'd just won a fight he'd been dreading. "We have to figure out what the wraths want with Liv, and what their ultimate goal is. And we have to act before they make their next move."

"We take the fight to them," Kat said, nodding.

"And they lead us to Malquin, or at least whoever he has in charge over here," Cedric responded. "Tonight." He leaned forward, his determined eyes meeting those of everyone at the table. Liv thought he suddenly looked like a general during the inspirational monologue scene of a war movie—an effect that was only slightly hampered by the sausage grease stain on his T-shirt.

"We should return to the area around the museum again. It's the last place we knew for sure the wraths were tracking us," Kat said.

Cedric nodded. "If the wraths are still looking for us there, it should not be too difficult to find them."

"Did you know the word 'Malquin' brings up thirty-three thousand hits online?" Shannon interrupted, looking up from her phone and around the table. "I mean, I don't think any of them are relevant to you guys, but . . ."

Everyone stared.

"Just trying to be helpful," Shannon said, shrugging. Liv smiled, for what felt like the first time in hours. She was so happy Shannon was here.

"Anyway," Cedric said, "the wrath Kat questioned before did not know where Malquin is or what he is planning, but *one* of them has to. We just have to keep looking until—"

"Oh my God." Shannon shot up in her chair, hand gripping her phone.

"What is it now?" Kat asked, exasperated.

Shannon turned to Liv. "It's your sister . . . Daisy. Maisy. I assumed she'd be in Nicaragua with her parents, but I just checked her Instagram, and . . . she's here. In LA."

"Are you sure?" Liv reached out and took Shannon's phone. On the screen was a sun-drenched image of a tennis court, an image posted by one "daisystar02." The text below the image read *#Saturday #bored*.

"That's the tennis court in the Ratners' backyard. I saw an aerial shot of it in *Life & Style*."

"Shan, your borderline stalking abilities are finally paying off."

"It's not stalking. She's got, like, forty thousand followers."

"What does all of this mean?" Cedric asked.

With difficulty, Liv pulled her focus away from the screen. More than anything, she wanted to keep scrolling through Maisy's pictures to get a better sense of her life. But the utter confusion on Cedric's face forced her to be in the present moment.

"Mai—Daisy is here, in LA," Liv said.

Kat shook her head. "What does that matter?"

Shannon's mouth dropped open. "What do you mean, what does that matter? Do people not have hearts on whatever planet you're from?"

Kat raised one cool eyebrow. "We have more heart than the people here, I assure you."

"Not as far as I can tell, Ice Queen," Shannon shot back.

Merek laughed, but Liv just rubbed her temples. A plan was swirling around in her head, a crazy plan. One that would go against everything she'd promised Joe. And would surely piss him off.

Not to mention how much it would piss off everyone at this table.

Liv looked back down at the screen in her hand. A piece of her sister, so close. It felt impossible, to finally know where she was, after all these years. Liv could just go over to Maisy-Daisy's house, introduce herself, and explain everything. . . . How could she not do it? She looked up at Cedric and Kat.

"It matters because I thought my sister was safe, and now we know she's not. She's here, in LA, where any wrath or Knight can find her. We need to warn her."

Cedric shook his head, and Liv's stomach sank. "We have already decided on a plan," he said carefully. "To track down the wraths tonight and finally determine what Malquin is after. Why his wraths are after *you*."

"And if they get to my sister first? She is a scroll just as much as I am, you know. And if you've vowed to protect me, you should protect her, too."

Cedric sighed. "It is unlikely the wraths will find her."

"Unlikely? I don't want to bet my sister's life on 'unlikely.'"

"And we cannot bet our lives for hers," Kat said. "Every day we stay here is dangerous. We need to use the knowledge we can get from the wraths to go home and free our parents."

"But you need me for that, don't you? *I'm* the scroll." Liv dropped her voice low, wanting to make her point very clearly. She knew this was the one card she had left to play. "And I won't help you get home unless I know my sister's okay first."

Kat's eyes flared with anger. Merek looked at Liv with an appraising stare. But it was Cedric's reaction Liv dreaded most.

"If that is what it will take," he finally said.

"This is not a good idea—" Kat started.

"We need Liv's help," Cedric said. "Now she has asked for something in return."

"And what is to stop her from asking for something else?" Kat asked.

"I won't," Liv said.

Cedric nodded. "We can still move forward with our first plan. Kat, are you up for taking another trip to the museum to see if you can track any more wraths?"

Kat looked at Liv with eyes that could spear right through her. "Of course."

"Merek can go with—"

"Merek can speak for himself, thank you," Merek replied. He looked to Kat. "I assume you do not need my help?"

She shrugged. "I can track perfectly well on my own."

"Good," Merek replied. "Because I would very much like

to see more of this 'Beverly Hills,' where an orphan girl of low birth might rise to live in a palace."

Cedric looked confused, but Liv smiled, remembering their conversation at the observatory. "I think you'll be impressed. And I'll just ignore that 'low birth' comment."

With everyone's part in the plan sorted, Liv stood up to collect the pizza boxes from the table. Her entire body felt heavy and slow, as if she'd just run a marathon on three hours of sleep.

Liv headed toward the house with the trash in her hands. Without saying a word, Shannon got up and followed her. As soon as they were safely alone in the kitchen, Liv collapsed against the counter.

"So . . . rough week?" Shannon asked, leaning up against the wall across from Liv.

Liv shook her head and managed a half-laugh.

"How are you doing, really?" Shannon asked.

"You're the one who just found out about other worlds and killer demon creatures. How are *you* doing?"

Shannon gave an exaggerated shrug. "Oh, you know me. I like to roll with the punches."

"Oh yeah." Liv laughed. "That's definitely your reputation. Shannon 'Taking-It-Easy' Mei."

"Are you being sarcastic? Because I *am* easygoing. Sometimes." Shannon grinned. She looked so much like a part of Liv's regular, familiar world, with her chunky wedge shoes, hot green nails, and wide smile, it almost hurt.

"Seriously, though," Liv said. "How are you handling all this?" She motioned at the window behind her, toward where

Cedric, Kat, and Merek were probably cursing her name in new and creative ways. "I know it's a bit . . . insane."

"Seriously?" Shannon said, winding one short strand of black-and-red hair absentmindedly around her finger. "I don't know. I mean, yes, on the one hand it's completely insane. But on the other . . . it doesn't seem that strange at all. All those years we spent watching movies about zombie apocalypses and alien invasions or whatever . . . it's like, it prepared me, in a way? Like, I spent so many hours training for crazy without even realizing, and it would almost be weirder if something like this *didn't* happen at least once in our lives. You know?"

Liv smiled. "I actually think I do."

"Besides," Shannon continued, "I can totally use all this for motivation when I'm cast in the next Peter Jackson movie."

Liv laughed, then turned and looked again at the group sitting outside. From this distance, they looked so normal. Well, aside from the sword resting against the table. Cedric was talking, his hands making large but calculated motions. For a moment, Liv just watched him, the intensity of his movements, the way his mouth moved when he spoke. Her mind wandered to the night before . . . to the two of them alone on that motel bed . . .

She shook the thoughts from her head and turned to Shannon. "So what do you think—have some free time to accompany me to Beverly Hills?"

"Like you have to ask."

Liv grinned.

Shannon's gaze shifted to just over Liv's shoulder, and her

eyes narrowed. "Who's that?"

Liv whirled around. Through the other kitchen window that faced the side yard, she saw a quick-moving blur. Liv moved closer to the window to get a better look and saw a thin girl with long, snarled hair moving along the side of the house.

Liv threw open the window. "Hey," she called out.

The girl's head snapped up. Her face was pale white and streaked with dirt, and her eyes were round as marbles. Liv saw the shabby clothes she was wearing, recognized the desperation in her eyes. A runaway. Before she could say anything, the girl darted away, moving toward the street.

"Hey!" Liv yelled. "You don't have to go—" She cut herself off. Ordinarily, she would welcome the young girl to the squatter house. After all, she'd been in that same position before. Lost, torn, alone. She looked at a box of half-eaten pizza and felt guilty.

But then her gaze moved past the pizza boxes to the backyard, and she realized there was more danger for the runaway here than anywhere else.

"Who was that?" Shannon asked, joining Liv at the window.

"Just a street kid, looking for a place to crash probably."

"Anyone you know?"

"No," Liv said. "She could have been anyone. Once upon a time, she could have been me. Or my sister."

Except that wasn't true, not anymore. Liv no longer had to wonder where her siblings were, or worry that they were living on the streets. They were alive, and they were cared for, and she was going to see one of them.

Today.

THE STORMING OF THE CASTLE

Liv drove slowly westward, watching as the lawns became greener, the houses larger, and the palm trees more neatly tended on the sides of the streets. With every mile they passed, her rusting clunker of a car stood out more and more amid the BMWs and Priuses.

Liv thought about Maisy growing up in this world. She tried to imagine what her sister might look like now, as a thirteen-year-old girl, but all she could see was the tiny child in pigtails who used to eat bubblegum-flavored ice cream until half her face was stained pink and blue.

Cedric stared out the window at the houses as they passed.

"They're kind of grossly excessive, aren't they?" Liv nodded to one giant mansion situated far back on a manicured lawn and fronted with a Greek-style colonnade.

Cedric continued to stare, and Liv wondered if he was icing her out for basically forcing him to change his catch-a-wrath plan. He was sitting as close to the window as possible, his body angled away from her. The moment they'd shared at the hotel seemed so far away, almost like it had happened between two different people.

Then Cedric turned to her, and his mouth lifted on one side, into its customary half-smile.

"I have seen grosser."

"Don't expect him to be impressed," Merek said from the backseat. "He does live in the largest castle in Caelum."

"You want a castle?" Shannon asked. "Wait till we get to the Ratners' house; now that place is a palace. It has, like, gold-plated everything. Even the plungers are platinum. Can you imagine?"

Merek stared at her blankly.

"Guess not," Shannon breathed, turning her attention back out the window.

Liv looked down at the *Map to the Stars* guide she'd picked up at a 7-Eleven. The Ratner-Cole residence had a giant yellow star marking its location.

"I think it's here," Liv said. She slowed the car down.

Everyone turned their head to look out the right-side windows, but all they could see was an eight-foot-high hedge. Liv eased the car along the side of the road, finally stopping just before an enormous iron gate with an intercom.

"What do we do?" Shannon asked, catching Liv's eyes in the rearview mirror.

Liv shrugged. "You're the resident celebrity stalker. Any ideas?"

"Would you stop with the stalker talk already? Geez, you try to get backstage to see Justin Timberlake one time . . ."

"Maybe we should just go up and ring the buzzer?" Liv asked.

Cedric craned his neck upward. "I could vault that gate."

"Yeah, I'm not sure that's the best idea . . ." Liv began.

Her words were cut off by a rumbling sound. She turned in her seat and watched as a red double-decker bus crested the small rise in the road and slowed as it approached the Ratners' front gate, eventually coming to a wheezing stop. A sign on its side read "Star Tours" in glittery letters, and Liv could see the faces of tourists pressed up against the windows.

"Ooh, I've always wanted to go on one of those things," Shannon said. Liv raised an eyebrow in her direction. "Okay. Maybe I am kind of a stalker."

"What is it?" Cedric asked. His gaze rose to the second story of the bus, which featured more tourists sitting on plastic seats in the open air.

"It's, um . . ." Liv struggled to figure out how to explain the nature of Hollywood celebrity to Cedric, who was looking at her expectantly. "You see, there are people here who are really famous, mostly for being in movies. And then other people come in from out of town and take these tours to see where the movie stars live. . . ." She let her voice trail off and shrugged, thinking she wasn't explaining it right. But instead of staring at her blankly, Cedric gave a knowing nod.

"Like petitioners."

"What?" Liv asked.

"In Caelum, petitioners come to our palace on a daily basis. They are often townspeople making complaints, and my father sets some time aside every morning to hear them. But sometimes, they don't have legitimate complaints. They just want to get a look at the inside of the throne room or gossip about what my mother is wearing."

Shannon leaned up from the backseat. "Whoa. You have a throne room?"

Cedric gave a sheepish shrug and turned his attention back to the tour bus. Merek scoffed. "Nice false modesty, Highness. It is most becoming."

Shannon rolled her eyes at Merek. "Jealous much?"

Liv looked back at the bus, where a tour guide with a microphone was talking animatedly to the tourists on the top deck. With a sweeping gesture, she pointed toward the Ratners' house. Liv rolled the car window down to hear.

". . . and as you all know, Michael Ratner and Shana Cole have come a long way since they met on the set of *Meteor* in 1995 . . ."

"Ooh, I love that one," Shannon said.

"The Ratners married in 1997 and moved to this mansion in 2000. They also have homes in Malibu, Rome, Hawaii, and Austin, Texas. Since their marriage, they have adopted seven children from all over the world—"

"Yeah, and changed their perfectly good names into stupid flowers," Liv muttered. Shannon leaned up from the backseat to shush her.

"Look," Cedric whispered.

Liv followed his gaze through the iron bars, where two security guards dressed in white polo shirts and pressed black pants appeared seemingly out of nowhere to man the gate. They looked over the bus with bored but watchful expressions.

"Whoa, where did they come from?" Liv asked.

"Just there." Cedric pointed to a small structure to the left of the gate. It was covered in ivy, and Liv had previously taken it for an extension of the hedge. But looking closer, she could see that it was actually a well-disguised guard hut.

"Well, there goes our vault-the-gate plan," Shannon said.

"Not necessarily," Liv said, her eyes bouncing between the guards on one side of the gate and the group of tourists snapping photos on the other.

Liv put the car into drive and eased it around the group of tourists. She followed the hedge for another hundred yards or so until it came to an abrupt stop, then pulled the car over once again.

"Look there." Cedric pointed to the edge of the hedge. It turned a ninety-degree angle at the corner of the yard, running up the side of the lawn toward the house. But between the edge of the hedge and the neighbor's fence was a narrow gap of space, maybe eight inches wide.

"You want us to go in there?" Shannon asked, eyes wide.

Liv cast a glance to the bus, which revved back to life as tourists began to put their cameras down and look away from the house. She knew another tour bus would come along and distract the guards eventually, but didn't want to wait that long.

"It's the best shot we have. And we have to go now."

She pushed open the door and ran quickly around the edge of the car, stopping in front of the narrow gap. On her left, the wooden fence rose up maybe eight feet, so it was nearly level with the hedge. The two ran parallel to each other down the entire length of the yard, so when Liv stared down the gap she could see only a constant stretch of white and green, white and green, with no end in sight.

Merek cast a dubious glance into the gap. "That looks a bit tight . . . are we sure one of us should not wait here?"

Shannon pulled on Merek's arm. "Come on, oh complain-y one."

Liv sucked in her stomach and took sideways steps into the narrow gap. Her back pressed against the hard wooden fence on one side, while the leaves from the hedge tickled her face and arms. Still, she tried moving quickly through the passage and ignored the pain as little sticks and branches tore at her clothes and skin.

She also tried—less successfully—to ignore how close Cedric was pressed in on her right side. He had his sword-in-a-garbage-bag clutched in one hand.

"I think we should go up this way," Cedric said, his voice low. He put one arm up against the hedge and pushed on it. It held firm. He crouched down and laced his hands together, then held them out flat, motioning for Liv to step into them.

Liv settled one of her Chucks into Cedric's hands. She gripped handfuls of leaves from the hedge as Cedric lifted her up past the top of it. The moment she could see the entire house, her breath caught in her throat.

It was enormous. At first glance, it really did look like a castle out of a fairy tale—one covered with satellite dishes and enormous bay windows, of course. In the back of the house, a clear-blue pool sat next to the tennis courts.

Liv pulled herself up and over the top of the hedge, counting to three before dropping down to the other side. Shannon and

Merek followed. They landed heavily next to Liv on the bright green grass. Cedric pulled himself up and over the hedge last.

Liv saw one of the guards start to make his way down the front walk of the house.

"Get down!" she hissed, pulling Shannon to the ground as Cedric and Merek dropped behind her.

But the guard didn't even look in their direction as he paused beside a giant fountain to speak into a walkie-talkie. His eyes were still on the front gate.

"Now," Liv said. She crab-walked over to a row of lemon trees that bent low to the ground and lined the entire left side of the massive house. The others followed her, and they waited as the guard scanned the yard, put his walkie-talkie back into his holster, and walked back to the small hut near the gate.

"What now?" Shannon whispered.

Cedric's eyes were trained on the back of the retreating guard. He gripped his sword through the plastic garbage bag. "There are only two of them. I can disable them easily—"

"No!" Liv whisper-screamed. "We're already trespassing. I don't think we should add another assault and battery to your list of charges."

Cedric wrinkled his forehead in confusion, and Liv rolled her eyes. "No. Swording."

"What are we going to do, just go up to the door and knock?" Shannon asked.

Liv shrugged. "Guess so." She slowly rose. "On my count . . ."

"What are you doing in my yard?" A clear, girlish voice rang out across the grass.

Standing near the corner of the house was a short teenage girl. She wasn't the same pigtailed girl with ice cream smeared around her face that Liv remembered. She had the same eyes, the same round face and spattering of freckles, but she wasn't the same Maisy. Her mouth was set in a scowl; her hands were on her hips. She tapped her foot in its designer shoe impatiently against the ground.

This was Daisy.

And she was a total stranger.

THE REUNION

"Daisy . . . Ratner?"

Daisy raised her eyebrow expectantly, seemingly not surprised that complete strangers would know her name. "Yes?" she asked, impatient. "How the hell did you get in my yard?"

"Um." Liv struggled to come up with something to say. The whole ride over, she'd tried to figure out how she was going to explain to her sister that she was in fact a secret scroll who could open a portal between worlds. She hadn't thought that this part, the introducing-herself part, would be just as hard.

Daisy crossed her arms and looked toward the front of the yard and the guard hut. "You have three seconds to explain yourselves before I call over Andre and Tim—"

"Wait! I—I'm Olivia Phillips." Daisy's expression remained blank. Liv took a deep breath. "But it wasn't always Phillips. They changed it, when . . . well, when our parents died . . . I'm your sister. Your, um, biological sister."

Daisy's lips parted in surprise, and for a moment, the

tough expression dropped from her face. Then she shook her head slightly, as if trying to clear something from her mind. "That's . . . no way. Who are you really? What do you want?" Daisy peered at each of them, but especially at Cedric, who held his Hefty bag behind him. "You can't just sneak in here to get photos, it's private property—"

"I'm telling you the truth," Liv continued. "I can explain everything if you give me a chance. But you have to believe me. You do remember me, right? Even just a little?"

Daisy's eyes dropped to the ground, her forehead wrinkling. Then she reached into her pocket and pulled out a small, square device. She pushed a button on it and raised it to her mouth. "Andre, it's D. I need you to come up here—"

"Wait!" Liv said, desperate. "I know about the tattoo."

Daisy's mouth fell open in surprise, then snapped shut again. Cedric's eyes darted to Liv, his eyebrows raised. Liv could just barely hear Shannon mutter "oh crap" under her breath.

"The one on your back," Liv continued. "It's written in a strange language, isn't it?"

For a moment, Daisy just stared at her, shaking her head. "No one knows about that. My parents made sure of it." Her face burned red.

"I have the same one," Liv said. Turning quickly, she slipped down the shoulder of her T-shirt, revealing the top of her markings to Daisy. When she pulled her shirt straight and turned around again, Daisy was looking at her with wide eyes.

"Daisy? Daisy, you copy?" A male's voice cut through the air, and it took Liv a second to realize that it was coming from the small walkie-talkie in Daisy's hand. Daisy brought the box up to her mouth slowly, her eyes never leaving Liv.

"We mean you no harm," Cedric said.

"Just give me ten minutes to explain, please," Liv said. "I don't want anything from you. Promise."

"Daisy?" The voice came through the walkie-talkie again.

Daisy paused for a few long moments before she pressed her finger on the button again. "Never mind, Andre. Everything's cool."

Daisy pocketed the device and turned to Liv, beckoning her toward the massive front door of the mansion. "Ten minutes. And if you try anything funny, we also have a guard dog." She shot a side-eye glance at Merek and Cedric. "A hungry one."

They turned a corner of the house and climbed a set of wide marble steps lined with different kinds of flowers. Liv spotted a set of cameras mounted on stakes in the rosebushes. They swiveled to follow her as she reached the front door of the mansion. Behind her, Shannon let out a low whistle.

Daisy pushed open one of the heavy double doors, stepping into a brightly lit foyer. Once inside, Liv couldn't keep from looking up, down, and all around at the stark white walls, the marble-tiled floors, the chandeliers hanging from the ceiling, and the pieces of expensive-looking modern art framed on the walls.

Daisy ignored the group's gawking stares and kept walking, into the largest kitchen Liv had ever seen in her life, complete with shining wood floors and a kitchen table that might have easily seated sixteen people.

Cedric, Shannon, and Merek filed into the room after Liv.

Daisy's attention fixed on Cedric as he moved through the doorway, her eyes roving from his face to his arms and back again. She tilted her head and blinked her eyes, which Liv could see were covered with glittery glue-on lashes.

"So, what's in the bag?" Daisy asked Cedric. Liv froze, but then she realized Daisy's voice wasn't so much suspicious as . . . flirtatious?

"A camera stand," Liv answered, a little too quickly. "We're making a movie."

Daisy rolled her eyes. "Who isn't? Is it about me?"

"No, it's about . . . something else." Liv tried not to make a face at her own terrible lie.

But Daisy's eyes were on Cedric. "Why'd you bring it with you?"

"It's too valuable to leave in the car," Liv said. "Cedric insists on carrying it."

Cedric grinned at Daisy, and her glittery lashes fluttered. He tapped the edge of the bag and lowered his voice to a conspiratorial whisper.

"If it's with me, I know it's safe."

Liv took one look at the expression on Daisy's face and knew her sister couldn't care less what was in that bag. As Cedric moved past her, Daisy ran a hand through her hair and pulled down on her already too-tight tank top. Oblivious, Cedric wandered farther into the room, his eyes raking over stainless steel appliances and Pottery Barn-perfect cabinets.

"You can sit here," Daisy said, pointing to a low couch and chairs grouped at the far end of the room around an enormous stone fireplace. She flopped down on a comfy-looking orange chair that faced a group of monitors set up high in the opposite wall. The monitors showed every side of the yard, and Liv realized Daisy must have been watching from the kitchen as they dropped over the hedge.

"If you want drinks or something, you can help yourselves," Daisy said, motioning lazily toward the giant refrigerator.

"That's okay." Liv sat carefully on the couch, which was angled perpendicular to Daisy's chair. Cedric sat down next to her, careful to tuck his garbage bag out of sight. Only Merek wandered over to the refrigerator and opened it, giving a long whistle. He reached inside.

"All of this food is so . . . cold," he said.

Cedric turned to face him. "Merek."

Daisy shrugged. "He can take whatever he wants. It's not like anyone will miss it." She smoothed down her hair again. "Are you sure you don't want anything?"

Cedric gave her a smile and shook his head. "No, thank you. I am fine."

"Yes, you are," Daisy said with a little grin.

"Daisy," Liv hissed, then sat back abruptly. She was surprised by how easily her tone had slipped into a sort of annoyed familiarity, the kind she usually only reserved for Shannon when she was being particularly Shannon-ish.

Daisy's sharp eyes shot from Cedric to Liv. "So you say you're my sister, huh? They told me I had one, but I don't really remember," she said, matter-of-factly.

Liv swallowed down her disappointment. "That makes

sense. You were pretty young when . . . well, you know, with the fire."

Daisy's eyes lowered, and her fingers picked absently at the orange cloth of her chair. "When my parents died," she finally murmured.

"Our parents," Liv said gently.

"So you don't consider the Ratners to be your parents?" Shannon asked. Liv shot her a warning glare. But Daisy only shrugged.

"They are when they're here, I guess." She flipped her hair then, as if she'd just made the most casual statement in the world. As if she'd spent years practicing the exact motions needed to come across as a jaded child of movie stars.

At that moment, Merek pulled what looked like a block of tofu out of the refrigerator. "Should I even ask what this is? Honestly, how many types of food do you have in this realm?"

"Realm?" Daisy asked, looking between them. She looked over at Liv. "Are you, like, part of some weird cult? Because Mike and Shana are already raising me as a vegan atheist . . ."

Liv shifted uncomfortably in her seat. "We're not a cult. We actually came here because I have to tell you something important." Liv looked around the room, her nerve slipping by the second. "Basically, we think you might be in danger."

"Sounds like something a cult member would say." Daisy raised an eyebrow at Liv.

"No, Daisy. Liv is telling the truth," Cedric added.

Daisy's round cheeks reddened briefly when Cedric spoke her name, but she covered with another hasty hair flip.

Liv took in a deep breath, unsure, once again, of where to start. "It's about our . . . tattoos," she said. "They make us special, sort of. We were born with them."

"Born with them?" Daisy asked, eyebrows furrowing. "That doesn't make any sense. My parents told me an old nanny gave me the tattoo. She was deported immediately, of course. We've tried to have it removed, but . . ."

"But you couldn't. Your parents lied to you," Liv said. "Or maybe they just saw the marking and assumed your nanny gave it to you. But she didn't. You were born with it."

"You can't be born with a tattoo."

"We were. And it's not *really* a tattoo."

Daisy just shook her head. "That's crazy."

"Yes, but it's also true. And it's not just us. Cedric here is special, too. In a different way." Liv turned to Cedric. "Maybe you can show her?"

He smiled. "Are you sure?"

"Seeing is believing."

Cedric stood up from the couch and extended his hand to Daisy. She grinned and took it, then hopped up from her chair. Cedric led her over to a large, sliding glass door at the back of the kitchen, one that looked out over the tennis courts.

"Do you see that ball there?" Cedric asked, pointing through the window into the backyard.

Daisy squinted in the direction he was pointing, finally spotting a yellow tennis ball a few hundred feet away. "Yeah?"

"Keep an eye on it."

Without waiting for a response, Cedric opened the door,

braced himself, and then raced across the yard. Like when he was fighting, he moved with a speed that was faster than human. Just outside the realm of belief.

In the space of a breath, Cedric was back in the doorway. He held the bright yellow tennis ball up to Daisy.

Her eyes widened, but she stood her ground. "So you're really fast? That's the big thing you had to show me?"

"He's more than really fast," Liv said. She bit her lip—this wasn't working. It had taken her not one, but two near-death experiences before she'd believed Cedric's story. How could she expect any different from Daisy?

"Cedric isn't like regular people," she said. "I'm going to tell you some things. More things that are crazy, but also true."

Before Daisy could interject, Liv took a deep breath and started talking. She wanted to be as open with her sister as possible, and started her story the way it had begun for her—at the side of the LA River. She explained meeting Cedric, learning about who he was and where he was from, and then discovering the truth about the scrolls. When she reached the story of the night of the Knights—with some light editing, of course—she tried to stress the extent of danger they were all in.

When Liv was finished talking, Daisy just stared at her, fingers once again twitching, this time at a loose strand of thread at the bottom of her tank top. Nervous, Liv waited and watched for her sister's reaction.

But instead of responding to Liv, Daisy's eyes slid to Cedric. "So you have actual superpowers?"

"Daisy—" Liv started, leaning forward.

Daisy ignored her, still intent on Cedric. "You do, you have superpowers. You're, like, an Avenger or something. That's so hot."

"Uh . . ." Cedric looked to Liv for help.

"Did you hear that last part? About how people are searching for us? Dangerous people. And other . . . things. And you might not be safe staying here, especially not if you're by yourself."

Daisy gave a dismissive wave of her hand. "This is the safest place in the world. You saw the guards out front. I could call for more whenever I want."

Liv tried not to sound exasperated. "But the creatures and the people who are after you, they'll be stronger than those guards. And faster, too."

"Faster than him?" Daisy asked, nodding in Cedric's direction.

"Well . . . no," Liv responded.

"Then it sounds like as long as he stays here, I'll be safe." Daisy grinned.

Shannon smothered a laugh. Liv looked to Cedric for help. Before he could respond, though, Liv's phone rang.

"Joe." Liv sighed, looking at the screen. She couldn't leave Joe hanging, not at a time like this. "I have to take it."

"Joe who?" Daisy asked.

"My . . . I guess, *our* caseworker."

Daisy's eyes widened. "I remember Joe!"

"How do you remember Joe and not—never mind." Liv shook her head and answered the phone.

"Liv, are you okay?" Joe's voice sounded far away.

"Yeah, I'm okay. We all are."

"Good. I'm almost to Fresno. Just wanted to check in—"

"Can I talk to him?" Daisy popped up by Liv's elbow and reached for her phone. Liv dodged away.

"Who's that?" Joe asked.

"I haven't seen him since I was little, I want to talk to him," Daisy said, her voice bordering on a whine.

"Liv," Joe said, his tone serious. "What did you do?"

"Um . . ."

"Is that Daisy?"

Daisy reached for the phone again, and Liv tried to spin away. This time, Daisy was faster. She plucked the phone from Liv's hand and pranced across the kitchen.

"Joe! Do you remember me?"

Liv couldn't hear what Joe was saying, only Daisy's side of the conversation.

"What? . . . Oh, pretty good. . . . No, they're out of town right now. . . . Yeah, that's what she said. . . . She's really my sister? . . . I guess, but I think she might have some real mental probs . . ."

Daisy went quiet for a while, listening. Then she held the phone back to Liv. "He wants to talk to you. He sounds kind of mad."

Liv took her phone back. "Joe, give me a chance to explain—"

"Oh, you better."

Liv took a few steps away from the group and lowered her voice.

"When I found out she was still in town, I had to see her.

She deserves to know she might be in danger."

"She's a thirteen-year-old girl, Liv."

"She's . . . mature for her age. Plus, if I had known the truth at thirteen, maybe I would've been a little more prepared for all this."

Joe sighed.

"She's all alone here. I mean, she has security, but . . . she's alone."

There was a pause. "And you're going to stay with her until I get back?" Joe asked.

Liv cast a look to Cedric, knowing he wouldn't be pleased with that idea. "Yes."

Another pause. "Good. I'm almost to Fresno now. I'll try to talk Peter into coming with me, and we'll hopefully be back in LA first thing in the morning. Just . . . stay there. Stay together."

"I will."

After Liv hung up with Joe, she turned around to face the others.

"Looks like we might need to stay here tonight."

Daisy looked to Cedric and grinned. "Sounds good to me."

"Your parents won't mind?" Liv asked.

"Don't see how they'd even find out. Most of the family's in Nicaragua. Or maybe Nepal . . . except for my older sisters—they're at boarding school, and the baby's with the nanny in Texas. No one'll know you're here, except for Andre and Tim, and they do what I say."

Daisy's attitude made Liv uneasy, but at least she was okay with them sticking around. For now. "So we stay."

Merek, still standing by the refrigerator, bit into a celery stick and shrugged. Cedric, however, looked less thrilled.

"I know it wasn't the original plan," Liv said to him. "But we can call Kat and let her know to meet us here when she's done. It's just one more night."

"One night," Cedric repeated, though his eyes were still blazing. Liv gave him a weak smile.

"One night in a Beverly Hills mansion. I mean, think of what we can do!" Shannon said. There was a long pause as everyone stared at her. She turned to Daisy. "I mean . . . what *can* we do?"

Daisy shrugged. "We can order Thai food."

"Now that sounds like a fine plan," Merek said, his mouth full.

Cedric scoffed. "Food is not a plan. But of *course* you are only capable of thinking about your stomach at a time like this."

Merek's eyes narrowed, and Liv felt a twinge of guilt that Cedric was taking his frustrations with her out on Merek instead. Especially because Merek didn't seem to realize that's what was happening.

"You," Merek said, his voice dropping low, "have no idea what I am capable of."

"Okay," Liv said loudly, before Merek and Cedric continued to snipe at each other. "Maybe we'll get food later." She turned to Cedric. "For now, the *new* plan is to wait here until we hear from Kat and Joe. And it wouldn't hurt to stay busy while we wait."

Daisy yawned. "I've got the new PlayStation."

"Sweet," Shannon said, standing up.

"What is a PlayStation?" Merek asked, putting another hunk of food in his mouth.

Shannon grinned. "Oh, man. We are about to change your whole life."

THE COMPLICATION

While Shannon and Daisy showed Merek how to shoot two-dimensional zombies, Liv sat anxiously in the living room. Cedric had been out "scouting the perimeter" of the backyard ever since he'd called Kat to explain they were staying the night. Apparently Kat hadn't taken the change of plans all that well. But she hadn't yet found a single wrath, so she agreed to join them in Beverly Hills for the night and try again the next day.

Liv then spent two minutes getting an Uber for Kat, plus another ten minutes explaining to Kat—mostly unsuccessfully—how Uber worked. If Kat showed up at the mansion at all, it would be a miracle.

Liv got up from Daisy's game room, looking for a few minutes of peace to clear her mind. But as she walked out of the kitchen door and onto Daisy's expansive back porch, the frantic thoughts tumbling through her brain refused to go away.

She wondered whether or not they would be safe for the night. And if they were, what about tomorrow? Would they be safe for the week, the year, ever? Even if Cedric was able to take care of Malquin, the Knights would still be after her. Would she be on the run, always, because of some stupid symbols on her skin?

Being outside didn't help Liv answer any of these questions, but she did find she could breathe a bit easier in the night air. A strong breeze lifted her hair off her neck—the first of the Santa Ana winds kicking off the end of a sticky hot summer. Liv made her way over to a stone bench that was propped against the wall of the house and sat down.

"Sorry to disturb."

Liv glanced up to the edge of the brick patio, where Cedric was standing in the doorway, looking at her.

"If you want to be alone . . ."

"It's okay," Liv said, and scooted over on her bench. Cedric crossed the distance between them in three quick strides and sat down. Liv noticed that he kept a decent amount of space between them. Still, they were alone together for the first time in hours.

Liv's insides tightened. She hated how when she was around Cedric, her body felt completely outside of her control. Being near him made her feel like she was spinning around in circles, arms outstretched, but she couldn't find anything to hold on to to make it all stop.

"Seems like Merek is getting the hang of things here . . . getting used to things, I mean," Liv said, trying to keep her voice light.

"Three months of moaning and he has finally found

something in this world he can appreciate," Cedric said with a wry smile.

"Violent video games. Who would have thought?" She took a deep breath and looked sideways. "Speaking of which . . . on a level from zero to fake zombie maiming, exactly how angry with me are you right now?"

Cedric was quiet for a moment. Then he said, "I wish I *was* angry with you."

When Liv didn't answer, Cedric continued in a softer voice. "It would be easier if I hated you. Or even if I felt nothing for you at all. Then all I would have to think about is the fastest way to get home, even if . . ."

"Even if it meant tying me up in one place until it was time to use me to open a portal?"

Cedric shook his head quickly. "I would never do that." He turned to her then, and his hands were balled up into fists resting on his knees, like he was forcing them to stay still. "But I also would not be here, jeopardizing what is best for my own people if . . . if I did not care so much about what happened to you."

Part of Liv wanted to avert her eyes, to hide whatever emotions were visible there. With real effort, she turned to look at Cedric instead. There was little light on the porch, but his eyes shone from beneath the purplish shadow of his dark hair.

"You do?"

"I cannot stop myself from thinking about you. About whether you are in danger, or in pain, or upset. About whether you think of me . . ."

As Cedric spoke, Liv could feel herself tensing up with excitement—and with fear. What he said now couldn't be taken back, and if he kept talking, he'd be pulling her across an invisible barrier they'd only barely walked up to before. They'd almost crossed it in the motel, but he hadn't spoken to her like this since that night.

There was good reason to pull back—so many good reasons—but Liv didn't want to. She wanted Cedric to keep talking them both all the way through the barrier until they fell through the other side, together.

She was suddenly very conscious of her breathing, and her breath, and of the stale cookies she'd just eaten from Daisy's cupboard.

Very slowly, as if afraid he might scare her away with any sudden movements, Cedric reached out his hand and carefully brushed his fingers against Liv's temple, then ran them down the side of her face until they ended at her jaw.

"You are like nothing I have ever known," he whispered. His eyes traveled over her face, from the bridge of her nose to her cheeks to her eyes and back again.

Liv's first instinct was to crack a joke to ease the unbearable tension growing between them. But she was tired of jokes. She was tired of talking at all.

Cedric's eyes focused on hers again, and then he was moving closer, closer, his hand resting on her neck now. She could see his eyelids dropping, and his lips as his mouth drew nearer and nearer to hers.

Then he was kissing her, first slowly, and then completely,

with one hand still on the back of her neck and the other reaching to her waist.

Liv's whole body felt fizzy, soft around the edges. And then Cedric's hands were running gently along her neck, the rough skin of his fingers drawing little invisible lines that made the small hairs there rise up, up, up.

She leaned into him, deepening the kiss and letting out a small sigh when it went from gentle to something more. Cedric gripped her harder. She ran her hand down the length of his chest, her fingers playing at the hem of his shirt. She carefully lifted it, hand shaking just a little, and let her hands run over the flat edge of his stomach there.

Cedric made a low noise and leaned forward more still, and then they were both falling until Liv landed with her back against the hard stone of the bench, with Cedric on top of her. His lips stopped moving for a moment and he pulled away just a few inches, and Liv knew without opening her eyes that he was checking to see if she was okay. But there was no need to respond, they were beyond words now, and she reached up hungrily and pulled his head back down toward hers.

Their bodies pressed against each other while their legs draped lazily down to the concrete ground. Liv was completely lost in him, in his mouth and his ragged breathing and his hands that ran from her shoulders, down her arms, and to her hips. She didn't know what would come next, but she didn't want to stop. She couldn't believe that this was happening, that this was Cedric and it was her and this was real. . . .

Cedric moved down to kiss her neck, and as he did so she

felt something tiny, cold, and hard fall against the skin just above her collarbone.

For a moment, Liv closed her eyes even tighter, willfully ignoring the small, circular thing that pressed deeper into her skin. But she knew what it was; she had known the second it fell against her, and ignoring it wouldn't work for long.

The warmth in Liv's insides faded away, and for the first time she really felt the hard stone bench beneath her, pressing into her shoulder blades. She put her hands against Cedric's shoulders and lightly pushed him away.

It took him longer to realize what had happened. He pulled back a few inches, his eyes confused, and then he saw it. His betrothal ring, dangling on a chain between them.

"It fell," Liv said. Her voice came out sounding smaller than she had intended.

Cedric's eyes were fixed on the ring. Then, with one swift, sure movement, he pulled himself up and off Liv, all the way into a standing position at the side of the bench. Farther away than she could reach. She could still feel the warmth of his skin on hers.

"I—I am sorry," Cedric said. She couldn't meet his eyes. "I did not mean—"

But that was too much; that was the worst possible thing for him to say. Liv held up one hand and shook her head, trying and failing to smile. She stood up from the bench and straightened her shirt. The space between them felt enormous; an entire parade could have marched through it, with her on one side and him on the other.

"I should get back inside," she finally said.

Cedric nodded, but stayed rooted to his spot. Looking at him hurt her eyes.

Liv turned around and walked back inside while making as little sound as possible. Once the door was closed, she stood in the middle of the kitchen and tried to catch her breath.

It wasn't so hard to do now.

"What the hell happened to you out there?"

Shannon had taken one step into the kitchen, seen the look on Liv's face, and without a word, dragged her by the elbow into the nearest bathroom. Her hand was still tight on Liv's arm, her eyes worried.

"Wh-what do you mean?" Liv stammered, trying to act casual.

"I mean, you're all flushed and weird-looking," Shannon said. "Are you okay? Did you see something out there, or—" Shannon stopped talking as Liv pursed her lips together and shook her head. Shannon's mouth curled into a smirk, and she raised one eyebrow. "Or maybe it was something else entirely?" she finished.

Liv thought about denying it, but she suddenly didn't have the energy to lie. She looked down at the pristine bathroom tiles, then back to Shannon. "Cedric kissed me," she said.

Shannon's eyes widened, and she started to grin.

"And then I kissed him," Liv continued. "And then there was . . . more kissing."

Shannon's fingernails tapped lightly on Liv's arm. "For how long?"

"For a while."

"And?"

"And . . ."

"Oh please, you are *not* holding out on me. What was it like to kiss an alien?"

Liv smiled despite herself and rolled her eyes. "He's not an alien."

Shannon shrugged. "Whatever. What was it like?"

Liv flashed back to an image of herself and Cedric on the bench. She wasn't sure how to put it in words . . .

"That good, huh?" Shannon smirked.

"It really was. And then . . ." Liv trailed off, the smile dropping from her face.

"Ugh." Shannon rolled her eyes and grabbed Liv by the shoulders. "Why do you make me drag things out of you? Just tell me what happened."

Haltingly, Liv explained to Shannon about Cedric's ring and what it meant, and how once it became a real and visible thing between them, it was impossible to ignore.

Shannon crossed her arms over her chest. "So? So what if he's getting married at some far-off, future date? He's clearly into you *now*."

"I don't know. I think he was about to say that he didn't mean for it to happen—the kiss. I think he regretted it . . . and I can't just forget about Kat," Liv replied, her eyes on the bathroom tiles. "I mean, she's going to be his wife someday. And also, have you seen her?"

"Kat? I mean, she's okay-looking," Shannon said with an unconvincing shrug.

Liv smiled. "You don't have to do that best friend thing where you lie and tell me a girl's not pretty when she clearly is. I mean, have you seen her skin? I bet it would even look good in HD. Plus, she and Cedric have this whole past, not to mention a future, and she's also a *literal ninja,* and I'm just . . ."

Shannon put one hand flat in the air. "All right, stop right there. Number one, you're obviously awesome, or else I wouldn't be your friend. So that's not your problem. And number two, I don't think Kat's your problem, either."

"Really." Liv remembered how the betrothal ring had felt on her skin. How cold the metal was, like it knew it didn't belong anywhere near her.

"Really. The problem is you." Shannon leaned back on her heels, head tilted, as if daring Liv to make her continue. Liv took the bait.

"Me? What happened to me being awesome? You just said it, like, four seconds ago."

"You are awesome, except about this one thing, where you can kind of suck."

"I have no idea what you're talking about."

"Did you tell Cedric how you felt? About kissing him, about the betrothal ring? Did you talk about it at all?"

"Um . . ."

"It was a hypothetical question. I already know the answer."

Liv could feel her cheeks flame. "I'm pretty sure he knows how I feel."

Shannon shrugged. "Maybe. It's possible reading minds is one of his superpowers. But on the off chance it isn't, you're going to have to do the hard work of saying it out loud. Which I know you hate."

"I don't—"

"Please. Getting you to open up about anything other than camera angles and box office figures is a miracle most days. I mean, it's obvious to *me* that you're into him, but that's only because I've known you for years. He might need you to spell it out. Open up."

"I've opened up to plenty of people, including Cedric," Liv said, without thinking.

"So I'm wrong? You've told him how you feel? About him?"

Liv crossed her arms tightly over her chest and tried to go back over what had happened with Cedric over the past few days. She was sure he knew how she felt—it was obvious, wasn't it? Except she couldn't remember actually saying the words to him. Not on the stone bench, not in the motel room, not in the car. Not ever.

"I don't know why, but I think I'm . . . afraid. To say it out loud," she finally said.

Shannon nodded, as if that was obvious. "Yeah, I know." She leaned in close, and very gently, she pulled Liv's arms apart and away from her chest. "The thing is, though . . . so is everyone else."

Liv couldn't think of a single thing to say. Shannon reached over and opened the bathroom door.

"So why not go tell him now? The words will come. Just try to get it all out there before the making-out part starts up again, okay? It confuses the brain."

Liv grinned. "Thanks, Shan. I know you'll probably be grounded till graduation, but I'm really glad you're here."

"Me too."

Liv stepped out into the kitchen. She could talk to Cedric about her feelings. How hard could it be?

But when Liv looked through the glass kitchen door, she could no longer see Cedric on the porch. She turned to rejoin the others, but the monitors on the wall caught her eye.

On the screens, Liv could see various parts of Daisy's yard, now lit up with greenish lights. One screen showed the tennis courts, another highlighted the front of a four-car garage. But it was the middle screen that drew Liv's attention. She moved closer to it, her eyes scanning it over. With each step, she hoped that what she was seeing was a mistake. A trick of the light.

On the middle screen was the guard hut. And at the entrance to the hut was a small, indistinct mass. A grayish, unmoving blob. Liv moved to stand right in front of the screen, her nose inches from it. The blob had arms, and legs in dark pants. It was one of the security guards, knocked out—or maybe, Liv thought, stomach dropping, maybe worse—on the ground.

"Shannon!" Liv called, her voice tight. After a moment, Shannon's head popped back into the kitchen, her face falling when she saw Liv.

"Someone's here."

THE ENEMY AT THE GATE

Cedric sat at the top of a large staircase inside Daisy's home, lightly spinning the ring around the chain on his neck. He knew he should go and check on the others, make sure Merek was staying put, see if Liv—

Liv.

He couldn't afford to think about her right now, because once he started, he wouldn't stop. And that was really the whole problem. He didn't want to think about facing her again, and he had no idea what he might say if he did. His fingers pulled tighter and tighter on the chain, until the hard metal ate into the skin on the back of his neck.

Cedric heard a yell coming from behind him. Torn from his thoughts, he jumped up and immediately moved through the confusing hallways of the house toward the sound of the noise.

He found Liv and Shannon in the kitchen, looking at the wall. Or no, they weren't looking at the wall, but at a series of rectangles placed there—*teevees,* he remembered they were called.

"What is it?"

Liv looked to him, and her eyes were huge. "Someone took out the guards."

"Took out?"

Liv shook her head, flustered, and just pointed to the screen. On one, Cedric could see the small image of a man lying on the ground.

Merek and Daisy burst into the kitchen at that moment.

"What's going on?" Daisy asked.

"We have to lock all the doors. And call . . ." Liv looked to Cedric. "Who should we call?"

Cedric immediately went to the giant glass door in the kitchen and looked out into the night. He could see nothing but shadows and trees.

"Wait. What's happening?" Daisy asked again, her voice pitched higher. Then she looked at the screen, and her hand flew to her mouth. "Is that . . . Andre?"

"We need to secure the yard," Cedric said, his hand on the door handle.

Liv stepped toward him. "Wait! We don't even know if we're facing wraths or Knights! And what if they're just waiting for us to come outside, so they can attack?"

"Or," Shannon said, voice shaky, "what if they're already inside?"

Everyone fell silent. Unconsciously, their heads moved up, down, and all around, as if they could see through the walls and ceiling. Merek moved to the doorway opposite and peered into the hallway. A creaking noise sounded out from the room to the right, and everyone jumped.

Cedric went quickly to where his sword was still resting by a chair. He ripped off the plastic covering and held the hilt close.

"Daisy, were any doors unlocked?" Liv asked. "Daisy?"

But Daisy's eyes were glued to the screen, to the image of the unmoving guard. Suddenly, she whirled on Liv.

"What did you do?"

Liv took a step back, surprised by Daisy's ferocity. "Wh-what?"

"What do you want with me? Why are you doing this?"

Liv shook her head, at a loss for words. Cedric moved cautiously toward Daisy, who jumped back from him as though he were brandishing fire. "We do not want to harm you," he said, trying to keep his voice calm. "But we are all in danger—"

Daisy's eyes drifted down toward his sword.

"Oh God," she murmured. "Oh God, oh God." She backed up until her shoulders hit the wall.

"Daisy," Liv said, shaking herself into action. "We weren't the ones who hurt the guard. We've been here the whole time."

"No, you weren't!" Daisy yelled. She looked between Liv and Cedric. "You left, you went outside and . . ." She looked to the screen again.

"I promise we didn't do this," Liv said. "Remember, I explained everything earlier? Remember what I said, about the wraths and the Knights—"

"But none of that is real!" Daisy screamed. "I didn't *actually* believe you!"

"But . . . Joe, he told you I was telling the truth, didn't he? Don't you believe him?"

For a moment, Daisy wavered. Then her eyes landed again on Cedric's sword. "You lied. You said that was a camera stand and . . . oh. Oh God."

"Wait . . ." Liv reached for Daisy then, but Daisy dodged her outstretched hand, pushed off against the wall, and sailed past Merek, down the hallway. In seconds, she was streaming out the front door of the house.

"No!" Liv yelled. She turned to Cedric. "We don't know what's out there!"

Cedric nodded once, briefly, before setting off after Daisy. Liv followed, though he outpaced her easily. When he reached the front door, he saw Daisy's small frame move across the lawn, arms pumping, running toward the body of the guard near the gate.

"Daisy, wait!" he yelled, then immediately cursed himself for giving away his position to whoever had "taken out" the guards.

But it didn't matter anyway. They were already waiting.

Just as Daisy bent down to the motionless guard, a hulking figure stepped out of the dense bushes near the guard hut. A wrath, with a shock of gray-white hair and thick shoulders that looked like someone had just attached slabs of rock to each side of his neck. Cedric recognized him from the alley—Chath. The white-haired wrath lifted Daisy off the ground in a single swift movement.

Daisy gave a small scream—more a yelp of surprise—before the wrath turned and ran with her toward the edge of the yard, into a thicket of bushes and trees.

Cedric shot off toward the pair. He could barely feel the

ground and could only make out the blurred edges of trees as he passed. Ahead of him, he saw the wrath pull Daisy up and over a fence. Cedric followed and pitched himself over the fence, landing in the center of still more trees. They seemed to be part of a private garden that wove in and around itself.

"Daisy?" he yelled out. He was surrounded by trees and shadows and blackness.

"If you want her, come and take her," a low voice said from just to his right.

Cedric turned toward the direction of the voice and spotted Chath and Daisy, the wrath with one hand over her mouth, underneath a tree with gnarled, twisting branches.

A knot of uncertainty tightened in Cedric's stomach. How had the wraths known to find them here? How could they have been following all this time? Cedric held his sword out in front of him, prepared to use it. The wrath didn't even flinch, but instead let out a long, low whistle.

"Let her go," Cedric said.

Chath threw his head back and laughed toward the night sky. "Threatening me? The little warrior prince with his pointy play toy. All alone in the woods, threatening me."

Cedric tightened his grip on the sword hilt and took a step toward the wrath.

"Put her down, or I'll show you what a toy can do."

It was then that Cedric noticed the shadows around the edges of the clearing start to move. Dark shapes morphed into arms and legs and heads as they came into the light of the clearing. The blacks of the wraths' sunken eyes were lost in the shadows but low growls escaped from their throats. Three extra wraths emerged from the trees, two at Cedric's sides and one more cutting off the exit at his back. He was surrounded.

"Why don't you show them first?" Chath said.

"How did you find us?" Cedric asked, trying to buy himself time to think. He hoped that Merek had stayed in the house with Shannon and Liv. He hoped they'd found a way to hide.

Chath cocked his head. "Does Your Highness not like his first taste of betrayal?"

Cedric narrowed his eyes. "You lie. No one has betrayed me."

Chath's grin split wider—impossibly wide. He looked less human with every second. "If you say so, Highness."

He's trying to confuse you, Cedric thought, gritting his teeth. But something in the back of his mind caught on that word—betrayal—and didn't let go. His thoughts kept snagging there, like cloth on a tree branch.

The wrath on his right shifted forward, and Cedric lashed out, turning on the ball of his foot and swinging his sword. It connected with the creature, who let out a howl of pain and gripped his shoulder, falling to the ground.

The other two wraths advanced on Cedric at once. He whirled around and struck out at the female wrath approaching from behind. She dodged at the last second, twirling away from the edge of the sword as it sliced down.

Arcing his sword arm back up, Cedric repositioned himself against the wiry wrath whose black eyes bulged out of his small-sized head. The wrath carried his own sword, one that was at least twice as long as Cedric's. He grinned as he lunged with it toward Cedric's midsection.

Cedric swung his sword to meet the wrath's. When they hit, reverberations moved up Cedric's arm, and he gritted his teeth. The wrath with the sword was stronger than he appeared.

A small, strangled sound came from the edge of the cluster of trees, and Cedric looked up to see Daisy struggling against Chath. The wrath moved calmly away, carrying Daisy with him.

"Stop!" Without looking behind him at Chath's friends, Cedric ran toward Daisy across the lawn. The wrath stopped when he reached a row of tall, sparse bushes that stood in a line. Through them, Cedric could see what appeared to be a street. How far had they run? Daisy's green eyes, so much like Liv's, looked around in terror. Chath smiled as Cedric approached, sword out.

The wrath tightened his grip on Daisy, and she let out a panicked, choking noise. Cedric advanced with his sword pointed out, inches from the wrath's face. Chath didn't even flinch.

"As long as I am alive, you will never take her," Cedric said, breathing heavy. "And a handful of wraths will not be able to kill me."

Chath's black eyes suddenly lit up with color, first reflecting bright red, then bright blue. Flashing lights, getting bigger and bigger, brighter and brighter, until they caught on the surrounding tree trunks and bushes as well. Looking down, Cedric saw the colored flashes on his own skin, lighting it up first blue, then red, then blue again.

The wrath grinned. "Who said anything about killing you?"

THE PANIC AND THE TERROR

By the time Liv got outside, both Daisy and Cedric were nowhere to be seen. She scanned the front yard fruitlessly for a few moments with Shannon, while Merek went to search the back.

Liv felt more and more panicked as she searched through the shadowy spaces of the front lawn. She knelt down to check on the fallen guard. His left arm was twisted underneath him at an odd angle, and a trickle of blood ran from a cut somewhere above his hairline. She reached a shaking hand over to check his pulse, and found a slow beat.

She exhaled in relief. But where was the other guard? And Daisy? As Liv looked around in the dark, her eyes were caught on the approaching red and blue lights of a police cruiser. The car stopped a few hundred yards down the road from Daisy's property, and Liv's first thought was, *Thank God, the police.*

She ignored her second thought, which was, *Who called them?*

Shannon joined Liv, and without a word, the two ran past

the guard hut and the now-open front gate and continued quickly toward the police car. With the headlights still shining in her eyes, Liv couldn't make out the expressions of the officers behind the windshield.

The two cops didn't seem to be focused on her, though. Instead, they both got out of the car and headed toward the line of shrubbery that guarded the property of one of Daisy's wealthy neighbors. Before they reached the edge of the road, though, a figure came flying through the bushes, as if it had been thrown. In the flashing lights from the top of the police car, Liv saw the figure was Daisy. Someone else came crashing after her with almost as much force. Cedric.

Daisy hit the pavement, and Cedric knelt over her, head bent down.

"Son," a voice boomed out across the night. Liv jumped as one of the officers, a mustached man who looked slightly too large for his snug uniform, approached Cedric with his arm outstretched. He held something small and dark in his hand. "Step away from the girl, now."

Cedric looked up, confused. He blinked rapidly in the lights. Tears streamed down Daisy's face.

"Step. Away. From the girl," the cop repeated.

The harshness in the cop's voice threw Liv for a moment, until she saw the metal in Cedric's gripped hand. His sword hung down like an extension of his arm, and Liv could see even from several feet away how sharp its edges were as they glinted in the headlights.

Cedric slowly stood up. In an instant, Liv saw how the

situation must look to the cops—a boy with a weapon chasing a girl through a quiet, dark, and superwealthy neighborhood. And even she had to admit that beneath Cedric's confusion, his face was all anger. His eyes blazed in the swirling blue and red lights.

He looked frightening.

"Put the weapon down," the mustached cop repeated. "This is your only warning."

Belatedly, Cedric looked down at the sword in his hand. His grip loosened, and Liv felt sure he was going to release it. But then his head swiveled rapidly to the woods behind him, as though he had suddenly heard a noise there. His eyes searched through the darkness, his chest heaved, and his grip tightened on his sword hilt once again.

The mustached officer raised his other arm to meet the extended one. He wrapped both fists around the small black object Liv had noticed before. This time, Liv realized what it was.

"Cedric, please. Drop the sw—"

But she was too late. Liv didn't see the cop pull the trigger, and she didn't see the current of electricity as it left the stun gun and traveled across the few feet of pavement and into Cedric's chest. She could only see Cedric stiffen all over as his head snapped backward. The sword finally dropped from his fingers as he fell to his knees, then continued to pitch forward. He landed face-first on the street with a crack.

Liv screamed with a force that frightened even her.

The mustached cop made his way toward Cedric's still jerking figure on the ground, while the second officer came and put a strong hand on Liv's shoulder.

"You're okay now," he said in an oddly soft voice. Looking up into the officer's face, Liv saw that he was only a few years older than she was. Tufts of baby-fine hair stuck out from beneath his cap.

"Don't hurt him," Liv said, her words coming out in a tumble. "He's not dangerous, he's my friend. He's . . ."

The mustached officer said something into his walkie-talkie that Liv couldn't quite catch, though she caught the word "apprehended." A squawking voice replied, "Copy."

The officer hooked the walkie-talkie back into his belt and bent toward Cedric. He picked up Cedric's limp arms and put handcuffs around his wrists before lifting him up off the ground. Cedric's legs and arms drooped down out of the officer's grip, and his head flopped back as he was lifted.

"What are you doing? Where are you taking him?" Liv took a few steps toward Cedric, but was pulled back by a pair of arms. One arm belonged to the young officer who had just tried to calm her, the other to Shannon.

"He'll be fine, miss," the young officer said. "The effects of the Taser are temporary. He'll probably be awake before we get to the station."

"The station? But, but . . . he has rights . . ." Liv tried to think of the perfect words to say, the single line of *Law & Order* dialogue that would somehow get them all out of this . . . but her mind was blank.

The mustached cop pulled open the backseat of the police cruiser and lowered Cedric inside, then slammed the door. Liv could no longer see Cedric's face through the tinted glass.

Daisy made her way slowly to where Liv and Shannon were standing. In the flashing police lights, her movements looked jerky and off-kilter, like one of her video game zombies.

The mustached cop approached. "I'm Officer Bartley, this is Officer Cooper," he said, pointing to the young cop. He pulled out a small pad of paper and a pen from his pocket. "Can you tell me what happened here tonight?"

Before Liv could respond, Daisy mumbled something, low.

"What was that?" Officer Bartley asked.

But Daisy didn't look to the officer. Instead, she turned to Liv. "The man came after me . . . he had . . . he had all-black eyes, just like you said . . . I couldn't get away."

Liv's breath caught. Not Knights, then. Wraths.

"You're okay now," the officer said. "We've got him."

"No you don't," Daisy said, her voice bordering on a yell. Liv moved toward her, instinctively.

"You have the wrong person," Liv said. "A . . . man attacked my sister—"

"More than one," Daisy put in. Her words sent a chill up Liv's spine, and she peered into the shadows of the surrounding yard.

The young cop, Cooper, turned to his partner. "I'll go check the area."

"Wait!" Liv yelled. Officer Cooper stopped and looked at her. She thought again of the officer in the alley outside of the museum. The one who'd been thrown against a brick wall by a wrath, as easily as a child might throw a toy.

"They're dangerous," Liv said. She wanted to stop him, but how could she tell the cop he was surrounded by monsters without getting locked up in a psych ward for the night?

Officer Cooper only paused a moment before heading through the shrubs.

Bartley ushered the girls to stand in front of the car, near the side of the road. If Liv couldn't stop the cops, she at least had to try and get Cedric out of that car. Then they could all get in the house, lock the doors, and . . . what? Her mind whirled.

"You have to let Cedric go," Liv repeated. "He didn't do anything wrong."

Bartley looked at her, impassive. "The young man in the car, how well do you know him?"

"Very," Liv said, without hesitation.

"Do you know that he's wanted for questioning in connection to an assault on a police officer? And you saw that he was armed?"

"But that's . . ." Liv started. But how could she explain? "He was protecting my sister."

"With an eighteen-inch blade?"

"He had to! That man had claws!" Daisy yelled.

Officer Bartley looked from Daisy to Liv. "Have you kids been drinking tonight?"

"No," Liv responded.

Daisy scoffed. She crossed her arms and looked at the officer with contempt. "Are you calling me a liar? Do you even know who my parents are?"

The officer was unfazed. "No, but I think it's a good idea to get them involved. Do you live here?"

"There," Daisy said, pointing at her mansion next door. "But my parents are out of the country."

Liv inwardly groaned. There was no way the cop was just going to leave them here by themselves. Would he take them to the station, with Cedric? Maybe that was the best plan. . . .

"Is there any adult home that I can talk to?" Bartley asked.

Daisy's eyes widened, as if she'd just remembered something. "Andre! You have to help Andre. He's my guard, and he's hurt . . ."

Daisy started pulling on Bartley's arm then, leading him over to her front gate. Liv looked once more at the cop car, but still couldn't see Cedric through the all-black windows. She turned and followed Daisy and the officer, with Shannon just behind. But when they reached the section of street before the open front gate, Daisy came to an abrupt stop. The injured guard was nowhere to be seen.

"He was . . . he was right here," Liv said, looking to the officer. For a moment, she wondered if the guard had managed to pull himself away.

Officer Bartley's eyebrows rose up. "Why don't we get inside? I'll call the station—"

A figure emerged suddenly from behind the hut, but it wasn't the guard. Liv's body pulsed with fear. She reached for Daisy and gripped her arm.

Chath moved slowly closer to the group of them, a smile stretched across the bottom of his face. Even from this distance, in the dark, Liv could see the wrongness of his mouth, with its too many, too sharp teeth.

Officer Bartley didn't seem to see those teeth. Or if he did, he didn't let on. He moved to block Liv, Shannon, and Daisy, and put one hand out toward the advancing wrath.

"Sir, do you live here?" Bartley said.

"I am here for the girls," Chath responded, his grin spreading farther.

Bartley reached for his two-way. "Stop where you are—"

In an instant, Chath raised his hand high and brought it down in a slashing motion toward the officer's chest. Daisy screamed as Bartley stumbled back. Whether or not he could see Chath's thick, clawlike fingernails in the darkness, he could certainly feel them. Before he could reach for his weapon, Chath slashed out again.

And Bartley fell.

"Run," Liv choked out. She managed to get her feet in motion, pulling Daisy and Shannon behind her. Only, she didn't know where to go. Chath was blocking the entrance to the house, and the street was long and dark—they wouldn't make it far before Chath caught up to them. And wherever Officer Cooper was, he wouldn't be able to help them any more than Bartley had.

Then Liv remembered her car, still parked near the hedge that bordered the lawn. She broke into a sprint, pulling the keys from her pocket as she moved. For a moment, she thought of Merek. Was he still in the house, or had the wraths found him? There wasn't time to look.

"Get in, get in!" she yelled, pushing the Unlock button on her key ring. She didn't hear a click over her frantic breathing, but the door opened anyway, and after she jumped inside, she slammed the door behind her. Shannon did the same on the passenger side, and Daisy threw herself into the back. Liv jammed the key into the ignition.

She turned the key. Nothing happened.

"No," she whispered, turning the key again.

"Liv? Now would be a time to get out of here." Shannon's voice was at full screeching capacity.

Chath strode past Liv's side of the car then, his pace deliberate, slow. He stopped right in front of her bumper, looked in through the windshield, and smiled his hideous smile.

Liv turned the key again, and again, her hands shaking. In the backseat, Daisy let out a low, keeling moan. On her fifth try, Liv dropped the keys. When she cast an arm down to pick them up, she felt the wires. Thin, plastic-coated, jagged-edge wires, hanging down below her steering wheel where they should not be. They'd been cut.

"No. No, no, no."

Liv looked up and saw that Chath was not alone. He was flanked on each side by another wrath. And more were coming.

Within seconds, the wraths had surrounded the car. They were close enough for Liv to see their grins as they circled slowly.

The wrath closest to Liv bent down, looked through her window, and smiled.

"We're going to be fine," Liv said, then reached out to grab Shannon's hand. "Everything's going to be fine."

The wrath scratched against the window with a long, dark object—a crowbar.

Shannon squeezed Liv's hand back, but shook her head.

"Liar."

THE LAIR

Liv couldn't move.

She floated in and out of consciousness, switching from disturbing dreams to an even more disturbing reality. For chunks of time, she didn't know which was which.

When she awoke fully it was with a jolt, her body hitting hard against the ground beneath her. Except it wasn't ground, not exactly. Liv felt the surface she rested on rattle slightly as it moved, then stopped, then started again. In her bleary state, she recognized the motion of a car moving over road. She tried to stretch out her cramped legs, but they knocked against a solid wall. Her arms were twisted awkwardly behind her back, the skin of her bound wrists chafing against what felt like cheap carpeting. Her confused mind cleared enough to piece together where she was—in a car trunk.

Liv's mind immediately jumped to the countless school assemblies and movies-of-the-week she'd seen that warned about abduction. She thought of the victimized female characters, usually past-their-prime TV stars slumming it on cable. They'd be bound and gagged and stuffed in trunks, and Liv remembered the grim lessons that followed: Never walk home alone. Never go to a second location. Liv had always secretly scoffed at these trusting, soft-looking actresses, knowing she was too smart to ever wind up like them.

So much for that theory.

Except she hadn't been tricked by a creep in a tan overcoat, she'd been . . . what? Liv tried to think. She'd been in her car with Daisy and Shannon. Daisy and Shannon! Liv twisted around, sending a shock of pain up her arms and across her shoulders. The trunk was too small to move much, but she was able to shift onto her back enough, twist her neck enough, to see behind her. The space was empty. She was alone.

The car suddenly picked up speed, rolling Liv toward the tail end of the trunk. She let out an involuntary gasp as she rolled back onto her side, then felt something hard cut into her thigh. Her phone. It was in her left pants pocket.

Liv struggled at the ties on her wrists, hoping she could maneuver one hand free to retrieve the phone. But they were bound tight with what felt like a cord. The more she struggled, the more the cord cut into her skin. She wanted to scream in frustration, especially as more memories flashed through her mind. Daisy's fingernails scraping against the fabric of the backseat as the wraths pulled her out of the car . . . Shannon's heels hitting the pavement as she tried to get away . . . the single punch she'd thrown at a large, boulder-fisted wrath who'd eventually forced a sweet-smelling white cloth over her mouth . . .

She could feel the car slowing down, making a turn.

Then stopping altogether. A car door slammed, reverberating through the walls of the trunk. After a few sickeningly long moments, she heard a metallic click, and then the lid to the trunk opened slowly.

Twisting her head, Liv could see two wraths standing behind the trunk. The gray-haired one, Chath, and another who was a bit smaller, with a blunted nose.

"Where are my friends?" Liv asked.

"I told you we should gag her," the short one said.

Chath merely shrugged. "Doesn't matter if she screams now. No one will hear her."

Liv looked past the wraths to the giant space behind them. The car was parked indoors, but she couldn't tell how large the room was. Was it a garage? A warehouse? Far above, large fluorescent bulbs hung from steel beams.

Chath leaned down and grabbed her roughly by her right arm. He lifted her up in a way that nearly wrenched her arm from its socket, then hoisted her over his shoulder and started to carry her across the room.

From her vantage point, Liv was able to take in more of the large interior space. Long pieces of wood and various tools lay propped against walls, and a handful of what looked like broken-down or disassembled boats were strewn across the concrete floor.

Chath carried her down a long hallway lined with wooden doors, some closed, some open. Through the open ones, Liv saw wraths. Wraths sitting and standing, laughing and talking, eating sandwiches and staring into space. More than a dozen of them, their low, abrasive voices rising into one indistinguishable din. Chath continued all the way down the hall to the last door. He pushed it open and walked in.

The warehouse room was large and dingy, mostly empty save for some barrels and boxes pushed up against the far walls. There were no other doors leading in or out. A single lightbulb hung down from the ceiling, and the corners were shrouded in darkness.

In the back of the room, Daisy and Shannon were sitting against the metal sheeting of a wall, each of their hands clasped in shackles that were bolted to the floor.

Chath dropped Liv down onto the concrete beside Daisy and Shannon. Liv hit the ground hard and winced in pain.

"Liv!" Shannon called out, scooting across the floor as much as she could. Her clothes were dirty and torn, the right side of her face swollen. Daisy looked relatively unhurt—her hair was a mess of tangles, but there were no cuts or bruises on her face that Liv could see. Liv tried to reach for her, but her arm was wrenched back by Chath, who cut through her rope binds with a long, dirty knife. He held her right arm tightly in one large hand, opened up another rusting shackle, and clamped it down over her wrist. The chain attached to the shackle was only a few feet long, and its other end was cemented to the floor. Liv gave it one sharp tug, knowing even before she felt the resistance that she was secured tight.

Chath laughed. "There's no getting out of that until Malquin says so." He leaned down, his face less than a foot from Liv's. "If you know what's good for you, you will do what Malquin wants, when he wants it."

Liv stared at him, her mouth fixed in a straight line. She still worked her wrist against the metal edge of her shackle. Chath gave a half-smile and stood up. "Only trying to help," he said, turning to leave. He shut the door behind him, leaving the girls alone. Liv heard the sound of three separate locks clicking into place.

"So . . . this is pretty bad," Shannon said.

"Are you okay? Are either of you hurt?"

Daisy shook her head.

"No," Shannon replied. "After I saw what they did to you, I stopped fighting. Some cars drove up to the street, and I saw them put you and Daisy in separate trunks. Then they did the same to me."

"Did they get to Cedric? What about Merek? Or the other officer?"

Shannon looked down. "I didn't even think to look . . . I was so freaked, Liv. . . ."

"It's okay," Liv said, reaching out to Shannon with her free hand. "I get it." As Liv moved, she felt the bulk of her phone in her pocket. She pulled it out. "We still have this, thankfully. Either the wraths didn't see it or were too stupid to take it from me."

"Or they figure there's no one you could call," Shannon said.

Daisy made a slight whimpering noise, and Liv raised her eyebrow at Shannon, who looked sheepish.

"Sorry," Shannon said, "but you saw what happened to that cop. The wrath was so fast, it was like . . . like he didn't even have a chance."

Liv thought of Officer Bartley, and she knew Shannon was

right. If she called 9-1-1, they'd send a couple of squad cars, maybe even three or four if she was convincing enough. But unless the cops showed up with silver bullets, they'd still be no match for the number of the wraths she'd seen in the building.

"There is one person we can call," Liv said, casting a look at the door. "I have to do it fast, before they come back."

She tapped at her phone's screen, and it lit up her face in a bluish tint. She clicked on the maps app and saw the small warehouse they were in was close to Venice Beach.

Liv hesitated a moment, then clicked on the Recent Calls list and pulled up the last number. It was to Kat's disposable phone, from when Cedric had called her at Daisy's house. Liv hit the Call button, and almost immediately, she could hear ringing.

"Please, please pick up," she whispered.

And then, Kat did.

The first noise Liv heard was scoffing. And then muttering.

"Kat? Kat, can you hear me?"

A pause on the other end.

"Hello?" Kat said cautiously.

"Kat. Put the phone closer to your ear. Like I showed you . . ."

Liv heard the light sound of rustling on the other end. And then Kat spoke, and her voice was clear and loud. Liv could hear what sounded like traffic in the background.

"Liv? This person driving said I am near to the address you gave me. Is Cedric there?"

Liv ignored the tightening in her chest, pushed aside the

image of Cedric lying unconscious on the pavement, his body still twitching from electric shock. "I . . . I think so."

"What? What do you mean?"

"We were attacked."

A sharp intake of breath. "Was it wraths?" Kat's usually cool voice rose in panic. Liv struggled not to join in as she quickly explained that the wraths had found them at Daisy's house.

"The police were there, too. They just . . . showed up, even though we didn't call them . . ." Liv's mind bounced over the events of the night. *How* had the police known to come at that exact moment? "I think, somehow, that the wraths were behind it. Maybe they planned for the police to distract Cedric, so they could get to us. It worked, mostly. Last I saw, Cedric was in the back of a squad car at Daisy's. He might be there still, or he might be somewhere here, with us. Merek, too. We're at this place in Venice. It looks like an old boat warehouse, Six Ten Rose Street—"

"I will find Cedric."

"Wait, Kat—"

But the line went dead. Liv sighed—for someone who'd never made a phone call before that afternoon, Kat was quick to master the fast hang-up.

"Is she coming?" Shannon asked.

Liv bit her lip. "I don't know." She pulled against her shackle, even though she knew it would get her nowhere. The chains scraped against the ground.

"Even if she was coming, what good could she do?" Shannon asked. "She may be a superteen, but she's only one superteen.

We need more than that. We need, like, an army."

"Oh my God," Liv murmured. "That's it. Shannon, you're a genius." Liv started typing into the phone.

"Duh. But who are you calling now?"

Liv palmed the phone, bit her lip. "Hopefully? An army."

Shannon craned her head, peering over Liv's shoulder and reading as she typed into the Google search bar.

"UC San Diego has an army?"

THE CAVALRY

The first things Cedric noticed when he opened his eyes were bars—thin, dark, and crisscrossing his vision. The second thing he noticed was that he hurt. Everywhere.

He was lying on a small bench in an enclosed space, he realized. A car. Only it wasn't moving. Through the window above his head, he saw shadows and the night sky. When he sat up, his head rocked with pain.

Cedric's hands were bound in metal circlets. It took him a while to position them correctly so that he might open the car door behind him. But the handle only lifted up and down, without opening anything. The crisscrossed bars acted as a barrier between Cedric and the front of the car. He was stuck. And there were wraths outside. He tried to remember—there had been four of them, some with weapons. He pulled again and again at the door handle, with no results.

A figure lurched toward the car and wrenched open one of the front doors. A young, uniformed man—an officer—who was bleeding badly from the head. The man reached for a square device in the car and brought it to his mouth.

"Officer down, I repeat, officer down. We've got a two-four-five, multiple assailants, request for backup."

The officer panted as he wiped blood from his face.

Cedric pushed against the bars between them, and the officer looked at him, startled.

"There are wraths out there. I can help."

But the square device was talking back now, and the officer pulled his eyes from Cedric to listen to the far-off voices repeating numbers and directions Cedric couldn't understand. The officer's eyes closed as he listened, and he looked unsteady, like he might fall over at any moment.

"Please," Cedric said. "You have to let me out."

The officer once again turned his head toward Cedric. He opened his mouth to talk—and then went flying backward, out the front door of the car. One moment, he was in front of Cedric, and the next, gone.

Cedric leaned forward, his head hitting the bars. He could just barely make out the officer's legs twitching on the ground. Then he heard a *thump* and a groan, and the legs went still.

Cedric threw his shoulder against the bars, the door, the window. But he was trapped. Panic bubbled up—

A dark head popped into the front seat. "There you are."

Kat grinned.

Quick relief fell over Cedric. He smiled back, then looked to the officer. "How hard did you hit him?"

Kat shrugged one shoulder. "Hard enough, but he will likely wake soon. Which means we need to get out of here now."

"Liv and the others—"

"I know," Kat broke in. "Liv managed to reach me on one of her phone devices. The wraths took her, Cedric."

Cedric jerked up, immediately ready to fight. But even if his fists weren't stuck together, there was nothing for him to aim them at. He threw his elbow hard at the wall of thin, interlocking bars that separated the front of the car from the back. Though the metal rings dug into the skin of his wrists, feeling the impact was worth it. For a moment.

"Where?"

"Liv told me where she is," Kat said, in a rush. "Though I do not know how to get there. The driver who brought me here left, and I do not know how to call for another."

"If you know where she is, I can only think of one way to get us there quickly," Cedric said, looking grimly around the car.

Kat raised one eyebrow. "You must be joking."

"I am not in a joking mood, to be honest. I think I know how to do it, from watching Liv . . . except . . ." Cedric held up his bound wrists as explanation.

Kat leaned close to examine them. "Wait! There's a keyhole here. Which means there must be a key."

She knelt down next to the unconscious officer and searched around, coming up with a key ring. After a few tries with the wrong keys, she finally used one to open the back door, then another to pop the latch on the metal circlets. Cedric pulled his hands free, rubbing his wrists.

After Cedric and Kat pulled the officer safely off the road and under some nearby shrubs, they searched the yard and house. Cedric's sword was missing. So was Merek.

"Maybe he was taken with the others," Kat said.

"Maybe," Cedric replied. But he couldn't stop his mind from stumbling over the same question. He kept picking and worrying at it like a loose tooth. "Or maybe he went with them willingly," he finally said.

"Cedric—"

"How did the wraths know where to find us tonight? It does not make sense. The wrath who spoke to me in the woods, right before the uniforms came, he said something to me about betrayal. About being betrayed."

Kat's eyebrows shot upward. "You think Merek betrayed us?"

Cedric walked back to the car and got inside, this time in the driver's seat. Merek's words sounded out in his head: *You have no idea what I'm capable of . . .*

"Merek could have told the wraths where we were going."

Kat got in the seat next to Cedric. She put one hand up to her temple, rubbing the skin there. "But why? Why would he do that? If Liv is our best chance at getting home, why hand her over to the wraths? Merek can be . . . challenging, but—"

"More than challenging. He has questioned me every step of the way. Of course he would try to take things into his own hands, the little—" Cedric smacked the round wheel in front of him. "Think about it. Merek argued for us to leave the museum. Not a few hours later, who led the group of wraths to the alley, forcing us to flee? He could have easily gone back to them the night the two of you returned to the museum. You separated for a while, did you not? That could have given him more than enough time to find the wraths and hatch this plan."

"I suppose . . ." Kat said, and sighed.

"We will deal with Merek later. First, we have to find Liv."

Cedric gazed at the wheel before him with a sinking stomach, and Kat fixed him with an expectant stare.

"Well?" Kat finally said.

"Give me a moment." Cedric breathed in once, deep, before putting his hands on the dangling set of keys on one side of the wheel. He tried to remember the series of actions Liv had taken each time she drove him somewhere. Moving slowly, he turned the keys, and held them there.

The metallic, churning noise sounded out. As Cedric continued pushing the keys, the noise turned into a high-pitched squeal.

"Aghh." Kat put her hands over her ears.

Cedric grimaced and looked down at the stick near his knee. "I think it's on." Remembering Liv's actions once again, he grabbed hold of the stick, pulling it from the *P* to the *D* position.

The car rolled forward, and Cedric remembered he had to do something with his feet. He looked under the wheel, trying to find the levers down there, when Kat yelped. Cedric whipped his head back up, just in time to see the car nearly sliding into the row of shrubs. He jerked on the wheel, and one of his feet landed on a pedal. The car lurched to a stop. Cedric tried the next pedal, and the car surged forward.

"Ah, got it now," he said, letting out a breath he didn't realize he'd been holding in.

Kat looked less than convinced.

Beads of sweat formed along the edge of Cedric's hairline as his eyes shot from one of the car's windows to another, always watchful for movements on the darkened road.

"Liv gave me an address," Kat said. "But how are we supposed to find it?"

Cedric glanced up at the small device that sat to his right, below the car's main window. It was nearly identical to the device he'd seen in Liv's car—the GPS she'd used to navigate on their visit to the professor.

"You have to use that."

Kat shot him an incredulous look. "Use it how?"

Cedric shrugged. "Turn it on? It speaks directions aloud to you in a human voice, so long as you push the right button."

"That is entirely unsettling."

As Kat struggled with the device, Cedric gripped the wheel tightly, eyes focused on the roadway. He was afraid to move, afraid to blink. And yet at the same time, controlling the movements of the car was almost . . . exhilarating. He forced himself to concentrate, keeping his foot rigidly on the pedal near the ground, the way Liv had done.

Kat cursed at the small box more than once, until it finally chirped out the correct location, and she slumped back in her seat.

The car hit against the side of the roadway, jolting hard against a fence.

"You are sure you know what you are doing?" Kat asked.

No, Cedric thought. "Yes." Cedric tried to keep all of his focus on the roadway and on his own movements. He followed the small box's instructions, and they drove into a busier, well-lit street. Pinpoints of bright, yellow light moved here and there as other cars navigated around them. Cedric tried to keep his hands steady on the wheel so Kat wouldn't pick up on the slight shaking in his fingers.

"What are we going to do?" Kat asked, in a small voice.

"First, not die in this contraption. Second, rescue Liv and the others."

Kat was silent for a moment. "And what are we going to do about Merek? If what you say is true . . ."

Cedric gritted his teeth and stopped the car at a red light so quickly that it jerked forward. "Then we will drag him home, where he can face the punishment he deserves."

"So you agree . . . that we need to get home? And soon?"

Cedric squared his shoulders. "We have to get Liv back first."

"Yes, of course. We will find the wraths and get Liv back so we can go home. . . . I know you wanted to stay and determine Malquin's plan, but he has been one step ahead of us here the whole time. We had access to the portals, and then he took them. As soon as we get them back . . . I don't want to risk that happening again. Risk getting stuck here. We must get back home and fight the wraths there."

"And leave Liv and her siblings here alone to face whatever comes for them next?"

Kat sucked in a breath. "I know you care about her. But there are more important things. Remember what our parents said? The day they gave us these?" Kat reached for the gold band that hung from a chain around her neck. "We are different, you and I. We have great advantages, but we also have a responsibility to Caelum. Do you remember?"

"I do."

"There was a time when I followed you and supported you without question. But that was when I knew that we had the same goal, of keeping our people safe. Do we not still?"

Cedric pursed his lips together. Kat put one hand over where his rested on the steering wheel. Their fingers blended together in the dark. "This is about more than one girl," Kat continued. "It is about everything, Cedric. Everything that has ever mattered."

New images rose up in Cedric's mind—Emme's laugh when she beat him at cards, his mother sewing in her sitting room, the color of the castle walls as the sun hit them every morning . . .

Liv's eyes right before he kissed her.

"So are we in agreement? As *soon* as we free Liv from the wraths, we use her to go back to Caelum?" Kat asked.

Blurred lights passed by all the windows as the car flew forward. Cedric remembered driving in the car with Liv on the way to San Diego, how she had pointed at the ocean as they'd passed by. It was the first time he'd ever seen it, a glimmering strip of blue on the right-hand side of the car.

"Isn't it beautiful?" Liv had asked, sneaking glances to catch Cedric's expression as he took in the sight for the first time.

"It is," Cedric had responded, a tugging feeling in his chest. "But it is not home."

THE MADMAN

As soon as Liv hung up the phone, she turned to see Shannon staring at her with wide eyes.

"Are you insane?"

"Possibly."

The metal door to the room creaked open, and Liv quickly tucked the phone into her back pocket. A pair of hulking wraths entered and stood on either side of the door. Neither of them bothered to speak to the trio of girls chained to the floor.

"And how are our guests faring?" a voice asked from the doorway. He was half-slouched, shielding one arm against his torso while the other hung down past his waist. When he stepped into the light, Liv could see his shoulder-length, stringy white hair. His deep brown eyes went right to Liv.

"A bit uncomfortable, to be honest," Liv said, rattling her chain.

The man chuckled. "I apologize for your rude reception, but I think you'll understand that these are exceptional circumstances." He gave her a small smile that only turned up the corners of his lips. "Allow me to introduce myself. My name is Malquin."

Cedric and the others had talked about Malquin plenty of times, but they'd never described what he looked like. Liv had always pictured someone large and imposing, like the villain in an Arnold Schwarzenegger movie. Or maybe Arnold Schwarzenegger himself. But in reality, the hunched form of Malquin couldn't have been more than five-foot-seven, and his twisted body couldn't take so much as an arm-wrestling match against Cedric. This was who they had all been so afraid of?

And yet, Malquin was the reason she was in chains.

"What do you want from us?" Liv croaked.

Malquin moved closer to Liv, pulling over one of the wooden crates with his leg and taking a seat.

"That, my dear, is a long and complicated story," he said. "But the short version is etched across your back."

Liv put all of her effort into not glancing at Daisy, though Malquin likely knew about her markings, also. She tried to slow her breathing, not wanting to show Malquin how scared she was. "How did you find us?"

"I was told where you'd be," Malquin said. "Loyalty is a funny thing. A fluid thing, I have found. Even those who are truly loyal, who love their friends, their family, their home . . . even they will break if the correct pressure is applied. Or the correct price is offered."

Liv's head snapped up involuntarily. "So you knew where we'd be tonight . . . and the cops . . ."

"The prince has an annoying way of slowing down my

soldiers, and I grew tired of waiting. Having the police separate him from you seemed an expedient solution." Malquin leaned forward, and Liv retreated in revulsion. "Delegation, dear, is the mark of a true leader."

"Who gave us up?" Liv asked. She ran through the possibilities in her mind, but nothing made sense. Kat would sooner fall on her own sword than betray Cedric. Then again, she hadn't exactly been shy about her dislike of Liv . . . would Kat give her up to Malquin if he promised her a quicker ticket home? And what about Merek? Would he think twice about double-crossing his friends?

Malquin gave his small smile again, one that showed no teeth. He waved one finger in front of Liv. "My own loyalty is not that easily cast aside."

Liv shook her head again, willing herself to focus. "Why? Why do all this?" She gestured to her chains. "You have to know I'll never do anything to help you."

Malquin's eyes slid slowly over first to Daisy, who cowered away, and then to Shannon. "Oh, I think you will."

Shannon returned his gaze and jutted out her chin, but Liv could hear her ragged, uneven breath. She saw the greenish-yellow bruises on Shannon's face and swallowed back a throat full of bile. How could she have gotten Shannon involved in this? How selfish. How stupid. And why? Because she didn't want to deal with it on her own?

"Leave her alone," Liv said.

"I'd really like to," Malquin replied. He clapped his hands together lightly, then held them under his chin, as though he was praying. "You needn't worry. I'm not going to ask anything of you that you cannot easily give. I only need you to help me open a portal."

Liv's gaze slid over to the two wraths who were standing on either side of the door.

"I know where they came from," Liv said. "And where you came from. What's wrong with the portal that got you here?"

Malquin sighed. "It's too small."

Liv shook her head in confusion.

"One person—one very special person—can open a door between worlds, it's true. But that's not the way the system was meant to work. I didn't understand that, at first. I had to learn it the hard way. I was foolish and arrogant and, well, young. Almost as young as you." Malquin smiled again, but his eyes were somewhere else, remembering. "I believed that because I was born special, I could use what power I had to go wherever I pleased. But the universe taught me otherwise."

Malquin brought his bent, withered arm in closer to his body. It seemed an unconscious movement, almost like a twitch.

"I paid for my arrogance."

Something clicked in Liv's mind. Arrogance. Her mouth dropped open, and her head jerked up in shock. Everything began to fall into place—how Malquin knew to use the police in his plan, how the wraths managed so easily in this world, as if someone was teaching them how. And now, with his own words, Malquin was as good as admitting it.

"You're not from Caelum. You're from here," she said. "You're Joe's brother."

Malquin just cocked his head and smiled. "I was. Once."

"Oh my God," Shannon whispered.

"You already know the beginning of my story, it seems," Malquin said.

Another idea came to Liv. Malquin seemed like the kind of man who liked to talk, like a scenery-chewing, veteran actor savoring every word of his monologue. If she could just keep him going long enough . . .

"I don't know everything," Liv said. "Joe said you died when you went through that portal."

Malquin laughed, then gestured to himself with one hand. "Clearly, that was not the case." He glanced again at his useless arm. "I almost died, though. I had no idea the portal would take so much from me. I didn't understand enough about it."

"And now you do?" Liv asked, keeping her voice steady, trying to sound controlled and curious.

"I know much, much more, now. There's a reason the children of the scrolls are always born in groups of three, for instance," Malquin said. "Those ancient Knights who turned the first humans into keys knew what they were doing. They divided the power up into three, both as a fail-safe—so no one man could permanently open up the distance between worlds—and as a necessity. Because human beings are fragile by nature, and one body alone cannot sustain the amount of magic it takes to control portal energy."

Malquin shook his head and let out a low chuckle. But it was one devoid of real humor. "I was foolish to open that first portal when I did." Malquin's face hardened. "Though if my brother had actually come through it with me when I needed him to, things might have gone differently. . . ."

Malquin shrugged and flicked his good wrist, as if batting away a fly. But Liv could see through him. The anger that had flared up in his eyes at the mention of Joe hadn't really faded.

"On the other end of the portal, I found myself in a new world. But I was broken. Even with all of the magic that Caelum possesses, it took me years to heal. And it wasn't the Guardians who took me in, those so-called paragons of virtue. No, they mocked me, called me insane. But not the wraths. And I discovered that for all its magic, Caelum was a lot like Earth. Those who were in power abused it, held their might over the oppressed. But I knew who could help the wraths find justice. Me."

Malquin's eyes flared again, but he didn't seem angry—he seemed excited, proud. Liv seized on the brief pause in his story. "You rose up against Cedric's family."

"The Guardians were due for an uprising," Malquin said. "Of course, there were other reasons to lead a rebellion. The royals had blocked off my first portal, the one I originally came through. They extended their palace walls around it so no one could touch it, like the greedy hoarders they are."

"So you went looking for it," Liv said.

"I honestly didn't know what I would do when I found it. I didn't know if it would work, or if it would try to crush me once again. For years, I'd searched Caelum for answers, until I found a mage—an old crone living in the Southern Hills. She explained why I wasn't able to open a second portal back to Earth on my own. As there is magic in Caelum, so there is on Earth. But here, it is older, and more dangerous. It is more powerful than any of the parlor tricks you'll find in Caelum. Humans don't know about magic because the Earth is so old, it has found ways to conceal those powers."

"The Quelling Theory," Liv breathed. She remembered Professor Billings's face across the desk in his office, his kindly and academic tone as he told her the theory of how Earth quelled its magic. It was odd to think of that version of him, now that she knew the truth of who he was.

Malquin's mouth split into a smile. "Been doing a little homework of your own? Yes, the Earth itself prevented me from opening a new portal on my own that would take me back here. As hard as I tried, I was blocked again and again. This damned place just doesn't want to let magic back in. The only option was to go back through the way I came, through the first portal. Which meant I needed a way into the palace."

"Because that portal stayed open?"

"Yes," Malquin tilted his head. "Opening a portal from Earth to Caelum is like splitting a window screen in half—it creates a permanent tear. Caelum wears its magic on the surface, and a portal's tear is visible and permanent. But Earth hides the tear. Those with magic can feel it, but no one can see it."

The words rocked through Liv's brain. The only portal she knew of was the one Cedric and his friends had come through—the one under the bridge at the LA River. The place where, years before, Joe had watched his brother disappear. The place had always felt special to Liv, in a way that felt intensely personal.

Could she sense the magic there, even though it was hidden? It was a disconcerting thought, that even before she knew what her tattoo really was, she was being slowly guided by forces she didn't understand.

Malquin seemed to mistake Liv's silence for confusion.

"The Earth quells magic at every opportunity, or else hides it well."

Something else clicked in Liv's mind. "The wraths . . ."

"Yes, it's also why the wraths are able to pass as humans in this world. As soon as they come through from the portal, their true appearance is hidden."

"Not hidden enough," Liv murmured, thinking of the coal-black eyes and sharpened claws of the wraths.

"They're well hidden from those who aren't tainted with magic as you are," Malquin replied.

There it was, again. Liv could see the wraths because she had magic in her, and she always had. She'd always been different.

"Once I was in the castle," Malquin continued, "I had intended to use the portal myself, after the Guardians were subdued. The royal children merely . . . beat me to it. As soon as the palace was secure and I sent a couple of wraths ahead of me safely to track them, I decided to follow. But I had discovered why the portal wouldn't cooperate for me as easily it had for the royals. It was mere coincidence that I discovered it—when one of my wraths was accidentally shot before the royals crossed over, and his blood spilled on the ground, it suddenly made sense. We humans can open the portals, but only those with wrath blood are allowed to cross through safely. Guardians, and the wraths themselves. That is why the first crossing nearly destroyed me. To cross unharmed a second time . . . I needed their blood."

"Wait," Liv said. She wanted to keep him talking, keep him going for as long as possible. Malquin remained seated. "If you were able to use the . . . the blood . . . and cross through the portal, bringing wraths with you here, what do you need me for at all?"

Malquin clasped his hands together again, the strong one over the weak, gnarled one, as if protecting it. "The portal I opened all those years ago on my own is very small—and unstable—and Earth's quelling magic only lets a few pass from Caelum to here at any time before it closes up again. Many of the wraths who tried to cross together were lost to the space between worlds. And I need more than just a handful of wrath spies and guards. I need an army of my own."

"An . . . an army?" Liv asked, suddenly feeling sick.

"Well, yes. I didn't help the wraths rise to power in Caelum out of the goodness of my heart, after all. We had a deal. I would use my knowledge of Caelum's main city to help them infiltrate its walls and defenses. And if the portal still worked, half of their forces would come through with me."

"Why?" Liv breathed.

Malquin narrowed his eyes as he looked at her. "This is the part I think you'll like very much. For years, as I rebuilt my strength in Caelum and dreamed of returning, do you know what was foremost in my thoughts?"

Liv shook her head.

"Not my parents, who never believed me when I told them I was special; not my brother, who abandoned me. It was the

Knights." Malquin again leaned forward, his face close to Liv's. He smiled, but it was an angry, dark smile.

"The Knights of Valere. I still remember the faces of the men who grabbed me off the street. I remember how they knocked my brother out with a single blow to the head. Eric was just eight years old, you know. When the Knight hit him, there was something in the man's expression . . . something almost like glee."

Liv remembered seeing the same expression on the professor's face as he told her, calmly, that he was going to kill her. She felt her jaw tighten with anger, and Malquin saw it. He nodded, pleased.

"This is why I know you'll help me. They want to destroy you, too. They hate magic, and they fear what they don't understand. They'll kill every child born with a scroll until the end of time to keep portals from opening on Earth—to keep magic repressed. So I returned—and with a wrath army, no less—to find every last member of the Knights of Valere and wipe them off the face of this world."

"But . . . if we could only talk to them, explain . . ." Liv said, her voice weak to her own ears.

"Talk? You think those child-killers want to talk? They don't want to hear what we have to say. They're the worst kind of monsters. The ones who think they are doing right."

"And what does that make you?" Liv whispered.

Malquin paused for a moment, as if considering her question. Then he slightly raised his withered hand. "I suppose you'd consider me a monster as well. But unlike the Knights, I'm a monster who's on your side. You're a child of the scrolls, dear. I would never hurt you."

Liv didn't know how to respond.

"I brought you here because it takes three scrolls to open the portal fully and allow my entire wrath force to cross through. I didn't know I would find you, honestly," Malquin said, cocking his head to the side. "I was looking for Joe to help me open the portal. But I also had a group of wraths hunting down the royals. I knew they would look for the scrolls and wanted to know if they found my brother before I did. To my great luck, they stumbled onto something even better. You."

Liv closed her eyes, remembering the second time she'd encountered a wrath in the alley beside the museum. The way it had sprinted off after getting a glimpse of her tattoo. She wondered if things could have turned out differently somehow, before that moment. What if she hadn't gone to the museum at all? What if she'd kept the sword and never seen Cedric again?

Was she always meant to end up here, pulled by the same magic that had attracted her to the river? Had she ever had a choice?

Not that it mattered anymore.

The crate Malquin sat on creaked slightly as he leaned forward to look at Daisy. "The three of us, together, can finally open the portal properly, the way it was first opened nearly a thousand years ago. Alone, I could barely punch a crack through the walls between worlds. You and I, my darlings, are going to open a highway."

"And what will that highway do?" Liv asked. She thought of Joe's warnings, of the bridge that came down around him after he watched his brother go through the portal. "Every time someone has crossed through the portal, there have been earthquakes. Cedric caused one when he came over, and then they kept happening all summer . . . which I guess was you and your wraths. If you open a bigger portal, people could get hurt."

Malquin narrowed his eyes. "You sound just like my brother. So overly cautious, too scared to act."

He reached out with his good hand, running one finger down the side of her face. Liv flinched away. Malquin withdrew his hand, but kept speaking. "You and I were born magical in a world that's been fighting magic for centuries. We're survivors. Special. Why waste time thinking about those who aren't?"

Liv shuddered. Malquin stood up abruptly, then, facing the wall behind Liv, Shannon, and Daisy. His eyes seemed to be taking something in, but the wall was blank.

"We already have the perfect place," he said, motioning to the wall. "Isolated, yet stable. We have the three scrolls." He gestured to Liv and Daisy on the ground. "I have the magic words, so to speak," he said, pointing a long, thin finger toward his forehead. "And we have the blood." Malquin snapped his fingers then, and one of the wraths nodded. It walked to a corner of the room and lifted up a piece of canvas that was cracked with dirt and age. The canvas itself looked like nothing, just a forgotten piece of rubbish in an old warehouse. But what lay underneath it wasn't spare parts or rags.

It was Merek. He was unconscious and bleeding, and he looked small against the concrete floor. Liv gasped as the wrath grabbed Merek roughly and hauled him up. It carried him over to Malquin's feet and dropped him on the ground. Liv could just barely make out the slight rising and falling of Merek's chest. If he was the one who had sold them out to Malquin, it looked like he'd been double-crossed.

"What did you do to him?" Liv whispered.

"Nothing, yet," Malquin replied.

"What did you promise him? To make him give us up."

Malquin's head twitched at that, and he smiled his creepy smile. "Ah, my dear. Maybe you are less insightful than I thought."

Then he reached into his pocket and withdrew a long, thin knife.

"No!" Liv said, pulling against her chain.

Malquin ignored her, and knelt down over Merek.

"Please," Liv said. "You don't have to do this." She could hear the naked desperation and helplessness in her own voice. Behind her, Shannon moved closer to Daisy, as if to block her view.

"Wrath blood is needed for us three to cross through the portal without being torn apart. You don't want to be torn apart, do you?" Malquin lowered the knife and pressed its point to the skin of Merek's exposed neck.

"Please!" Liv pulled against the chain until her shoulder threatened to pop. Her feet scrambled against the floor, but took her nowhere.

She watched as the knife pierced Merek's skin below his neck and drew across his collarbone, toward his shoulder. She couldn't tell how deep the cut went, but it was enough for him to bleed immediately. A steady trickle of Merek's blood fell over the side of his shoulder and ran soundlessly to the floor.

Liv's stomach lurched as she watched Malquin lean down

over the pooling puddle of blood and dip both hands in it. When his hands were coated in a dark red, Malquin stood. Behind him, Merek twitched, and his eyelashes fluttered. A powerful relief fell over Liv to see that Merek was moving, but it slipped away as Malquin made his way toward her. He ran two fingers over her forehead, and she jerked at the feeling of wetness they left behind. Malquin then went to Daisy and left a streak of red on her as well.

"Repeat after me," he said, without looking at them. *"Echgo libratum, echgo indux vitte. Echgo libratum, echgo indux vitte."*

The words sounded vaguely Latin, but more guttural somehow. A language Liv didn't know. Ancient and harsh.

"I said, repeat." Malquin reached into his other pocket and withdrew a small handgun. He aimed it at Shannon, and Liv's mind went blank.

Shannon shook her head and inched as far away from Malquin as her shackles would allow. "Please," she whispered, sounding more scared than Liv had ever heard her sound before. Shannon was directing her words to Malquin, but it was Liv who responded.

"Echgo libratum, echgo indux vitte." The words came from her mouth more easily than she would have thought. After a moment, Liv heard Daisy's voice join hers. Then, she could feel something beginning to grow—a pressure in her head, right between her eyes. A pulling sensation. As though she was connected to an invisible string—and maybe she had been her entire life—and only now was someone on the other end beginning to pull it tight.

Malquin chanted as well, his lips curling into a smile as he did. Liv turned around, slowly, to face the wall, and her breath caught in her throat. There, at her eye level, a small, black hole was opening up in the wall. Then it started to grow. Liv felt the hole drawing her closer, pulling her near. It wanted her. It felt heavy, purposeful. Inevitable.

A crashing, tearing sound ripped through the room.

But it hadn't come from the portal. Reluctantly, Liv stopped repeating the words, tore her gaze away from the growing hole in the wall, and turned around—only to see another hole. But this one was much larger, taking up nearly half the space of the wall across from her. Instead of opening up into pure darkness, it showed the orangy-black haze of the Los Angeles night sky. And standing there, in silhouette, were more than two dozen figures in dark red robes.

THE BATTLE

The portal was nearly five feet high, but had stopped spreading over the rusted wall.

"Don't stop chanting!" Malquin yelled, but his focus was soon pulled away from Liv and Daisy, toward the robed figures who were working their way through the room. Wraths poured in from the warehouse to fight the Knights back with knives, pipes, and other makeshift weapons. A small group of wraths formed a rough line that protected Liv, Daisy, Shannon, Merek, and Malquin from the clanging conflict. Liv could hear metal on metal and could smell blood in the room's enclosed space. But soon the line of wrath guards blocked her view entirely.

"Keep chanting!" Malquin screamed.

But chanting was the farthest thing from Liv's mind. And even Malquin was distracted by the pushing wall of dark red robes that was moving ever closer.

A wrath guard to Liv's left collapsed in a heap on the ground, a blade sticking out of its chest. It didn't get up again.

Liv realized, with a dimmed sort of triumph, that she had been right to call the professor instead of the police—the Knights knew how to fight wraths, and had brought silver blades. Now she could only hope that their fight with the wraths lasted long enough for her to figure out how to get away. . .

A yell tore through the room. Liv couldn't tell if it was human or wrath. She turned slightly and saw Merek struggling to rise. For a moment he looked up, eyes first on Liv, then on the portal. He got to his knees and started to crawl toward Liv, his teeth gritted in pain. Not a moment later, a battling Knight and wrath stepped in between them, blades and claws flashing. When they moved away, Merek was gone.

The fight went on. Blades flashed in the dim lighting of the warehouse, robes swirled, wraths growled. A trickle of blood made its way slowly across the concrete floor, toward Liv's foot. There was no way to tell if it was from a wrath or a human. It almost looked fake, like the corn syrup concoction she'd whipped up for her film shoot earlier in the summer.

Liv looked out over the fight and, for a moment, tried to convince herself the whole scene *was* fake. The wraths were stuntmen with dark contact lenses, the fights were choreographed, the weapons props. If someone called "Cut," everyone would stop. They'd pull back their hoods and go chat over a hummus tray in the corner. It could almost be true, if she imagined hard enough . . . it could almost be true . . .

The trickle of blood reached her foot, staining the edge of her shoe. A few feet away, a wrath crashed heavily into a pile of barrels, causing them to roll over onto the floor, spilling out a stream of pungent, familiar-smelling liquid. Liv knew there was no more pretending—this was a real fight, they were in real chains, and real gasoline had just been spilled.

Malquin called out and snapped the fingers on his good hand. Two wraths broke from the fray and approached.

"Unchain the scrolls," Malquin said. "They're coming through the portal with me."

"No!"

The wrath ignored Liv's scream and unlocked her from her shackles while another released Daisy. Every part of Liv's body wanted to sprint away, but the sight of Shannon, still in chains, stopped her. Within moments, the wrath who had released Liv from the shackles held her tightly by the arms.

Liv looked squarely into Malquin's eyes. "I did everything you asked. Let Shannon go."

Malquin squinted at her. "Once we are safely through the portal, my people have instructions to release your friend."

"Don't go with him, Liv," Shannon said. Her fingers were wrapped tightly around her shackle chain, pulling uselessly, the skin of her knuckles turning white.

But Liv wasn't sure she had a choice. She pulled against the wrath who held her, but its grip was too strong.

And then, a familiar face appeared at the edges of the fight. His eyes were puffy and bruised from where Cedric had hit him the night before, but it was impossible not to recognize him. The professor.

At first, Liv thought the professor's eyes were locked on hers. Was he going to kill her—right here, right now? But the professor walked right past Liv, his eyes sweeping past the portal and landing on Malquin.

"You," he sneered. "I remember you."

Malquin turned to face the professor, his face full of hate. "And I, you. It's hard to forget the face of the man who destroyed your family."

"Not sufficiently, it seems." The professor reached into his robes and pulled out a short, silver sword. "But there's time to correct that."

Malquin merely smiled, and lifted up his own handgun. "What is it they say? Never bring a sword to a gunfight? Or something like that. These things tend to fade from the mind when you're trapped in a medieval dimension for two decades."

The professor narrowed his eyes at Malquin. "Close the portal."

Malquin laughed. "I do remember the perfect Earth response to that: Make me."

Before Malquin could move, the professor thrust his sword at Malquin's good right hand, the one that held the gun. Malquin jerked back just in time to spare his wrist from the blade, but the gun was knocked to the floor. The professor swooped down to retrieve it.

"Not exactly my weapon of choice," he said, steadying it in his hand. "But it will do. You can't keep the portal open for long if you're missing a scroll."

Before anyone could react, the professor swiveled, pointed the gun at Liv, and fired.

Liv felt something crash hard into her chest, and she

dropped to the ground. For an instant, she was sure she'd been shot. But something heavy was lying on top of her—someone had managed to push her to the ground.

She shifted to see Cedric, his face inches from hers.

Cedric brought a hand up to her cheek and ran his thumb over her skin. "Are you okay?"

Liv nodded. Before she could say more, Cedric leaped up to face the professor. But as soon as he jumped up, he stopped, his eyes caught on the portal hole in the center of what was once a concrete wall. His legs gave a quick jerk, and for a moment, just a moment, Liv thought he was going to dive into the darkness. The darkness that would take him home.

Instead, Cedric turned back to the action of the room.

With a firm hand, the professor aimed the gun once again. This time, it was Malquin who jumped in front of Liv, batting at the professor's hand with his good arm. Cedric looked between Malquin and the professor, as if unsure which one he should try to help.

Malquin spoke through gritted teeth as he fought for control of the gun. "Go, through the portal!" He was still facing the professor, but Liv knew his words were directed to her.

"No way in hell," Liv replied, "am I going anywhere with you."

The professor rammed the butt of the gun into Malquin's face, then quickly turned and aimed it again—not at Liv, but at Daisy.

Daisy's eyes widened as she stared down the barrel of the gun, but she seemed frozen in place. The wrath who was holding her jumped away from the threat of a bullet. Before Liv could yell out, Cedric sprang into action. One moment he was standing next to Liv, and the next he was at the professor's side. He reached out to knock the gun from the professor's hands, and as he did, another shot went off.

This time, Liv knew immediately that the bullet hadn't met its mark. She saw sparks hit the wall where the bullet ricocheted off the cement, near the overturned barrels of gasoline. A bright orange flame flickered at the edge of the liquid, and in a matter of moments, the barrels were burning. The gun Cedric had knocked to the ground was consumed by fire.

"Oh God," Liv whispered. The fire spread quickly from barrel to barrel, lighting up the gasoline on the floor. Liv's brain swirled with panic. The smell of the fire and the rising smoke threatened to bring her back, back to her old, darkened bedroom, her old wooden house. Sitting on that lawn and watching it burn . . .

Shannon pulled on Liv's arm, shaking her back to attention. "Liv! We have to get out of here."

Liv took her hand from her mouth and coughed as the smoke hit her throat. "Daisy, run! We'll be right behind you."

Daisy looked back at Liv and gave a quick nod. She dropped down low and ran into an opening in the fray, away from the growing fire. Liv lost sight of her almost immediately. She turned and knelt next to Shannon, who was still in shackles.

Both girls pulled at the chains while keeping track of the quick progress of the fire. The flames had already spread to cover the entire spill.

Malquin, Cedric, and the professor continued to struggle a few feet away. Liv looked up when she heard a grunt, and saw Cedric doubled over at the waist. But he recovered quickly, his jaw set in a hard line. He shoved the palm of his fist up against the injured part of the professor's face and grimaced as the professor yelled out in pain.

Liv turned back to Shannon. She wrapped the chains around her hands and pulled again, so hard that she fell backward.

"Liv," Shannon said, her voice soft. "You have to go."

"No way. Not gonna happen."

"I can't get out of here," Shannon said, eyeing the fire. "And you don't have much time."

"Shannon—"

Liv was interrupted by a loud, horrific screaming. She looked up to see a Knight flailing around the room, his robes engulfed in flame. The wraths stepped out of his path, and not even his fellow Knights tried to help him. Within a few moments, the Knight had sunk to his knees, the fire growing brighter and larger on his back.

Liv coughed through the thickening smoke.

"Cedric!" she screamed out. "I have to get Shannon out of here!"

Cedric tore himself from the fight and dropped down next to Liv to help her pull on Shannon's chains.

Liv heard a choked yell and looked up. With Cedric gone, the professor was gaining the upper hand in the nearby fight. His hand wrapped around Malquin's throat. Malquin stumbled back, bringing both men closer to the wall—and the portal.

"Hurry," Shannon urged.

"It won't . . . budge," Cedric said, gritting his teeth.

Shannon let out a small, desperate sob that transformed into a cough halfway through.

"Please, please," Liv said, pulling the metal around Shannon's wrist with all her might. Her face and arms felt hot, and she knew the fire was growing closer. It was almost impossible to see the fight in the warehouse through the waves of dense smoke. The fire itself was growing louder, drowning out the cries of the men and wraths who fell into it.

Past Cedric, Liv could barely see Malquin and the professor as they still struggled. They were very near to the portal now, the fire at their backs. They grasped at each other, half fighting, half clinging for the support to stand.

Malquin's eyes scanned the fiery horror of the warehouse, and Liv could briefly see flames reflected in them. He looked to her, then, and she could read the defeat in his eyes. She knew, just a half-second before he moved, what he would do. Clinging tightly to the professor, Malquin pushed himself off the ground, backward into the portal.

The professor reached out, trying to keep Malquin from escaping. His hands clasped at Malquin's twisted arm, but instead of pulling Malquin back into the room, the professor was pulled forward. He stumbled for just a moment, eyes wide, before falling completely into the blackness of the portal and disappearing from view.

Cedric stared into the space where the two men had just disappeared. His back was completely rigid, and from her vantage point on the floor, Liv could just make out a sliver of his expression—of the horror there, and also the longing. On the other side of that black hole was his home.

Liv tried to call out to him, but instead sucked in a lungful of smoke and ash. She doubled over, coughing and retching.

The room tilted.

Liv was thrown violently to the right, and crashed down hard on her elbow. She reached to steady herself against the ground, but couldn't—the ground itself was shaking.

An earthquake.

Dust and debris fell from the ceiling, only to be swallowed by flames. Wraths and Knights alike tumbled to the ground. Several raced out of the building through the giant opening in the wall, until a chunk of corrugated metal from the roof tore free, slicing the air as it went and partially blocking the opening.

"Liv!" Cedric screamed. "You have to go!" His voice was swallowed up by the chaos and the noise. Liv had a hard time seeing him through the smoke. But she shook her head.

The world lurched again, once again throwing Liv to the ground. When she struggled to get up, she saw a large crack in the cement under her feet. The earthquake had pulled the floor apart.

Instead of pulling on the shackles around Shannon's wrists, Cedric instead pulled at where they were chained to the crumbling ground. The chain gave, and Cedric handed it to Shannon to carry.

Shannon rose, still coughing heavily. Cedric and Liv each supported her on one side and started toward the opening on the other side of the room. Beads of sweat ran down Liv's face, and her throat was raw. The heat of the flames was oppressive, overpowering.

They carefully made their way toward the other end of the room, weaving between the remaining Knights and wraths that still filled the space. They had to crawl over dark heaps of robes and clothes that Liv knew were collapsed bodies. She tried not to look down, instead keeping her eyes half-closed to keep out as much smoke as possible.

Once, Cedric glanced back over his shoulder, toward the portal. Liv risked a glance back also and saw, to her surprise, that it was growing smaller. As it did, the wall itself started to fall, large chunks of it crashing down to the ground.

They were almost across the room when Liv heard a screaming, tearing noise coming from above. She, Cedric, and Shannon all looked up, just in time to see the last remaining section of the metal ceiling swinging downward, trailing flames.

Cedric's arms wrapped around both Liv and Shannon now, propelling them forward. He lifted them off their feet and out through the ruined wall into the night. Behind them, the burning chunk of ceiling crashed down onto the floor of the warehouse with a deafening bang, sending sparks and pieces of charred wood flying. Cedric pushed Liv and Shannon to the hard ground, diving on top of them to protect them from the debris.

Heat raked up Liv's legs, and she struggled to breathe through smoke and ash. She turned back to the warehouse just in time to hear a groaning sound.

"It's going to collapse," Liv choked out.

Cedric nodded, unable to speak. Shannon's eyes were closed, though she continued to suck in huge breaths of air. Liv put an arm under Shannon's shoulder and hauled her up so the three could move across the small lawn. Liv knew that she should move her legs faster, faster, faster, but couldn't force her muscles to respond to her command. She just barely registered that the earth had stopped shaking.

They finally reached the spot where Daisy half stood, hands on her knees, and Kat held a still-bleeding Merek.

When Cedric saw Merek, his face went entirely still. He was covered in soot and ash, but his eyes burned through it all.

"You!" Cedric let go of Shannon's arm and launched himself forward, tackling Merek to the ground. He barely noticed that Merek, limp as a rag doll, didn't even try to fight back.

Cedric grabbed Merek's shoulders and shook until his head flopped backward. "Why did you do it? Why?" he screamed, voice catching in his throat.

"Cedric!" Kat yelled out. Liv could see that she was covered in dust and the knuckles of her hand were bloody—she'd been fighting, too. "Stop!"

But Cedric wouldn't stop, or couldn't. He slammed Merek's shoulders again into the ground.

"I . . . don't . . ." Merek coughed.

"You betrayed us! Why?" Cedric's lips were pulled back into a grimace, his eyes were wild. "Why?"

But Merek didn't just look scared—he seemed confused.

Even in her daze, something Malquin said before popped into Liv's head. *Maybe you are less insightful than I thought. . . .*

"Cedric, wait," she yelled, as loud as her smoke-charred throat would allow. "It wasn't him. Malquin told me . . . it was someone else."

Cedric's body tensed, but it took another moment for his fingers to release Merek's shoulders. He stayed there, hovering over Merek for some time.

"There is no one else," he finally said. "It had to have been him."

"I did not betray anyone," Merek responded. His voice was thin and raw. For the first time since Liv had met him, it was entirely devoid of sarcasm. Like the rest of the group that sat wheezing and sweating on the lawn, Merek was totally rung out, a hollow shell. A teenager who was in over his head. "I swear."

Kat leaned down and slowly coaxed Cedric away from Merek.

"We will figure everything out when we get away from here," Kat said. She bent over Merek, ripped the sleeve from her shirt and wrapped it slowly around his largest wound, the one from Malquin's knife. "Can you move?"

Liv's eyes shot back to the burning building. A few figures were still scattering into the night, some wearing flowing robes that flew out behind them as they ran. Any wraths and Knights who made it out of the fire weren't sticking around to see what happened next.

When the right half of the warehouse collapsed in on itself, it did so with a shudder and a bang. The crumbled remains of concrete walls stood brightly against the night.

There was no sign of the portal.

"Liv, look," Shannon said, nudging Liv's side. Liv followed her gaze past the ruins of the warehouse to the surrounding area beyond. She had a hard time processing what her eyes were telling her.

They stood in a field of rubble—and not just right outside the warehouse. For a full block, every building in sight had been completely leveled. Brought down to the ground.

Decimated.

THE DEBRIS

They moved as quickly as they could through the darkened Venice streets. Liv's lungs burned and her head pounded with each step, and she only wanted to sit down somewhere cool and clean. But they had to keep moving, away from the Knights and wraths fleeing the wreckage of the warehouse, away from the cop car Cedric had stolen, away from anyone who might try to stop them.

Getting away quickly was difficult, what with everyone still coughing up ash. Merek could barely even stand without Kat and Cedric on each side to prop him up. But still they moved, following Liv's lead. She was taking them to the only familiar place nearby—the ocean. When they reached the beach, Liv looked around, trying to get her bearings. It was nearly dawn, and sirens wailed in the distance. Liv wearily directed the others to turn right, toward the only structure that could provide some sort of shelter where they could stop and rest for a while.

As the Santa Monica Pier grew closer in Liv's line of vision, with its familiar buildings and Ferris wheel outlined against the sky, her body finally started to shed some of its panic. They collapsed into the sand under the rounded wooden pillars that supported the weight of the pier. The shadows would hide them well.

With Kat's help, Cedric was finally able to snap the shackles from around Shannon's wrists. Once that was done, he moved to sit a little away from the group, his arms wrapped loosely around his knees. He stared out at the water and avoided looking at Merek, who in turn stared at the sand, his expression dark.

Liv fell down next to Shannon and Daisy, noting their soot-streaked faces and thinking she must look just as dirty. Their throats must be as parched and dry as her own, too, after inhaling so much smoke. She wished she had water—or anything at all—she could give to them to make it better.

"Let's never do that again," Shannon said flopping down in the sand and rubbing her wrists.

"Are you okay?" Liv asked Daisy. Her sister looked up, as if startled by the question, and Liv saw that her eyebrows were furrowed. She regretted asking—of course Daisy wasn't okay. "I'm so sorry to pull you into this. I really wanted to keep you safe, not put you in danger. I shouldn't have come for you at all."

Daisy looked out at the ocean, not responding for a while. When she did say something, her words surprised Liv. "I'm glad I know the truth, even if tonight was, like, the worst thing that ever happened to me." She looked over at Liv. "I'm glad you found me."

"Me too." Liv smiled and turned her head toward the ocean. "We're going to need a way out of here. Time to call Joe."

Liv moved a little way from the others to dial, and Joe picked up on the first ring. "I'm glad you're all okay," Joe said when Liv was done explaining what had happened. His voice sounded strained. "Peter and I are just outside the city. Do you have somewhere safe you can go until we can get to you?"

Liv thought of the Echo Park house. It was likely that Malquin knew about it, and his wraths, too.

"No," she said. "There's nowhere safe left."

A pause. "Then stay where you are. I'll be there soon."

"Okay. And Joe? There's something else." Liv heard light static through the line as Joe waited for her to continue. But how could she tell him this? Not only tell him that his brother was alive, but also explain what he had become? There was no easy way.

But it had to be done, and there was no one to do it but her.

"Malquin isn't from Caelum. He went over there through a portal." Liv took a breath. "Twenty years ago."

Joe made a small noise of shock, and Liv knew he understood. "John," he whispered. When he spoke again, his voice was shaky. "Okay. Okay. I'll be there soon, all right?"

"Okay," Liv breathed. She hung up and turned to the exhausted group around her. "Joe's on his way to come get us. And as long as we're waiting, there are some things you guys should know."

Liv filled Cedric, Kat, and Merek in on everything Malquin had told her about his plan. When she was done, Cedric took his head from his hands and stood. His expression was carefully controlled. It was a scary thing, Liv thought, watching Cedric pull himself into leader mode like that. But it was impressive, too. "He fell through the portal. But now we know what he wants. He won't give up just because he lost a handful of wraths in a fire."

Liv closed her eyes, trying to block the sights and smells of the fire from her mind.

"We can't let him open a giant portal," she said. "You saw what happened to those buildings, and that portal was only open a few minutes. If it had been longer . . ." Liv swallowed.

"We will not let that happen," Cedric said.

"But it's worse than just that. The portal closed on this side, but Malquin explained that they stay open on the other end, in Caelum. He could still use it to bring wraths through . . ."

"Better the wraths come here than stay in Caelum," Kat said, her voice cold.

"Nice," Shannon shot back.

"No," Cedric said, his voice again eerily calm. "Expelling the wraths to this realm is not the solution. But now that we know Malquin's plan, we can stop him. We can find him in Caelum and intercept him before he can cause more damage to either world."

"You really think you can do that?" Liv asked. "Stop him before he comes back?"

"Yes," Cedric said. "I can."

"Why should we trust you now?" Merek said, his voice rough and shaky. He coughed and spit into the sand. "Look how far trusting you has ever gotten us."

Cedric winced. "I know I could have done things better,

Merek. No one knows that more than I. We acted rashly tonight, going to get Daisy, and then . . . *I* acted rashly. . . ." Cedric's voice faltered, and he swallowed hard. "But I will not make that mistake again. We will make sure the scrolls are safe here, we will follow Malquin home to Caelum, and we *will* stop him."

For a moment, no one spoke.

"Look," Daisy said, pointing out toward the sea. A thin shimmer of lighter blue was beginning to rise from the horizon, with just a hint of pink underneath it. "It's morning."

While everyone looked out over the water, Liv's head swiveled to Cedric. The almost-morning light was not yet bright enough to reflect in his eyes, and his features looked dark. He seemed very far away, like he was slipping from her. Soon, she wouldn't be able to reach him at all.

Liv pushed herself up from the soft sand and walked over to where he stood.

"Can I talk to you? Before Joe gets here."

Cedric nodded. "Of course."

He followed her as she started to walk away. Kat watched them go with careful eyes, but didn't make a move to join them.

Liv led Cedric out from under the pier, up the beach a few paces to the worn, wooden stairs that led from the sand to the main pier entrance. In the early darkness of morning, the pier was empty. Its boards were cool to the touch, though Liv knew they would be baking hot later, under the summer sun.

"Where are we going?" Cedric asked. He looked around at the closed-up shops and restaurants, the Ferris wheel frozen in place at the far end of the pier.

Liv led him across the width of the pier to the railing on the other side. They were near enough to keep an eye out for Joe on the road, but far enough to be out of sight of the others. Liv leaned her arms up on the splintery railing and listened to the splashing of waves against wood.

"Liv?"

"I wanted you to see this," she said.

The strip of sky at the horizon of the ocean was growing larger, and the sky was getting lighter with each second.

"Do you have oceans in Caelum? Or piers like this one?"

Cedric shook his head. "We have a sea. But nothing like this."

"I know you've seen a lot of terrible things since you've been in this world," she continued. "But I'd hate for you to think it is all bad. That after everything, you still thought it was . . ." Liv trailed off, the word *hell* on the tip of her tongue. With the images of the fire still bright in her mind, she couldn't bring herself to say it.

"I do not think it is all bad," Cedric said softly, looking out over the waves. "Not anymore. There are a lot of dangerous things here, but there are dangerous things in Caelum as well. It's just the unknown that is frightening."

"But this place, it's at least a little less unknown than it used to be?" Liv struggled to keep the hopeful tone from her voice.

Cedric's mouth twitched a little, just a hint of his half-smile. "Yes," he replied. "And not everything that was frightening turned out to be bad."

Liv swallowed hard, trying to summon back the courage

she'd felt at Daisy's house after her pep talk with Shannon, just before the wraths had attacked. Even if it was ill-timed, she knew this would be her last chance to say something real. *This is the moment*, she yelled inside her head. *Do it now.* Her stomach clenched, and she turned back to look at the ocean.

"Cedric, you and me . . ." She faltered. Why was it so hard? Why, after everything else . . . ?

"Liv," he said, carefully. "You do not have to—"

"No, that's the thing. I do have to. I really do. Because what we have between us, it's new to me. It's all scary and . . . unknown. But that's no reason to be afraid of it, right? It's no reason to shut down. I know this is completely the wrong time, but if you really are going to go soon, I don't want to regret never telling you . . ."

Cedric's eyes bored into hers, searching. But Liv couldn't tell what he was thinking.

" . . . how much I care about you. Because I do, so much." The words were tumbling out of Liv's mouth now, and she let them. She knew if she stopped talking, this moment would pass away like all the others had and she'd never be brave enough to get it out.

"I just want to explain, I want to be clear so there's no doubt . . . whenever we're around each other, it's like you're the most important thing in the room . . . and I just need you to know . . ."

Liv didn't wait for Cedric to interrupt her. She leaned in quickly and kissed him hard. His mouth tasted like salt and smoke. After a split second, Cedric began to kiss her back. He reached up to the back of her head, and his fingers tangled up in her bedraggled hair.

With effort, Liv pulled away. "I just need you to know that . . . I need you to know that I want you to stay."

Cedric's hands remained in Liv's hair, but his eyes were fixed on the wooden pier beneath their feet. Time ticked by for what felt like minutes, hours, even, and Liv had trouble remembering to inhale and exhale. Even though her feet were on solid ground, she felt like she'd just taken a running jump off the pier, and she was falling, falling, falling into nothing. . . .

Cedric stepped away, releasing Liv and tucking his hands into his pockets. He cleared his throat.

Liv landed, hard.

"I can't," Cedric said.

Liv took a half-step back, looking to the ocean so Cedric couldn't read the emotion in her eyes.

"Everything that happened tonight, it was my fault," Cedric went on. "Someone could have died in that fire. I may not know how we were betrayed, but in the end, it was still my decisions that led us there."

Liv thought about the day before, when she had pleaded with him to go to the observatory, and then to find Daisy. When Kat had called her out on manipulating Cedric to get her way. She shook her head. "It was my decision to go to Beverly Hills. If it's anyone's fault, it's mine."

"No. You wanted to go, but the decision ultimately falls on me. That is what it means to be a leader. That is what Kat has been trying to tell me." Cedric breathed out heavily and ran a hand through his hair. "I fought for so long, against my father's wishes, against my future. All I wanted was to fight, not to rule. But I can't run from it—I have to be a leader. Their leader. There's no changing what I was born to be. Even if I wanted to . . ." Cedric paused. "I can't."

Liv stayed completely still as Cedric went on. He sounded weary now. "I was born to protect my people, and these past few days, I have not been doing that. I should have put the welfare of Kat, Merek, and my family first, but instead all I could think about was . . . you."

She looked hard at him in the rising daylight. There were his hands that had picked her up to run from the wraths. There was his mouth that she had kissed just minutes before. . . . He was standing right before her, but the possibility of him was drifting farther away with each second.

"Having you around, it confuses things," Cedric continued. "My priorities shift when you are close. My priority becomes you. And it cannot be you. Not now, when we need so desperately to get home, and not soon, when we have such fighting ahead of us. And not later, when I have to take up my responsibility to my family and my kingdom. Not ever, Liv."

Cedric turned away from her then.

A hundred responses formed on Liv's mouth. That it wasn't fair. That she understood. That she didn't understand. That he was taking the coward's way out. That he was brave.

In the end, she said nothing. She saw the resolution on Cedric's face, and she knew she wouldn't sway him. The hurt was sinking in, like a fresh wound that stings just before it begins to throb. Her words were out there now, and so were his. There was no taking any of it back.

The wind swirled Liv's hair around her face. She could just see the sky turning bluer over the water. The darkness seeped away by the second.

"I am sorry," Cedric said.

"Don't," Liv said, shaking her head. "Please don't apologize."

Cedric nodded. "I will make sure that you, Daisy, and your brother are hidden from Malquin. It is in the best interest of both our families that he does not get what he wants. We'll figure out the safest way to keep you from him, but meanwhile . . . I think it would be best if you and I kept our distance."

It took a good amount of Liv's energy to keep her voice steady as she said, "Okay."

Cedric stood awkwardly for another moment, as though he wanted to say something else. Then he turned and walked away.

Liv wanted to call out to him, to scream that this wasn't the way things were supposed to go. She had summoned up the courage and made her declaration. Granted, it hadn't been in a last-minute dash to the airport or on top of the Empire State Building, but she still knew what was supposed to happen next. Happily ever after, with the credits rolling over the two of them, together. If the world worked the way it was supposed to, that's what should have happened.

But Liv couldn't force the universe to give her a proper happy ending any more than she could force Cedric to turn around. She heard the sound of his shoes hitting the wood as he walked down the pier steps.

Soon, she would have to turn around too. Walk down the pier. Wait with the others. Soon, she would leave this moment behind and wait for it to become a painful memory. But for now, she stared out over the ocean's waves, the water's cold, salty spray blowing into her face and stinging her eyes, mixing there with her warm tears. And for once she didn't bring a hand up to stop them or hold them back or blink them away, but just stood still and let them fall.

THE ROAD AHEAD

Cedric tried to keep his mind blank as he walked down the wooden steps and back onto the cool sand of the beach. The sky was a light blue now, and in the distance he saw cars driving along the roadway. He wanted to turn around and get one last look at Liv, see her outlined there in the morning light, but that would only make things harder.

Instead, Cedric looked forward, to where Kat and Merek rested on the sand. Merek swayed where he sat, his eyes dark hollows. A part of Cedric felt guilty when he saw Merek's injuries, and another part of him still wanted to shake his quasi-friend until he told the truth. Even if Merek hadn't betrayed them, Cedric believed he knew more than he was telling. At some point, it would be up to him to figure out what that was.

But for now, he was so tired.

Cedric's lungs ached, and the skin of his arm tingled where the hair had burned off. Walking across the sand was difficult. As

Cedric trudged over to where Kat was sitting, he saw movement out of the corner of his eye. He looked up to see that people were starting to make their way down the beach, toward the shore. A few men carrying fishing poles, some older couples in large hats, one lone girl with dark hair and pale skin.

Cedric stopped in his tracks.

Suddenly, he couldn't feel anything—not the scratches on his skin, not the pounding of his heart. He stared blankly at the girl who was striding, poised and calm, in his direction. She wore a long-sleeved gown, and her feet made tracks in the sand. She stopped not ten feet from where Cedric stood.

"Hello, Brother," Emmeline said, grinning wide. Cedric's little sister closed the space between them, like a vision come to life, and embraced him.

"Emme?" Cedric's voice came out strangled and rough. He stood frozen in place. Could this be real? Or was this dreaming?

No. Kat jumped up and rushed forward to embrace Emme. This was real. Emme was here, on Earth. On this very beach. Cedric couldn't form words.

But Liv could.

"You're Cedric's sister?" Liv exclaimed. She was close, walking quickly across the sand, though Cedric hadn't noticed her behind him. "But . . . it's you," Liv continued. "You were outside the house yesterday!"

Cedric heard the accusatory note in Liv's voice, but her words barely sank in. He could only see Emme. Emme was everything safe and good in the world. Emme was his home. And now, Emme was here.

How was she here?

"W-what are you doing in this realm?" Cedric finally stuttered. "How did you find us?"

Emme's shoulders fell a few fractions, and he could see the disappointment on her face. A face that, if he was to be completely honest with himself, part of him had expected to never see again.

"And what sort of welcome is that, Cedric?" Emme smiled, and that's when Cedric noticed the changes in her. Her voice was still playful, but her face had lost some of its youthful softness. It looked harder around the edges, somehow. And she hadn't answered his question.

"It was you," Liv said again. "You overheard everything. You were at the house yesterday, when we were talking about getting Daisy, our whole plan. It wasn't Merek who was working with Malquin, it was you."

Emme scowled at Liv, but Cedric shook his head. It wasn't possible. He remembered the way Emme had looked at him before he'd fallen through the portal, how scared she'd been that entire night. His baby sister. "No," he said.

But Emme didn't deny it. "I have had to do a lot of things to keep our family safe," she replied, her voice suddenly sharp.

Cedric thought his heart had stopped. He couldn't tell whether he was breathing or not.

"Emme, what are you saying? *How are you here?*"

"I followed you, of course."

Cedric just stared at Emme as her eyes locked onto his, and her face broke open in another smile.

"And now, finally, it is time to bring you home, Big Brother. Today."

⁂

Liv paced in the sand until the muscles of her legs ached. She couldn't help but glance at the roadway every few minutes in search of Joe's minivan. She knew that once he got here, he'd be able to help. He'd help them figure out what to do next.

And he'd have Peter with him.

Liv looked over to where Emme sat in the shade under the pier, her dress splayed out across the sand like a girl in a medieval painting. She was just inches from Cedric, who stared at her as if she were a Christmas gift he had just opened but was afraid would disappear from before his eyes if he blinked for even a moment.

Whenever Cedric had talked about Emme, he had done so with such a lightness in his voice. But looking at her now, Liv felt nothing but anxious. Emme had been spying on them—for Malquin.

"Emme," Kat said, voice gentle, "tell us again. How long have you been here?"

"A few days," Emme replied. "Malquin had people following you—"

"You mean wraths," Merek interrupted. He slumped against a wooden support beam, eyes narrowed and arms crossed. He seemed to be the only person aside from Liv who doubted Emme's every word.

"Yes, of course," Emme said, her face coloring. "I have not forgotten what they are. But here, in this realm, they look so little like monsters. They look more like . . . us. It is odd, is it not?"

"Emme," Cedric said, his voice low. He reached out and touched her hand, and in that one moment, she seemed to soften. "Please tell us everything. We need to know."

Emme nodded. "He knew you were staying at the . . . what is it? The museum? When you left, he had you followed. And he knew you were in possession of a scroll. He only needed to separate you from . . . her."

Emme turned her eyes to Liv, then looked away quickly. Liv felt her stomach knot. She moved a few feet away, closer to the bottom of the pier steps. Shannon was there, and Daisy, too. Both were trying to follow the conversation while swaying with exhaustion.

"He asked me to come and get more information. The wraths were too conspicuous. Malquin said that even in human form, they lacked . . . subtlety. He warned me not to be seen, and when *she* caught me, I was terrified . . ."

"I didn't know who you really were," Liv said, her voice cold.

Emme continued as if Liv hadn't spoken. "I went to Malquin and told him what I heard, that you were splitting up and going after another scroll. He knew it was his time to take his chance and acquire them both." Emme bit her lip, and her eyes welled with tears as she looked down at her hands in her lap. Liv was distinctly reminded of Shannon, who forced herself to cry whenever her parents tried to punish her for sneaking out or lying or doing anything else Shannon-like.

If Cedric thought Emme's tears were forced, he didn't show

it. He squeezed her hand tighter. On Emme's other side, Kat looked equally sympathetic.

"I did not want to do it," Emme said. "But he said it would all end, Cedric. He could not give us the castle back, but he promised you would be safe, and he would release our parents—all of our parents."

Cedric looked to Kat, twin hopes flaring up in their eyes.

"They are still in the dungeon," Emme continued. "I was there with them, for a long time. Then Malquin came to me one day and asked for my help. He had a task for me. At first I didn't want to help him, but he said I would get to see you again, Cedric. And if I did just as he asked, he would let us all go."

"And you . . . believed him?" Kat's voice was gentle.

"What other choice did I have?" Emme's shoulders shook. "It is so cold down there . . . and Mother, she is not taking it so well. . . ."

"Is she ill?" Cedric's voice rose with concern.

"She is . . . struggling. She has always been so strong, but we have been locked up for months, with no word of you or of the kingdom, no idea what was happening outside of those damn stone walls."

Emme took a deep, shuddering breath. "I agreed to help him, Cedric, but I did it for our family. Please understand."

Cedric looked down for a long moment. "I understand," he finally said.

"Oh, so when it is your sister who's the traitor, you 'understand,' but when you thought it was me, your first thought was to flatten me to the ground," Merek said. Liv noticed that the skin of his face looked a few shades paler than it had just moments before.

Cedric took a deep breath. "I truly regret my mistake, Merek."

To Liv's—and everyone's—surprise, it was Shannon who jumped up. "*Mistake?* That's it? I mean, look at the guy." She motioned to Merek. "Sure, he's a jerk, but he didn't deserve to be throttled like that."

Merek, perhaps equally surprised by the outburst, nodded at Shannon. "Thank you." He turned to Cedric. "You should not have suspected me in the first place. Especially after this—" Merek pointed to his collarbone, which was covered in the crusty bandage Kat had wrapped around it earlier. He pushed himself off the ground, swaying a bit.

Shannon stepped toward him, steadying him. "Come on, we should really wash that out with some water." She peered at Cedric and Kat. "And maybe give Cedric a moment to come up with a better apology."

Merek haltingly followed Shannon down to the shore.

Cedric turned back to Emme. "What exactly did Malquin want of you?"

"I waited with him, at the warehouse. I stayed hidden in a back room while the wraths brought the two scrolls—"

"Liv and Daisy," Liv interrupted. "You keep calling us scrolls, but we're people. And those are our names."

Emme gave the briefest of sharp looks to Liv before softening once again. "Of course. He'd figured out a way to keep a portal open on Earth, he said, though he wouldn't tell me how. He just needed the two—you two. Malquin said once the new portal was opened, we would all be able to go home. But then it all went so badly."

Emme's face hardened. "I heard the fighting, but Malquin had told me to stay hidden at all costs. Then, I smelled the smoke, and saw the fire . . . I ran from the building just before it collapsed."

Cedric gripped Emme's hand, and she gave a small smile.

"I am all right. After a few moments, I saw you, all of you. You were running away. So I decided to follow you here. For a while, I lost sight of you, and thought I might be stuck here alone. But then I looked up, and saw you standing down by the water . . ."

"What did you mean earlier, when you said it was time to go home?" Cedric asked.

"Malquin's plan failed," Emme said. "But his portal *did* open. I saw it in the warehouse, before I ran the other way. I saw him go through it. Which means he is back there now, with our parents. And if he does not get the scrolls, he will keep them locked up, Cedric. He told me he will." Emme's voice went quiet. "We have to bring them to him."

Liv fought against her instinct to throw or punch something. Finally, Cedric looked up at her.

"We're not going." Liv moved closer to Daisy, who was still slumped against the stairs. "I'm not taking my sister through any portal."

"He is going to kill my parents!" Emme cried. Her tears dried quickly as she turned angry eyes on Liv. "My family is at stake."

Liv stood firm. "So is mine."

The silence grew thick as Emme stared down Liv.

"We will find another way," Cedric finally said.

Emme turned to him, and her mouth dropped open.

"Emme, listen," Cedric continued. "Malquin cannot be trusted. We have no way of knowing whether he would keep his promise to spare our parents. He has no reason to let them go once he gets what he wants. But we do know that his plan hinges on Liv and Daisy, and so we have to keep them from him. We will find another way to free mother and father. To free everyone."

Emme shook her head in disbelief. "Cedric . . . we must do this. We must. . . ." Emme looked to Kat. "Kat, please. Help me talk sense into him. Your parents are at stake as well. Please."

Kat hesitated, and for a moment, Liv wondered if she would argue against Cedric. She briefly looked to Liv before she spoke. "Cedric is right. Liv and her sister cannot come to Caelum. Malquin cannot win."

Emme put her head in her hands and shook it back and forth. This time, Liv believed her tears were real. "No," Emme whispered. "Please, no. He'll kill them . . . please . . ."

Cedric stared at his sister with a kind of helpless terror. He wrapped her in his arms and held her tight. When he gazed over her shoulder with pleading eyes, he didn't look to Liv, but to Kat. She moved closer to Emme, putting an arm over her as well.

Liv turned away from the sight, and when she did she saw a familiar van in the beach parking lot.

Joe was finally here.

Liv raced across the sand, with a suddenly alert Daisy on her heels. She skidded to a stop just as Joe got out of the minivan. Liv's eyes focused on the passenger-side door, which swung open. A pair of Chuck Taylors hit the ground, and Liv's heart sped up. She reached for Daisy's hand as a lanky teenage boy with oversized glasses and a T-shirt decorated with a picture of twenty-sided die shut the door behind him.

Liv opened her mouth, but Daisy beat her to it. "Peter?"

The boy looked between them, his expression uncertain. Liv raced toward him, her hand still in Daisy's, and threw her free arm around her brother. After a beat, Daisy did the same. Peter's face broke into a smile.

"I remember you!" Daisy said. "I didn't think I would at first, but then I saw you and I did, I remembered!" Daisy smiled—a real smile—for the first time all day.

"I remember you, too," Peter said, and his arm clenched tighter around Liv's shoulder.

Joe came around the side of the van. "I know you guys have a lot to talk about, but I don't think we should stay here for long out in the open. If the wraths or Knights find you . . ."

"Wraths. Knights." Peter shook his head, but was still smiling. "I still can't believe it. I mean, I can; it makes so much sense. Of course all this stuff is real . . . it's just so . . . awesome."

Liv pulled back slightly from her brother. She looked to Joe, who sighed. "I've been filling Peter in. He believes me, but maybe doesn't understand the . . . severity of the situation."

"Of course I understand the severity," Peter said, pushing his glasses up his nose. In that one moment, Liv instantly saw the overly serious, imaginative eight-year-old boy Peter had been when she last saw him. Her chest tightened. "That doesn't mean it isn't exciting."

"Um . . . right," Liv said.

"If the wraths know where you are, we need to get everyone out of here, and soon," Joe said.

Before Liv could respond, Shannon ran up to them, her shoes slapping against the sand. Liv took one look at Shannon's ashen face, and her heart dropped.

"It's Merek," Shannon said. "He just fell on the beach, and he won't wake up."

THE DAMAGE DONE

Cedric had never been in a room like this one before. The walls were painted in muted colors, and the smell was impossible to describe. It was a bit sour, but it also burned his nose every time he inhaled in a way that was only slightly more pleasant than breathing in ash and smoke the previous night.

But even worse were the people. People perched on tiny, colorful chairs. People pacing, running their hands through their hair. People in uniforms running up and down the brightly lit halls. People crying.

Cedric hated it.

But he had to wait with all the others to hear whether or not Merek was seriously injured. The horrible smell of the place—what Joe and Liv called a "hospital"—combined with Cedric's own guilt to form a small pit of nausea in his stomach. Liv had tried to get all of them to eat a few "snacks," but the extremely orange, perfectly square crackers she offered up made Cedric's stomach clench. If she had offered him roasted boar with plum sauce, he wouldn't have been able to take even a bite.

How could he eat when Merek might be dying?

And it was all his fault?

For the twentieth time, Cedric stood up and left the group sitting on the hard plastic chairs—all except Joe, who was talking to the healers—to walk to a large window on the other side of the room. He couldn't stop picturing the position of Merek's body where it had fallen down in the wet sand, or the bone-white color of his face as they'd lifted him into Joe's vehicle.

Merek had hardly been breathing then. His eyes fluttered open, but it was as though he couldn't see any of them. If they'd been in Caelum, Merek would have been taken to the healers' quarters, a long, airy space on the outer edge of the castle. But in this realm, they went to the hospital, and Cedric had no idea if these busy people in their thin, colored uniforms would be able to help his friend.

The friend Cedric had, just last night, slammed against the ground again and again, too angry to care that he was already injured.

Cedric stared out the window at the trees and buildings and hills of LA, but he didn't really see any of it. Someone came up to stand right behind him and he knew, without turning, who it was.

"You look tired."

"I am tired," Cedric replied.

Kat looked out the window. "It's almost beautiful, from up here. When you cannot smell the trash or hear the noise, it's . . . peaceful. Now that we are so close to going home, even I can admit not everything about Earth is terrible."

Cedric refused to meet her eyes. "How can we go back there without . . . if Merek does not . . ."

"He will. He was a bit knocked about, but we all were. He will be fine. Very soon, we are all going home. Together."

The fierceness in her voice almost made Cedric believe her. He longed to, he did. But at the same time, his stomach roiled with guilt. Because it was not just Merek on his conscience. He could never tell Kat about that secret, small part of himself that didn't want to go home at all. The part that had opened up the second he met Liv. Possibly even before—possibly when he was running through the streets of this strange world, lost and confused and . . . free. The part that thought, just for a moment, that he might have a purpose in the world other than the one he'd been born to. Every second he'd been with Liv, his true life had felt so far away. Living in his princely suite, hunting in the forests, having banquets with his parents and the townsfolk. Marrying Kat. All of that seemed, for the first time, changeable. The future hinted at other things, and it had felt . . . good.

But that feeling had clouded his judgment, and now they were here.

"He really will be fine," Kat said, misinterpreting Cedric's silence. "And when we are home, we can deal with what Emme has done."

Cedric started. Even though Emme now sat, improbably, just twenty feet away from him, he hadn't given her much thought since the moment Merek collapsed.

"We should not be too harsh," Kat said, her voice low. "I cannot imagine what it must have been like for her, locked up in a cell all this time."

"Do you think she is right? That we should barter Liv and her siblings for our parents' freedom?" He didn't dare to look at Kat while waiting for her answer.

She sounded hesitant when she answered. "Are you having doubts about your decision to keep them safe?"

Cedric sighed. "I doubt everything. If I were a stronger leader, I would trade over Liv, her brother, and sister without hesitation to free our families."

"Then you would be an idiot."

Surprised, Cedric looked over to Kat. Her jaw was set, determined.

"Why do you think I supported your decision?" Kat asked. "Have I ever struck you as being overly fond of Liv?"

Cedric gave a small smile. "Not particularly."

Kat continued, "I trust you, Cedric, but I know you have feelings for her. And when we open that portal and part ways, I will be happy to never hear the name Liv Phillips for as long as I live."

Kat moved to stand in front of Cedric, so she was facing him. "I supported your decision because it was the right one. What assurances do you have that Malquin would even hold his promise to Emme? Why would he free the king and queen? It makes no sense. And once he has what he wants . . . who knows what he will do then? The scrolls are our greatest leverage against him, and we cannot just hand them over." Kat paused before adding, "I think your father would agree."

Cedric's eyes fell to the floor. Just hearing the word *father* was like taking a blow to the stomach. And was it true? Would his father agree with him? Would his father approve of anything he'd done since falling out of that portal and landing in the middle of this foreign world?

Probably not. Still, Kat believed in him. That meant something.

"Thank you," he said.

"Of course," she said, then turned back to face the window. "It has been a rough few days. A rough few months, really. But we have all survived. And soon, everything will be as it was. You will see."

Cedric wished he could believe her—and even more, he wished that her vision of the future could provide some bit of comfort. But he was beginning to suspect already that some things, once changed, could never really be the same again. Not Caelum, not Merek, not Emme. Not even himself.

Liv knew she was exhausted, but a prickly sort of energy kept her from dozing off in the waiting room chair. It had been only a few days since she'd sat here, alone, waiting to hear about Rita's fate. Now she was in a similar position, but somehow, impossibly, she was surrounded by her family.

It seemed crazy to have Peter on one side of her and Daisy on the other. Daisy slumped against her plastic seat back, eyes falling shut every few moments. But Peter was wide awake and sparking. He wanted to hear everything about what had happened to Liv. She told him in hushed tones, while Cedric and Kat whispered by the window, and Emme stared at her, warily, from a few chairs over.

"It's all so hard to believe," Peter said, for the millionth time.

Shannon, who was sitting next to Peter, responded before Liv could. "Believe it."

"But there's a whole other world. Isn't that intense? Scientists have been looking for other worlds for who knows how long, and now we know of one that exists. And we can get there any time we want."

"It's not that simple," Liv said, a bit uneasily. She thought of Malquin's damaged arm, and his even more damaged plan. She thought of earthquakes and fire and holes in the world. But she didn't say any of this out loud. She didn't want to scare off her brother, now that she'd just gotten him back.

Peter uncrossed his long arms and leaned forward in his chair, his legs bouncing with jittery energy. "Things like this are rarely simple . . ."

"You have a lot of experience with traveling between worlds, do you?" Shannon cut in.

Peter pushed his glasses up his nose again. "Not actual experience, no. Not yet."

Liv was about to ask what Peter meant when Joe was suddenly there, standing at the door of the waiting room. She jumped up and ran over to him, but she wasn't as fast as Cedric and Kat.

"Merek is stable," Joe said right away. "But he's not out of the woods entirely."

"Woods?" Cedric asked, his voice tinged with panic.

"I'm sorry, I meant to say that Merek should be fine," Joe responded. Like everyone else, he had dark circles under his eyes. "He had a pretty significant concussion—a type of wound caused by a knock to the head—and the blood loss and smoke inhalation didn't help. The doctors want to keep him here for another day at least, but probably more."

Cedric breathed out, slowly, and Kat put an arm on his shoulder.

"We will stay here then," she said.

Joe shook his head. "Unfortunately, you can't. The police are already on their way to question me about what happened to Merek. I can try to answer their questions as best I can, but with all of you here—especially you, Cedric—it will be too difficult."

"Why especially him?" Liv hadn't even noticed that Peter had come up to stand behind her until he spoke.

"Cedric is currently wanted by the police. And even if that weren't true, it's too dangerous having you all here, out in the open where anyone could find you or ask questions. If your names and descriptions got into the wrong file, the Knights could track you down all over again."

Liv nodded, but Cedric shook his head. "We cannot just leave Merek behind."

"I'm not suggesting you leave your friend behind," Joe said. "Just let me handle this situation and lie low for a couple of days. It's the only way to keep you from behind bars."

Even Cedric seemed to understand that expression.

"But where will we go?" Liv interjected.

"My place is too risky," Joe said. "I have no idea if Malquin knows where it is, or if he still has wraths here doing his bidding."

Joe's eyes shot to Emme, but she was all wide eyes and innocence.

"Plus, there are the Knights. If they haven't connected me

to the three of you yet, they surely will soon. You need a better place to hide," Joe said.

"Hide?" Peter exclaimed. "Aren't these the villains who killed your little brother, Joe? We should fight them."

None of the group, still tired and covered in a layer of ash and bruises, answered him.

"I think I might know of a place," a voice piped up from the plastic chairs behind them. Liv turned, surprised, to see that Daisy was fully awake and standing. "I mean, if you don't mind the beach."

"The beach?" Peter asked.

"My parents have a house in Malibu," Daisy said. "It's not super big, just, like, four bedrooms, but it's pretty secluded."

Liv's eyes didn't go to Joe's, but to Cedric's. He stared at her for just a moment before giving a brief nod and turning away.

Liv nodded, too. "Malibu it is."

THE CITY'S END

The Malibu beach house was surrounded on three sides by an iron fence, even though there wasn't another house nearby for nearly a half-mile in each direction. The fourth side of the estate sat on a rocky bluff that faced the ocean. A winding set of stairs ran from the back door of the "not super big" house down to the pristine, empty beach.

The room where Liv was now resting with Peter and Daisy was equally pristine, though Daisy claimed it hadn't been used in months. She'd been able to get inside the gates with a code, though they'd had to break into the actual house by smashing through a window since Daisy couldn't risk going back to her old house for the key. Before leaving the hospital, she'd asked Joe if he could at least check up on what had happened to the two security guards at her parents' estate. As for what he'd tell her parents or even the police—Liv could only guess.

Cedric and Kat didn't want to leave Merek completely alone while Joe talked with police officers, so Shannon had agreed to stay on in the waiting room. She, after all, had parents who could vouch for her, even if they would be furious with her for sneaking out of the house—again. So Liv had hugged Shannon tight, thanked her, and apologized (though how could any thanks or apologies ever be enough?), and left her behind, taking Joe's van along with the others out to Daisy's beach house.

And even though Liv hadn't slept in who-knew-how-many hours, and was now sitting on the softest mattress she'd ever felt in her life, she still couldn't force her eyes to close.

There was no way she could sleep, not with Peter and Daisy there in the same room with her. Daisy was curled up against a pillow next to Liv, her feet swinging over the edge of the bed. She was cleaned and showered, and unlike the others, had barely a scratch to show for the horror movielike experience she'd just been through. For the first time in hours, Daisy seemed more like her regular self—like the girl who had stood with her hands on her hips and challenged a group of strangers trespassing on her lawn.

"Can I see your tattoo? Or whatever it is," Liv asked Peter, who was sitting on the twin bed opposite.

Peter shrugged and half turned, lifting up his shirt to show his markings. It was an exact replica of Liv's.

"Joe said that you must have had it when we were kids," Liv said. "But I don't remember . . ."

"I kinda do," Peter replied, pulling his shirt back down over his lanky torso. "Mom was really worried, and we went to a few doctors. I didn't understand what was happening, really."

"Do you remember the fire?" Daisy asked. The way she asked it, so lightly, was jarring to Liv. Then she realized Daisy probably had no memories of it, and was thankful for that.

Peter exchanged a quick look with Liv. His expression, so serious, tugged at the corners of her memory in an unpleasant way. It wasn't just that he was so similar to the eight-year-old boy Liv once knew—it was that he was a mix of that boy and their father. Liv could see it now, and it brought back images of her father she'd been pushing down for years. The sweep of his hairline, the ears that stuck out just a bit too far, the mouth that was just a bit too big for his face.

"Yes," Peter responded. "I do."

Daisy looked like she was about to ask more questions about it, so Liv cut her off, trying to keep her voice light. "So what have you been up to, Peter? Where do you live? Where do you go to school? I want to know all about you." Liv shot a glance to Daisy. "About both of you."

Peter leaned back heavily against the wall, stretching his legs out horizontally over the edge of the bed. "Not much to know, really. I've been in a bunch of foster homes, most of them in Fresno. Four different high schools. It was hard to make friends that way, until I got into D&D."

"D&D?" Daisy asked.

"Dungeons & Dragons. It's this role-playing game . . . kind of hard to describe. But there was always a group of kids who played it in every high school I went to, which was nice. Like, wherever I went, I had a kind of home, you know?"

Liv nodded.

"But now, looking back on it, I wonder if there was more to it," Peter continued, his eyes taking on a far-off look. "I always kind of felt like I was preparing for something. Like I always knew the world had more to offer me than trig tests and crappy foster parents. I always had this feeling like I was kind of, I guess, different somehow. More than other people. And now I know that's true."

Peter smiled, but a chill ran down Liv's spine. Peter's words called Malquin to mind, sitting in that warehouse and putting a gnarled finger to her face. *We're survivors. Special. Why waste time thinking about those who aren't?*

"I don't know if being different has worked out for us so far. If we're going to stay safe, we may need to go into hiding." Liv looked to Daisy. "How Joe is going to convince your parents of that, I have no idea . . ."

"I doubt Mike and Shana will mind," Daisy said, shrugging. "They've been trying to get me to go to boarding school for years. Or to start building off-Broadway cred in New York." Her eyes drifted. "I wonder if anyone's told them yet, about . . . what happened. At the house."

Liv reached over to carefully touch Daisy's shoulder. She was worried her sister might pull away, but she didn't.

"Do you get along with them? Your parents?" Peter asked, either not sensing Daisy's sudden sadness or trying to distract her from it.

Daisy shrugged one shoulder. "I mean, they're great and everything. They got me this moped for my birthday, had it painted pink and all. But sometimes I wonder . . . I don't remember my birth parents at all. Our parents. What were they like?"

Thankfully, Peter spoke first.

"I wish I could tell you what they were like, as people," he said. "But I only knew them as a kid. I didn't know if they were smart or funny or cool. They took care of me when I was sick and told us stories at bedtime." He shrugged. "They were . . . parents."

Daisy nodded, as if this answered her question. She swung her legs up onto the bed and lay back on her pillow. "I'm glad I found you guys, even if this has been the weirdest night of my whole life."

Liv smiled. "Me too. Hopefully, things won't get too much weirder."

"I hope they do," Peter said, flopping back onto his own pillow.

Liv gave a weak smile. She couldn't fault Peter for thinking all of this was exciting. After all, he hadn't been in that warehouse. If he had actually seen the portal in front of him, seen Malquin's face, seen the wraths for himself . . . he'd probably think a little differently.

Liv lay down next to Daisy and tried again to shut her eyes. Somewhere else in the house, Cedric, Kat, and Emme were also trying to get a little sleep. She wondered if they were more successful.

Before Liv finally, finally fell asleep, a memory came to her. She, Peter, and Daisy were much smaller, riding in the backseat of their parents' car. It was dark out. The radio was on low, and heat blasted gently from the radiator, wrapping her in warmth. Her parents murmured in the front seat, and Peter's sleeping form slumped against her shoulder. She didn't know how old she was or where they were going, but she remembered the feeling of it, of being surrounded by family. Being safe.

⊱⊰

Liv woke up to the sound of the world coming apart.

She was pitched from her bed and landed with a violent crash on the floor. Her first coherent thought was *earthquake*, but she couldn't remember exactly where she was. Was she back in her bedroom at Rita's? Or still in the Echo Park house? Liv crawled toward where she believed the doorway to be, but instead smacked hard into a bedpost. Then something heavy with elbows landed directly on top of her. Daisy.

Everything snapped into focus.

"Daisy!" Liv screamed as the bedroom shook around her. A lamp crashed down to the floor, and the windows rattled. "We have to get to the doorway!"

Daisy scrambled up and to the doorway, with Liv close behind. She put her hands up over her neck to protect her head—a lifetime of earthquake response training kicking into gear.

The bedroom window shattered inward, and both girls screamed.

A terrible thought struck Liv, and she looked over to the opposite twin bed. "Peter!"

The bed was empty, the sheets trailing onto the floor.

"I have to go find him—" Liv started to move out of the doorframe, but Daisy grabbed her wrist.

"No, don't go!"

Liv wrapped her free hand around Daisy's and huddled close to her. In the hallway outside, a picture frame smashed to the floor. The ground shook for what felt like minutes before finally petering out.

By the time the world was still again, both girls were surrounded by wreckage—the broken pieces of a bookshelf, the shards of a lamp.

"We have to get to the others," Liv said. She pulled Daisy up, and they slowly worked their way down the glass-strewn hallway. Liv needed to make sure everyone else was okay, but most of all, she needed for her gut feeling to not be true. . . .

They walked into the main living room, which was a giant mess of furniture and debris. Afternoon sunlight streamed in through the paneless holes in the walls. Joe entered the room through the kitchen, looking shaken. Liv realized he must have arrived at the house while she was asleep.

"Is everyone okay?" he asked.

"I don't know," Liv said. "Where are Shannon and Merek?"

"Still at the hospital."

Kat raced down the stairwell. "The earth moved again," she said, her voice shakier than Liv was used to hearing it.

"Another portal?" Joe said.

No, Liv wanted to say, but couldn't find her breath.

"Where's Cedric? And Peter?" Joe asked. He picked his way across the living room toward Liv.

No, no, no.

Kat looked pale. "Cedric would never—"

"Cedric would never what?"

Everyone turned to see Cedric walk in through the front door. His eyes were wild, desperate. They scanned the damage, took in the figures in the room. "Where's Emme?"

"Liv, Cedric . . . look." Joe pointed to the opposite wall of the room. Someone had taken a marker and written over the white wall in large letters. Liv held her breath as she silently read the words, and her worst suspicions were confirmed.

Dear Cedric, it began, *I hope you understand why I had to do this. Peter came willingly, and I hope the rest will follow. I promise he will be all right. We all will, so long we do what Malquin says. Please forgive me, your Emme.*

Beneath her message was a shorter one, scrawled out in messy letters:

Liv and Daisy, this was something I had to do. I hope to see you both soon.

Liv's knees buckled beneath her, and she took an involuntary step back to steady herself. Cedric walked slowly to the wall and ran his hand over Emme's words.

"How could she do that?" Cedric asked. His voice was low, as though he was talking to himself. "How could she just . . . leave?"

No one answered.

They all gathered closer to the words on the wall, and Liv focused on her brother's messy scrawl. She remembered the gleam in his eyes when he'd talked about being special . . . had Emme overheard him talking in the hospital waiting room? Did she know then he would be an easy target? His handwriting on the wall was heartbreakingly familiar. It was the same as it had been when Peter was small.

"I'm going after them," Liv said. She was surprised by the force of her own voice.

Cedric spun around. "No." He looked around the room, as if searching for support—first to Kat, then to Joe.

"That's exactly what Emme wants you to do, Liv," Joe said. "That's why she convinced Peter to go with her—she knew you'd follow and she could hand you over to Malquin. But you can't."

"Yes, I can. He's my brother. I just got him back, and I'm not losing him again."

"We already agreed," Cedric said, moving closer to Liv. "Malquin only needs two scrolls. If he has Peter, and he gets you . . . we cannot let that happen."

"He's right," Kat said. Cedric nodded.

"You can't stop me." Liv moved closer to Cedric. She straightened and looked up into his eyes. They burned with intensity, but she didn't care—hers felt just as bright.

"I'm a scroll, remember? I can open a portal anytime I want. I'll go alone if I have to, to get Peter back. I will."

"Liv," Joe started, walking up toward her. She spun to face him.

"I will. You'll have to chain me up, Joe, I swear. And even then, I'll find a way." Liv put every ounce of conviction she had behind her words. "He's my family, Joe. My *brother*."

Joe flinched, and Liv knew she'd hit the right nerve. He'd let his own brother go, all those years ago, back when Malquin was just John. Liv knew the kind of person that Joe was, and knew how it must have eaten him up inside to not go after his brother. He'd had two once, and lost them both.

When Joe spoke, he was quiet. "If you open the portal alone, it will chew you up, just like it did to John."

"Not if we do it right, if we all open it together and use . . . blood." Liv looked to Cedric briefly, then barreled on. "I'll be the only one who crosses through, but if the three of us open it together, it should work right. I saw how Malquin did it."

"But Peter didn't," Joe said. His expression was all sympathy, which Liv could barely tolerate. "He must have opened a portal for him and Emme alone, without knowing the right things to do. There's no way to know if he . . . survived."

The pit of fear in Liv's stomach spread. She shook her head. "No. He's alive, he has to be." She couldn't accept that he wasn't. That she had found Peter again, after all these years, to have only a few hours with him . . . it wasn't possible that he was gone, forever. It wasn't.

"I have to find him," she managed to say.

"So you could get hurt, too? Even if the three of us open a portal safely and you cross through, you'll be all alone—"

"She's not going alone," Cedric said. When he looked at Liv, his eyes weren't just hard. They were angry. She never imagined he could look at her that way. She forced herself to look away. "We will go with her, obviously."

"What about Merek?" Kat said.

Cedric kept his eyes, and his anger, on Liv. But his words were directed at Joe. "Is there any additional news on Merek's condition?"

"The doctors want to keep him under observation for a few days. I won't be able to get him out until he can walk on his own, which might be a while . . ."

"We don't have time," Liv whispered. She held Cedric's stare. "We know Merek will be okay, at least. But Peter? If he's . . . hurt, I need to find him and bring him back now."

"What about me?" Daisy suddenly stepped up. "I want to go. He's my brother, too."

Liv exchanged a panicked look with Joe, then turned to her sister. "I can't risk you, too. Besides, you have people here who care about you."

Daisy rolled her eyes and muttered under her breath, but her face looked unsure.

"I know it might not seem that way, but your parents do care. They cared enough to adopt you, to raise you."

Daisy swallowed.

"You can't just leave them behind," Liv said. She walked over to Daisy and pulled her into a hug. "Besides, I won't be long. I'll find Peter and be back here before you know it." Her words caught in her throat as Daisy gripped her back, hard.

She hoped she sounded convincing.

THE HOLE IN THE SKY, PART TWO

They walked down the beach for a long time, following the narrow strip of sand between water and cliff. Joe led the way, followed by Liv and the others. The nearest neighbor to Daisy had a fire engine parked outside, and Liv hoped the morning's earthquake hadn't caused too much trouble. She thought of the ruined buildings surrounding the burned warehouse in Venice. Joe had told her they were mostly boat storage units, and no people had been on the scene other than the Knights and wraths. Still, Liv didn't want too much more destruction on her hands.

After a half hour of walking, they stopped in front of a long stretch of cliff.

"This seems to be pretty isolated," Joe said. "Minimal damage."

Liv nodded, but she knew there was no way any of them could be sure that was true. So much harm had already been done. She looked to Daisy, who looked so young, so small standing there. If she left, how could she be sure Daisy would stay safe?

Was it worth it to go?

Her eyes met Cedric's then. He stared her down, his blue eyes nearly translucent in the bright morning light. And she realized what it must be like for him, all the time—having to make the hard decisions.

Liv wished she had a script she could follow, beats laid out to let her know she was on the right track. But there was no way to know which choice was right until after it was already made. The only way to decide, in the moment, was to determine which path was the one she could live with the least, and then take the other one.

Liv turned back to Joe. "Let's do this."

"Wait," Daisy said, stepping toward Liv. "I have something for you." She thrust out a small black backpack. "It's an earthquake kit."

Liv smiled. "Thanks, but if this actually works, you might need that more than me."

Daisy pushed the backpack into Liv's hands. "It has water and a flashlight and walkie-talkies, just in case you run into . . . stuff." Her voice wavered, and for a moment, she looked uncertain, younger than thirteen.

Liv smiled and put on the backpack. "Thanks, Daisy."

Daisy shrugged, then stood taller, suddenly looking more like herself. "No big deal. We have, like, four more of them back at the house."

Liv looked to Joe. He gave a brief nod and stepped between Liv and Daisy, so the three of them faced an empty stretch of air between the surf and the cliff.

"You remember the words Malquin spoke?" Joe asked Liv.

"Yes," she said. She didn't know how she'd ever forget. "And there's the second thing we need."

"Blood." Cedric's voice was flat. "Our blood."

Liv nodded. "So I can go through without being hurt. Hopefully."

Kat handed Cedric a knife. He quickly put it against his palm and slit downward. A drop of his blood leaked out through his clenched fingers and spilled to the sand.

Fighting the rising bubble of fear in her stomach, Liv reached out toward Cedric. She took his injured hand in hers—the first time they'd touched since the pier. And possibly the last time they would. Sure, he'd agreed to take her to Caelum, but she knew his resolution from the pier still stood. He'd keep his distance.

The blood felt warm against her palm, and she pulled her hand back quickly.

"Thank you," she whispered.

Liv turned back to Joe and Daisy. She thought about the swirling portal in the warehouse, the surging, open blackness.

She breathed in deep. "Repeat after me. *Echgo libratum, echgo indux vitte.*"

She felt it immediately, a light buzzing under her skin that surged quickly. Magic.

"Echgo libratum, echgo indux vitte."

Liv heard Joe's deep voice and Daisy's higher one joining in. Or no—not heard, but felt. Their voices were energy, mixing with her own. She repeated the words over and over in her mind, no longer even sure she was saying them out loud. The world around her took on a brief technicolor focus, then went fuzzy around the edges.

Then she could see it—a small hole right in front of her, a pinprick. It slowly opened upward. Or rather, it tore. Through the air, it shimmered and grew, until it expanded outward in a rough circle. The portal. She had created it.

Liv exhaled. She'd done it.

She felt exhausted, spent. All the energy she'd brought up inside of herself had been expelled, and was now swirling around in thin air before her.

A tear in the world.

Cedric stepped up behind Liv—she could feel his presence there without turning around.

"Time to go," he said.

Joe and Daisy stepped aside, and Kat assumed their place. Her face was bright as she looked at the portal.

"Home," she said, a smile on her lips. She turned to Cedric. "See you there." She took off at a light run and jumped through the portal.

Cedric was next. He turned to Joe. "Thank you, for all your help. With Merek and . . . everything."

"Of course," Joe said. He met Liv's eyes.

"Look after each other, and Shannon. Till I get back," she said. It hit her how sad it was she had so few people to say goodbye to. And would Shannon understand why she'd had to leave her behind? "Tell her—"

Liv's words were cut off by a huge, smashing noise. The ground shook beneath her, but right before she fell to the sand, she saw that a large portion of the nearby cliff was cascading downward.

"We have to go, now," Cedric said.

The ground shook again, and was followed by another noise—but this wasn't the crashing of rocks. It was a wheezing, straining noise, like air being let out of a balloon.

"What is that?" Joe asked. "The portal?"

Liv didn't know—she hadn't heard the noise when the portal was open at the warehouse. She barely had time to shake her head before Cedric reached for her.

"Liv," he said. She grabbed his hand. Together, they moved to the swirling black hole.

Liv turned her head once, to say good-bye to Daisy and Joe. But they weren't looking at her anymore. They were staring at the sky above them . . . the sky that was roiling, darkening, changing from light blue to orange and then red. Thick clouds moved impossibly fast across the ocean, and with their burnished color, they looked like a spreading fire.

"Wha—"

Liv's voice was swallowed by the great expanse of darkness as Cedric pulled her farther into the portal. The last thing she saw was the fear on Daisy and Joe's faces as they stared at the impossibly vivid sunset.

Liv's final, confused thought was, *But it's the middle of the day . . .*

Then, there was nothing.

THE NEW WORLD

Liv was lying on the ground. Hard ground, familiar ground.

It didn't work, she thought. *I'm still home.*

Relief flooded through her, then shame. She hadn't realized how big a part of her wanted to stay on Earth until she'd failed to leave it.

Liv opened her eyes to see a bright sky. It was whitish-gold and clear.

Her ears were ringing, and she focused on her own breathing. What could she feel? Her body beneath her, intact. She raised her palm to her face and saw streaks of dried blood there. Cedric's blood.

Liv started to sit up, and her muscles groaned. She felt as though she'd just done five hundred sit-ups. She was lying next to a crop of spiky blue flowers. They were larger than any flower Liv had ever seen in person. What were they?

She sat up farther.

And gasped.

There, in front of her, was a giant mountain range, with points that reached up into the sky. They seemed to go on forever—farther than Liv could see—before fading away into a white haze. And ten feet away from her, punching a hole through the air right in front of the picturesque vision of the mountain range, was a dark portal.

This wasn't home.

Liv slowly struggled to her feet. She was in a giant meadow full of blue flowers, some of which grew up to her waist. Everything was large, and wrong somehow. Like she was in a dream. But the pain in her body told her she was awake.

"Are you okay?"

Liv turned at the sound of the voice, and saw Cedric standing near her.

"I think . . . I think so," Liv said. She looked around again. "Holy crap."

A few steps from Cedric, Kat was spinning in place, grinning. She bent down to the ground and picked up a handful of dark soil.

Cedric turned to Liv, and though she knew he was still angry with her, his blue eyes were shining.

"Welcome to Caelum."

ACKNOWLEDGMENTS

Acknowledgments, wow. This may be the closest I ever get to giving some version of an Emmy award speech, so bear with me. At least no orchestra can play me off when I start to ramble—

—and I'm being told to hurry this along, so okay. First and foremost, my deepest thanks to Reiko Davis, my kind and talented agent, who not only thought my writing was worth spending time on, but who made it better and stronger from the beginning. I would literally not be writing these words without you, and yet I feel like there aren't words strong enough to express your awesomeness.

Also awesome beyond words—Jess MacLeish, my cool, amazing editor, who knows what words to cut, what words to leave in, and what restaurants to go to in New York. This book is so much better because you worked on it. Thanks also to the entire HarperTeen team for all the work put in at every stage of bringing this manuscript from a file on my laptop out into the world.

Special thanks to my very first readers, Sarah Ratner and Ariana Jackson; your suggestions and also your words of encouragement were really crucial at the beginning stages of all this. Eric Luper and Elissa Sussman also provided fantastic notes that helped me shape early drafts. Thanks also to the other members of my writing group, Christopher Bosley and Elysse

Applebaum, for the support, for making me a better writer, and for the donuts.

A lot of people provided guidance as I worked on this book, both on a personal and professional level. Thanks so much to Erica Phillips for listening to me blather on about every single step of this journey, and for telling me I deserved it even when I didn't think that was true, and thanks to Josh Sathre, who got me my first TV job in LA, for which I will always be grateful. And big thanks to Chuck Pratt, for offering encouragement, giving me a job, and teaching me how to always write to a killer act break.

So much thanks and love for my family and friends in Michigan, the magical place that will always be my home no matter where else I go in this life. My grandparents, aunts, uncles, and cousins—you are far too many to name (seriously, that would take up a whole other book)—but you are each so important to me. And to Erica Blalock, Daina Graves, Lisa VanderPloeg, Paula DuBose, and Kim Syrios—I wouldn't be who I am without you.

No life is complete without sisters, and mine definitely wouldn't be without Alli Klingele and Sarah Boyle, my best friends and partners in crime. Worlds of thanks to my parents, Steve Klingele, Robyn Boyle, and Toby Boyle, who taught me how to be a human, and who let me read as many books as I could ever want.

And finally, to Phil—I always thought getting a book published would be the best thing to ever happen to me (and honestly, it's pretty great), but it's nothing compared to getting to spend every day with you. So thank you for that, and for every other little thing.